Praise for The First Blast of the Trumpet

"Marie Macpherson's well-researched novel captures the period which led up to the Reformation in Scotland, in which decay and despotism led eventually to a new regime. She leaves the reader much better informed about the rivalries between the Scots nobility, and the way in which they used the late medieval church as a power base to consolidate their hold on power. In addition, she skilfully escapes the constraints of the known facts to give her readers an intriguing fictional tale of the early life of John Knox. The violence and brutality of life in sixteenth century Scotland is well captured, along with the struggles among the vying dynasties to supplant a weak monarchy. Her romances are earthy rather than ethereal, her nobles far short of heroic and the result is a book which portrays the main players in Scotland's Reformation as flawed human beings rather than the goodies and baddies which partisan history has often made them."

---**Rev Stewart Lamont**, *author of "The Swordbearer: John Knox and the European Reformation"*

"In this novel, set in one of the most turbulent periods of Scottish (and English) history, much historical, ethnological and linguistic research is in evidence, which – importantly – Marie Macpherson delivers with a commendable lightness of touch. Descriptions of contemporary superstitions, medicinal cures, and religious practices are impressively handled and closely linked to an engrossing plot and finely drawn, convincing characterisation. The over-riding theme of the novel is Keep Tryst and all the central characters are confronted with the issue of fidelity of some kind, with its breaching or betrayal resulting in an acute sense of loss and/or guilt. The novel well documents the corruption among church officialdom and the blatant misogyny of many of those in positions of power, yet the author handles these issues sensitively. I enjoyed this book enormously and would be more than happy to read it a second time. I'm sure such an accomplished debut novel will enjoy considerable success."

---**Charles Jones FRSE**, *Emeritus Forbes Professor of English Language, University of Edinburgh*

"With style and verve Marie Macpherson whirls us into the world of sixteenth-century Scotland: its sights and smells, sexual attraction, childbirth and death, and of course the ever looming threat of religious strife. Few are the known facts of John Knox's first thirty and more years, but this vivid creation of a fictional life for him not only entertains but raises many questions in the reader's mind about the character and motives of a dominating figure in Scottish history."

--- **Dr Rosalind Marshall**, *Fellow of the Royal Society of Literature, research associate of the Oxford Dictionary of National Biography, to which she has contributed more than fifty articles, and author of biographies of Mary, Queen of Scots, Mary of Guise, John Knox, Elizabeth I and Bonnie Prince Charlie.*

THE FIRST BLAST OF THE TRUMPET

THE FIRST BLAST OF THE TRUMPET

The Knox Trilogy
Book One

Marie Macpherson

Best wishes
Marie Macpherson

KNOX ROBINSON
PUBLISHING
LONDON • New York

KNOX ROBINSON
PUBLISHING

3rd Floor, 36 Langham Street
Westminster, London W1W 7AP
&
244 5th Avenue, Suite 1861
New York, New York 10001

Knox Robinson Publishing is a specialist, international publisher of historical
fiction, historical romance and medieval fantasy.

First published in Great Britain in 2012 by Knox Robinson Publishing
First published in the United States in 2013 by Knox Robinson Publishing

A CIP catalogue record for this book is available from the British Library.

ISBN HC 978-1-908483-21-8

ISBN PB 978-1-908483-22-5

Typeset in Bembo by Susan Veach
info@susanveach.com

Printed in the United States of America and the United Kingdom.

Download the KRP App in iTunes and Google Play to receive free
historical fiction, historical romance and fantasy eBooks
delivered directly to your mobile or tablet.

Watch our historical documentaries and book trailers on our channel on YouTube
and subscribe to our podcasts in iTunes.

www.knoxrobinsonpublishing.com

This is dedicated to the one I love — for keeping faith

Contents

CAST OF CHARACTERS

★ Denotes fictional characters

House of Hepburn

Elisabeth Hepburn	daughter of 1st Earl of Bothwell; Prioress of St. Mary's Abbey, Haddington
Margaret Hepburn	Meg, sister of Elisabeth; married Archibald Douglas, 6th Earl of Angus
John Hepburn	Prior of St. Andrews Priory, later Bishop of Moray; uncle of Elisabeth
Janet Hepburn	Prioress of St. Mary's Abbey; sister of John Hepburn
Patrick Hepburn	1st Earl of Bothwell; married firstly, Joanna Douglas; secondly Margaret Gordon
Margaret Gordon	1st Countess of Bothwell; mother of Meg & Elisabeth
Adam Hepburn	2nd Earl of Bothwell; son of Patrick Hepburn & Margaret Gordon; married Agnes Stewart
Patrick Hepburn	3rd Earl of Bothwell, dubbed the Fair Earl; married Agnes Sinclair
Joanna Hepburn	daughter of Patrick Hepburn & Joanna Douglas; half-sister of Elisabeth; widow of Lord Seton; founder of St. Catherine's Convent
Agnes Stewart	Nancy, 2nd Countess of Bothwell; natural daughter of Earl of Buchan; former mistress of James IV & mother of Jenny; widow of Adam Hepburn & mother of Patrick
Patrick Hepburn	Prior of St. Andrews, later Bishop of Moray; uncle & tutor to Patrick, 3rd Earl of Bothwell
Harry Cockburn	stable lad at St. Mary's Abbey
★ Katherine Hepburn	Kate, orphan of indeterminate parentage; mistress of James IV
★ Betsy Learmont	nursemaid to the Hepburn family
★ Isabelle Campbell	orphan adopted by Elisabeth Hepburn
★ Jamie Campbell	brother of Isabelle

House of Douglas

Archibald Douglas	5th Earl of Angus, dubbed Bell the Cat
Archibald Douglas	6th Earl of Angus, his grandson; married firstly Margaret Hepburn; secondly Margaret Tudor
Elizabeth Drummond	widow of George, Master of Angus; mother of Archibald, 6th Earl of Angus

Janet Douglas	Jinty, sister of Archibald; married firstly John Lyon, 6th Lord Glamis; secondly Archibald Campbell of Skipness
George Douglas of Pittendreich	brother of Archibald, 6th Earl of Angus
Elizabeth Douglas	sister of Angus; wife of John, 3rd Lord Hay of Yester
Margaret Douglas	daughter of Archibald Douglas & Margaret Tudor; married Matthew Lennox; mother of Henry, Lord Darnley
Janet Douglas	Jessie, Mistress of the King's Wardrobe to James V

House of Stewart

James IV	King of Scots 1488–1513; married Margaret Tudor; sister of Henry VIII of England
Margaret Tudor	widow of James IV; married secondly Archibald Douglas, 6th Earl of Angus; thirdly Henry Stewart
Janet Stewart	Jenny, natural daughter of James IV & Agnes Stewart; half-sister of James V; married Malcolm, 3rd Lord Fleming
James V	King of Scots 1513–1542; married firstly Princess Madeleine of France; secondly Marie de Guise-Lorraine
Sir David Lindsay of the Mount and Garleton	tutor to James V; poet, playwright
John Stewart	2nd Duke of Albany; grandson of James II; Regent of Scotland 1514–1524
Marie de Guise	widow of Duke of Longueville; married James V
Mary, Queen of Scots	daughter of James V & Marie de Guise
Margaret Erskine	mistress of James V; wife of Lord Robert Douglas; mother of James Stewart by James V
James Stewart	natural son of James V & Margaret Erskine
Matthew Stewart	4th Earl of Lennox; descendant of James II; married Margaret Douglas; father of Henry, Lord Darnley
Henry Stewart	son of Andrew Stewart, 1st Lord Avondale; distant cousin of James V; later 1st Lord Methven; 3rd husband of Margaret Tudor
Antoine D'Arcie	Duke of Albany's French lieutenant in Scotland

House of Hamilton

James Hamilton	2nd Earl of Arran; Governor & Regent of Scotland 1543–1554
Jean Hamilton	Jeanie, his daughter; pupil at St. Mary's Abbey

| James Hamilton of Finnart | dubbed the Bastard; natural son of 1st Earl of Hamilton |

Catholics

David Beaton	Abbot of Arbroath; later Cardinal of Scotland
Katherine Beaton	his sister; nun at St. Mary's Abbey
Lady Marion Ogilvie	mistress of David Beaton
Sister Maryoth Hay	nun at St.Mary's Abbey; sister of John, 2nd Lord Hay of Yester; aunt of John 3rd Lord Hay
John Hay	3rd Lord Hay of Yester, dubbed the Wizard of Goblin Ha'; husband of Elizabeth Douglas: nephew of Sister Maryoth Hay
Andrew Forman	Archbishop of St.Andrews
Dr. John Winram	Sub-Prior of St.Andrews
★ Sister Agnes	French nun at St.Mary's Abbey
★ Father Dudgeon	Parish Priest at St.Mary's Collegiate Church, Haddington

Reformers

John Knox	son of Margaret Sinclair & William Knox; godson of Elisabeth Hepburn
William Knox	older brother of John
George Wishart	former priest; protestant reformer
Widow Ker	housekeeper to John Knox

James Balfour of Pittendreich
Henry Balnaves of Halhill
John Cockburn of Ormiston
Hugh Douglas of Longniddry
William Kirkcaldy of Grange
John Leslie of Parkhill

| Norman Leslie | Master of Rothes |

James Melville of Halhill

| John Rough | Ayrshire preacher |

Ladies at Court

Janet Kennedy	mistress of James IV & Archibald Bell the Cat Douglas, *inter alia*
Isobel Kennedy	daughter of Janet
Mariota Hume	widow of John, Earl of Crawford
Elizabeth Hamilton	widow of Matthew, Earl of Lennox

HOUSE OF HEPBURN

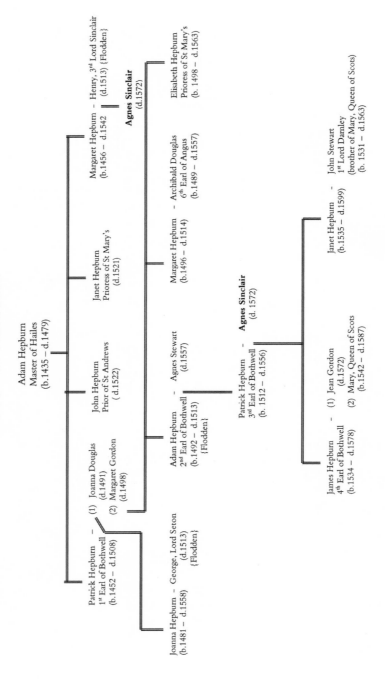

Adam Hepburn
Master of Hailes
(b.1435 – d.1479)

Patrick Hepburn   –   (1) Joanna Douglas
1st Earl of Bothwell   (d.1491)
(b.1452 – d.1508)   (2) Margaret Gordon
                                          (d.1498)

Joanna Hepburn – George, Lord Seton
(b.1481 – d.1558)   (d.1513)
                                    {Flodden}

John Hepburn
Prior of St Andrews
(d.1522)

Adam Hepburn   –   Agnes Stewart
2nd Earl of Bothwell   (d.1557)
(b.1492 – d.1513)
{Flodden}

Patrick Hepburn   –   Agnes Sinclair
3rd Earl of Bothwell   (d. 1572)
(b. 1512 – d.1556)

James Hepburn   –   (1) Jean Gordon
4th Earl of Bothwell   (d.1572)
(b.1534 – d.1578)   (2) Mary, Queen of Scots
                                          (b.1542 – d.1587)

Janet Hepburn
Prioress of St Mary's
(d.1521)

Margaret Hepburn   –   Archibald Douglas
(b.1496 – d.1514)   6th Earl of Angus
                                          (b.1489 – d.1557)

Janet Hepburn   –   John Stewart
(b.1535 – d.1599)   1st Lord Darnley
                                          (brother of Mary, Queen of Scots)
                                          (b. 1531 – d.1563)

Margaret Hepburn – Henry, 3rd Lord Sinclair
(b.1456 – d.1542)   (d.1513) {Flodden}

Agnes Sinclair
(d.1572)

Elisabeth Hepburn
Prioress of St Mary's
(b. 1498 – d.1563)

HOUSE OF DOUGLAS

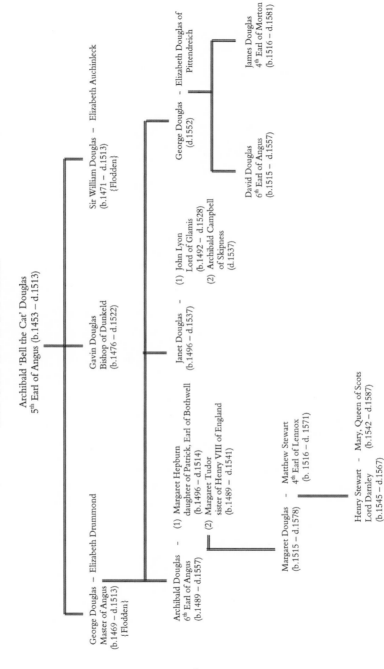

Archibald 'Bell the Cat' Douglas (b.1453 – d.1513)
5th Earl of Angus

George Douglas – Elizabeth Drummond
Master of Angus
(b.1469 – d.1513)
{Flodden}

Gavin Douglas
Bishop of Dunkeld
(b.1476 – d.1522)

Sir William Douglas – Elizabeth Auchinleck
(b.1471 – d.1513)
{Flodden}

Archibald Douglas – (1) Margaret Hepburn
6th Earl of Angus   daughter of Patrick, Earl of Bothwell
(b.1489 – d.1557)   (b.1496 – d.1514)
                         (2) Margaret Tudor
                              sister of Henry VIII of England
                              (b.1489 – d.1541)

Janet Douglas – (1) John Lyon
(b.1496 – d.1537)   Lord of Glamis
                        (b.1492 – d.1528)
                   (2) Archibald Campbell
                        of Skipness
                        (d.1537)

George Douglas – Elizabeth Douglas of
(d.1552)   Pittendreich

Margaret Douglas – Matthew Stewart
(b.1515 – d.1578)   4th Earl of Lennox
                        (b. 1516 – d. 1571)

David Douglas
6th Earl of Angus
(b.1515 – d.1557)

James Douglas
4th Earl of Morton
(b.1516 – d.1581)

Henry Stewart – Mary, Queen of Scots
Lord Darnley   (b.1542 – d.1587)
(b.1545 – d.1567)

HOUSE OF STEWART

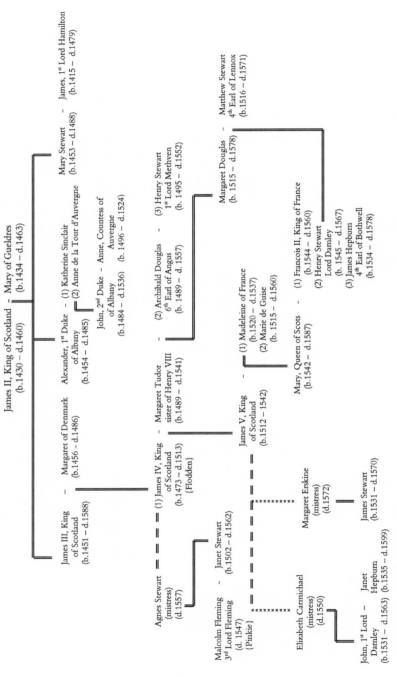

HOUSE OF HAMILTON

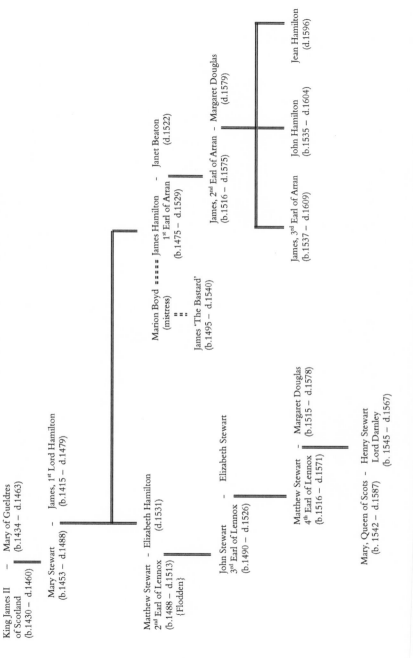

Map of Central and Southern Scotland 1500-1548

PART ONE

I

Hallowe'en

> The night it is good Hallowe'en
> When fairy folk will ride;
> And they that wad their true-love win
> At Miles Cross they maun bide.
> *The Ballad of Tam Linn,* Traditional

Hailes Castle, Scotland, 1511

"There's no rhyme nor reason to it. Your destiny is already laid doon."

Hunkered down on the hearth, Betsy jiggled the glowing embers with a poker and then carefully criss-crossed dry hazel branches on top. Huddled together on the settle, the three girls drew back as the fire burst into life, the crackling flames spitting out fiery sprites that frolicked their way up the chimney. Betsy wiped the slather of sweat from her flushed face and scrambled up to plonk herself down beside them by the ingleneuk.

"Doom-laden?" Elisabeth queried, her head dirling at the thought. "So where's the use in making a wish?"

"Wishes – and hopes and dreams," Betsy added, "are what keep us going. You make a wish in the hope that it'll come true, but you'll never flee your fate. Now then, my jaggy thistle, when the flames die down, cast your nut into the fire and wish on it," she instructed. "And mind, be wary what you wish for."

Elisabeth delved her hand into the basket and pulled out two nuts coupled together.

"Ah, a St. John's nut." Betsy nodded slowly. "That's a good omen."

"That my wish will come true?" Her ferny green eyes glinted in the firelight.

"Nay, lass, but it'll guard you against the evil eye. Don't fling it, but keep it safe as a charm against witches."

With a doubtful glance at her nurse, Elisabeth slipped the enchanted nut into the pocket of her breeches and chose again. "I will never marry," she began, pausing to savour the astonished gasps before throwing her nut onto the red-hot embers, "unless for love."

"Don't be all blaw and bluster, Lisbeth my lass. It's a wish you've to make, not a deal with the devil. And in secret, otherwise it'll no come true," Betsy warned.

"Then I'll make it come true," Elisabeth retorted.

Betsy shook her head. "You'll have no say in the matter. You maun dree your weird, as the auld saying goes." Then, seeing Elisabeth's quizzical frown, she added, "You

3

must endure your destiny, my jaggy thistle. And never, ever tempt fate by having too great a conceit of yourself. Forbye, if you marry for love, you'll work for silver."

"We'll see," Elisabeth replied, quietly determined that she wouldn't share the lot of those lasses, sacrificed at the altar for the sake of family alliances and financial gain. Leaning forward, her brows drawn tightly together, she glared at the hazelnut, willing it to do her bidding. The nut twitched around the embers before splitting open and spitting out its kernel.

"Sakes me!" Betsy muttered.

"What does it bode?" Elisabeth tugged impatiently at Betsy's sleeve.

"That your peerie heid and nippy tongue will lead you into bother, my lass," Betsy cautioned.

"And that no man will touch a jaggy thistle such as you."

Elisabeth twisted round ready to repay Kate's stinging remark with a sharp nip, but a dunt in the arm from Meg stopped her.

"Even the briar rose has thorns, mind," Elisabeth snapped instead. "Bonnie you may be, but blithe you're not."

"Tsk, tsk," Betsy chided. It made her heart sore to hear her three wee orphans, her bonnie flowers of the forest, bickering. She shook her head as her jaggy thistle, the sharp-witted, spiky-tongued Lisbeth lashed out at fair-haired, pink-cheeked Kate who, like a pawkie kitten, kept her claws hidden until provoked.

Ignoring their squabble, Meg leant forward and cupped her chin in her hands to gaze wistfully into the fire. She lowered her hazelnut gently into the embers where it sizzled and sputtered, before slowly fizzling out.

"Oh, dearie me," she moaned, sucking her top lip over her teeth to stem the tears.

"Don't you fret, my fairy flower." Betsy patted her knee. "That's a sign of a quiet, peaceful life."

"Is it Betsy? Truly?" Meg's watery blue eyes – the shade of the fragile harebell – glistened with grateful tears. Fey, frail Meg had no desire to marry but secretly craved the contemplative life of a nun, sheltered from the hurly-burly of the world behind a protective wall. Let not matrimony and maternity be my destiny, she prayed.

"My turn now." Kate had been rummaging through the basket, picking over the nuts until finding one to her liking. Smooth, flawless and perfectly round.

"We ken fine what you'll wish for," Elisabeth taunted. "And since it's no secret, it'll no be granted."

Kate's eyes blazed in the firelight. "Make her stop, Betsy."

While Elisabeth and Meg were daughters of the late Patrick, 1st Earl of Bothwell, Kate's parentage was vague. An orphan of one of the minor scions of the family – though tongues wagged that she was a love-child – the "lass with the gowden hair"

4

had been taken in by the earl and brought up with his own daughters at Hailes Castle.

Pernickety and petulant, and endlessly teased by Elisabeth for being a gowk, the cuckoo in their nest, Kate aspired to improve her lowly position through marriage. But, knowing that Kate had set her heart on their brother, Adam, the young Earl of Bothwell, Elisabeth had set her teeth against it.

Taking her time, Kate inspected the bed of embers before deciding where to place her nut. They all bent forward to watch as it hopped and skipped about, before being spat out to land on the hearth. Instinctively they drew their feet back.

"You'll have to throw it back in at once for your wish to come true."

Betsy glowered at Elisabeth, but was too late to stop Kate who'd already picked up the sizzling nut. And dropped it again with a piercing yelp of pain.

"Cuckoo! Cuckoo! Feardie-gowk!" Elisabeth goaded her.

"Sticks and stones may break my bones, but names will never hurt me," Kate recited and sucked on her smarting fingertips to soothe them.

"You were the clumsy kittok for dropping the nut and now your wish is forfeit."

"I don't believe you. You're only saying that because you don't want me to marry Adam. Well, you'll see. I'm no common kittok. I shall be a great lady one day. I shall be the Countess of Bothwell." She flicked back her golden hair and glared at her tormentor.

"Over my dead body, brazen besom," Elisabeth muttered under her breath. She couldn't abide the thought of her cousin becoming her brother's wife and a titled lady, for she suspected that, beneath her simpering mannerisms and ladylike demeanour, skulked a scheming wench.

"While no-one will waste a glance on a rapscallion like you," Kate was saying, "a gilpie no a girl." She tilted her head to look down her snub nose at Elisabeth, clad in her brother's cast-off riding breeches, her copper hair tousled and unkempt.

Seeing her jaggy thistle about to snap, Betsy clamped her hand across her mouth. Only when Elisabeth nodded, to indicate that she'd keep her mouth shut, did Betsy let go.

"Wheesht, wheesht, my fairest flowers," she crooned, "this is no a night for bickering."

"These daft games are tiresome." Kate stood up abruptly and wrapped her shawl tightly around her shoulders. "I'm away to bed."

"Afore the witching hour? On your own?"

Elisabeth's deep menacing growl had the intended effect. Kate glanced round, horror-stricken by the sinister shadows cast by the flickering tallow candles, before stammering, "Well, why not? I ... I ... "

"There's no telling who or what you'll meet on Hallows Eve," Elisabeth continued in her spooky voice, fluttering her fingers in front of Kate's anxious face. "When ghosts and ghouls and boglemen walk the earth."

"Don't you be scaring the living daylights out of her," Betsy chided. "Don't fret, Kate, you'll meet your match soon enough. Come, now, and sing us the *Ballad of True Thomas*." She leant forward to stoke the fire with more logs. "Coorie in my bonnie lassies, and listen."

With a hostile glare at her cousin, Kate tossed her fair curls and began crooning softly in her linnet-sweet voice, which, though she'd die rather than admit it, Elisabeth loved to hear.

> "True Thomas he pull'd off his cap,
> And louted low down to his knee.
> All hail, thou mighty Queen of Heaven!
> For thy peer on earth I never did see."

The girls listened spellbound to the legend of Thomas the Rhymer, lured by the Queen of Fairies to Elfland where he disappeared for seven long years, although it felt like only three days to him. Before he left, she gave him two gifts: a tongue that never lied and the power to see into the future.

"Betsy, have you the second sight?" Meg asked, her whisper breaking the mort-cloth of silence that had fallen over them after Kate's eldritch song. Betsy Learmont came from an old border family descended, so she told them, from this very Thomas of Earldoune, half minstrel, half magician, famed and feared for his sorceries. Betsy stared into the fire for a few moments before answering.

"I jalouse we all have in some way or other. We've all been given a sixth sense, a third eye, some cry it, that sees beyond the veil, but more often than not, most folk pay it scant heed. For where's the use in being able to peer through the dark veil smooring the future with no power to change it? And those who are truly foresighted would say it's more of a curse than a blessing.

"But at certain times of the year, like tonight, All Hallows'' Eve – or *Samhain* as the auld, Celtic religion cries it – the thin veil between this world and the next is drawn back. Nay," she said, shaking her head at Meg's raised eyebrows, "not your Christian paradise. Nor thon limbo where the souls of unbaptised bairns and pagans linger for eternity, but the twilight world between heaven and earth where the fairy folk and the unquiet dead dwell."

"The unquiet dead?" Meg murmured.

"Wheesht!" Betsy put a warning finger to her lips, for to mention them risked rousing them. She lowered her voice to a faint whisper. "The restless spirits of folk that have been murdered or have taken their own lives, who roam the earth, looking for unwary bodies of the living to possess." Her chilling words sent a shiver through Meg. "On this night our own spirits can leave our bodies, too. That's why you're able to see the spectre of the man you'll marry."

6

The blustery wind soughed down the chimney, gusting smoke into the chamber and rattling the shutters. The cold draught at their backs sent shivers skittering down their spines. The girls drew their thick woollen shawls more securely over their heads and huddled in closer together. As the mirk and midnight hour approached, Betsy set about making hot pint. She plunged the scorching poker into a kettle of spiced ale sweetened with honey until the toddy sizzled and simmered merrily, rising to the top in a smooth, creamy froth.

"This will give you good cheer and good heart," she promised.

While they blew on their courage-giving draught to cool it down, Betsy scraped some soot from inside the chimney to rub on their faces as a disguise to fool the malevolent spirits of the unquiet dead. It was nearly time to ring the stooks.

"I'll just bide here by the fire." Kate shivered. "It's far too cold and dark to be wandering about."

"You mean you're too feart. And what will Adam think when he hears the future Countess of Bothwell is a feardie gowk?"

Ignoring Elisabeth's taunt, Kate smeared her pink cheeks with soot and then wiped her clarty hands on Elisabeth's breeches. Betsy deftly stepped in between to foil any reprisal from the jaggy thistle and handed them each a branch from the fairy tree.

"These rowan twigs will ward off evil spirits. Hold on to them for dear life. Or else." She lit the taper in the neep lantern and passed it to Elisabeth. Its ghoulish grin of jagged teeth glowing in the dark would scare the living never mind the undead.

"Now, mind and go widdershins round the stooks," Betsy said, before adding, "and beware of tumbling into thon ditch, my jaggy thistle."

The snell blast as they stepped out from the shelter of the castle walls caught their breath. Hearing the wind whistling and howling like a carlin through the trees, the girls hesitated. Top-heavy pines swayed back and forth in the wind, threatening to fall over and crash down on them. Trees stripped of their leaves were transformed into blackened skeletons with gnarled, wizened fingers pointing in menace. Leaves whirled and reeled madly like hobgoblins at Auld Clootie's ball. Clouds scudded past the furtive moon, casting unearthly shadows. Striving to make no sound that would alert evil spirits, the girls stepped lightly, but the crisp, dry leaves crackled and crunched underfoot.

By the glimmer of the neep lantern they skirted round the ditch filled with fallen leaves until they came to the crossing point. In the cornfield, the harvest straw gathered into sheaves stood like rows of drunken men leaning into each other for support. Kate hung tightly to Meg but kept looking round, convinced that they were being followed.

"Aagh! What's that?" She stopped to brandish her rowan switch.

"Wheesht! You'll wake the unquiet dead with your screeching," Elisabeth growled.

"Look over there." Kate was pointing with her twig. "Isn't thon a bogleman?"

All three huddled together to peer at the eerie shape frantically waving its tattered limbs as if in warning.

"Thon's a pease-bogle, you daft gowk," Elisabeth sneered as the scarecrow keeled over in the strong wind.

Stopping beside the nearest haystack, they bickered about which way to circle it. "Betsy said mind and go widdershins," Meg said, her teeth chittering.

"The devil's way? Against the sun? Will that no bring bad luck?" Kate shivered.

Meg shrugged her shoulders. "Not at Hallowe'en. For this is the witches" night and we'll vex Auld Nick mair if we go sunwise, says Betsy. Now shut your een and hold your arms out in front. Circle three times and on the third turn your sweetheart's spectre will appear."

"I … I… I'm no sure I want to do this." Kate was looking round, still certain that some malevolent spirit was stalking them.

"We'll do it together," Elisabeth suggested, for she, too, was feeling uneasy.

Having no wish for a spouse in any form – body or spirit – Meg held the lantern while the two girls, eyes tight shut and arms stretched out like sleepwalkers, began to circle the stook. Willing herself to see the image of the one she loved, Elisabeth squeezed her eyelids tight against her eyeballs until colours flashed and flared in her head.

As they came round for the third time, leaves disturbed by a field mouse or vole rustled nearby. An owl or bat whooshed past her, and then a high-pitched scream rang out, chilling her blood. In the shadows of the trees, Elisabeth could make out two shapes stumbling across the cornfield towards them. As they loomed nearer, she drew back, alarmed to see two bogles, the whites of their eyes gleaming in blackened faces.

"Beware the unquiet dead!" a menacing voice rumbled.

"Or the quiet undead!" another echoed.

When one of the ghouls darted forward to reel her in, Elisabeth turned tail. She flung aside her rowan switch and stumbled over divots towards the ditch.

Suddenly the burn bubbled up and a torrent swept her off her feet. As she was tossed and spun in the murky water, shadowy figures whirled around her. She tried to grab hold of a hand but the rotting flesh fell away from the fingers. A severed head spun towards her, its fronds of hair streaming out behind, its face stripped of flesh. With greenish-black pus gushing through the empty eye sockets and its jaws locked in an eternal grimace, the skull leered at her. The burn water thickened and darkened to blood red, brimming into her lungs. As the whooshing sound in her ears died down, she opened her mouth to gulp down air. From far away she heard an unearthly voice murmur, "She's coming to herself."

When arms lifted her up and propped her against a dyke, Elisabeth snorted to clear the stench of decaying leaves in her nostrils, but as she wiped the glaur from her eyes she let out a yelp. Behind the neep lantern with its jagged teeth, another ghastly head, with soot-stained mouth and bone white teeth, was yawning wide. She jolted backwards but, as she jerked forwards, her forehead whacked the fiend's nose with a loud crack.

"Ouch!" The bogle's hand darted to its face. "*Nemo me impune lacessit.* You're well named, my jaggy thistle. Who'd dare meddle with you? Your snite is worse than your bite. And there was I, ready to bewitch you with a kiss," he mumbled, dabbing at the streaks of sooty blood trickling from his nose. "Pity."

"She hasn't broken anything." Meg had knelt down in the glaur to massage her sister's ankles with fingers cold as the grave.

"What about me?" the ghoul wailed. "Not only my nose but my poor heart is sore."

"She's well enough if she can skelp him like that," Kate hissed, but, seeing the other bogleman approach, she widened doe eyes at him. "Forbye, this spanking wind is whipping the skin off my cheeks," she whimpered.

"Come, then, afore it flays the hide off you." The fiendish Earl of Bothwell was holding out one crooked arm to Kate who, needing no further coaxing, linked her arm through his. But when he offered his other arm to Meg, whose very bones were trembling with cold, Kate's face darkened to a glower. Meanwhile the other ghoul was helping Elisabeth to her feet.

"You ... you ... scared me half to death, Davie Lindsay," she scolded.

"Better not let the cold kill the other half then."

Lindsay pulled her into the shelter of his cloak but the acrid smell of soot from his blackened face began to prickle her nostrils. As she screwed up her nose to stifle a sneeze, he pressed his finger hard against her top lip.

"Squeezing is better than sneezing, my jaggy thistle. And kissing can wait. But keep in mind whose spirit you've seen tonight, otherwise the devil knows who you'll marry."

II

A Cursing

The eldest she was vexed sair,
And much envied her sister fair.
Into her bower she could not rest,
Wi grief and spite she almost brast.
The Ballad of The Twa Sisters, Traditional

Hailes Castle, January 1512

Elisabeth lay on top of the bed, cradling a hot stone wrapped in cloths to soothe the dull ache in her womb. The curse of Eve, her monthly bleed had begun and, though her eyelids were heavy and she craved sleep, she feared falling into the terrifying dwam.

"No wonder you were scared," Betsy had said. "Didn't I warn you about the fairy hole? You were lucky – the wee folk could have dragged you away. But I fear the fairy blast may have dinted you with the falling sickness. Keep the St.John's nut with you always to spare you from it."

At Hallowe'en Elisabeth had tumbled across a threshold, from girlish innocence to the darker, mysterious realm of womanhood. Ever since then she felt as if the unquiet spirits had taken over her body, making her tetchy and tearful – not like herself at all – and, reliving the moment when Lindsay had bundled her tightly in the folds of his cloak, made the tiniest hairs all over her body tingle. Was that what was meant by falling in love? Head-over-heels. Tapsalteerie. Whigmaleerie.

Elisabeth rubbed her eyes. A strange, oval cloud had appeared high above. Everyone was looking upwards expectantly. To the sounds of creaking, cranking and whirring, the egg-shaped cloud slowly cracked open. A huge bird spread out its elaborate wings and hovered above them before gliding down to earth. While the crowd clapped and cheered, Elisabeth pushed her way past legs and skirts to where the bird had landed. Her eyes grew huge and her lips rounded into an O. Never in her ten years had she seen anything like this. Feathered and festooned in gold and emerald plumage was the most glamorous woman: tall and wide-hipped, with skin the colour of a burnished chestnut and lips as plump as plums.

The thrilled spectators were now crowding round to congratulate Sir David Lindsay, Master of the King's Revels, on his breathtaking spectacle. The flight of the Moorish Maiden was the highlight of the Tournament of the Wild Knight. Brimming with excitement, Elisabeth swooped at him, demanding to soar and fly like the Lady

Bird. With a great whoop, he picked her up and whirled her round and round, her petticoats billowing outwards. She screamed in delight as the world swung round, a whirligig of gaudy colour. Gaily coloured tents and pavilions adorned with banners of silver and gold and flying pennants flashed past her eyes in a trice.

Back down to earth, she'd staggered around drunkenly for a while, her head still reeling with dizzy exhilaration.

"Steady now, steady." Lindsay held her firmly to stop her from keeling over.

"Nay!" she cried out, holding up her arms, "Mair birling! Mair birling!"

"Are you pestering our court jester?" her brother Adam chided, before turning to wink at his friend. "Our jaggy thistle is thrawn and never takes nay for an answer. She'll never let you stop, even if you make her puke."

"Indeed?" Lindsay laughed. Picking her up again, he whirled her round until giddiness made him wobble and lose his balance. He set her down gently, keeping her steady until her head stopped spinning. After blinking a few times, she focussed her eyes on him and solemnly put the question.

"Davie Lindsay, will you marry me?"

"Since when did maidens do the speiring?" His grey eyes were twinkling but, on seeing her face about to crumple, he knelt down on one knee and took her hand.

"Your proposal may be most precocious, but it's the best I've had all day."

"Most precious? Truly?"

"Aye, and precious too," he nodded, his face serious. "Now, no flashing those green eyes at anyone else or you'll make *me* green. With envy. You're promised to me, mind."

Had Lindsay meant it or had it just been a ruse to quieten a tousie ten-year-old lass? Had he been sincere when he'd tried to steal a kiss at Hallowe'en? Or only teasing? Elisabeth was startled out of her dwam by the shrill screech from the next room that sent needle-sharp shards of pain shooting through her skull.

"Not only is that shameless whore a bastard, but the mother of one. Hurled out of the bed of the king who's had his fill of her, the flaggartie slattern smickers at Adam. How dare she? Does he ken where she's been fyking? Does he ken she's already had the king's bairn? How could he! For all he kens she may be carrying another royal bastard."

At the end of January Adam was to marry – not Kate as she'd wished – but a former mistress of the king. Agnes Stewart, or Nancy as she was known, was not only the natural daughter of the Earl of Buchan, but mother to one of James IV's ill-begotten daughters. Kate felt severely wronged. Brazen beyond belief, the harpy had swooped down behind her back and carried him off. Hell hath no fury like a woman scorned and Kate seethed, angrier than a cowped wasps" byke.

"And yon cow-clink is to become the Countess of Bothwell! It cannot be! You must make Adam change his mind," she hissed.

As the bearer of bad news, Meg was bearing the brunt of her cousin's temper.

"But how? What can I do? He never made a promise to you, did he?" Her face pinched tight with fear, Meg fluttered helplessly around her cousin, like a mother hen trying to calm her chick. Kate gripped her by the forearms and dug her sharp nails into her shilpit flesh.

"Nay, but he's your brother and you saw how he flirted with me. You can't say he was only trifling with me. He cannot marry yon ... yon strumpet. I won't stand for it."

Kate's eyes, swollen from salty tears, bulged in her puffy face as she shook frail Meg back and forth until her bones creaked.

"Leave her be, you skirling shrew!" Elisabeth pounced on Kate and hauled her away from her sister who reeled backwards, stunned by her violent tirrivee. "If Adam has made up his mind to wed Nancy, then he will – and he'll do so because he loves her," she went on, further stoking Kate's blazing fury.

"Love? How could he love that tawdry trollop?" Bitter tears had stained her cheeks and her perfectly groomed golden hair spilt untidily over her shoulders. For a split second Elisabeth felt sorry for her – slighted love was sair to bide – until Kate's face warped into an ugly mask of rage and she poked an accusing finger at her.

"He's been dintit, smitten, and it's your fault. You never wanted me to marry him. You've put a hex on him, you witch – some spell of Betsy's, some potion in his ale. You must have done something to beglamour him, you cankart carlin. How else could he ... "

Kate clenched her fists, as if desperate to lash out at something. Or someone.

"How dare you cry me a witch, you cuckoo in the nest," Elisabeth snapped. "I had no hand in it. Forbye, what would my brother want with a vauntie-flauntie like you who thinks that, just by fluttering her eyelashes, men will come flocking? Much good your joukerie-pawkery has done you. Och, dearie me, my heart's all aflutter. I fear I may fall into a swoon," she drawled, raising a limp hand to her forehead in mockery. "That may draw their attention, but it won't hold their interest."

"She's jealous. Because I can attract admirers," Kate boasted to Meg who, still dazed by her outburst, was massaging her bruised arms.

"Even a festering corpse can draw maggots," Elisabeth retorted.

"That's not true. Plenty of suitors dangle on my every word."

"Aye, but that's all they do. Dangle. While Nancy kens how to reel them in."

In a fit of frenzy, Kate launched herself at her tormentor. Elisabeth grabbed her wrists and, as they wrestled, the blood whooshed in her ears. The flesh on Kate's face seemed to dissolve, unveiling the skull beneath: Elisabeth blinked and stumbled backwards onto the settle. She gave her head a good shake and, when she dared to look again, Kate was bleating and rubbing her wrists. Her face was puffy and tear-stained but not macabre. Elisabeth stood up warily and swayed unsteadily towards her. She sniffed a few times and then ran her fingers over the greasy blotches smearing Kate's cheeks.

"What's that muck on your face?"

"Goose fat," Meg volunteered quietly before positioning herself between the two adversaries to keep them apart. "Betsy says it's good for the complexion."

"Much good it has done you," Elisabeth sneered and wiped her hands up and down the front of Kate's woollen gown.

Arching her back, Kate hissed and spat like a cornered wildcat and her eyes narrowed to demonic slits. "If I were a witch, I'd cast the evil eye on all you Hepburns."

"Oh, Kate, you should never cast such a cantrip." Meg's pale face drained to a deathly pallor. She reached out to restrain Kate who waved her hand away impatiently.

"I'd curse you standing; I'd curse you sitting. I'd curse you in bed … I'd curse every hair on your head to be nit-infested, every bone in your body to crack and every breath that you breathe to throttle you till the last gasp."

As she let fly with the cursing, her whole being blazed: her face aflame, her lips frothing with bile, her eyes dirling with blood-red fury. Meg closed her eyes, murmuring a prayer and making the sign of the holy cross. Elisabeth fumbled in her pocket for her charm against the evil eye and rolled the St. John's nut between her fingers. Kate faltered for a moment before bursting forth with a final blast.

"The devil swarbit on you! Just wait. You'll see. I'll have my revenge."

III

The Wedding Feast

Was never in Scotland heard nor seen
Sic dancing nor deray.
Christis Kirk on the Green
Anonymous, 15th Century

Hailes Castle, 31 January 1512

"No expense has been spared, I see."

Prior Hepburn glanced round appreciatively as he warmed himself by one of the two huge log fires blazing at either end of the Great Hall. The bare flagstone floors had been strewn with heather and the rough, stone walls bedecked with seasonal red-berried holly and green-leaved ivy. But, more importantly for the Prior of St. Andrews, the oaken trestles buckled under the weight of the nuptial feast. The aroma of roasted meats and fowls was stirring up his digestive juices. Conducting the marriage ceremony had been hungry work indeed.

The prior cast his keen blue eyes over the lavish spread: gigots of venison and wild boar, all kinds of roasted birds and a sheep's head, its skull stuffed with boiled brains. He rubbed his podgy hands and smacked his fleshy red lips, drooling in anticipation of cramming his belly. Already ensconced at the trestle, his sister jiggled her head in approval. Even stouter than her brother, Dame Janet, the Prioress of St. Mary's Abbey, goggled with greedy eyes at the honeyed cakes and sweetmeats piled up on ashets in front of her.

"They say the king himself paid for the bride's gown," she said. "And her daughter Jenny is to be stabled in the royal nursery with all the rest of the king's bastards."

"Small recompense for services rendered," the prior sneered. "As the foremost earl in the land, Adam could have skimmed off the cream of Scotland's maidenhood, yet he chooses the brock from the king's table."

"Aye, it's a sorry trait in the Hepburn men to be dintit with the kings" quines. Adam's grandfather, whom he was cried after, laid siege to Mary of Gueldres, widow of James of the fiery face, and afore that Patrick Hepburn of Hailes was champion of Queen Joan, the widow of the first James. And even Adam's father, our brother Patrick, God rest his soul, had to share his own wife ..."

"Don't be casting up that old clishmaclaver." Prior John's violet eyes flashed with anger. "Whatever wagging tongues may say it was not the *Countess* of Bothwell whom the king dabbled with but the flighty *Lady* Bothwell. Thon wanton, Janet Kennedy, wife to a few and mistress to many, freely bestowed her favours for land and title. As the mistress of Bell the Cat Douglas – though *she* claims she was his

14

wife – she received the barony of Bothwell, which *he* claimed was his to give. Then she has the brazen cheek to mislead everyone by styling herself *Lady* Bothwell. Nay, our brother's wife, Countess Margaret, was a fine, modest woman who had to thole that scandal and she did so with dignity. May her soul rest in peace."

"Pardon me, brother." Dame Janet rolled her eyes in mock apology. "Well, let's be thankit that Adam hasn't fallen for the queen."

The prior snorted. "What full-blooded Scotsman would? The Tudor rose has lost her bloom and grown blowsy and stout."

Opening her mouth to retort, Janet thought better of it and closed it again. "Let's hope Adam kens what he's taking on," she remarked instead. "Nancy Stewart is a spirited lass. Men may be drawn to her, as bees to heather, but her like are rarely content with just the one loun. Young Adam will not be the last, I fear. She'll be lowping the dyke afore long."

The prior frowned at her. "They've only just taken their vows."

"And when did that ever stop folk?" Dame Janet's chin disappeared into her plump shoulders as she shrugged. "Forbye, it's only the plain truth I'm telling." Her bulbous eyes swelled even more as she nudged her brother. "Well, what toothsome dainties have we here."

The three girls hesitated on the threshold of the Great Hall. With her head held high, Kate surveyed the guests with a defiant look. Dressed to rival the bride in a gown of rich, ruby red velvet, she stood with one hand on her thrust-out hip as if in challenge. Let Adam Hepburn have his slattern: she would show everyone what he'd missed.

"Thon one looks set to become a besom." Dame Janet grinned. Then, seeing the prior's eyes light up at the sight of Kate's well-developed bosom straining the laces of her bodice, testing the limits of decency, she said, "Pop your een back in for a moment, brother. Thon bonnie flowers you're ogling so randily are your nieces."

Bashful and self-conscious, Elisabeth kept her eyes down as she fiddled with the white fur trimming on the sleeve of her mistletoe-green velvet gown. Meg – nunlike in a plain robe of palest cream wool – shimmered like a will o" the wisp between the two rivals. While the comely Kate flaunted herself in her low-cut bodice, Elisabeth felt awkward. Tall and gawky, with bones poking out at all angles, Lisbeth was indeed a gilpie of a lass, more comfortable in her brother's cast-off leather breeches and jerkins than laced into confining corsets and restrictive skirts.

Though her figure was beginning to fill out, putting more flesh on her bones and softening the sharp edges, she still felt too spiky. Like a skittish colt, she had frisked and fretted while Betsy mercilessly brushed the tangles out of her unruly hair until it rippled, a mane of burnished copper, down her back. Alarmed at how immodestly high the tight lacing of the bodice pushed up her meagre bosom, Elisabeth had swaddled herself in a shawl.

"How swiftly time flies! How quickly they have grown." The prior became pensive. He hadn't seen them since they were babes, not since he'd fallen out with his older brother.

Dame Janet's attention was elsewhere, drawn to one of her favourite dainties. As she sank what remained of her teeth into the delicacy, her eyelids quivered in ecstasy. She then sucked her fingers languorously, one after the other, to savour every last globule of grease. Meg and Elisabeth, their eyes like collops, exchanged glances.

Dame Janet smacked her lips. "Just how I like them: soft, squidgy and sweet. Tastier than a strumpet's teats. Taigle your tongues round these, my lassies, for your hair to curl and your juices to flow."

But she could tempt neither sister with her treat of stag testicles, slowly poached in a honeyed sauce. Indeed, the sight of a guest scooping out the greyish skirlie from the grinning sheep's head was making Elisabeth feel quite queasy.

Prior John crooked his pinkie at them. "Let's have a keek at you." As his saturnine eyes scrutinised them closely, he gave a low whistle. "By Christ's blood, if she isn't the very image of her mother. She has her eyes."

He dabbed at the beads of sweat glistening on his brow with a silk napkin. Leaning forward he tried to remove Elisabeth's shawl for closer inspection but she grasped it even more firmly and glared boldly at him.

"Ha! Shielding your modesty are you? No harm in that. How old are you now, my bright young virgins?"

Meg had just turned seventeen and Elisabeth was nearly fourteen. Already? And what of their future? What provisions were being made? Dame Janet shrugged her plump shoulders. On his father's death, this had been Adam's responsibility, but he had been too taken up with his own marital matters to make plans for his sisters. Hepburn flashed an angry rebuke at the prioress.

"Then it's high time we stepped in, sister. And the sooner the better."

While the trestles were being cleared away, Elisabeth scanned the hall for the groomsman. Ever since Hallowe'en she'd been like a hen on a hot girdle. How could she have dunted Davie Lindsay on the nose! What must he think of her? A daft, foolish lassie, no doubt. Or away with the fairies as Betsy believed. There he was, talking to one of the king's men. She picked up a goblet of wine and quickly downed it to stop her heart from racing. The tight lacing on her gown constricted her breathing and her hands were clammy with perspiration.

While waiting, she checked her sleeve where she'd hidden the magic talisman Betsy had given her. Then she shrugged her shawl downwards, lowering it just enough to expose her shoulders. Hands clasped, she worried at her hangnails until Lindsay dismissed the servant. With a final pat on the talisman, she took a deep breath and started towards him. At that moment, Kate swished past her to strut in front of Lindsay.

"Ah, the very man. I have a favour to ask of the groomsman," she said coyly, batting her eyelashes and simpering in the way that seemed to please men but which stuck in Elisabeth's craw. If he put his arm round Kate's waist, if he whirled her round the floor, she wouldn't be able to thole it. Whatever it was that Kate was requesting, Lindsay was shaking his head in response. Good. He'd snubbed her and now she was moving on to more lucrative quarry: a swarm of admiring young studs.

Summoning all her courage, Elisabeth stepped forward and tapped Lindsay on the shoulder. "Will you dance with me, Davie?" she asked, trying to control her wavering voice.

He looked her up and down, his expression puzzled.

"What? Can this be my jaggy thistle? Why, I hardly recognise you in your finery." Then, wagging his finger, he gently chided her. "You may have blossomed into a bonnie flower of the forest but your manners are still rough-hewn. Did they never teach you that it's unseemly for a lady to ask a gentleman to dance?"

Elisabeth's cheeks flamed as crimson as Kate's gown and her courage ebbed away. Another mistake. She would have slunk off but he took her hand and squeezed it firmly. "Stand firm, my jaggy thistle, and mind your motto: *Who dares meddle with me?*"

He bent down to pick up her shawl that had fallen to the floor, but instead of draping it round her, he flung it over his own shoulder. "If my lady does not spurn my advances," he gave a knowing wink, "I shall be honoured to be her knight this evening. And I claim this shawl as my token." He bowed low with an exaggerated flourish.

"Forgive me for cracking your nose," Elisabeth blurted as they waited for the musicians to strike up. "I didn't mean to." She began to fiddle nervously with her fur-trimmed sleeve where she'd hidden the sprig of mistletoe that Betsy assured would bring good luck in love. Stretching up on tiptoe, she swiftly pecked him on the cheek. Lindsay took an exaggerated step backwards in surprise, his eyes crinkling with laughter.

"What's this? A kiss under the mistletoe! Why, what a little pagan you are! First you invite me to dance, and then you kiss me like a wanton hussy. What next I wonder? But once smitten twice shy," he said, pointing to his nose.

Helpless desperation gagged her sharp tongue and she felt as jiggly as one of the jellies on the banqueting table. Why hadn't she paid more attention to how Kate flirted?

"You have much to learn, my guileless thistle." Lindsay brushed her cheeks lightly with his lips and then, as the music struck up, he gripped her tightly round the waist and whirled her into the throng of dancers. Giddy and breathless, her cheeks glowing, her flesh tingling at his touch, she willed this whigmaleerie to go on forever and ever.

"Stop the music! Stop the music!"

The reeling throng of dancers gradually wound down, bodies bumping into each other as they came to a chaotic halt. Who had dared to give such an order? The lackey Lindsay had been speaking to earlier was swaying unsteadily on a trestle table, and waving his arms.

"Harp and carp, Davie Lindsay! Harp and carp! You're the groomsman and it's high time for the bedding. Get on with it, man."

His speech was a slurred drawl but the guests congregating around the shoogly table clapped and cheered.

"Who does yon flunkey think he is, giving orders like that?" Kate remarked loudly. "Why doesn't somebody pull the drunken oaf down?"

Dame Janet's fingers dug into her bare arm. "Have you not heard of the Guiser, my lass?" Kate winced as the prioress yanked her in closer. "*That's* who *thon* is. It's the king's fancy to dress up as a commoner and gad about the land. He thinks he's well buskit. As if anybody could be fooled. Thon foxy red hair and long neb stick out a mile," she snorted. "Yet we must feign ignorance and yield to His Grace, as do the lasses he lowps on. One of the royal privileges." She gave a knowing wink.

"That is King James?" Kate's round eyes widened, first in astonishment, then in admiration. So, the king was attending the wedding after all – despite what Lindsay had said. No doubt he'd had to keep it secret.

"The time is ripe. And so is the bride. And I'm as impatient as the groom to …" the lackey smacked his lips and cackled lewdly, "loosen her snood."

"Why are they needing a bedding? The whole world and its mother ken that the bride's cherry has been picked long ago," Dame Janet trilled, her shrill voice rising above the hubbub. "And by no less than the monarch himself," she added under her breath.

"Aye, my lady prioress, you're right. And if the king himself were here he could vouch for the bride's chaumer skills," the lackey yelled back.

"It's a great pity His Grace has not deemed it worthy to grace us with his presence," Dame Janet placed her hand on her bosom and sighed, rolling her goggle eyes dramatically.

"Aye, but he has." The lackey pulled off his cap triumphantly to reveal the straggly, pale-reddish hair of King James himself. "And he's come to measure the groom's knack and see if it's up to regal standard. So, stand proud, my Lord Bothwell, and, by royal command, let the bedding begin."

As the drunken crowd around her hooted and howled, Meg looked bewildered.

"I don't understand. What does he mean?" she asked.

Dame Janet leant over and grinned, baring the jagged remains of her blackened, rotting teeth and belching fumes of claret in her face.

"You chaste young damsels have been living a life more sheltered than in my cloister, I fear. Time to school you in the ways of the world. What he means is that the menfolk will carry off the bride, while the ladies lead the bridegroom to the marriage bed. There they'll be stripped naked and hurled together on the bed. Where," she broke off with a vulgar, coarse laugh, "they shall dance the reel of Bogie until we're all satisfied that the deed is done." The prioress cackled with glee.

"*Consummatum est!*" Prior John pronounced irreverently.

"Adam and Nancy are to be gawked at? By everyone?" Meg gasped. The idea that this drunken, rowdy mob should witness such an intimate act was shocking.

"Aye, by the whole clamjamfray." Prior John's lips contorted into a repulsive leer. It was the part of the nuptials that he enjoyed most. The spiritual union – the marriage service – was never as satisfying as blessing the newly-weds" bed and drooling over their physical union.

Dame Janet patted Meg's hand. "There's no need to be so mimsy-mou'ed, my lass. Sonsie Nancy is no modest maiden. She kens a thing or two about tail-toddle. Aye, and you'll have to learn about it ere long."

At her aunt's warning, Meg's horrified face swiftly drained of any colour, becoming even paler than her gown.

"Look at all the toadies, falling over themselves to bend the knee in front of their monarch," the prioress sneered.

In the midst of them all was Kate who, now that she had been enlightened, had revised her opinion of the insolent fool. She fussed with the neckline of her bodice, tugging it down lower to reveal even more of her charms. Meanwhile, the monarch was becoming impatient.

"What's the delay, Davie? You cannot tell me the bride is unwilling."

"Forbear with me, Lisbeth," Lindsay said and draped the shawl round her shoulders. "I must obey His Grace's bidding. The king's pleasure aye comes before my own." His breath soft and sweet against her cheek as he whispered softly, "Wait for me, I'll be back as soon as I can. You promised me a kiss, mind."

"A song! We need a song," the king was shouting. "To cantle up the bride and groom for the marriage bed."

Kate stepped in front of the drunken rabble and began to sing, her strong soprano soaring high above their discordant chorus:

"Fye, let us all to the bridal,
For there will be lilting there;
For Jockie's to be married to Maggie,
The lass with the gowden hair."

Meanwhile, Meg had stumbled towards the doorjamb for support. She leaned against it, one arm hiding her face, the other clutching her stomach. Turning her ashen face to Elisabeth, she whispered, "Oh, Lisbeth, I pray I never have to wed. I couldn't thole their jibes and jeers."

Nor could she contemplate her fragile virginity being breached. Shrinking into herself she shielded her womb. "How I wish mother were still here with us."

Seeing the pained look flicker across Elisabeth's face, she clutched her arm.

"Oh, Lisbeth, I didn't mean ... You mustn't think I was casting it up to you."

But Elisabeth had no such thought for she knew well enough that there was not a spiteful bone in Meg's delicate body. Winding her shawl round her sister's shuddering shoulders she led her away.

IV

Annunciation

> I have thee luvit loud and still,
> Thir yearis two or three.
> *Robin and Makyne*
> Robert Henryson, 15th Century

Hailes Castle, 25 March 1512

Betsy had opened the shutters wide to air the chamber, fusty and stale with wood-smoke after the dark, damp winter. By the fireside, Meg sat curled up in the Orkney chair, a gift to her father when he was appointed Lord of Orkney and the Shetland Isles. With short, stumpy legs and a high oaten straw back with a hood to keep out chilling draughts, the chair suited Meg perfectly. Weary after rising early to attend Mass of the Annunciation at the nearby abbey, she supped Betsy's milk brose. Never mind that it broke the Lenten fast, Betsy insisted she needed it to restore her strength after all that knee bending.

Meg shivered as Elisabeth burst in, leaving the door wide open. Still dressed in her breeches and riding jerkin after her morning ride, she prowled up and down, anxious and edgy. Usually her fidgeting would kittle up Kate, but she seemed not to notice. She sat idly with her embroidery in her lap, staring into the middle distance as if in a dwam, quietly humming to herself.

Elisabeth scrambled onto the window bunker and poked her head out of the window of the west tower. Far below, the waters of the River Tyne tumbled through a ravine before flowing more calmly in front of the castle. Further along the riverbank to the west, masons were clambering up and down the scaffolding erected for the construction of the new bell-tower at St. Mary's Abbey, but her eyes were drawn northwards. Across the Tyne and beyond the rise lay Garleton, the Lindsay family seat.

Just then Betsy came hirpling in with her lopsided gait, the result of a childhood ailment that had left one leg shorter than the other.

"Dicht yourselves, my bonnie lassies, for you have a visitor," she said, giving Lisbeth a playful skelp on the seat of her breeches.

Wabbit at the thought of company, Meg snuggled deeper into her chair, while Kate, a secret smile flitting across her face, picked up her sewing and began stitching tiny crosses. Elisabeth sprang from the window seat and bounded to the door like an exuberant puppy, colliding unceremoniously with their visitor. Thrown off balance, she backed into the room again, flustered at the sight of the king's herald resplendent in a red tunic with the lion rampant emblazoned in gold. Every day since Adam's wedding, Elisabeth had ridden out by Garleton, hoping for a chance encounter with Davie Lindsay, but she'd always been disappointed. And now here he was!

Graciously refusing Betsy's offer of refreshment, he bowed courteously to them all. In vain Elisabeth tried to read the expression on his face, but Lindsay, in his rôle as professional courtier, was inscrutable. Not a glimmer of a smile or even a wink as he requested permission for a private audience with one of the ladies. Black affronted at her untidily braided hair, Elisabeth pointlessly brushed at the mud on her breeches.

She was about to step forward when Lindsay strode past her and held out his hand – to Kate, who gazed up at him demurely from under her eyelashes. Her backward smirk as she flounced out of the room on Lindsay's arm ruffled Elisabeth's temper. Why did he want to speak to Kate? What could he possibly have to say to thon gowk?

"Surely he's not going to ask for her hand?"

"Wheesht, wheesht, my lass," Betsy said to calm her. "He's on the king's business, so he told me. He wouldn't be wearing thon tabard otherwise."

"But what has the king to do with Kate?" Elisabeth grumbled, gnawing at her hangnails until slapped down by Betsy. She thrust her hands under her oxters and stomped up and down the room. When at last Kate appeared, she paused dramatically in the doorway before making her announcement in a newly acquired, haughty tone.

"I have been chosen to be one of the queen's ladies. And I am to leave for Edinburgh immediately. Betsy, you shall help me to gather my belongings."

As she pranced off, Betsy raised her eyebrows at her command. Leaning forward, hand on her chin to gaze into the fire, Meg heaved a sigh.

"What a grand privilege for Kate! To be invited to the court of the Thistle and the Rose! Oh, Lisbeth, do you mind the poem that was written for the queen's arrival into Scotland?"

"Aye, all thon rigmarole about the mighty English king's daughter being *a princess most pleasant and preclare.*" Even their father, the Earl of Bothwell, who'd acted as proxy bridegroom at her betrothal, had praised her beauty and regal bearing. "Telling us she was the fairest of the fair, when she wasn't even bonnie," Elisabeth snorted.

Meg sighed. It was true. Even she had been disappointed when they had met the queen, Margaret Tudor, at the Tournament of the Wild Knight.

"Aye, I mind it was the Moorish lady that took your fancy. While all the ladies of the court scanced at her for being a coarse blackamoor, you kept saying you'd never seen anyone so sonsie."

And, with her glossy chestnut skin, shimmering corbie-black hair and teeth as white as caller oyster pearls, Black Ellen, as she was cried, was majestic. In contrast, Queen Margaret was a dowdy dunnock.

"Short and squat and skrinkie-faced with froggy eyes. And a mouth like this ..."

Elisabeth pursed her lips together and pushed them out in grotesque imitation. "Not a princess but a puddock."

"Just as well she didn't hear what you said about her; otherwise she'd have had your eyes out." Meg gave a little chuckle.

"Even if she had, she wouldn't ken what a puddock was."

"Oh! I'm sure Her Grace would soon have been enlightened by one of her toadies," a male voice broke in.

Startled, Elisabeth swung round. Lindsay was leaning against the doorjamb, arms crossed, the corners of his mouth crinkled into a mischievous smile.

"Well, whoever wrote that poem about her was telling barefaced fibs," Elisabeth maintained though her cheeks were reddening.

"Have you no poetic soul, my dear lass? I'll admit that eulogy is not one of the makar's best. William Dunbar has written much better verses than those."

"Like the *Twa Marrit Women and the Widow*?" Elisabeth giggled while Meg gave her a cautionary look. Nancy Stewart had often dropped tantalising hints about this bawdy poem but always refused their pleas to recite it for them.

"It's not for the ears of two unmarried lassies like you. Once you're both old hen-wives, perhaps."

"But then it'll be too late. Surely we need to ken now so as to …"

"Be acquent with the sleekit tricks wives use to deceive their husbands?" Lindsay suggested.

"Nay. To learn how to be a lady. Like Kate." Elisabeth pouted and, thrusting her hips forwards, tucked her hands into the pockets of her old breeches.

"That," he began, slowly eyeing her up and down, "could take some time."

"Oh, stop scarting and nipping, you two." Meg yawned. "You're tiring me out."

Lindsay winked. "Just sharpening our tongues for a bout of flyting."

"Well, take her out for a walk, Davie, and douse her feisty temper."

With a Kate-like toss of her braids, Elisabeth flounced out of the chamber.

Leaving the castle by the postern gate, she waited until they had scrambled down the steep riverbank before challenging him.

"Where have you been, Davie Lindsay? You gave your word that you'd come."

"So my jaggy thistle is still prickly, with no kind word for her sweetheart. O cruel maid, does it not please you that I am here now?" He tried to slip his arm round her waist but she wriggled free.

"Only to speak with Kate, it seems." She refused to look at him and kept her arms firmly folded. "How long would I have had to wait otherwise?"

"I beg forgiveness, my dearest Lisbeth, but it's not so easy to escape from court. The king's affairs aye keep me busy."

When he tried to sweep a straggly hair out of her eye, she shied away.

"So, no hope of claiming that kiss, then? Pity." And, with a nonchalant shrug of his shoulders, he turned round and walked off.

Elisabeth wanted to scream in frustration. Her childish peevishness was driving him away and she had no artful tricks to lure him back. She ran after him and clutched at his arm.

"Don't go, Davie. I'm sorry. Look, you can kiss me now."

She squeezed her eyelids tightly together, puckered up her lips and waited. Aware of a slight movement from him, she screwed up her face more enthusiastically. Instead of feeling his lips pressing against hers, she heard a peculiar, strangulated sound. Baffled, her eyes flew open to see Lindsay's shoulders quivering and his face red and contorted as he choked back tears.

"Are you unwell?"

"Nay ... Aye ... I mean nay. I'm s ...s ... so sorry." He pressed his hand hard against his mouth. "It was just that you put me in mind of that puddock you described. The way you ..." he managed to blurt out, before doubling up in a fit of laughter.

Elisabeth's cheeks burned, affronted at his cruel mockery.

"Well, then, it's your loss. For all you ken, I might have been turned into a princess."

Before she could stomp off, he grabbed her round the waist and pulled her in close. Catching her unawares, he kissed her firmly on her parted lips. Not a short peck or a swift smack, but a long, lingering kiss full on the mouth. He hugged her tightly, squeezing out her life-breath and making her heart race. When he let her go, her head was reeling: the whole world spinning and wheeling like the day he'd birled her round and round. Tapsalteerie. Whigmaleerie.

"Now, that," he insisted, "is a kiss."

Instinctively her arms flew up and clasped his neck in a stranglehold.

"Have I so offended you that you want to throttle me?" he burbled, breaking free from her grasp. Only when he felt her relax in his embrace, did he kiss her again. "Aye, there's a chance that this puddock may turn into a princess."

Reluctant though he was to leave her, he'd have to go. Kate wouldn't take kindly to be kept waiting. Elisabeth gazed around in a daze before dashing off up the slope. So, a kiss had transformed his jaggy thistle into fluffy thistledown, to be wafted away on a slight breeze? His powers of enchantment were more potent than he thought.

"Watch this!" At the top of the slope she fell onto her front and began tumbling over and over downhill, recovering her balance just in time to avoid splashing into the river. She was scrambling to her feet when something caught her eye. She bent down to pick it up and then, holding one hand cupped over the other, she ran towards Lindsay.

"I've made a wish, Davie," Elisabeth said, struggling to suppress a cheeky grin. "I cannot tell you what it is but I've cast a cantrip that, if you ever kiss another lass, you'll turn into this." As she lifted away her top hand, a tiny pond frog with jigging feet sprang from her palm. "And then," she wagged a warning finger at him, "I swear I'll cut off your legs."

Watching Kate ride off in triumph with Lindsay, Elisabeth scowled, while Betsy's face clouded for a different reason.

"Poor Kate. Our wee rosebud thinks she'll be living a life of idleness and luxury but she'll have a rough furrow to plough. The puddock queen, as you cry her, is soon to be brought to childbed. I jalouse that it is the monarch himself has summoned Kate. To keep the royal bed warm."

V

Holy Orders

Blame nocht thy Lord, sae is his will;
Spurn nocht thy foot againis the wall;
But with meek heart and prayer still,
Obey and thank thy God of all.
The Abbey Walk
Robert Henryson, 15th Century

St.Mary's Abbey, Haddington, May 1512

Raising a goblet to his wine-stained lips with one podgy hand and stuffing bread into his mouth with the other, Prior Hepburn ate swiftly and methodically. Elisabeth nudged Meg with her elbow.

"Like a blind mowdiewort shovelling dirt," she whispered from behind her hand. Meg, who was picking at her food, anxiously wondering what important news he had to tell them, stifled a nervous giggle. Dame Janet glowered at her brother who was chomping on roast capon and swilling it down with huge draughts of claret as if it were his last meal.

"You'll dig your own grave with your teeth. A crammed kyte makes a crazy carcase, mind," she warned, while her stubby teeth nibbled incessantly at a plate of candied fruits.

The prior belched, wiped his lips with a linen napkin and then winked across at Elisabeth. She looked away, embarrassed for she could still taste the soggy kiss from those lips, fleshy and tender and fringed by his bushy beard, when he'd greeted her. But it was the prior's eyes that were disconcerting. Of the most intense, violet blue they brooded, all seeing, all knowing, beneath beetle-black brows.

While the prior dallied with the serving lass, the girls followed Dame Janet along to her inner sanctum where she hoisted her great bulk onto the deep, goose-feather mattress. She sank into the soft down pillows with a groan.

"Ah that's better. Now the weight is off my feet. Soft bedding's good for sore bones."

Though it was unlikely that, being upholstered in so much flesh, her bones would feel anything, Elisabeth thought. She gazed in wonder at the ornately carved four-poster bed hung with rich brocade curtains and piled with fluffy pillows. Embroidered tapestries lined the walls and finely woven rugs covered the floor. The light from the fat beeswax candles suffused the chamber with a rich warm glow. Such luxury in a nun's cell was surprising. The furnishings were far more sumptuous than anything at Hailes Castle, where coarse rushes and dried heathers covered the floors and foul-smelling tallow tapers glimmered in the passageways. Hailes lacked a mother's touch.

An intricately embroidered cushion depicting a fabulous golden bird, with wings outstretched to escape the flames of a fire, had caught Meg's eye.

"Thon's a bird of paradise. If you like it, take it," Dame Janet said, before adding quietly, "for your sister will be getting all the rest." Then, turning to Elisabeth who was admiring a wooden kist, she said, "That's made of the rarest rosewood. Go on. Open it."

The large carved chest was cedar-lined and delicately scented with juniper sprigs to ward off moths and preserve the abundant collection of gowns in silk, satin and velvet. In her youth Dame Janet had worn these underneath the nun's habit – her small rebellion against being forced into the abbey. Now that her ample frame had outgrown them, Janet proclaimed her defiance by adorning herself with worldly baubles, powdering her face with white lead and rouging her lips.

"But this is more magnificent than a bride's plenishment!" Meg exclaimed.

Dame Janet chuckled. "Aye. Nothing but the best for one of Christ's consorts." She untangled the expensive necklace and bracelet buried in the podgy folds of her neck and wrists to show her.

"Speaking of which," the prior said as he ambled into the chamber, "if you ladies have tired of fashion and furnishings, it's time to discuss more important matters. Your brother Adam has been sluggish in settling the plans for your future, but no more time must be wasted, my bonnie lassies."

He settled into a chair and began massaging his paunch to ease his digestion. "It has been decided that one of you is to be married and the other will enter the nunnery."

The girls exchanged worried glances before Elisabeth spoke up.

"It will be the answer to Meg's prayers to take the veil, uncle, and I would fain be wed. To a man of my own choosing," she added hastily.

Scowling at her, Prior John raised a hand. "It's not your advice, I'm seeking, lass but your obedience. You'll do as you're bid. Both of you." His blue eyes darkened. "Now tak tent. A marriage to the heir of the Earldom of Angus, one of the foremost titles in Scotland, has been arranged."

Elisabeth furrowed her brow. "You surely don't mean Archie Douglas? The grandson of kenspeckle Bell the Cat Douglas?" she splurted. "Some might say he's one of the bravest lads in the land, but he's also one of the wildest. I wouldn't marry him if he were the last man on earth."

From the depths of her feather bed Dame Janet sniggered quietly. Fain be wed indeed.

"And neither you shall, Elisabeth." Prior John narrowed his eyes. "As I was saying, this most favourable marriage has been arranged – at great effort and even greater expense on my part – for your sister, Margaret."

Meg let out a tiny, startled gasp.

"And since you, too, would fain be a bride, Elisabeth, your wish shall be granted. You shall become a bride of Christ, here at St.Mary's where you'll be ordained in due course."

Elisabeth sprang to her feet."But, uncle, I fear you've mixed us up! It's Meg who wants to be a nun, not me. She says her prayers every day. In Latin! She never misses on Sundays and holy days – unless she's poorly. Meg is the holy one. She has the temperament."

"Aye and you have the temper, that much is becoming clear." Dame Janet had hoisted her weight onto her elbows."Pay heed to your uncle! You'll have to learn to curb thon nippy tongue when you come here. Or be made to take a vow of silence."

Like a startled hare, Elisabeth looked from one to the other. "But I have no wish to be a nun. Ask Adam. He'll tell you."

"Did you ever hear such a thing?" Dame Janet scoffed. "She has no wish! As if her wish was of any account. And don't think your brother has any say in the matter, either. He's not your keeper and you're certainly not mistress of your fate. Gey few women, if any, have that privilege. I, for one, had to bend the knee. And your eldest sister, Joanna, was married off. To Lord Seton no less, and none the worse for it. Now Meg is to be wed, and your fate, my dear lass, is to be a bride of Christ, like me. And there's an end to it."

"But … but … " Elisabeth was floundering until a thought floated past her like a piece of flotsam. She grasped at it greedily. "I have no call from God. He hasn't chosen me."

"That's of no import. Neither was I privy to the voice of God. Not that you'd listen if the Almighty bawled in your ear, my lass. You've a mind of your own."

"Aye, she's a lass of mettle," the prior nodded, "and that's no fault in a Hepburn, but now it's time to do as you're bid. You've been ganging your own gait for too long."

"Is this what is meant by Holy Orders?" Elisabeth sniped, giving him a sidelong glance.

Meg, who had sat in stunned silence throughout, gasped at her sister's insolence. Elisabeth was too bold, too brazen to be a nun. Although she would gladly change places with Lisbeth, she wouldn't wish Archie Douglas as a bridegroom on anyone, far less her own sister. Whatever happened, sacrifices would have to be made.

"Perhaps more gentle persuasion is needed."

A forced smile stretched across the prior's sensuous lips as he pulled her behind him into the garderobe. In the small intimate closet, he began to rub his fingers up and down and then across the wooden panels until he heard a click. He pushed open the panel and led her into a low-roofed, sloping passage – built to allow Dame Janet to be carried along to services in the chapel, her uncle explained. Directly in front of them, a door opened to a turnpike staircase leading up to the newly constructed bell-tower.

The sun, still high in the luminous evening sky, lit up the fertile fields, magnifying the lush green of the growing grain and the grass of the grazing fields. As the prior waved his arm, proudly pointing out granaries, mills, breweries, and orchards, he scared a couple of cooing doves roosting on the parapet. They flew off, clumsy and slow in contrast to the swifts, swooping and swerving as they scooped up clouds of midges.

"All that you can see, my dear Elisabeth, and more, belongs to the abbey." He fell silent for a few minutes to make a mental calculation of the value of the view. "I've been endowing the lands of Haddington for some time in the knowledge that you'll inherit this post one day. As prioress of the abbey, you'll be a rich and powerful lady."

Elisabeth winced as his podgy hand squeezed hers. She stared ahead, fearing to look at those spellbinding eyes that threatened to weaken her resolve. She wouldn't make it easy for him to win her over. The promise of land and riches would not tempt her away from her love for Lindsay. Hepburn could sense her stiffening beside him.

"I was hoping to keep certain facts from you, but your thrawn reluctance leaves me no choice." He dropped her hand abruptly. "You may not wed, my dear lass, for the simple reason that you have no tocher. No dowry has been settled on you, because you were, to put it kindly, born on the wrong side of the blanket."

With his hand shading his eyes from the sun's glare, the prior avoided looking at her. He cleared his throat before continuing. "Your mother, God rest her soul, was taken in adultery – during one of your father's long absences – and you are the fruit of that union. When she died, Patrick agreed to bring you up as his own, so as not to shame your mother's memory, but he didn't settle on you the same rights as his legitimate daughters, including Meg."

"But, uncle," Elisabeth began and tapped him patronisingly on the arm, as if speaking to a doited half-wit, "Kate is the love bairn, not me. She's the cuckoo in the nest."

The prior chortled. "Aye, the saying is true enough: It's a wise child that kens its own father – and mother, forbye. But don't be dirling your head about Kate. She'll have more to do at court than sing for her supper. It's *your* fate that is being decided."

Elisabeth's head was indeed dirling. She'd often mocked Kate for being ill-begotten. Surely it couldn't be true that she, too, was a love child? A bastard?

"Then who is my father?" Her voice dropped to a whisper.

"Your father," he began and then broke off. In the silence she could hear his breath whistling between his teeth. "Your father was a buttery-lippit blackguard who was slain in a border foray. That's all you need to ken." As his breathing became more laboured, beads of sweat broke out on his brow. "But don't fret, you're not alone. You join a merry band of distressed gentlefolk who have to make their own way in life. As the fourth son, without land or wealth, I couldn't make a suitable match: the only path open to me was the Church. And like you, I was reluctant, for I had no calling and would have fain followed a worldly career. But needs must.

"When I was offered the priory of St. Andrews with all its benefices, I didn't hesitate. Your Aunt Janet has also made a comfortable life for herself, as you can see. As prioress, she manages this property with all the monies pertaining to it, but she'll not live forever and there *must* be a Hepburn to control these lands." He drew her in close, his intense blue eyes scrutinising her face.

"My dear niece, you may not have a vocation in the spiritual sense, nevertheless, it is your duty to take over as prioress of this abbey one day. With your strong will and quick wit you're truly deserving of what I have to offer. If you go against my wishes and wed, you wed with nothing." His stout arms squeezed her so hard that she struggled for air. "And to a nobody, for no lord or high-born gentleman would consider marriage to you without a tocher."

That could not be true. Davie Lindsay wouldn't care whether or not she had a dowry, Elisabeth was sure, but would he overlook her ill-starred birth? Would he be as generous as Adam had been with Nancy and love her despite that?

"This news will have ca'ed the feet from under you, no doubt," the prior continued, "but in time you will understand the significance of what I am saying and the importance of what I am giving you. All this," he declared with a sweep of the arm, "is my legacy to you, my dearest niece. This abbey is your birthright. Accept it with good grace."

He leant forward and smacked his fleshy lips against her forehead, leaving a damp sticky stain.

VI

Matrimony

It, that ye call the blest band that bindis so fast,
Is bare of bliss, and baleful, and great barrat wirkis.
The Treatise of the Twa Marrit Women and the Widow
William Dunbar, 15th –16th Century

Hailes Castle, August 1512

Meg carefully lifted her mother's bridal gown from the kist and shook it out to show Nancy. A headless wraith, the dress swished and rustled as she held it up against her. Even though the fragile oyster silk was greying with age and the lace trimming was yellowing, she insisted on wearing it to her own wedding – to feel that her mother was with her, watching over her, and to help her thole the dreaded ordeal. A solution of vinegar would whiten the lace and the slight tears and rips along the seams would be mended when it was taken in, Betsy had assured her. The dress swamped Meg, whereas it was a perfect fit for Lisbeth.

"That's another sign that she should be the bride, not me," Meg said mournfully.

For, however much she feared sexual intimacy, she was terrified at the thought of giving birth. Her slim hips weren't suited to childbearing and her delicate constitution would make her more susceptible to the fever that took away their mother soon after Lisbeth's birth. Childbed had been her deathbed.

One of her first memories was writhing in Betsy's arms and being made to put her hand on her mother's icy forehead. How she had howled. Why, she asked years later, had such a young bairn been made to touch her mother's corpse? So as to prevent her spirit from troubling her, Betsy explained. Well, it hadn't. Ever since then her mother's quartz-white face had haunted Meg's dreams. Now another nightmare was about to begin, she was panic-stricken.

"But you're not doomed to share your mother's fate," Nancy said. Ripe and ready to drop with her second child, she had little inkling of Meg's distress. "Have you ever ridden astride a horse?" she asked. "Losing your cherry would be easier, if you had."

Meg shook her head. Only Lisbeth dared to do so: another reason in her favour.

"Never mind. The first time may be a bit sore and you may bleed a little," the well-seasoned Nancy reassured her, "but no more than you do every month."

The first time! In front of a gawping crowd! Her deflowering to be made public! It was unbearable. Meg flinched at the thought.

"I'm not hurting you, am I?"

"No," Meg whispered. Quite the contrary. The way Nancy brushed her hair with

30

long, languorous strokes was soothing. She didn't tug or yank at the tangles but teased them out with gentle fingers that tickled her neck and shoulders. Meg closed her eyes, luxuriating in the warmth of her touch. Would Archie make her feel like this? From the smirks and sneers of his boorish brothers, she guessed that Archie had been initiated into the secrets of the bedchamber, but in their brief betrothal they'd never been alone together, never mind dally in anything more intimate.

"A man comes to the boil fast – too fast, oftentimes, while a woman needs gentle coddling before she starts to simmer." Nancy's lips were soft against the crease of her neck. "At least your brother has learnt that, otherwise I'd never have agreed to wed him. As for King Jamie ... well ..." she rolled her eyes, "you lie with the king not for pleasure but for reward." She jiggled the expensive jewel-encrusted gold bracelets on her arms. "Pleasure you must seek by other means."

It was clear from Meg's wide eyes that this was new to her.

"Have you never fondled your lips down below?" Nancy knelt beside her and gazed at her with deep, sensuous eyes the colour of rich heather honey. No wonder Adam had fallen for the voluptuous Nancy. Meg blushed and shook her head. "Down below" was a gash, an open wound, which bled once a month. Betsy had given her a lotion to smear "down there" beforehand, but she felt queasy about applying it.

"Well, my dearest sister, time to learn the secrets of *The Twa Marrit Women*."

"*The Twa Marrit Women*!" Meg gasped. "You've heard it?"

"Heard it? I could have written it! If I could scrieve!" Nancy's remark made them both shake with laughter till their cheeks were sodden with tears.

"That's better."

After pouring them each a generous goblet of wine, Nancy heaved herself onto the bed and patted the space beside her. They lay together quietly sipping their wine, until Meg's eyelids began to droop. When Nancy pulled her in closer, Meg nestled into her soft, comfortable body to rest her head on Nancy's heavy breasts. Drowsy with wine and lulled by the steady beating of Nancy's heartbeat, Meg's mouth slackened and she began to doze.

With her free hand, Nancy began to caress her neck, moving in little circles down to her slight breasts. Taking her time she lowered her hand and tweaked at Meg's nightgown. As Nancy leisurely stroked her thighs, Meg purred contentedly but when her hand brushed against her Venus mound, her eyes flew open.

"Trust me," Nancy murmured. As her hand crept higher and began to fondle her secret-most places, Meg quivered. "Come. Touch yourself. There's nothing to fear. Close your eyes and feel how soft your quim is," Nancy coaxed, guiding her hand to touch the soft folds of skin. "As tender as your lips," she purred. "Now frot gently with your finger until it throbs."

She moved her hand away to let Meg take over. "Keep going," Nancy urged. "Till you feel the love sap flowing in your womb. A man's seed will shrivel in a dry bed. It needs your moist milk to flourish and thrive."

Tentatively at first, Meg began caressing the cleft between her thighs while Nancy gently caressed her nipples. A deep flush spread over Meg's skin, sending a delicious warm glow through her belly. As waves of painful pleasure surged through her, she arched her back moaning and gasping like a shameless strumpet.

"That's it," Nancy urged. "That's the way, lass."

As Meg lay back exhausted in the crook of her arm, Nancy lightly brushed away the strands of damp hair clinging to her brow and nuzzled her earlobes to whisper, "Now you ken how to warm up yourself for Archie. Forbye, you have no need to wait for him. You can pleasure yourself any time you feel like it."

On the last night of her maidenhood Meg lay as still as a corpse trying not to cough and disturb Lisbeth who was snoozing peacefully beside her. Though Betsy's sleeping draught had deadened her limbs, it had failed to calm her reeling mind. Her ordeal was as nothing compared to the cruel torture of the early Christian martyrs and saints, she scolded herself, but that brought cold comfort. If only she could change places with Lisbeth. If only she could enter the convent, she would be a good and faithful sister.

She was not the only one who had considered such an exchange. Lady Douglas, who'd been expecting more smeddum from a future Countess of Angus, made no secret of her contempt for her son's betrothed and had suggested that a marriage to her younger sister would be preferable. Sturdier in character and constitution, Elisabeth was clearly the hardier stock, but the prior would have none of it. Furthermore, the arrangement had been signed and sealed and could not be rescinded without serious loss of honour.

Fearing that they were being fobbed off with the runt of the litter, Lady Douglas had been unrelenting in negotiating the dowry. She should not fret unduly, one of her friends confided, oft-times marriage was the making of a lass like Meg. A man would soon bring her to life; put the roses into her cheeks. Once wedded and bedded, the bonnie bluebell would bloom.

To the groom, Archibald Douglas, the marriage was little more than a formality – the signing of a contract between two powerful families. On the day of the wedding, his first duty, after meeting his betrothed at St. Mary's chapel door, was to announce the terms of the dowry. Business over, he led his bride, her face hidden by a veil, into the chapel where the ladies shook their heads and exchanged disapproving glances:

Meg had chosen to be married in her late mother's bridal gown. Not a good sign, they muttered. It bodes ill.

After the *Sanctus,* the couple knelt in front of Prior John to exchange vows and receive the marriage blessing. As Archie lifted the veil from the bride's face, Prior John's upraised hand stopped in mid-air. His face blanched.

"What the deuce do you take me for? The Abbot of Unreason? Who dares to play hunt the gowk with me?" he blustered, his brow bulging with veins as purple as his robes. "I'm no fool. I will not marry this woman to this man."

For, standing in front of him, about to exchange vows and rings with Archie Douglas was not Meg, but Elisabeth.

"Compose yourself, Hepburn. There's no jape being played here," Archie's grandfather, the fearless Bell the Cat, barked at him.

Weakened from a rasping cough, Meg could hardly stand, never mind walk up the aisle. To postpone the wedding would risk giving the Douglases an excuse to call it off and so, in great haste, Betsy had altered the dress again – this time to fit Lisbeth who had agreed to stand as proxy for her sister – but only at the wedding, not at the bedding, she insisted. Secretly Elisabeth could hardly wait to see the look on her uncle's face when the veil was lifted. And he did not disappoint.

"The devil dryte on you, Douglas," Prior John hissed. "You never thought to tell me! For a while I thought … I thought …" But what he thought was left unsaid.

Among the lady guests, tongues wagged and heads waggled meaningfully. Meg was poorly because she was already with child and suffering from the sickness of the early months. No-one was shocked. On the contrary, was that not a good sign, proving that she was fertile?

Regaining his composure, Prior John carried on with the ceremony, though he paid particular attention to the wording of the marriage rite in case there was some other joukerie-pawkery going on under his nose. Elisabeth's mischievous smile and those fern green eyes with hazel glints peeking out from under long eyelashes, so disconcerted him that he almost faltered over the irrevocable words, "I now pronounce you man and wife."

VII

Education

Howbeit that nuns sing nichts and days,
Their heart knows nocht what their mouth says.
Ane Satire of the Three Estates
Sir David Lindsay, 16th Century

St.Mary's Abbey, Winter 1512–1513

Sister Maryoth's thin lips clamped together in a disapproving grimace. The girl could not recite the *Ave Maria* or even the *Pater Noster*: nor, indeed, any prayers at all. Elisabeth knew next to nothing about Scripture: she had never said her beads and had no idea how to behave at holy Mass. Christmas and Easter were the only occasions she had attended the chapel. Unlike Meg, whose faith was a comfort and solace to her, Elisabeth skipped Sunday Mass, preferring to go hunting and hawking with the Hepburn men. Why bend the knee themselves, they'd say, when they gave money, land and benefices to the sisters of St.Mary's to do their praying for them?

"Are you sure you've even been baptised?" Sister Maryoth wouldn't be surprised that, with thon heathen Betsy as her nurse, she was still a pagan. She heaved an impatient sigh. Being one of the few literate nuns at the abbey, she'd been given the task of turning this wild child, this spawn of Satan, into an obedient, compliant novice, who – and the thought stuck in her craw – would be prioress one day. A position that, as Dame Janet's scribe and keeper of the financial records, she believed she deserved.

The cell where Elisabeth was incarcerated was as cold as a tomb, with no floor coverings and no warming fire. Inky patches of damp spattered the walls. The bed was a hard board covered with coarse woollen blankets that itched the skin like fleas.

"This is how we all live," Sister Maryoth declared. "You are to be treated no differently from the other sisters."

No fear of that. Stupefied from lack of sleep, Elisabeth dragged her feet to the chapel three times a day. Matins in the early hours – so early it seemed to be the middle of the night – was particularly tortuous with Sister Maryoth pinching her arms to keep her awake. Genuflecting, crossing herself, telling her beads, reciting *Pater Nosters, Aves, Glorias* and *Credos* daily, forever and ever. *Amen.* Interminable Latin chants that made no sense to her. Nor did Sister Maryoth make any attempt to explain them but seemed to take a perverse pleasure in listening to her struggle. And, if she made a mistake, it was a venial sin. Whatever that was.

Sister Maryoth's particular devotion was to St.Mary, the patroness of the abbey, and she spent hours praying to the miraculous statue of the Black Madonna and Child.

During the great flood of 1358, when the Tyne overflowed its banks, a devout nun had snatched up the statue, threatening to throw it into the water, unless Our Saviour and his Holy Mother saved the abbey from destruction. At that very moment, the surging waters shrank and the river once again flowed peacefully within its banks. What proof of the power of faith!

Since then pilgrims had come with their humble offerings to beseech the Mother of God to intervene on their behalf to her Son. At the Lady Altar, where candles burned night and day, screwed-up scraps of paper scrawled with prayers from petitioners were strewn at her feet and an assortment of tattered rags, trinkets and amulets dangled from her arms.

"To be worthy of your calling, you must first learn the joy of suffering," Sister Maryoth informed the novice.

Which meant kneeling on cold flagstones while the Holy Mother and Child gazed down with glazed eyes, indifferent to her torment. The tale of the statue's miraculous appearance was often recounted. While cherubim and seraphim may have flown the Holy Family's house from Nazareth to Loreto in Italy, their Black Madonna had sailed from the east in an oyster shell to her chosen resting place near the abbey. Whoever dared suggest that the icon had been carved from a blackened log washed up in the River Tyne was derided as an unbeliever. Over the years, the original paint had flaked off and attempts to restore it had resulted in rendering the Madonna more as a vulgar old courtesan than the Mother of God.

Elisabeth's whinging that her knees ached was music to Sister Maryoth's ears: proof, if any were needed, that she was unsuited to be a nun and unworthy of becoming prioress.

"I do what I can," Sister Maryoth whined to Dame Janet and Prior John when they asked about her progress, "but the girl has no calling. Not one iota of religious feeling. She can't understand the difference between superstitious nonsense and religious rite. Marriage would smoor her high spirits."

"That's not for you to judge," the prior retorted. "If she is to take over as prioress one day you must persevere with her."

Bowing her head in submission, Sister Maryoth pressed her lips more tightly together to suck back the bilious envy welling in her craw.

During Matins, one bright spring morning, Sister Maryoth had caught Elisabeth gazing with longing at the dusty motes dancing in the sunbeam that lit up the gloomy nave. Used to a life outdoors, Elisabeth suffered greatly from being cooped up in the suffocating, cloying confines of the cloister but that should not excuse her, Sister Maryoth scowled. She was about to scold the irreverent novice for being distracted from her prayers, when a divine flash inspired her. After the service she took her aside.

"Since I can abide your wretched moans no longer," she complained, "I will allow you to go out riding."

Elisabeth gawped at her in disbelief. There were two conditions, however: a strict time limit of one hour and the stable lad Harry Cockburn as escort.

"But," Sister Maryoth added, placing a conspiratorial finger to her thin lips, "this must be our secret. If your aunt and uncle hear of it, they'll soon put a stop to it."

VIII

A Courting

> Or, what is love, or to be lo'ed?
> Fain would I learn that law.
> *Robin and Makyne*
> Robert Henryson, 15th Century

The Garleton Hills, Spring 1513

Elisabeth squinted as she followed Lindsay's finger pointing out all the landmarks that could be viewed from the crest of the Garleton Hills. To the east, the shimmering Craig of Bass was circled by squawking seabirds, and to the west, the lion couchant of Arthur's Craig guarded the sloping silhouette of Edinburgh Castle, skirting the skyline above the smoky haze of Auld Reikie.

The whole of central Scotland may be laid out before them, but taking in the scenery was not Elisabeth's priority. Knowing that Sister Maryoth could just as capriciously curtail the privilege she had so generously granted, she was edgy and impatient. After riding out from the abbey to Garleton, she had left Harry Cockburn at the kitchen door. The lure of bread and ale and the company of saucy scullery maids, who teased and flirted with him mercilessly, would keep him occupied during the precious hour she was allowed alone with Lindsay.

"And do you see straight ahead there?" Lindsay pointed across the wide bay of Aberlady and over the Forth estuary. Though the sky above them was clear, a shower of rain was falling on the twin paps in the Kingdom of Fife. "Thon's the Mount of Lindifferon, lands I inherited from my mother."

"And does Garleton also belong to you?"

"Aye, it does. Do I see that busy brain of yours calculating how much I'm worth?" He squeezed her shoulders. "I'll take you to the Mount one day so you can see for yourself."

"Do you promise? Cross your heart? Before they make me take my vows."

Lindsay pulled her into his arms and she nestled closer against his chest, pressing against him to intensify the needle-sharp prickles of raw pleasure zigzagging up and down her spine.

"Och, a wee pagan such as you could never be a nun," he replied, planting kisses, soft as a dusting of pollen, on the top of her head.

Elisabeth wasn't so sure. She wriggled round to face him, her brow wrinkled. "Davie, would you marry a lass without a tocher?"

"That would be foolish. For what other reason would a wise man wed?"

"Oh." Her heart thudded against her breastbone. Seeing that she was taking his flippant remark seriously, he tilted her chin to give her a stern look.

"Do you question my honour as a gentleman? Why, of course I'd marry the lass I loved, whether she had a dowry or no."

Blushing, she lowered her eyes before daring to ask, "Do you love me, Davie Lindsay?"

Taken aback by her forthright question, the seasoned courtier hesitated. Did he love this jaggy thistle, this scamp, anxiously awaiting his answer? When pinned down like that, aye, he supposed he did. Her face lit up but swiftly clouded again as she put another question:

"And if we were wed, they couldn't force me to take my vows, could they?"

"Nothing would please me more, Lisbeth. When the time is ripe I shall ask Adam for your hand."

"It's not Adam's permission we need," she said quietly, "but my uncle's. And if we go against his wishes, I'll no be given a tocher."

He frowned. The fact that she had no dowry didn't disturb him so much as the idea of provoking the legendary wrath of the formidable Prior Hepburn. If he ever found out about their clandestine courtship, Lindsay was under no illusion that he would have him gelded at the very least. He pressed his thighs together tightly at the thought.

But there was another way, Elisabeth explained. They could elope.

"Elope? What a fanciful notion! So you'd like to be whisked away like some gypsy ganging over the march." Lindsay raised an eyebrow.

"And then we could be handfasted." According to Betsy, the ancient border custom of handfasting required only the exchange of promises in front of two witnesses. "We don't even need a priest."

"What! You want us to plight our troth in the middle of the forest. Like tinkers and common folk!"

"I'd rather be an honest gypsy who gives her heart freely than a nun languishing in a cell, locked up against her will," she retorted and pushed him away rather too brusquely, judging from his raised eyebrows. Why couldn't she learn to curb her reckless reactions? Not without cause they cried her the "jaggy thistle". She let out a deep breath and lowered her eyes, gazing at him sideways from under her eyelashes affecting the kind of plaintive, appealing expression that Kate employed – often to great effect.

"Enough of making calf's eyes at me, Lisbeth, it doesn't suit you."

She tossed her head and turned away, her elbows folded in a sulk but he pulled her back. "Lisbeth, listen to me. I understand your plight, but I would be loath to steal you under cover of darkness like a roving gypsy. We shall be wed in the proper way." The naked yearning burning in her eyes caused his heart to lurch, and he regretted having to douse her hopes. "When the time is right. But these are difficult times, my dearest love. There are grave matters concerning the safety of the realm to deal with before I can begin to think of my own personal happiness."

"What about my happiness? Our happiness. Don't you care about that? Don't you care about me?" she snivelled, wiping her nose on her sleeve.

"That I do, my cherished one. More than you can know. But first and foremost I'm a servant of the king and he has entrusted me with a special mission. The king's will comes before my own."

"I care not a fig for the king." She began beating her fists against his chest in frustration, salty tears of disappointment stinging her cheeks. He grabbed her by the wrists to stop her flailing hands.

"Listen to me, Elisabeth." His harsh tone made her take heed. Stubborn to the point of being thrawn, his jaggy thistle could vex him beyond his patience at times. "This is no time for starry-eyed romantic fantasies. Henry of England is threatening our borders. The country is about to go to war."

"All the more reason for us to wed before you go," she blubbed. "Please, Davie, don't let them send me back to the abbey. What if something should happen to you?" She licked away tears with the point of her tongue. "At least if we were handfasted, I'd be your relict, wouldn't I? And I would have a home in Garleton, if …" she trailed off.

Relict indeed. He pulled her in close and gently rubbed her back. His lips fluttered like moth's wings against her cheek.

"I'll speak to the king himself. He has a soft heart and will intervene for us. Don't fret. As soon as this is all over, we shall be together. Forever."

Back at the abbey stables Elisabeth had just dismounted when she heard a voice say, "Dame Janet has been looking all over for you. You are to come at once."

Sister Maryoth had been skulking in the shadows and had snuck up behind her silently, without warning. With her soundless steps, her aunt's secretary had mastered the uncanny knack of appearing from nowhere. A chill seemed to accompany her spectral presence – even her breath was cold. Harbinger of doom rather than herald angel, Elisabeth thought. Sister Maryoth may have been renowned for her piety, but she couldn't abide her mim-mou'ed holiness.

With her head to one side and a smile as warm as a late spring frost, the nun delivered her message and then, just as she was about to flit away, she added, "I trust you enjoyed your little jaunt."

Something about her insinuating smile disturbed Elisabeth. She marched over to Harry, rubbing down her horse in the stall. He looked sheepish and uncomfortable.

"Have you been blabbing, Harry?"

His face flared redder than a rowanberry as she glared at him.

"Naw … naw … nothing," he stuttered. "I'd never do that."

"For if you clype on me, I'll tell on you – for wenching yon scullery maid."

"I give you my word, Lady Lisbeth," he stammered, "that I will never, ever betray you. I'd cut off my right arm before I did that."

Propped up on huge goose down pillows, Prioress Janet was languishing in her soft feather bed. Her chubby fingers dipped incessantly into a bowl of comfits that she sucked slowly, one after the other. Since she could neither chew nor stomach strong meat, she would complain, sweetmeats and honeyed liqueurs were her only sustenance.

"Sister Maryoth tells me yon stable lad has a fancy for you. She's seen how his eyes gobble you up. Harry Cockburn may be a strapping lad with a fine set of limbs but you must not let that turn your head. You're over flichtersome, lass. Glowering at the moon, you don't want to be falling in the midden." Dame Janet chortled, her thick rouged lips slowly parting to display stumps of teeth in wrinkled gums.

Elisabeth breathed a sigh of relief. She'd been worried that they'd found out about her meetings with Lindsay.

"But just in case you're tempted," Dame Janet continued, "I've a few words to say about this blissful state of marriage that most women hanker after. This sacrament created by the Church fathers to sanctify the messy business of procreation. Go forth and multiply, they tell us," Dame Janet mimicked her brother's sermonising voice, "not just once – or even twice –but every year of your life while you're still broody. When you're not bleeding you're breeding."

"Aye, it may seem a lofty and worthy aim to produce souls to keep God company in his lonely heaven, but that's never in a man's mind when he dances the reel o" Bogie with his wife every night. Every man is in thrall to his pistle, with never a thought to what their womenfolk have to thole: a few spurts of pleasure for them means untold grief and agony for us. Our punishment for Eve tempting Adam to commit the first sin, they tell us." She snorted with unconcealed contempt. "Well, it behoves the Almighty ill if he made such a weak, fushionless creature as Adam in his own image." She paused for a moment to ponder this possible blasphemy and then popped in another comfit, smacking her lips together with a satisfied slurp.

"Seeing his gross error, Almighty God showed more gumption when he created woman, yet he has scant regard for our sex. All very well to spare the Virgin Mary the indignity of being bedded, but she still had to bring forth the bairn in a byre with the kye and the yowes. I ask you, if God in is wisdom deemed that good enough for the Mother of his beloved Son, what chance is there for the rest of us? Even the beasts in the field suffer less than a woman in childbed.

"That's if you don't part with a bairn before it's time. Or you may carry it in your creel, only for it to be stillborn. And many's the bairn that has failed to thrive and countless more have lived for a few months or a few years before being struck down by some affliction. God's little angels we cry them, doomed to strum harps for eternity. Humph." She took a sip of cordial and then wiped her sticky lips delicately with an embroidered napkin.

"All too often the price to be paid for bringing a child into this world is the life of its own mother. Her death then leaves a wheen of mewling orphans and a feckless, grief-stricken father. And even if you are spared, you'll be troubled with ailments that even Job himself wouldn't thole. Then, as soon as one has been weaned, another will be sown in the womb. You'll aye be heavy-footed and old before your time. Your man may find you comely enough now, but when you're baggy-eyed, with your firm young skin hanging loose in a paunch, he'll look elsewhere for his comfort. They all do." She nodded knowingly, though years of over-indulgence rather than childbearing had bloated the voluptuous figure of her youth.

"Marriage does not mean, as you might think, my dear niece, freedom and independence. Not for nothing is it called wedlock. You have no wish to be cloistered, but see what other choice awaits you: to be beholden to a mere man. In pledging her marriage vows, a woman must promise to love, honour and obey her husband. Like a slave to its master, a wife is expected to do her man's bidding, whether she wants to or no. Tell me, what would be your preference? To be kilted to some puddock prince, or to be a bride of Christ and, one day, prioress of this abbey?"

The air in the chamber, stuffy from the heavy scents of pomanders and cloying confectionery, and the heat from the stoked-up fire, was making Elisabeth drowsy. She sat on her hands, waiting impatiently for her to finish. Dame Janet's words flowed over her, as meaningless as the Latin Mass. Nothing to do with her, for she knew better. Not once had her aunt mentioned the achingly delicious tingling that left Elisabeth weak-kneed and soft-limbed with desire.

"Why did you no tell Meg of this?"

Dame Janet scowled at her bold question. "Do you think she'd have gone up the aisle willingly if I had? Meg is one of those doomed to bear the burden of carrying on the human race. I'm telling *you* so that you ken what a fortunate escape you've had."

"But what if you love someone? Surely that must make marriage worthwhile?"

Dame Janet's piggy eyes, scarcely visible in the folds of flesh, glared at her. A grotesque parody of female beauty with her powdered face and plucked eyebrows, she bore a striking resemblance to the crude icon of the Black Madonna.

"Marriage for you has never been an option. As for love!" she harrumphed. "Love only happens in fairy tales, my lass. Who do you know who has ever married for love? However," she leant forward as much as her bulk would allow, confiding, "if you itch, then by all means scratch. If you fancy a tumble in the hay with the stable lad, make sure you're not bairnt. Och aye, there are ways and means," she nodded. "Betsy's the one to ask." Dame Janet readjusted her great weight on the bed. "Tak tent of what I've telt you, lass." Exhausted by her sermonising, the prioress yawned deeply, sank back into her pillows and closed her eyes.

Elisabeth had no intention of going to her grave a dried-up, withered old virgin, never knowing the sweet pleasures of being cherished by a man. *That* was what it meant to be alive. The passion of Christ, the celestial consort, was no consolation for forgoing the passion of a warm-blooded man. Pining prostrate on cold flagstones in front of a wooden-hearted Madonna was for the likes of pious Sister Maryoth. Elisabeth would not bend the knee. Taking the veil would not be her fate. She would flee the coop and escape from this dovecot of fasted women.

IX

Rumours of War

By Flodden's high and heathery side,
Shall wave a banner red as blood,
And chieftain's throng wi meikle pride.
The Ballad of Thomas the Rhymer, Traditional

Hailes Castle, 15 August 1513

Every able-bodied man between the ages of sixteen and sixty with victuals for forty days had been summoned to muster at the Boroughmuir on 18ᵗʰ August, but not the Earl of Bothwell's men. They had been spared traipsing into Edinburgh only to tramp back out again and would join the main army on its way past Hailes to the south.

Lindsay had ridden non-stop from the city to deliver the king's marching orders to Adam, one of the chief commanders of the campaign, and now surveyed the makeshift camp set up between the River Tyne and the high road. Men in ill-fitting hauberks and brigandines scurried about hither and yon like ants whose nest had been disturbed. Canvas tents had been set up and fires burned where blacksmiths sharpened swords and shod horses" hooves. At the risk of being dishonourable, Lindsay could not help but voice his private concerns.

"This is more than folly, Adam, it's sheer madness." He wiped his brow, dusty and sweaty from his ride. "I worry for the king's wits. And I'm not alone. Bishop Elphinstone, among others, is against this ill-advised campaign, and that old seasoned warrior, Bell the Cat Douglas, has spoken his mind."

And received no thanks for it, but an unmerited insult from his monarch that, if he were afraid he should go home. Black-affronted, Douglas had done just that and taken his grandson Archie with him but leaving his two sons for honour's sake.

All this because of James IV's promise to their "Auld Allies", the French, to come to their aid if attacked by the English. When Henry VIII landed an army on French soil, Queen Anne had sent James a turquoise ring, appointing him as her chosen knight.

"I cannot deny her," James had declared. "A lady in dolorous plight, she has laid it on me as her bounden champion to march into England for her sake."

Such a pompous utterance, displaying more ill-judgment than chivalry, dismayed Lindsay. This *coup de foudre* was in danger of ending up as an ill-fated *coup de grâce*, but neither reason nor unreason swayed James's decision. Not even the apparition of St. Andrew at St. Michael's Kirk in Linlithgow that had warned the king against leading an army into war and dallying with women. Nor the phantom herald that had appeared at the Mercat Cross in Edinburgh on the stroke of midnight and listed the names of all those earls, lords, barons, gentlemen and sundry burgesses of the city who would appear before his Satanic Master within forty days. Despite his highly superstitious nature, James paid no heed to these doom-laden portents. Nothing, it seemed, would dissuade him from his misguided mission. Lindsay was in despair.

"Nor should it," Adam affirmed. "There have been too many of these auld wives" tales for my liking, Davie. Why, I wouldn't be surprised if you had set up these tricks yourself, sleekit showman that you are," he quipped, jabbing his finger at the heraldic crest on Lindsay's embroidered tabard.

"Queen Margaret, too, has been afflicted with fearful dreams of his bloodied corpse pierced with arrow."

Adam snorted. "That doesn't surprise me. Not only is she the king of England's sister, but a jealous wife, riled by her husband's rally to a rival queen's cause."

"You misjudge her," Lindsay replied, "for all her faults, she is concerned that the royal succession rests on an eighteen month-old infant. This reckless undertaking puts the monarchy in jeopardy. It's not worth the 14,000 crowns the French are contributing."

Adam laughed. "Never mind auld wives" tales: you sound like my own wife!"

For Nancy, too, was critical of the king's reasons for going to war.

"All for some high-bendit notion, he's prepared to sacrifice us all: to save a damsel in distress. Hardly. She's twice-marrit and twice his age. Huh. James's head swivels too easily – thither and yon and back again. It's no wonder he can't see straight. I should ken better than most! I've borne him a daughter. God forbid that Jenny should have her father's flichtersome wits."

Anxious about her daughter's safety, Nancy had begged Adam to fetch her from Edinburgh, but he'd shrugged off her concerns. If Jenny were his own flesh and blood, would he be so uncaring, she reproached him, her tawny eyes flashing and her Stewart temper riled. Despite Lindsay's reassurance that the court had already fled to a secret refuge where her Jenny would be far from danger, Nancy had banished Adam from the marital bed. Sulking in her chamber she had refused to come and admire the muster and, scanning the display of arms with a critical eye, Lindsay could hardly blame her.

"A woeful wappinschaw," he groaned.

"Have faith, Davie." Adam placed a hand on his shoulder. "Since Henry is in France with the bulk of his army, we have the edge over the English. Our artillery is among the finest in Europe. Why, our guns are bigger for a start."

"But they're too heavy and slow," Lindsay pointed out. "They can only fire one shot a minute, while the English guns can fire three. I have it on good authority."

Adam wagged his head. "You may be the diplomat, Davie and no doubt your spies are well-informed, but I'm the soldier and I can tell you that not only do we have more men but they are better armed."

Surveying the straggly line of untrained farmhands, sulky stable lads and half-hearted quarter-men struggling with eighteen-foot pikes staffs, Lindsay questioned his friend's judgment. "Your men seem ill at ease with thon long lances, Adam. How are they going to use them?"

"To topple riders from their horses – in the way the French commander, D'Aussi, has advised."

"And can they?" Lindsay replied, looking doubtful.

Adam dismissed his concerns with a wave of his hand, reluctant to tell him that, though D'Aussi may have given his advice, he had neglected to give them any training.

"I wish I had your confidence, Adam." Lindsay rubbed his chin.

"I put my trust in hard steel, Davie," Adam replied with a cheery slap on his friend's shoulder. "And the 14,000 gold crowns from the French coffers," he winked. "Besides, what do you know about warfare, master poet? Away and prepare your pen to write a triumphal ode to commemorate our glorious conquest of the English."

An ode to victory was the last thing Lindsay felt like writing: he feared it would be an epitaph he would be penning. With a heavy heart he mounted his horse and rode off.

St. Mary's Abbey

"If the invaders reach this far, retreat to the fortalice of Nunraw," Prior Hepburn said, giving his marching orders to his sister. "It will be easier to defend. Begin making plans now. In the meantime, lock all gates here at the abbey. No-one is to enter or leave."

"Lisbeth, for one, will champ at the bit for having her wings clipped," Janet mumbled, savouring a *bonbon* of exotically sweet *marche de pan*.

Hepburn frowned. "What do you mean?"

Her mouth slackened, dribbling tiny morsels down her chin. Too late, Dame Janet realised she had blabbed. "Well, our peerie-heided niece would rather flee about the countryside than mind her lessons. She's a lass who craves fresh air and exercise," Dame Janet gabbled, seeing his face turn purple with rage. "Forbye, she's not alone. The stable lad aye goes with her."

"What? You let her go out riding with Harry Cockburn? How could you be so lax?"

"She's safe enough with Harry."

"An uncouth stable lad, with nothing between his ears, and a brainless quhillie-lillie between his shanks! I despair of you, Janet. With all this talk of war, bands of brigands will be scouring the land, looting, pillaging and raping. Sheep, cattle, women. It's all the same to them."

"And do you think that locking her up in a nunnery will keep her safe and out of reach of marauding men? Why, it's the first place they'll come to." Prioress Janet sniggered gleefully, as if relishing the thought. "Unless we all slash off our noses and lips, like the nuns of Coldingham, to slake the lust of barbarous invaders."

This prospect sent shivers up the spine of Sister Maryoth who was lurking with her ear to the door. She jumped back, caught off-guard when the door suddenly burst open.

"Bring my niece," Prior Hepburn thundered. "At once."

Sister Maryoth pressed her hands together. "It grieves me greatly to tell you," she said, trying to suppress a smile cracking her face. "But the novice Elisabeth has eloped."

X

Handfasting

Lovers beware and tak gude heed about
Whom that ye love, for whom ye suffer pain.
The Testament of Cresseid
Robert Henryson, 15th Century

Hailes Castle, 18 August 1513

"Damn and blast! Where do you think you're going?" Adam bellowed, waving his arms furiously. The horse galloping full pelt along the riverbank had scattered the disorderly lines of the wappinschaw to all the airts before slowing down.

"Adam, you mustn't go to war," Elisabeth blurted. She leapt down from behind Harry and flung herself at her brother. "I had a dream."

"Not another one." His scorn mixed with angry annoyance, Adam tapped his foot impatiently as he listened to her garbled account of her recurring nightmare: bodies swirling round in the flood, the severed head, the leering skull that had left her with an abiding sense of foreboding, throttling her so that she could scarcely breathe.

Elisabeth laid a hand on his arm. "So you see, Adam, you mustn't go."

"Not another doom-monger," Adam groaned. "A creditable performance, Lisbeth, but hardly credible."

Her eyes opened wide in alarm. "What other portents have there been?"

"Ask him, he'll tell you." Adam pointed towards the stables where Harry Cockburn was rubbing down a steaming stallion. "For I wager the hellish herald and the spirit of St. Andrew are but figments of the court jester's fertile imagination," he scoffed.

Elisabeth looked puzzled until she saw Lindsay coming out of the stable leading a fresh horse. She rushed up to him. "Davie! Is that true? Have there been other omens?"

Lindsay placed steadying hands on her shoulders. "There are aye portents when folk in peril try to make sense of the unknown, Lisbeth. Fear plays strange tricks with the mind."

"Aye, and if we listened to every old wife and her havers, we men would never go to war," Adam snorted.

"That would be no bad thing," Elisabeth maintained. She tore herself away from Lindsay to grab hold of Adam. "Don't you see? Your lives are in mortal danger?"

"Women know nought about warfare." He frowned, trying to prise off her fingers clinging limpet-like to his arm. "Now I must see about getting these men back into some sort of order and getting you back to the nunnery. Where's thon Harry Cockburn? Till I slap his sappie head for putting you in peril."

"You're not going with them, are you, Davie?" Lindsay's non-committal shrug of his shoulders told her otherwise. "But if there's a war, men will be killed and wounded. You and Adam might be ..." she trailed off, recalling the horrific images of her nightmare. She trembled at the thought that she might never see him again. This might be their last chance. She stretched up on tiptoe to whisper in his ear. "What about us, Davie? Have you spoken with the king?"

Lindsay shifted uncomfortably, for he'd not yet kept his promise. "It would be imprudent to pester His Grace with our personal plight when he has more important matters on his mind." Seeing her disappointed face droop, he went on, "Come, now, my thrawn thistle. Stand firm. Until this war is over ..." he faltered, gaining time as he mulled over what to do. She was to bide at Hailes with Nancy and her bairn and, as soon as it was safe to leave, he would send for her. Not to Garleton, for that was undefended, but to Edinburgh, where Lindsay had some rooms in a tenement in St. Mary's Wynd, just off the High Street. Elisabeth's face lit up.

"So it'll be no fib that I'm off to St. Mary's! To Edinburgh! If you think that's for the best, Davie." She became pensive again, her voice low. "But mind what I said about handfasting. Let's do it before you go to war. Please, Davie. Then surely they cannot make me go back to the abbey."

The alarm in her voice and dismay on her face touched him. He hugged her tightly to his breast and burrowed his face in her hair. He'd done his best to put a stop to this senseless battle. How he yearned to forget all thoughts of war and death and ignore the king's feckless orders that were making life more uncertain than ever. All he desired was to keep her safe. His spiky Lisbeth, always determined to grasp the thistle, was ready to follow him to the four corners of the earth. He may never see his love again. Why shouldn't they pledge themselves to each other?

When Elisabeth asked her brother to be a witness to their handfasting, Adam shook his head.

"You're courting trouble with Davie Lindsay. He'll not make you happy."

"How can you say that? He's a man of honour and your best friend. And I love him."

Adam brushed her unruly hair back from her face and tilted her chin up to look her in the eyes. He had shaved off his bushy beard – for greater ease in slipping his metal helmet on and off – and cut his hair *en brosse* to keep it lice-free and to prevent the enemy hauling him by the hair. Clean-shaven and bristle-haired, he looked like a newly hatched baby bird, naked and vulnerable, and no longer the fierce, bearded warrior.

"That's why I am well acquent with his nature. That you love him, I'm in no doubt, but, as your brother and guardian, it's my duty to shield you from harm. For I fear that you'll never be first in his heart. Two loves already possess Davie Lindsay."

"What? He has other paramours?" she yelped, but then how could she be so naïve as to imagine that she would be the first and only love of Lindsay, an experienced courtier and man of the world.

"Nay, Lisbeth, he has no mistress that I know of. Nay, Davie Lindsay is first and foremost the king's man. He would lay down his life for his master. And his second passion is poetry. Every spare second you'll see him scribble, scribble, scribble. You'll never be foremost in his thoughts, I fear, and that will never suit you. For, my jaggy thistle, you can be a demanding and wilful lass. Forbye, he's o'er old for you. Davie's already a man of six and twenty and you're a maid of only fifteen summers."

"Sixteen," she corrected him. "Why, Margaret Tudor was barely thirteen when she wed King James. And he was already thirty."

"The marriage of the thistle and the rose was a union of two countries, not loving hearts. And that English rose has turned into a thistle, a constant thorn in the king's side. Jaggy thistle though we cry you, you're still a rosebud, not yet full blown. I'm your guardian, mind, and I know what's best for you. Now, I'll get Harry to take you back to the abbey."

While he went off to find Harry, Elisabeth ran with her tearful tale of woe to Nancy who was sulking in sullen seclusion in her chamber.

"Men," she muttered, rising from her bed to hug Lisbeth and brush the tears from her eyes. "They may boast that they ken all about war, but they ken naught about love. Let's see if he'll agree to the terms of my truce."

Adam would be allowed back into her bed, but only if he gave the couple his blessing. When he readily agreed, Nancy gave Elisabeth a broad wink and whispered, "See how easily these warriors surrender in the battle of the sexes."

Betsy was more difficult to win round. Elisabeth had taken for granted that she would share her joy but her nurse kept shaking her head and muttering, "Away with the fairies. It's far worse than I thought."

Their handfasting in the Great Hall of Hailes was not a joyous occasion, with Betsy beating her breast, struggling to keep back the tears and Adam drumming his fingers against his thigh, impatient to be off to enjoy his own coupling with the merciful Nancy. Oblivious to their witnesses" qualms, the lovers plighted their troth, promising to be faithful to each other for a year and a day when they would be lawfully married. From his pinkie, Lindsay eased off a gold ring, a gift from James IV, and placed it on the fourth finger of her right hand.

"And in a year's time, when we are truly wed, I shall give you a wedding ring and place it here." He stroked her middle finger.

"I vow never to take this off until then," Elisabeth murmured.

Following Betsy's instructions, they had to lick the thumbs of their right hands and stick them together to seal their solemn vow. Betsy then gave them each a blue ribbon tied at the ends in a lover's knot.

"*Keep Tryst* is the Hepburn slogan," Elisabeth said as she looped her ribbon round Lindsay's neck.

"And *Endure Fort* is ours," Lindsay replied, doing the same. "You will have much to bear in the coming months, my thistledown. Mind our motto and stand firm whatever happens," he urged before lowering his head to kiss her.

They were about to raise a cup in toast to the newly betrothed couple, when baby Patrick toddled up to his father, whimpering and tugging at his elbow. Adam stooped to attend to him, but the infant, not recognising this smooth-cheeked stranger, howled and flailed his chubby arms and knocked the goblet out of his hand. The sight of the wine spilling out and staining the flagstones blood red was too much for Betsy who let out a long, low wail.

That evening, as she was brushing the white petals from Elisabeth's hair and preparing her for the bridal bed, Betsy crumpled.

"Oh, my wee lassie! My wee thistledown," she moaned. She threw her pinny over her face and rocked back and forth, on her stool, making an eerie, keening sound.

"Betsy, you're giving me the cold creeps. Why the dirge? This is not a wake! And this is my nightgown, not my shroud!"

For the handfasting ceremony Elisabeth had put on the only gown she owned, the one she'd worn at Adam's wedding. Of mistletoe green. How could she tell the hapless Lisbeth that it was bad luck to be married in the pixies'' colour? Or, that the spilt wine was another ill omen? Instead, Betsy thrust something wrapped in a damp cloth into her hand.

"Here, take this. Stap it in your quim afore bed."

Leaving Betsy to her lamentations, Elisabeth went to the privy. She unwrapped the cloth and screwed up her nose. A ball of sphagnum moss soaked in red wine. How was she expected to stuff that inside her? And what would Lindsay think?

However anxious and expectant she was, her groom lay fully clothed and fast asleep on top of the bed. Not too old, perhaps, but too tired? She crawled up to him and tried to nudge him awake but he only snored more loudly and turned onto his side. She lay down and curled her backside into his groin, bringing one of his arms round her belly and the other round her breast.

"I'm not leaving this bed still a maiden," she whispered. Behind her she felt him stirring.

"You're just a lass, Lisbeth," he croaked, his voice groggy with sleep. "It isn't fair to love you and leave you. Nor do I wish to harm you. There will be time enough."

"This is the time. This very night. Teach this nun to be a wanton, for then the convent will spurn me. Unless, of course, you're a monk and have taken a vow of celibacy – or a larbar, Davie Lindsay," she snickered mischievously.

"What? Where did a lass like you learn such a word? Who's been teaching you the wicked ways of the *Twa Marrit Women*?" He rolled her over to face him. "Do you ken what it means?"

Her hazel eyes twinkled. "An impotent old man."

"Older than you, I grudgingly admit to be, but impotent I am not. Rest assured on that." As he pushed himself up onto his elbows, a satirical smile quirked the corners of his lips.

"Larbar you cry me? I'll show you I'm no eunuch. And certainly no monk."

In the chilly hours of dawn they were awakened by the martial sounds of men-at-arms bawling, armour clanking, drums banging, horses snorting. Lindsay was about to slip out of bed – he couldn't bear to say farewell – but the touch of her hand caressing the sensitive skin between his waist and hips melted his resolve. He moaned softly and turned to her. For their first time, he'd been cautious, not wishing to cause hurt but she had opened up to him like a flower. No longer the jaggy thistle but a pink-tipped gowan unfolding its delicate petals to the sun.

Now the noises of war and nearness of danger sharpened their arousal and they clung to each other in a desperate attempt to wring out every last ounce of pleasure, before coming together in a climax of doomed ecstasy. As if making love for the very last time, Lindsay thought gloomily as their passion subsided and they fell back to lie spreadeagled side by side. He clasped her tightly to his chest and buried his head in her bed-tousled hair.

Once Lindsay had gone, Elisabeth had lain hugging the pillow, tearfully trying to salvage what she could from their brief honeymoon. After their initial nipping and scarting, he had slowly and gently stroked her skin with feather-light fingertips until she thought her very bones would melt. Only then, when he sensed she was ready, did he lay claim to her. The initial shock was breathtaking but, whispering soothing words and guiding with skilful hands, he'd brought her to such an intensity of pleasure that made her cry out. So as to memorise every blissful second she squeezed her eyelids shut and chronicled every kiss, every caress, every stroke of their lovemaking. This way she hoped to staunch the self-pity and frustration that threatened to engulf her.

Bleary-eyed and dazed, she dragged herself up to the battlements of the west tower where Adam was dandling his crabbit year-old son up and down in his arms to soothe him. He gave her a knowing wink.

"And this," he said, holding up the snotty-nosed toddler, girning for sleep, "is what you can expect from your dallying."

Rubbing her teary eyes, she attempted a weak smile.

"Look, Patrick!" Adam had caught sight of the cloud of dust that signalled the approach of the main force coming along the high road from Edinburgh. The snivelling infant seemed unimpressed by the cavalcade of weaponry which his father began to tot up: the five cannon and two culverin of the Seven Sisters cast by Robert Borthwick the king's master melter, drawn by thirty-six oxen; the numerous wagons of cannon-balls and powder casks. Even without the mighty gun, Mons Meg, they could not fail to win with such a vast array of armoury.

"The Seven Sisters?" Elisabeth sniggered. "With thon long-nebbed barrels are they not brothers?"

"To the cannonars deafened by their muckle mouths, they are most definitely female," Adam replied, giving her a withering look. "Forbye, with this vast array of armoury, we cannot fail to win."

Clasping her hand to her mouth to stifle her unseemly mirth, she glimpsed the ring on her finger. Of the rarest Scottish gold, Lindsay had told her, from a mine in the Leadhills. As she twirled the ring she gave a little gasp. Peering closely she could make out the king's initials encircled by the *memento mori* - a skull and crossbones. Her stomach lurched uneasily and she felt slightly sick. No more omens, no more portents she decided.

Curious to see her shiny plaything, little Patrick squirmed round and tried to grab it with his chubby fingers until his father pulled his hand away to wave at the procession. How could this warrior's son not fail to be amazed at his first sight of military might? Lords and lairds and knights in full armour, their metal breastplates and helmets gleaming in the morning sun, rode on horseback. Behind them marched the remaining soldiery; mercenaries and conscripts with pikes and staffs and, straggling at their tail, bondagers and byre-men – untrained, unkempt and some unshod – wielding pitchforks and scythes as if they were sauntering to the harvest.

Bringing up the rear lumbered the camp followers. Carts and haywains laden with cauldrons and kettles, pots and pans, sacks of meal and sundry victuals trundled past, drawn by scraggy nags. Barefoot children, chasing scabby-coated curs, scampered alongside the carts driven by their mothers dressed in sweepings from battlefields. Though some of the women wore canvas jackets tied with military belts and buckles, most were clad in garments cobbled together from ragged remnants: motley cloaks and shawls patched out of tattered flags and banners filched from the fallen of past forays.

Elisabeth's heavy-lidded eyes sprang open and she pulled herself up. Women going to war! There was something she could do after all! She could help to load weapons, fetch food and water, cook and even tend the wounded.

Reading her mind, Adam put a restraining hand on her shoulder.

"Nay, Lisbeth, you'll have no truck with them. Those women are nothing but whores and scavengers. They earn their living swyving with the soldiers first and then ransacking their butchered carcases afterwards."

When the time came for Adam to lead his troops off to battle he looked up at the ramparts where the remorseful Nancy was holding up Patrick and waving his tiny hand for him to bid his father God speed. Elisabeth was giving her brother a last hug when Betsy hirpled up to him.

"Afore you go, take this my brave laddie."

She pressed a polished stone into his palm and curled his fingers round it. "To protect you from harm." Her eyes clouded over. "And mind, beware the burn."

Elisabeth looked puzzled.

"Water," Betsy replied, her misty eyes seeing beyond the present. "It's a prophecy of True Thomas. He foretold the flooded field and the hidden burn."

"I swear to you, Betsy, that we will brook no hidden burn, for are we not Hepburns!" Adam laughed gaily. Grasping the talisman tightly, the warrior waved his fist in the air, a signal for the drums to start beating and the men to follow.

XI

Confrontation

Ane false intent under ane fair pretence
Has causit mony innocent to die.
The Puddock and the Mouse
Robert Henryson, 15th Century

Hailes Castle, August 1513

Hilter-kilter down the brae she somersaulted, head over heels, tumbling over tussocks and divots, before landing in the mire at the foot. High overhead black birds circled the air. Corbies. Birds of ill-omen, the ravens flapped their deathly wings like black flags. She splayed her hands and feet to try and stand up, but she kept sinking in the bog. Underfoot the land was sodden and swampy, fed by a reddish brown burn burbling half-hidden among the bracken.

As they wheeled round and round, the crows" shrieks became more strident before they plunged headlong downwards. Across the burn a thin mist obscured shadowy figures, waving their arms, whether in greeting or warning she couldn't tell. Kilting up her skirt she began to wade across the burn but her feet kept slipping on slimy pebbles.

Suddenly the burn bubbled up and a torrent swept her off her feet. As she was tossed around in the murky water, body parts whirled past. A jagged limb, the hand with the rotting flesh and, worst of all, the severed head spinning towards her, baring its teeth. She opened her mouth …

"Where is he?" Prior John was louring over her, his fiercesome eyes blazing as he yanked the blankets off her bed.

Still woozy from her horrifying nightmare, Elisabeth cowered into a tight ball. Was she still dreaming? She wiped the sleep from the corners of her eyes.

"Where is thon sleekit tod slouching?" He'd drawn out his dirk to stab at the blankets and was kneeling down to search under the bed. After hauling himself up, he kicked open the lid of the kist, pulling out clothes with one hand and thrusting his dirk into them with the other. Breathing heavily, he slammed the lid shut with a juddering bang.

"I trust you're not plucking at any crow to scouk your obligation, my lass. If this is some girlish fancy, another bee-heided ploy on your part to flee your fate, then let me tell you that when I lay my hands on that rapscallion who has dared to defile you, I'll send him off with more than a flea in his ear. This is what I will do to him."

Elisabeth braced herself, hugging her knees closer to her chest as he loomed over her, his hooded eyelids shading his violet eyes, his full red lips spluttering.

"I will gladly put my hands on his thrapple like this …" His clammy hands ringed her neck and his thumbs pressed firmly on her gullet, "until he is choking for breath. Then I shall cut off his pistle and stuff it into his gob to gag the cringing coward's whimpers. After that, I shall ram a rod up his sliddery arse and slice him in two. His belly I will slash in front of his eyes, gralloch him like a deer and pull out his gizzards.

"I will then take great delight in wrenching him limb from accursed limb and cast his remains to the howling beasts. That's what I shall do to the man who has dared to cross me and make off with my precious jewel. If he has any sense, he'll get himself killed in the fray. An arrow straight through the skull from some merciful archer."

Snorting and grunting like a fierce bull in full charge, the prior's primal wrath was magnificent to behold. Elisabeth's mouth was dry: she swallowed hard. How had he found out? Who had told him? The prior was now leaning over her, his breath hot and steamy in her face as he waggled his head in disbelief.

"It can't be true my niece would run off willingly with such a wastrel as yon stable lad."

"Stable lad?" She felt herself go limp with relief. "You mean Harry Cockburn?" She tittered nervously. "That gangly, tongue-tackit lad?" Whose spotty baw face turned as red as his hair every time she looked at him. "Oh, uncle, how could you think for one moment that we were running away together?"

"Nay, but I was led to believe …" he broke off.

Kneeling on the bed she clasped his hands.

"Dearest uncle, you must understand. I had to say farewell to Adam. Before he went off to battle. And Harry offered to take me."

"Aye, that is what I was afraid of."

"Uncle! How can you think so ill of him! Harry would defend me with his life." His eyes narrowed with suspicion as she beamed a smile of pure innocence.

"That's as may be, but I am taking steps to make sure that neither he nor anyone else needs to. While you, my taiglesome lass, will now have to learn to graith the harness."

XII

The Miracle of the Flood

Hail, mother and maid without macle
Bright sign, gladding our languishing
By might of thy miracle.
Ane Ballat of Our Lady
William Dunbar, 15th–16th Century

St.Mary's Abbey, 8 September 1513

The statue of the Black Madonna swayed ungracefully on the bier at the head of the procession meandering its way down to the river. Too stout to walk the short distance from the abbey, Prioress Janet swung heavily in a litter strung between two ponies that picked their way gingerly over the uneven ground. Trudging behind, Prior Hepburn wished that he, too, could have been borne in a litter. Soaked through by the constant drizzle, his lavishly embroidered vestments weighed heavily on him.

Every year on the Nativity of the Blessed Virgin Mary, he celebrated a Mass of Thanksgiving to the patroness of the abbey. The 8th of September was also the anniversary of the Miracle of the Flood that had occurred in 1358. Then the calm waters of the Tyne had become a raging torrent that had destroyed houses and bridges, swept away newly-harvested sheaves from the fields, drowned kye and livestock and carried off huge oaks and trees down to the sea. A great many folk lost their lives trying to save their meagre belongings.

But for the intervention of a pious nun from St.Mary's Abbey, who implored the Mother of God to save them, much worse could have befallen them. And much worse may, in future, befall those who neglected to pay their tithes. As usual, Prior John had intended to remind his flock of their obligations but this veiled threat exasperated Dame Janet.

"Not this year," she had remonstrated with him. "The women cannot pay on time."

"Then I shall threaten to excommunicate them. That will strike the fear of hell and damnation into their souls."

Dame Janet's head wobbled from side to side on her fleshy neck. "Much good your curses will do you. Show some mercy, brother. The women have been left to gather in the harvest while their menfolk have answered the king's call to arms. These braw lads may be paying for the safety of the realm with the ultimate sacrifice – their lives – and it will be solace and consolation their women are seeking from the clergy, not hell and damnation. You'd do better to pray for victory in the coming battle – that's what the folk want to hear – and for another miracle. A sign that heaven is on our side would not go amiss."

The mood among the crowd – mostly women, children and old men – on the Abbey Bridge was tense. Hunched against the rain, they silently watched the procession come to a halt by the water's edge where the statue was slowly lowered to the ground. Robed in the rough brown habit of a novice, Elisabeth knelt down before it, clasped her hands in prayer and bowed her head in an attitude of humility. Dame Janet tugged at the prior's chasuble.

"Behold, brother. It seems our niece has taken heed of her lesson."

"Aye, she plays her part well. Perhaps she has the makings of a nun after all."

While Prior John blessed the Black Madonna with oil of chrism, the young curate swung the golden thurible back and forth on a heavy chain. The smouldering incense used to smother the stench of the unwashed and enshroud the ceremony in mystery, was making Elisabeth's eyes stream and the acrid smell was catching in her throat. Choking back a desire to retch, she bent down to pick up the statue. To the strains of the choir chanting *Salvemus*, she lurched towards the river. The Black Madonna seemed to be growing heavier and heavier by the second and her arms ached as she struggled to keep it aloft. Raindrops streamed down her face like tears as she strove to utter the magic prayer:

"Holy Mary Mother of God, help us in our hour of need. Protect thy house from the waters. Save us from peril ... or else ..."

The crudely painted, egg-shaped face of the Madonna swirled before her eyes, its enigmatic smile distorting into a ghastly grimace. Go on, I dare you, it taunted. The booming sound in her ears grew louder and the world began to spin round. In a bid to be rid of this unholy burden, she pitched forwards onto her knees and cried out, "Or else Thy Divine Image shall be cast into the waters."

What, in the name of the Virgin most holy, was the wee pagan doing now? With supernatural effort, Sister Maryoth picked up the skirts of her habit and shot forwards. She made a frantic lunge for the statue as it rolled down towards the river where it teetered teasingly for a moment on the brink before tumbling in with a scornful splash.

The crowd gasped as the statue sank, their "Oooh" of horror changing to "Aaah" of relief, as it bobbed up again out of the murky depths. Desperate to save the icon from a sacrilegious dunking, Sister Maryoth flung herself into the water and floundered towards it. Stumbling on the stony riverbed, she steered the icon towards the side where choirboys were waiting to haul it out. Spluttering out slimy river water, the sodden saviour of the Madonna crawled out of the sludge onto the marshy bank.

"Trust Maryoth to fling herself body and soul into the task," Dame Janet remarked, "Baptism by total immersion. John the Baptist himself will be waggling his sainted head with pride. Will this impress the faithful, do you think?"

Prior John, however, was not amused. "It's bad enough with those two competing to making a bauchle out of me without your jibe, Janet," he muttered. But his sister's perceptive comments made him reflect. Once Elisabeth was tucked in beside her aunt to be taken back to the abbey in the litter, the prior turned to address the crowd. Arms outstretched he proclaimed. "Let us give thanks to God the Father and his Holy Mother for granting his humble servants another miracle. Behold how the Black Madonna floats on water! This sign from Our Lady of the Flood pledges victory over our enemies. On the field of the coming battle we shall prevail," he declaimed triumphantly.

XIII

Flodden

And wond'rous weel they kept their troth;
This sturdy royal band
Rush'd down the brae, wi'' sic a pith,
That nane could them withstand.
The Ballad of the Laird of Muirhead, Traditional

St. Mary's Abbey, 13 September 1513

The sound of raindrops drumming non-stop against the window shutter woke her early. Elisabeth groaned. Since the day of the miracle of the flood, the rain had never ceased. The constant downpours not only seemed to be confirming her guilt but were conspiring to make her punishment more difficult. Three times a day she had to get down on her hands and knees and wash the chapel floor. Already the skin on her hands was chapped and raw from wringing out the cloth in a bucket of cold water and the scabs on her knees never had time to heal. More rain, more pain.

As she splashed through the puddles on her way to the chapel, she noticed that there seemed to be more beggars than usual sheltering in the courtyard. Heaps of tattered rain-soaked blankets stirred and, from deep within one huddled pile, a child whimpered.

At Mass that morning, Prior Hepburn was raising the sacred chalice for the Eucharist when a bedraggled, glaur-ridden figure came staggering up the aisle to the high altar. Elisabeth's heart sank at the muddy trail left by his tattered footcloths.

Sister Maryoth rose from her knees. "How dare you break in to our service! This is a house of God. We are at prayer."

The lad slumped down at the altar steps and burst into sobs.

"Aye, and all your prayers will be needed on this woeful day. Scotland is lost. Our king and countrymen – all wede awa'!"

The nuns fluttered round him, anxious for news of their kinfolk. The noblest lairds of the land had fallen on the fatal field of Flodden, among them the gallant twenty-one-year-old Earl of Bothwell, cut down while leading the bold men of East Lothian into the fray.

"My nephew! Slain? The king's army routed?" Hepburn's florid face grew pale. "May God have mercy on their souls."

Some of the nuns followed his lead and began to pray but, when one of the older nuns began keening, others joined in this more ancient custom, their doleful lament drowning out any religious prayers.

"And who brings these terrible tidings?"

With his tattered clothing slathered in gore and glaur, and his face gaunt with exhaustion, the lad was scarcely recognisable.

"The cream of the country perish, but you survive?" the prior accused. "How is it that you escaped? Or did you flee the field afeart, Harry Cockburn?"

The prior lumbered down from the altar and began kicking the stable lad as he lay crumpled on the steps. Meanwhile, Sister Maryoth had hurried off to the kitchen where the abbey watchmen, men too old for warfare, were keeping their pelts dry but slaking their drouth with ale.

"Coward and sneak thief that you are, Harry Cockburn! Scum such as you don't deserve to live. I'll have you scourged until the skin flakes from your back like the bark of a birch."

Grabbing Harry by the scruff of the neck, Hepburn signalled to the watchmen who tied his hands behind his back and marched him down the aisle. While Sister Maryoth led the little procession out of the chapel, the prior shuffled back up the altar and flicked through the pages of the Holy Missal. The Mass in Time of War for the salvation of the king's servants and the extinction of his enemies was no longer right and fitting.

"*Requiem eternam.*" He growled the opening words of the Mass for the Dead.

Outside the chapel, clusters of stragglers and camp followers who had come seeking food and shelter lay sprawled around the abbey courtyard. Their forty days" supply of victuals had been used up long before the battle, leaving their menfolk too weak and hungry to fight. As she passed among them handing out weak ale and bread, Elisabeth tried to glean any scraps of information about Adam or Lindsay, but there had been too much carnage, too much butchery for the slain to be identified.

Removing their shoes to keep their footing as they charged down the slippery brae, many of the men had tripped over their unwieldy pikes and were trodden into the marsh by those coming behind. Others had been trampled to death as they stumbled to cross the burn.

"There was a burn?" Elisabeth gave a jolt. Hadn't Betsy warned Adam of a burn?

Tragically, that was their undoing. In their plan of attack, the officers hadn't foreseen the marshy stream hidden among reeds at the foot of the brae.

"And yet the rout was foretold," a woman with a bairn suckling at her breast declared, "but they paid no heed. Did it never cross their mind why the accursed field was named Flodden edge? And now the burn is running crimson with their blood."

"It was thon French general's fault." Hauching phlegm in her throat, a sturdy woman dressed in ill-fitting breeches, spat out a slimy gobbet to show her contempt. "Arming our menfolk with waffly bits of stick. For, if thon fancy French spikes didn't shatter in the rumption, the English billhooks smashed them all to smithereens. Waving a handful of thistles would have been wiser. At least they could have stung their arses."

Her vitriol unleashed a communal catharsis of grief among the women who began to pour out their harrowing descriptions. How could they begin to identify their loved ones scythed down in battle? They'd had to leave the butchered carcases of their loved ones strewn about the field, to be feasted on by flocks of corbies and gnawed at by curs and rats.

Elisabeth pinched her wrists to keep from fainting and swallowed hard to keep the brash from rising in her throat. And when they described how crows pecked out the eyes from cloven heads and gorged on minced brains, her hand flew to her mouth. Did they howk out Adam's bonny blue een?

And what about the king's herald? Was there any news of him? In his red and gold tabard he would have stood out on the battlefield, but the women shook their heads wearily. The chaos was such that many were still unaccounted for. Could he have been taken prisoner? Nay, they jeered. Knowing that the English would grant no quarter, the Scots had fought to their last breath. Few, if any, had surrendered.

When the camp followers had tried to bury their dead, the triumphant English had chased them from the field, mercilessly stripping the bodies naked of anything valuable. These sluts and whores, as Adam had cried them, began beating their breasts with guilt and remorse that their menfolk hadn't been given a decent burial. It was true that the Abbess of Coldingham had shown some Christian charity by allowing the fallen to be buried in the abbey graveyard, but only the corpses of the few identified as highborn. Those of the common soldiers were left as fodder for the corbies.

"And King James? What of him?" Elisabeth feared the reply, for she was sure that Lindsay would have shared his fate. He would never, ever have left his monarch's side. Reports were contradictory. That the king had fallen under his own banner; that Lord Hume had carried him off the field, wounded but still alive; that the English had taken him prisoner. So there was still hope.

But not for Sister Maryoth. The sisters took it in turns to press their ear against the door of the chapel, listening to the sounds of wailing and lamentation within. Consider how his sacred flesh was scourged to shreds, she howled, how his divine head was crowned with thorns, the blood gushing down his heavenly face. Consider how the nails impaled his hands and feet.

In penitential sackcloth, Sister Maryoth was following Christ on his final journey to Golgotha. The coarse cloth chafed at her skin while around her waist she'd fastened a heavy chain that cut into her flesh, forming angry-looking weals. After dragging herself on her knees around each station on the *Via Sacra*, she flopped, face down onto the cold flagstones to contemplate the horror of the Crucifixion.

These acts of self-mortification she endured for the sake of her brother, John, Lord Hay of Yester. Though Maryoth believed that he'd be given martyr status for sacrificing his life at Flodden and go straight to heaven, she shouldn't dare to presume divine will. Offering up her suffering, however, should ensure a plenary indulgence for his soul's immediate release from purgatory or, at the very least, a considerable reduction in his sentence there. Hell wasn't an option.

Witnessing this display, the sisters swithered from being awe-stricken at her extreme piety to being worried that she'd lost her wits. Her lamentations, however, left Elisabeth cold. Her own scullion hands and skinned knees were testament to her thrice-daily penance. What a pity Sister Maryoth had not put her self-indulgent breast-beating to better use by giving the chapel floor a good scrubbing while on her knees.

Two days and nights Sister Maryoth fasted and kept vigil until very early on the third morning, while the rest of the convent slumbered, she fell into a swoon. Flashes of light zigzagged in front of her eyes and illuminated her soul with a revelation: that the slaughter of the flower of Scottish manhood was not the fault of the foolish and misguided King James. No, Almighty God was taking revenge: casting his Son and Mother into the waters had been an act of blasphemy.

Coming out of her trance, Sister Maryoth sat beneath the feet of the Black Madonna to interpret this divine disclosure. What had possessed this wild child to commit such a sacrilege? An evil spirit or, heaven forfend, Satan himself? After all, Elisabeth had been brought up by that old witch, Betsy Learmont. What black arts had she taught her? The Prince of Darkness was amongst them and God in his wisdom had entrusted his humble and obedient servant Maryoth with the task of purging this evil from their midst.

XIV

Ordination

Then would I say: "If God me had ordained
To live my life in thraldome thus and pain
What was the cause that He me more constrained
Than other folk to live in such ruin?"
The King's Quair, James I, 15th Century

St. Mary's Abbey, 9 November 1513

Arrayed in the virginal white of a novice with a wreath of embroidered flowers crowning her chestnut hair, Elisabeth approached the altar and genuflected. Prior Hepburn smiled indulgently.

"Her recent loss seems to have purged our bee-heided niece of all her daft notions."

"Aye," Dame Janet replied. "Now that her fiery temper has been smoored, you'll find our niece more ready to accept her fate."

A few days before, at the Requiem Mass on All Souls" Day, as Prior Hepburn read out the roll call of the fallen at Flodden, Elisabeth fumbled for the talisman she'd hidden underneath her sark. Looped onto the blue ribbon were the king's ring and the St. John's nut, its kernel pierced with a needle. To help her *endure fort* when she heard Adam's name being read out, she pressed it against her heart. Still, the shock made her ears buzz and, yawning deeply to clear them, she just caught the name – Sir David Lindsay. Her heart shoogled.

"*Dies Irae, Dies illa.* Day of Wrath, that dreadful day," the choir chanted, "*Lacrimosa dies illa.*"

Though her heart longed to scream out in anguish, she kept her head bowed, fearful that the ever-watchful eyes of Sister Maryoth might detect her distress. But the words of the Gospel made her raise her head: Thy brother, Jesus said, will rise again. Would that it were true.

Since then Elisabeth had been confined to her cell where she'd spent the last few weeks in prayer and fasting to cleanse her soul in preparation for receiving the sacrament of Holy Orders. The regime must also be purifying her body for she hadn't needed to ask for monthly cloths. That, the washerwife pointed out, was one of the benefits of fasting. It staunched the accursed monthly bleed. "And another," she added with a conspiratorial wink as she gathered up the linen for washing, "is that it'll put you in Sister Maryoth's favour. For it's a sign of devotion in her eyes."

As he anointed her on the forehead with holy chrism, the prior noticed that his niece's downcast eyes were red and swollen and her face pinched and pale. Janet was right. Much of her fire had been quenched. He must have a word with Maryoth not to be so harsh.

After Elisabeth had pledged her vows, he presented her with two gifts. From a velvet-lined box he took out a string of rosary beads made from freshwater pearls with an exquisite silver crucifix that glinted in the candlelight. He draped it over her wrist and placed in her hands a *Book of Hours*, expensively illustrated with a jewel-encrusted cover and gold clasp. The newly ordained nun could only nod her thanks.

The sacrificial lamb was led in to the sacristy where Sister Maryoth tore off the wreath and put away the pearl rosary beads and the gaudily engraved *Book of Hours* for safekeeping. Then she set about cutting her hair. She grabbed it in tufts and hacked at it clumsily, cropping it back almost to the scalp, all the while muttering prayers and incantations under her breath to fend off evil.

"Lord, she is not worthy. Lord, forgive me for this shameful offering. Cast out the horned Prince of Darkness from this child of Satan."

"What's this?" Maryoth's hand had become entangled in the blue ribbon round Elisabeth's neck. "A holy scapular?"

Though she had no idea what a scapular was, Elisabeth gripped hold of it and nodded.

"Though I doubt it. For a heathen such as you, it's more likely to be a lucky charm."

Before she could stop her, Maryoth had tugged at the ribbon, snapping the love knot and sending the ring and the nut clattering onto the flagstones. Elisabeth dropped to her knees, splaying her fingers to search for them but as she crawled about, Maryoth stamped on her knuckles and then crunched the nut underfoot. The ring had rolled away unseen.

"As for this," she declared, dangling the blue ribbon as if it were a venomous viper. "The only way to be rid of this devil's tail is to burn it." With that, she held it over a candle, watching intently until it shrivelled to cinders. The vicious look in her narrowed eyes betrayed a desire to dispose of her rival in the same way.

Meekly the newly shorn lamb obeyed Maryoth's order to strip off her white lace gown and stood shivering in the cold vestry, hugging her tender breasts. Elisabeth closed her eyes as the dun-coloured habit was pulled down over her head, prickling her scalp and scratching her skin. Only when Maryoth tugged the hempen cord and knotted it tightly until it dug into her waist did Elisabeth flinch.

For now that she had lost Lindsay and her only connection to him had been severed, nothing mattered any more. She didn't even have the St. John's nut to protect her from the evil eye. Covering her shaven head with the wimple and securing the ties, Maryoth thrust a heavy wooden crucifix, crudely carved with the figure of the dead Saviour into her hands.

"You are a bride of Christ, now. Kiss your holy spouse, Sister Elisabeth."

XV

Birth

> The Lord God formed man
> of the dust from the ground
> and breathed into his nostrils
> the breath of life;
> And man became a living soul.
>
> *Genesis* II:7

St.Mary's Abbey, 30 November 1513

Her head bowed under her cowl against the skelping wind, Elisabeth scurried across the courtyard. Sheltering in the chapel porch, the regular gaggle of beggars squinted suspiciously at the straggly line straying in to their patch. Cripples on homemade crutches hobbled alongside the feeble and infirm being hauled on makeshift litters of ragged sheets, while other, less fortunate souls, had to shauchle along on their hands and knees, dragging their scruntit bodies through the grime and glaur.

"There's o'er mony for the money," the beggars grumbled uncharitably, though they had no need to fret. For the pilgrims, who'd trudged through hail, wind and sleet, hadn't come to poach their alms but to press their lips to the holy relic.

After the humiliating rout at Flodden, doubts about the miraculous powers of the Black Madonna had been spreading like a plague of boils amongst his flock. To rekindle their faith, Prior Hepburn was sending a precious bone of Saint Andrew to the abbey. To touch it may, or may not, procure a cure in this world, but would certainly guarantee a plenary indulgence – total remission of their time in purgatory – in the next, so he promised. The parish priest, Father Dudgeon, had argued for the relic to be displayed in the larger Collegiate Church of St.Mary's since it could accommodate more of the faithful. Prior Hepburn had refused. The precious relic would be shown in a pavilion in the grounds of the abbey for, if any miracle did occur, he wanted the glory to go to his convent.

Waiting their turn to venerate the relic, the pilgrims huddled together against the snell wind, teeth and tongues chattering. Which part of the sainted apostle's body would it be? His upper-arm bone or kneecap, perhaps, or even a finger from the cathedral's collection? When word came through that the tiny silver reliquary contained not a forefinger, a thumb or even a pinkie, but a tooth, the pilgrims choked back their disappointment. Size should not matter as they puckered their lips to kiss the magic box containing the blackened stump of a molar.

Sister Maryoth's lips also puckered – in disgust at the sight of all those filthy mouths covered in suppurating sores defiling the sacred relic. She sniffed deeply into the pouch scented with rose oil to stave off the stench, before turning her wrinkled nose to where the professional paupers were squabbling and jostling for position. As Keeper of the Priory Purse she organised the alms distribution, an act of charity she begrudged, for it tugged at her heart strings to undo the abbey purse strings and dole out to unworthy scroungers. Gathering the nuns round her she dispensed coins and warnings:

"Keep your distance, sisters, or you risk being infested with lice. Do not be fooled by thon feckless leeches who elbow their way to the front. So as to wheedle alms the sleekit sluggards rub their sores with buttercup sap to keep them pus-ridden."

Elisabeth kept her head down to avoid the louring looks, not only from Sister Maryoth but from the knot of tight-lipped women with whimpering weans on their hips and pinched-faced toddlers clinging to their skirts. Shivering in sullen silence, these widows of Flodden were black affronted at having to ask for charity. They carefully counted up the meagre offerings being doled out and grumbled that it was a lot less than the tithes exacted from them at harvest time: the lives of their menfolk worth hardly a groat.

She was emptying the last of the coins from her pouch when a sudden squall sent the beggars scurrying for cover and the sisters scuttling back to the abbey. Feeling faint from fasting for the feast, Elisabeth lagged behind the others when she felt a hand tug at her cloak. A young lad, no more than four or five years old was hopping from one bare foot to the other to keep them from the freezing ground. His pleading eyes loomed huge above sunken cheekbones as he held out his hand.

"Poor wee Willie," a woman muttered, "his father fell at Flodden and his mother's baggit with another bairn."

"Aye, she's in travail at this very minute. She'd no money for a skeily-wife and the howdie is doing all she can. But they've sent over to Hailes for Mistress Learmont."

"Aye, Betsy has the knack. She'll see her through."

Betsy was here! Elisabeth gave the lad a coin and asked him to take her home. Let Maryoth in her mercy chastise her for carrying out an act of charity.

She followed the lad through Giffordgait, past rundown hovels that became more and more dilapidated as they neared the Nungate Bridge. Smoke from peat fires hanging heavily over the turfed roofs blurred her vision, making it difficult to avoid stepping into what could be either mud or dung or both. The recent rain had enriched the sharp, sour stench rising from the gutters swilling with sewage. Scraggy hens squawked and squabbled on sodden midden heaps until scattered by a pack of feral dogs. The lad stopped at the broken-down door of a but-and-ben, squatting at the edge of the Tyne in the shadow of the magnificent Collegiate Church of St.Mary's on the other side of the river.

The door scraped open and she had to stoop to enter. The reek from the mutton-fat tapers stung her eyes, blinding her for a few moments. When her eyes had adjusted to the murky light she saw the lad on his knees, blowing onto a log to rekindle the flame under the cauldron of tepid water suspended on a swey. Muffled sounds came from the corner where a woman with a cloth stuffed into her mouth was writhing on a pallet of chaff. The howdie, a local woman who helped out in childbirth, was leaning over her, trying to wipe the sweat from her brow as she tossed her head from side to side. At the other end, Betsy was busy wringing out blood-soaked cloths. With her eyes smarting and her nose itching, Elisabeth strove unsuccessfully to stifle a sneeze. Betsy whirled round.

"Sakes me, Lisbeth, what are you doing here? This is no place for a young lass. Away you go."

"I heard the lad's mother needed help."

Betsy sighed. "Well, lass, you might as well make yourself useful. You mop her brow while Annie boils up the brew." She handed the howdie some dried leaves wrapped in muslin.

"Why is she gagged like that?" Elisabeth whispered. "To stop her screaming?"

"Nay, lass, it gives her something to bite on other than her own tongue. It helps her to thole the birthing showers, the spasms that push the bairn out. But I fear her travail's been over long. She's losing strength."

When the howdie untied the gag and tilted her head forward, the woman let out a shriek.

"Wheesht, Maggie, wheesht! Have a wee sip of this if you're able," Betsy urged. "It'll help ease the bairn through."

But, convulsed by another contraction, the woman grimaced with pain. Betsy fumbled around in the large pockets of her skirt and produced a poke, a small muslin bag containing a powder. Since the raspberry leaves weren't working, something more drastic was needed.

She shook some of it onto her palm and cautiously dabbed Maggie's tongue with tiny specks, for deadly nightshade, in too powerful a dose, could be just that. Deadly. The miniscule dose Betsy administered would, she hoped, put the mother to sleep and leave her to get on with prising the reluctant babe from the womb. Within minutes Maggie stopped struggling, closed her eyes and went limp.

"Now we can get on with it." Betsy thrust her head between the woman's thighs and, after much twisting and turning, she yanked out what looked like a haunch of mutton.

"Ah, the canny moment." Annie sighed and clasped her hands. "Praise be to the Virgin!"

Betsy carefully untangled the cord that had twisted round the baby's neck and bit it off, spitting it out into a bowl. Elisabeth's stomach somersaulted.

"What have we got Betsy? Lad or lass?" the howdie asked.

Betsy examined the infant and frowned. "A wee laddie," she said brusquely, more concerned about the faint bluish tinge round the tiny puckered lips. Wiping away the traces of birthing blood and mucous with a cloth, she threw him over her shoulder and thumped his back a few times, but the infant stubbornly refused to take his first breath.

"Has this one taken a scunner to life already? Well, perhaps that's for the best," she murmured, preparing to swaddle him in his shroud.

"No, Betsy, you can't just let him …" Elisabeth exclaimed. Though the messy, beastly process of birth was curdling her stomach, the thought of letting the bairn die revived her.

"Here then, lass, take the wean and blow into his mouth. I'm jiggered. There's no puff left in me. Now don't be feart to give him a fair good blast."

Betsy passed the infant over to Elisabeth who gawped in panic at the wizened face, thrawn and twisted from the efforts of being born. With his eyes tightly shut, fists clenched and lips pursed, he seemed to be defying life. Tentatively she covered the baby's lips with her own and puffed gently into his mouth. Again, she blew — more strongly this time — filling his tiny lungs with her own breath until she sensed a slight movement in his chest.

"That's the way, lass." Betsy leaned over and trickled some liquid into the bairn's mouth. He wrinkled his nose and, as the strong spirit hit his gullet, he gave a plaintive cry.

"That's something at least. I was afeart the cord might have throttled him. He'd better not get a taste for the *aquavitae*, mind. He's better off with this," said Betsy, laying him at his mother's breast where his toothless gums instinctively latched on to her nipple. Woken by her infant's cry, the mother laid a hand on Elisabeth's arm.

"Sister," she mumbled, "will you shield him from the fairy blast? Will you be the bairn's godmother and make sure he's christened soon? Afore the fairies spirit him away?"

"Aye, she will that, Maggie," Betsy answered for her. "I'll see that she does."

Once she'd fallen asleep with the bairn suckling at her breast, Betsy brought out the flask again.

"I reckon we need this ourselves now. Not only to wet the bairn's head but to quicken our own spirits. Here's good health and long life to us all." After taking a long, satisfying swig, Betsy wiped the rim and passed the flask to the howdie.

"And you too, Lisbeth. For though his mother may have borne his body into this world, you breathed life into him and stirred his soul. And from now on, you and thon laddie will aye be thirled together. For as long as you both shall live."

Elisabeth raised the flask to her lips but instantly recoiled. Throughout the laborious birth, she'd struggled to quell her queasiness, but now just a whiff of the sharp spirit brought waves of nausea welling up from the pit of her stomach. Holding her hand firmly to her mouth, she rushed outside to retch agonisingly into the gutter.

XVI

Baptism

The bairnie she swyl'd in linen so fine,
In a gilded casket she laid it syne,
Mickle saut and light she laid therein
Cause yet in God's house it hadna been.
The Ballad of the King's Daughter, Traditional

St. Mary's Abbey, 8 December 1513

Standing at the baptismal font, Elisabeth gently pulled back the shawl swaddled round the bundle snoozing in Betsy's arms and peered at the crinkle-faced bairn.

"Will you keep hold of him, Betsy?"

While Elisabeth may have been nervous about being a godmother and handling such a tiny newborn, her uncle had no such anxieties. As well as christening the bairn, Prior Hepburn had agreed, in the absence of anyone else, to stand as his godfather. With practised hands, he vigorously massaged the bairn's ears and nose with his own saliva and then dabbed his finger with salt before inserting it into his tiny mouth. To open the portals of evil to the odour of sweetness and sanctity, he explained.

Betsy winced. What kind of religion decreed that this wee mite was a child of darkness and sin, the devil's bird, until a gob of spittle and a splash of water transformed him into a blessed son of God, she wondered. Where was the joy in such a faith? And when the prior asked, "Dost thou renounce Satan and all his works?" she shook her head. What a daft question for a week-old wean. Betsy unwrapped his swaddling and handed him naked to the prior who dunked him in the baptismal font, splashing them all with holy water.

"*In nomine Patris, et Filii, et Spiritus Sancti …* "

After the third dunking his watery eyelids flickered but still he made no sound. Brusquely Betsy snatched the infant and rubbed him dry before wrapping him up again. When at last he gave a plaintive whimper, her chest heaved with relief.

"That was chancy. Better than nothing, I jalouse," she muttered, swiftly withdrawing the pin she had sneakily inserted beneath his swaddling. For if the bairn hadn't cried out, it would have been a bad omen, that he wouldn't be long for this world. While the holy water may have exorcised the devil, the pinprick had cast out the evil eye.

Meanwhile, the prior was blessing their new godson three times to bring him into the Christian fold. "*Ioannes Cnoxus,*" he said, christening him in Latin. John Knox.

PART TWO

I

Absolution

Next in the dance followit Envy,
Filled full of feud and felony,
Hid malice and dispite.
The Dance of the Seven Deadly Sins
William Dunbar, 15th –16th Century

St. Mary's Abbey, 18 December 1513

The sudden ray of sunlight through the slit window struck the gold leaf and sent glittering shafts skipping around the cell walls. Elisabeth rubbed her eyes. The *Book of Hours* with its lavishly illuminated illustrations was wondrous to behold, but she could make no sense of the mystifying squiggles that made up the text. Even if it were not written in Latin, she still wouldn't be able to understand it. If only she could read.

She loosened the hempen cord digging into her waist and chafing her skin. Peering at the illustration of the Annunciation, she could readily sympathise with the Virgin Mary's plight. Betsy had confirmed that she was with child but was at a loss what to do about it.

With one hand rubbing her belly, she was so completely absorbed, that she didn't hear Sister Maryoth slithering into her cell. Her uncle was on his way, the harbinger of doom warned, just as Prior Hepburn loomed up behind her.

"Cantle up your spirits my precious jewel, and confide in me. I am your confessor." Prior John's face was puckered with concern and he spoke in the wheedling tone he used in the confessional to encourage the penitent to unburden his heart. Elisabeth hesitated, caught off-guard by his solicitous manner. She grimaced. Stomach cramps were making her feel queasy, but her uncle's cloying sympathy was just as nauseous.

"He took you by force, didn't he?" he said, taking her hand. "Thon sleekit skite, Harry Cockburn did indeed violate my precious jewel! Why didn't you tell us the truth? I should have libbed him when I had the chance. But have no fear, I'll scour the land till yon poltroon's found," he said.

He squeezed her hand tightly to stem his fury at the loss of his prey. While Harry was being transferred to the deep pit dungeon at Hailes Castle, those old watchmen had let him slip through their incompetent hands and denied the prior the pleasure of a scourging.

Elisabeth inhaled deeply. Now was the time to tell the truth. Now was the time to confess that the father of her child was not the dim-witted Harry, but Sir David Lindsay. What would it matter now that he was dead? She couldn't let the lowly stable lad take the blame and bear the brunt of her uncle's wrath. Harry didn't deserve that.

Behind the prior's back, Sister Maryoth was smirking quietly to herself. Silently she gave thanks to God that her scheme had come to fruition. Ever on the alert for tell-tale signs, her vigilant eyes had spied Elisabeth's broadening girth. Soon her prayers would be answered, leaving the way open for her ambition to be fulfilled. Prioress Hay of St.Mary's Abbey! Dame Maryoth! While the prospect made her quiver with excitement, she must not let herself be seduced by the sin of pride.

But Elisabeth was now whimpering like a helpless kitten and the prior was drawing her to him in a comforting embrace. Sister Maryoth panicked. He was on the brink of showing mercy, of forgiving his niece. And jeopardising her future.

"We shall be sorry to lose our dear sister Elisabeth," she blurted, "but of course it would be unseemly for a future prioress to bear a child. Forbye, virginity is a prerequisite of our order and chastity our most important vow." She narrowed her lips to prevent them from breaking into a gloating, self-righteous smirk and cast her eyes downwards.

Her gesture of humility didn't fool Elisabeth. So that's what she was scheming.

"Don't be too hard on Harry, dearest uncle," she began. "He's a simple soul."

"Not so simple that he doesn't know what to do with his pistle," the prior growled.

"But Harry thought that I hankered after him and that, when I tried to push him away, I was only teasing and jiggling him. But he's a strong lad and, well …" Elisabeth turned away to hide her blushes.

"Wheesht, wheesht, my precious pearl, it's not your fault. I'm sure you wouldn't lead him on." As Hepburn pulled her into his arms, his wiry beard scratched her cheek. She tried not to wince.

"I didn't, uncle. He truly believed I was giving him the glad eye because," she paused to glare over her uncle's shoulder, "Sister Maryoth told him so." There. *That* would take the starch out of her wimple.

Sister Maryoth's smooth oval face clouded over. "By the Holy Virgin, Mary, the Mother of God," she began, clutching her rosary with two hands, "I would never encourage such … such … lechery." Her eyes widened. "How can she say such a thing? After I took pity on her and let her go out riding! None of us could be her chaperone, so who better than Harry? I was only doing what I thought best and this is how she repays me." She drew a square of linen cloth from her sleeve and snivelled into it.

"Steek your gab, sister." The prior leapt up to jab a finger at her. "It's a pity silence isn't one of your vows. My niece has been ravished and it's all the fault of your wagging tongue. That you could suggest such a lout as yon stable lad could even look at my niece! To kittle him up so that he'd be bold enough to pluck her precious cherry!"

Sister Maryoth tried not to flinch as flecks of spittle splattered her face. The prior looked round, caught sight of Elisabeth's gilded *Book of Hours* and grabbed it from the shelf. Not the Bible, but the next best thing.

"Whatever is said within the walls of this chamber is sacrosanct. Do you hear?" He waggled a menacing finger at her. "Nothing that is discussed here will – on pain of your life – nay – on the loss of your immortal soul, be spoken of anywhere, to anyone, at any time. And, to make sure that you do ..." he said, holding out the book. "Swear on oath."

Rudely awakened from her afternoon nap, Dame Janet wiped the sleep from her bleary, blackened eyes.

"What's done is done," she said, her mouth gaping wide in a lazy yawn. "And a corbie is no whiter for being washed. And after your threats, brother, I doubt we'll see young Harry in these parts again."

"Our niece is more sinned against than sinning," the prior declared. "And since I have the power to absolve her, she is now as pure as the day she was born."

"Like Christ's Holy Mother? You're surely not saying there was no stain of original sin on Lisbeth's soul as well? Immaculate virgin and mother most chaste? That's quite a claim," she remarked with a little chortle. "So we're to have our very own virgin birth in our midst, brother? Now that will indeed be a miracle."

Still amused at the thought, she leant over to choose a *bonbon* from the box by her bedside so as to sweeten her mouth stale with sleep. Watching her plump shoulders shaking with laughter, the prior scowled. Flippancy was not appropriate at such a time. Meanwhile, Sister Maryoth, with no forbearance for blasphemy, hurriedly crossed herself.

As she led a forlorn-looking Betsy to the prioress's chamber, Sister Maryoth's fingers plied up and down her rosary to ward off the witch's evil miasma. With her folklore and superstitions and arcane knowledge of female problems, Betsy was at worst a godless heathen and at best a follower of the auld, Celtic religion. A witch in other words, though she'd never dare to utter this aloud.

"Away and tell your beads elsewhere, Maryoth. This is not for your ears." Prior Hepburn pointed to the door.

Hostility oozed like black bile from the holy nun as she passed the ungodly pagan on her way out. The prior waited a few moments, opened the door again and, satisfied there was no-one eavesdropping, said, "Well, Betsy, you're the canny woman, so tell us, what can be done about this?"

Thoroughly miserable, Betsy shook her head.

"It's no the bairn's fault it's misbegotten. If only I'd found out earlier when it was still a tottie wee mite, I'd have no fears about scouring it out. But Lisbeth is at least four months gone. Forbye," she said, raising her eyebrows, "is it no against the law of God to redd out a wean? Even if the mother's life is at risk and she's struggling to feed another four or five, it's the unborn bairn that must be saved, so the priests say. A canny wife like me could be put in the jougs for helping out a mother at her wits' end."

"Well, Betsy, rest assured that will not happen," the prior promised. "And the Church has the authority to overlook a minor indiscretion when the greater good is being served."

Shifting in her seat, Betsy looked at him askance. "You mean turn a blind eye when it suits them?"

II

Visitation

> The heartly joy God give ye had seen
> Was shown when that their sisters met!
> *The Tale of the Uplands Mouse and the Burgess Mouse*
> Robert Henryson, 15th Century

Tantallon Castle, Yuletide 1514

Etched against the darkening sky, the jagged outline of Tantallon seemed to be ablaze as a shaft of low winter sun flashed through the murky rain-clouds to set the castle's red stone on fire. Elisabeth sat bolt upright in the saddle, bringing her horse abruptly to a halt.

Betsy trotted up alongside on her pony. "What's wrong, my lass?"

"It looks ... eerie." A shiver of apprehension ran through Elisabeth.

Betsy nodded. "Aye, I ken fine what you mean. It gives me the cold creeps, too."

Their little entourage passed over the drawbridge and through the portcullis into the fortress perched precariously on cliffs overlooking the Firth of Forth. The huge iron gate of the impregnable Douglas stronghold clanged shut behind them. The last rays of the setting sun had long passed away and the deep shadows of towering walls cast a gloom even more terrifying than absolute darkness. Elisabeth had been looking forward to spending Yuletide with her sister at Tantallon, but now, gazing up at the high walls, she felt more trapped than she'd ever been in the convent.

Swaddled in a fox fur cloak, Meg scampered across the frost-covered courtyard to greet them, a vulnerable little dormouse against the backdrop of the castle walls.

"You've come at last!" she cried, flinging herself upon them.

"How could we turn down the invitation of such a grand lady! Countess of Angus, no less."

Squeezing her sister tightly, Elisabeth could feel her bones, as spindly and fragile as a wren's, even through her cloak and velvet dress. Though never big and buxom, Meg seemed to have shrunk and, despite her newly elevated rank and expensive clothes, was looking unhappily gaunt and woebegone.

"Thanks be to God someone is glad for me. Not everyone here is overjoyed." Meg cupped her mouth with her hand and glanced upwards at the shuttered windows. "My mother-in-law is sore affronted that she missed her turn to be countess."

Flodden had not only carried off her husband, George, Master of Angus, and his brother, but had cheated her out of her title. And then, while they were still in mourning, her father-in-law, the fifth earl, had died only a few days before, leaving the title to Archie.

"We aye thought that old Bell the Cat must have at least nine lives! But losing his two brave sons in such a stramash broke his heart. And Lady Douglas is seething that one of auld man's mistresses – Janet Kennedy who claims that he married her – has crawled out of her scutter hole, demanding a share of his estate. She's threatened to put a hex on the hizzie!"

"Aye, her long neb has been sorely put out of joint," Betsy remarked. "She'll no be using it now as a kirnstick to curdle cream."

The girls burst into giggles but when the frosty air caught their breath and Meg started coughing, Betsy hustled them inside. As they warmed themselves in front of the log fire, Elisabeth pulled open her cloak to reveal her bump.

"A bairn? You're going to have a bairn?" Meg seemed wonderstruck. "But, Lisbeth, how can that be? You're a nun! You've just taken your vows! You've never lain with a man! Have you?"

Elisabeth took a deep breath before relating her tale. When she finished and Meg asked where Davie was now, she had to bite her lip. "He was slain. Along with Adam."

"May their souls rest in peace," Meg murmured, crossing herself. "Oh, my poor, dear Lisbeth, what are you going to do?"

"It will all work out fine," Betsy replied, although quite how, she wasn't sure. Regular doses of raspberry leaf tisanes had failed to bring on her courses, and Elisabeth hadn't been able to keep down the hot toddy of juniper berries simmered in *aquavitae* long enough to do its work. The roots of the lesser meadow rue, usually a proven remedy, had only loosened her bowels. Hot mustard baths and even the vigorous ride from Hailes had failed to slacken her womb. More invasive procedures Betsy would not consider for her dear thistledown. Nature would have to take its course.

"But Lisbeth, you'll never be able to bring up a bairn in a convent. You'll have to leave. And come here. Aye, that's it! You can come here to have your bairn!" Meg leapt to her feet, clapping her hands together. "Perhaps this is God's will!" Her forget-me-not blue eyes flashed and two little crimson spots brightened her cheeks. "Are we not told that the Lord works in mysterious ways? It's true! This is one of his wonders!"

So far Meg had failed in her duty to produce an heir. Her fault, Lady Douglas had accused her, for being either frigid or barren, or both. But how could she conceive when Archie tumbled into her bed, stinking of drink and lust after evenings carousing with his brothers? She couldn't bring herself to practise Nancy's lessons but lay waiting, rigid as a poker. Then, if he hadn't fallen into a stupor, he would begin jabbing into her. Not an act of love, but a painful, humiliating assault that left her sore and sobbing while he snored away, insensible and insensitive.

And now the newly entitled Earl of Angus had abandoned her altogether. He spent all his time at court dancing attendance on the widow queen, leaving Meg a virtual prisoner in this fortress. Every night she went down on her knees, pleading with the Mother of God to bless her with a child and now her prayers had been answered. Not in the way she would have expected but, nevertheless, a baby had been sent. Borne in her sister's womb. She squeezed Elisabeth's hands.

"Lisbeth, you are indeed heaven-sent. God in his mercy has ordained this! I'll tell them that I'm with child. And when the bairn's born, I'll bring him up as my own. You have no need to fret."

For the first time in many dark months Meg felt alive. The little cherries on her cheeks ripened into apples and, as she began making plans for the confinement, Betsy took hold of her hands.

"I don't want to douse your hopes, my lass, but I fear you're winding yourself into a pirn. When did you last lie with Archie? And when did you have your last bleed?" she asked.

Meg's mouth drooped, her eyes dimmed. Months ago would be the answer to both questions.

"And you ken why, my lass, there's no meat on you. You're just a rickle of bones."

Meg picked up the bird of paradise cushion and pressed it to her stomach.

"Look at my belly now! And I'll make myself eat. If you'll feed me up, Betsy, I swear I'll eat for two!"

Meg prayed that the child would be a lad. Would this be tempting Providence? A son would raise her esteem in the eyes of the Douglas clan. Her mother-in-law wouldn't be so swift to look down her long neb if she produced an heir. Judging by the tenacity with which the unborn infant had clung to his mother's womb, despite all her attempts to scrape him out, Betsy was convinced it must be a lad in there but, worn down by Meg's constant pestering, she agreed to divine its sex.

She checked the three week-old hen's egg for hairline cracks and then tapped it against the side of the bowl. She was about to separate the yolk from the white when she sucked in her breath: a double yolk. Tutting to herself, she shook her head.

"What will it be, Betsy. Lad or lass?" Meg dared to ask, crossing her fingers behind her back.

"One or tother. Or both." Betsy was bewildered. She'd have to try another test. With Elisabeth stretched out on the settle, she held a knotted string over her womb, watching its progress intently as it swung back and forth and round and round. After putting her ear to her belly, she straightened up and tapped her chin. Seeing her nurse's bewildered expression, Elisabeth gave a nervous laugh.

"I hope you're no going to tell me there are two in there, Betsy!"

"Ah, well, now you might have hit on something there," Betsy frowned. "Twins, now, that might explain ... but I don't think so, for I can only hear one heartbeat."

"Twins! O Betsy, that would be wonderful." Her eyes feverishly radiant, Meg clasped her hands together. "A bairn each for Lisbeth and me! That *would* be a miracle!"

III

Epiphany

Thus made they merry while they micht nae mair
And "Hail,Yule! Hail!" Cryit upon high.
Yet efter joy ofttimes comes care
And trouble efter great prosperity.
The Tale of the Uplands Mouse and the Burgess Mouse
Robert Henryson, 15th Century

Tantallon Castle, 6 January 1514

Her shadow fell now before, now after her as she scuttled along the passage, dimly lit by torches flickering in sconces. Every now and then she spun round to see if she was being followed. Wheedled into playing a game of tig, it was Elisabeth's turn to be het and she was cheating. Jinty, as they cried Janet, the baby of the Douglas family, was about her own age but acted much younger. Airy-fairy Jinty, with her skellie eye that could make her look fey or sleekit or both, scampered about Tantallon, playing pranks and enlivening the dour castle with her high-pitched shrieks. She would only ever sit still, listening enthralled to Betsy's tales.

Weary of their game, Elisabeth had gone beyond their agreed boundary of the northeast wing, hoping to give Jinty the slip, but after all the twists and turns she was now lost. She should have brought a candle or left a trail but that would have given the game away, so now she groped her way uncertainly along the gloomy tunnels. The sounds of raucous laughter and shouting brought her to a halt. The Great Hall. She'd need to retrace her steps to avoid that den where the Douglas men gathered to carouse.

"Och, a bonny wee heir for Archie! An heir for the Earl of Angus!" the drunken chorus were yelling:

"Then durst no man come heirhand the king
But the surname of the doughty Douglas
Which so royally in this region did ring.
Ding doun Tantallon."

The Douglas menfolk, famed for breaking all bounds in conduct, hadn't allowed mourning for their grandsire to spoil their Twelfth Night festivities. And now they had joyous news to celebrate. An heir was expected! At long last the Countess of Angus was with child.

Elisabeth peeked round the door. Up in the gallery, the last minstrel standing was valiantly plucking out a tuneless melody on the lute and warbling words of either joy for the conception of a new laird or lament for the death of the old one. Down below, several bodies lay slumped across a trestle strewn with flagons and beakers, their heads buried beneath the scattered remnants of a feast. Others had collapsed onto the floor, among the dogs rooting around the rushes for discarded bones and scraps. Those still on their feet threw back their heads to empty their tankards and then howled their war cry: A Douglas! A Douglas!

A movement in the corner caught her eye. A pair of maggot-white hurdies were thrusting between the thighs of a serving wench pinned against the trestle. Elisabeth drew breath and slid away, hoping to sneak past unseen but her way was blocked.

"Who the deuce have we here, Geordie? Friend or foe? Or spy!" the henchman bawled and grabbed her by the wrist. "By Christ's holy blood! A nun! If you've come to say Grace, sister, save your breath. We're all hell-bound heathens here. And if you've been cast out of the nunnery, come and join our pagan revels instead."

Elisabeth tried to snatch her arm away. "I'll make my own way back."

"Not in our castle, you won't." Archie's brother, George, had risen unsteadily to his feet and was staggering towards her. His large beefy chest bulged out of his shirt slashed to the waist and his belly spilled over his loosened breeches. He scratched at the wiry black hairs on his chest and leered at her. "We'll have no strangers wandering around willy-nilly."

"I'm no stranger. I am sister to the countess."

"Ah, Meg's wee sister. And a holy one at that. Come in to our wee heaven on earth." He dragged her into the hall and bellowed to his cronies. "Do you ken that clerics deem women the very devil? And nuns the most wanton whores of all! Is it not every nun's dream to be ravished?" He thrust his leering face so close that she could see his red-veined eyes and smell his stinking breath. "We'll make sure you don't go to your grave wondering. It would be a great pity if only wriggling worms wammled their way into your virgin's womb." He twisted his forefinger suggestively.

"Aye, and we'll all be up and ready to tirl her at the pin," one of his henchmen shouted.

"Steek your gabs you crankous crew. You'll all get your turn."

George wrenched her round and crushed his lurid claret-stained lips down on hers. His tongue forced its way through her teeth, slithering like a slug round the soft, secret places of her mouth. When she tried to bite down on it, he quickly withdrew and whispered hoarsely in her ear.

"So you want something meatier to nibble on? Get down on your knees, wee sister," he growled and thrust her roughly to the floor. While he fumbled clumsily with the laces of his breeches, Elisabeth clutched the wooden crucifix hanging on the cord round her waist and ran her fingers over the lifeless figure.

"Don't waste your fondling fingers on the dead Christ. Here's something quick and lively that'll respond to your caresses. The answer to your maiden prayers."

She waited until the flaps of his breeches were hanging loose before lunging forward to stab the crucifix as hard as she could into his groin. George grimaced in pain, letting out an inhuman yowl as he crumpled to the floor. She scrambled up from her knees and looked round in alarm, fearful that the barbarous Douglas horde would round on her for humiliating their brother. The din was deafening as they whooped and howled, thumping the tables and clanging their pewter tassies together.

"That's some blessing she's given you, Geordie. That'll put a stop to your sinning for a fair spell."

While George squirmed and nursed his throbbing genitals, Elisabeth held the crucifix aloft to proclaim: "Begone from me, ye cursed. May ye be hurled into the everlasting fires of hell! And the devil take you all."

As she fled out the door she stumbled over the crouching figure of Jinty, her shoulders heaving with silent laughter.

"Our Geordie is het! All het up! Look at him lowping and whauping! Once his whang cocks up again, you'll be in for a walloping!" she sniggered, her eyes rolling disconcertingly in different directions. She grabbed hold of Elisabeth's hand and hauled her through the maze of dark passages.

At the sound of footsteps, they would press hard against the wall, holding their breath until they passed. Stopping at a narrow door, Jinty creaked it open. While she trotted up the winding stair like a goat, Elisabeth had to heave herself up on the rope handrail to the topmost turret where she leant gratefully against the wall to catch her breath.

"I brought Meg up here once," Jinty said, stretching up to look out over the parapet, "for I thought the sea breezes would blow away her cough, but it only made her worse."

Elisabeth could understand. Icy droplets from the splashing waves pierced her lungs like shards of glass. The five-storeyed tower of Tantallon was built on the edge of a cliff that fell away to the sea far, far below. Even the lofty west tower at Hailes was not so steep. The fierce waves licked eagerly at the cliff face, rising higher and higher, as if stretching up to pull her down. To stop her head from swirling, she focussed her eyes on the Craig of Bass encircled with a halo of swooping seabirds.

"This is the best spot in the whole castle," Jinty gazed longingly over the parapet. "I could stay here forever. It's the only place I feel free."

"You're not afeart of heights?" Elisabeth asked.

"Nay! I would fain fly off away here, like one of those gulls and soar across the seas, gliding with the wind."

Listening to her baring her soul, Elisabeth marvelled that the Douglas clan could produce such lyrical poets and such uncouth boors. Jinty had the poetic soul of her uncle Gavin, the poet and cleric, but not, thank goodness, her brother George's foul-mouthed tongue.

IV

Clishmaclaver

Wise women have ways and wonderful guidings
With great ingenuity to bejape their jealous husbands.
The Treatise of the Twa Marrit Women and the Widow
William Dunbar, 15th–16th Century

Holyrood Palace, April 1514

"I, for one, would wager that Angus has sired the bairn," Lady Crawford affirmed. "The king and queen weren't on the best of terms and hadn't bedded as man and wife for a long while."

"There was no dirrie dantoun with her and Archie Douglas," Lady Lennox retorted. Married to a Stewart and a niece of James III, Elisabeth Hamilton took her rôle as self-appointed guardian of the royal morals seriously, whereas Mariota Crawford was an ill-gabbit gossipmonger who revelled in muckraking. But then she was one of the border Humes, notorious rogues who, it was rumoured, had murdered their king after dragging him off the battlefield.

"Forgive me, but I've been a lady of the queen's chamber many a year," Lady Crawford reminded her. "And I can tell you, that, between blankets still dented with the form of the king now cold in the clay, she has lain with Cheeping Archie for her pleasure."

Of similar age and status, these life-long rivals had both been countesses until the deaths of their earls at Flodden. Shared widowhood hadn't brought these two senior ladies any closer together, however, and the other ladies settled back to enjoy their jousting.

"And who's to say that the king was indeed slain?" Lady Lennox's mouth set hard. "There was no iron belt on the body they say was his."

"You surely don't believe the tale that he's taken off on pilgrimage to the Holy Land to do penance for his sin?" Lady Crawford sneered.

"Who knows? But our men would never leave their fallen king to the mercy of the enemy."

"Seems they did. And there have been too many reports from those that swear he was fatally wounded: his throat gashed, his head hacked off and his left hand severed. What was left of him, the English carried off as a trophy of their victory: to present to the queen's own brother. As for taking up with Cheeping Archie, she's a Tudor, mind, with Tudor appetites and tastes, and couldn't do without a man in her bed for long. Innocent bride she may have been, but the king's grace soon had her prenticed in tail-toddle." Lady Crawford smacked her smug lips.

Perched on a stool in the darkest corner of the sewing room, Kate listened to the court ladies chattering at their needlework. Plucking out tunes on a lute, a minstrel provided background music to their tittle-tattle. As he sang smutty lyrics *sotto voce*, he kept leering and winking at Kate. On the pretext of stitching a tapestry cushion or tatting a lace collar, the ladies of the court were gathered together for their daily dose of gossip, as much a sport for them as hunting was for their menfolk.

Everything was fair game and they were merciless in dissecting their present prey, the widow Queen Margaret, and the young Earl of Angus. Her flaunting infatuation with a married man provided a tailor-made seam for them to work on. The fact that she'd given birth, only months after the Flodden rout was being embroidered with salacious tittle-tattle about the possible parentage of Prince Alexander.

Their smutty, scandalous talk helped to keep Kate from falling asleep as she tottered on the wobbly stool. She'd spent yet another night huddled in a blanket by one of the huge ingleneuks in the kitchen for she had nowhere else to go. On the king's death, Queen Margaret had flung her out of his private quarters, along with the other paramours he'd lodged there. Since then, a discarded mistress of the king, penniless, without husband or protector, Kate had been living like the burgh mouse in Henryson's fable, in perpetual fear of the house cat.

She would never condescend to return to Hailes to be treated as an unpaid skivvy by her gloating rival, Nancy. Nor would she accept the invitation of Adam's older sister, Lady Seton, who, having lost her husband at Flodden, was dedicating her widowhood to founding a convent in Edinburgh. Enter a nunnery! That would indeed be a living death sentence! She'd rather live a twilight life, lurking in the gloom of the palace, sleeping wherever she could, living off scraps from the table and fending off unwelcome attention from lowly lackeys and lewd lute players. She hadn't changed her clothes for months and her own smell repelled her. Her bonny golden hair had become dull and matted and unsightly plooks had broken out on her sallow skin. How would she be able to attract patronage in this state?

"Her Grace would never have cuckolded the king," Lady Lennox stated.

"Ah well, who knows, but a quick fyke can be over in the wink of an eye, leaving a troutie in the well." Lady Crawford's main sport lay in contradicting Lady Lennox at every turn. "And King James himself was no better. Buskit as a beggar, he'd stravaig about the countryside, rampant and ready to prod young maidens who dare not disobey their liege lord. The Guiser we'd cry him."

"That's as may be," Lady Lennox said, and drew back her humped shoulders before continuing, "but he had no need to command certain ladies of rank who willingly lined up to warm his bed." Her scornful glance fell on young Isobel Kennedy whose mother Janet could include the doubtful title of Lady Bothwell among her collection. In the past few months Janet Kennedy had lost four of her partners, including King James and Bell the Cat Douglas, but no commiseration was wasted on this woman who had been grooming her own daughter for the king's pleasure.

"Aye, for the rich rewards he bestowed," Lady Crawford sneered.

Lady Lennox's lips twitched in disapproval. She looked up from the panel she was embroidering with neat, even stitches and waved her needle menacingly in the air as if considering where to jab it. "Let's not forget that our king was no slouch in answering a queen's distress call. And that he was distracted from his honourable quest by a wanton English whore." Her rounded mouth blew out the word with revulsion. "A sleekit spy in the pay of the English Henry."

"Well, he should have listened to thon warning not to mell with any lady, nor let them touch his body," Lady Crawford retorted, tossing aside her rumpled linen square. She had no patience for fine needlework and her loose, erratic stitching often had to be unpicked. "While he frittered away precious time, dilly-dallying with Lady Heron, the English were able to muster forces. Our menfolk would still be with us and not strewn about the boggy field of Flodden, if he hadn't given her the glad eye."

Lady Lennox shook her head and wagged her sewing needle. "That dudron bewitched James into breaking his sacred vow."

"Aye, and we've all paid sorely for his sin. So let me not hear your praises of the king's prowess. It has cost us dear." Lady Crawford's broad, matronly face and neck flushed with anger.

"What sacred vow?" Isobel Kennedy ventured to ask.

There was silence. When James III was killed at the battle of Sauchieburn, rumours flew that his son, James IV, had ordered his assassination, but none of the ladies dared repeat this. Except the intrepid Lady Crawford who piped up, "Our dearly departed king, James o" the Iron Belt, took to wearing a heavy chain around his waist as penance for his father's murder."

"What you say is treasonable!" Lady Lennox hissed.

"Aye, but this was no humble penance," Lady Crawford continued. "By displaying it outwith his garments for all to see, he added the sin of pride to the list."

"He never wore it when ..." Isobel Kennedy, began to say. With her beguiling Celtic looks – raven black hair and porcelain pale skin – and disturbing resemblance to her mother, she had been one of the king's more recent conquests. Then, as all heads swivelled and ears twitched, she faltered, "At least so my mother told me ... "

"Wheesht!" Lady Crawford put her finger to her lips. "I wouldn't blow about that if I were you. And I wager your shrewd mother would tell you to ca" canny, my lass. She took trouble to keep you well out of the queen's sight, for she knew that if Her

Grace were to jalouse that you'd been bedded by the king, you'd be hurled onto the midden heap with the rest of them."

"Aye, she was greatly angered by his habit of showing off his gaggle of bastards at court," Lady Lennox sniffed, "and lost no time in redding them out after Flodden. With their various mothers. Most of them, anyway," she added. "The ones she knew about. Whores and wantons the lot of them." Lady Lennox looked pointedly at Isobel, who raised her haughty chin and unashamedly glared back.

Bastard. Wanton. The full meaning of those words, spat out so forcefully, stung Kate. For years she'd had to endure Elisabeth's taunts for being a cuckoo in the nest and so she'd leapt at the chance of coming to court, not, as it turned out, to become one of the queen's ladies, but as one of the king's concubines. At first she had been scandalised but when James promised to reward her with a dowry and a wealthy husband – she had reconsidered. Besides, it had done Nancy Stewart no lasting harm to her reputation or marriage prospects – perhaps even enhanced them.

With no other choice, Kate had given in, but then the king had been slain before he'd fulfilled his promise to provide for her future. And his widow would certainly not honour pledges made in the bedchamber. Now she was not only a bastard but an ill-cleckit whore with no rightful claim to a husband, home or family. She shrank back in her seat, hoping to blend in with the tapestry behind her.

"If Angus did indeed sire the child, then the prince may be a Douglas bastard."

Lady Lennox fumed. "I'd hold my ill-scrapit tongue if I were you, Mariota. Thon red-headit bairn was never a Douglas. A talebearer is worse than a thief. What you're saying is slander."

"Och, it's just harmless blethers. Life is dreich enough without a scouthering scold like you dousing our merriness," Lady Crawford scoffed.

"Margaret Tudor may be too shrewd to be baggit with another man's bairn," Lady Lennox affirmed, "but what's she thinking of, dallying with a Douglas? Troublemaking rabble-rousers with their swords aye drawn at the ready, the Red Douglases will stop at nothing to advance their kin. Ding doun Tantallon. The old saying is true," Lady Lennox gave a knowing nod for their slogan aptly described the inbred audacity of the Douglas clan to overstep the mark. "It's as clear as the neb on his face that what he's after is a share of the throne. The sheer effrontery of the blackguard."

"Unlike others who would stake their claim," Lady Crawford remarked.

Lady Lennox ignored this jibe. Angus was an upstart while her family had a rightful claim to the crown, but she wasn't going to demean herself by pointing this out to the ill-informed Mariota. Instead, she went on, "Forbye, Archie Douglas already has a young wife."

"And a bairn on the way," Lady Crawford reminded her. "Though that won't please Her Gr ..." she started to say when Isobel Kennedy nudged her.

The other ladies had gone quiet as the herald, David Lindsay, entered the sewing room unannounced. Since losing his beloved lord and master, the grief-stricken Lindsay wandered aimlessly and listlessly about the court: many were concerned he'd lost the will to live. He scanned the chamber as if looking for a familiar face and was about to leave when he stumbled over Kate cowering on her stool in the corner. As he leant forward to apologise, he peered at her closely before holding out his hand to raise her up.

V

Hunt the Gowk

Black Douglas, and wow but he was rough!
For he pull'd up the bonny brier
And flung it in St.Mary's loch!
The Ballad of the Black Douglas, Traditional

Tantallon Castle, 1 April 1514

The dreich, damp castle of Tantallon, high on a crag above the Forth and blasted at from all sides by the four winds, was aggravating Meg's frail health. Racked by fits of violent coughing, she stayed bundled up in bed to keep warm. The freezing sea mists weren't doing her any good, Betsy said, alarmed at seeing flecks of blood in the phlegm Meg whooped up. It grieved her to see her fragile harebell wilting and waning. The climate inland at Hailes would suit her better, she suggested, but Lady Douglas reared her long craig, bridling at her suggestion.

"This is her home now," she said tartly. "Meg is the Countess of Angus and here she will stay. The next earl will be born, as all the others afore him, here at Tantallon." And she herself would take care of her. Had she not brought up a wheen of bairns to adulthood?

When the physician diagnosed the croup, Meg implored Betsy to take Lisbeth away to Hailes. Her own health didn't trouble her so much as that of the unborn baby but Elisabeth was loath to leave Meg at the mercy of Lady Douglas.

"Don't fret. She'll not harm me. Not while she thinks I'm carrying an heir. Forbye, it will only be for a few weeks, Lisbeth, and when you come back it will be time for our confinement."

"And how will we keep your mother-in-law out of the birthing chamber?" Betsy asked. "She'll want to be there to make sure her grandchild is delivered safely."

Meg spluttered, coughing up rheum that Betsy gently wiped from her cracked lips.

"Tell her ... Tell her that I've got some kind of catching disease and that it wouldn't be safe for her to be there." With great reluctance Betsy and Elisabeth made ready to leave for, despite Meg's brave effort to reassure them, they doubted whether she could keep up the pretence on her own.

As soon as they had ridden away from Tantallon, Lady Douglas laid down the rules that her daughter-in-law must now follow.

"You must eat, otherwise you'll never be strong enough to bear my grandchild," she insisted, serving up rich dishes to put flesh on her bones. But Meg had no appetite for the rich puddings of honey and thick cream that curdled in her stomach. Whenever she tried to swallow, her gullet constricted and if she regurgitated; Lady Douglas's long nose twitched in undisguised disgust at the sickly mess.

Some days Meg could hardly raise her head from the pillow and her head reeled when she had to get up to use the chamber pot. Jinty was her only sympathetic visitor. Not only to gobble up the sweet puddings spurned by Meg, but to chatter cheerfully about the new arrival, a playmate for her to fuss over. But when she was caught cramming a slice of pie into her mouth, her mother banished her from Meg's chamber.

Mystified that Meg's belly was not swelling as it should, Lady Douglas summoned the physician from Edinburgh. The black-coated doctor hovered like a raven sizing up his prey before landing his talons onto her stomach and then, with chilled pasty hands, he kneaded her belly like dough, pressing it hard down against her spine. When he forced her legs apart to probe deep into her, she cried out as his dirt-encrusted claws scratched the tender inner folds of flesh. He then took Lady Douglas to one side. Had there been any unusual flux?

"Nay," she replied confidently, for nothing escaped her hawkish eye.

Sensing that the fiercesome mother-in-law might withhold his payment, the doctor refrained from airing his concern that the bairn might already have died in the womb. He could hear no tiny throb of a heartbeat. The remedy in that case would be to cut her open but not without great risk to the mother's life – and to his own reputation if she died. Then the child must be very small, he opined. To boost the baby's growth, he prescribed his own receipts for strengthening cordial and tonics. If nothing else, they could do no harm.

This judgement did not please Lady Douglas. Never mind that a puny heir would bring disgrace on the Douglas family, it would make it more difficult to procure a divorce for Archie, as non-consummation could not then be claimed. Now that her son was high in the widow queen's favour, it would be a pity if anything should stand in his way. She would dispense her own remedy.

Meg screwed up her face at the evil-smelling potion Lady Douglas made her drink, for it stung the tiny, bleeding sores that had broken out on her gums. The only saving grace was that it made her fall into grateful oblivion; painless darkness, where figures, formless but familiar gathered in the shadowy underworld. Was that her mother hovering over her? Had she come at last? Whether she was dreaming or dying she neither knew nor cared.

When she woke up, she was alone. No-one was keeping watch by her bed. Her breathing came more easily. No coughing. No fiery darts jabbing into her chest. No pain anywhere. She raised her head from the pillow and sat up for the first time in weeks. The fever must have passed.

She felt an urgent need to use the chamber pot and stumbled out of bed, but weeks of being bedridden had weakened her muscles. Her legs trembled and then gave way beneath her. She crawled towards the pot and squatted, holding onto the bedpost to keep from toppling over. Though giddy and light-headed, she didn't feel sick. Using the bedpost to haul herself up, she got to her feet, swaying slightly. The fuggy stench in the sick room caught her throat. Fresh sea air would cleanse her lungs. She would climb up to the high tower.

A pall of perspiration swathed her brow as she groped her way barefoot along the dark stone passageway and her nightdress slapped like a sodden dishrag against her skin, making it cold and clammy. The shivering started, slowly at first, and then increased, until her teeth were chattering and her very bones were trembling.

Shrieks and screams and the pitter-patter of feet running hither and yon echoed throughout the castle. She stopped, holding her breath to listen. Further along the passage she glimpsed a hazy figure, its head hidden beneath a gossamer veil. A guardian angel flitting in and out of the shadows: or the spirit of her mother in her bridal veil – one of the unquiet dead.

"Wait for me!" Her strangled cry brought on a coughing fit but fearing to lose sight of the spectre, she struggled on. Rounding the corner, she came to a halt. Flickering torches cast eerie shadows down the sides of a broad staircase. There was no sign of the angel. Looking down the steep flight of stairs made her dizzy and she grasped hold of the rope banister for balance. She glanced around anxiously. Something shimmered beside her, flimsy and light like an angel's wing, and hovered in the air before gently falling over her head. She heard a stifled giggle. Startled, she let go of the post and staggered around blindly, trying to tear off the veil.

"Hunt the gowk!"

Happit in the veil, Meg took an unseeing step sideways and teetered on the edge before being hurled forward into space and timelessness. A spine-curdling scream dinging around Tantallon was the last mortal sound she heard.

VI

Requiem

> I doubt that March with his cauld blasts keen,
> Has slain this gentle herb that I of mean,
> Whose piteous death does to my heart such pain
> *To a Lady*, William Dunbar, 15th–16th Century

Hailes Castle, May 1514

"This won't hurt," Betsy assured her as she rubbed her oil-smeared hands vigorously together before warming them over a candle flame.

Half-lying on the bed, her eyes looming owlishly over her bump, Elisabeth watched anxiously as Betsy then ran her oily hands gently over the swollen dome of her belly, so far hidden by the loose folds of her habit.

"You're not casting a hex on me, Betsy, are you?" she said with a nervous laugh.

"No fear of that, lass, I'm just making sure that the bairn's not tapsalteerie."

Tapsalteerie! Whigmaleerie! The thought more than Betsy's massaging fingers made Elisabeth's stomach lurch. That wasn't natural, was it, to be upside down? Did it mean the bairn was accursed?

"Nay, nay, my lass. Far from it. Them that are born heels-over-gowdie are well-favoured in life's morning march and are gifted with the healing power, so they say. But we need to coax the bairn into flipping over to come head first into the world! It will save you a lot of grief, too. So speak kindly to him. Tell the wee man to do a somersault."

"The wee man?" Elisabeth gave a start. "How do you ken it's a boy?"

"Och, lads are aye likely to be more carnaptious and contrary." As Betsy kneaded her distended belly she could feel the baby kicking. What to say to this wee mite about to start out on life's journey? In a quiet voice she assured him that, once he left the safety of her womb, her sister Meg would love him as her own and bring him up as heir to the Earldom of Angus. He'd be a grand gentleman one day.

Betsy gazed in sorrow at Meg's scrawny, lifeless body tightly swaddled in a linen winding sheet with only her pale, waxen face showing. Lady Douglas had arrived at Hailes and handed over her corpse as if it were a packet that had been delivered to the wrong place.

"We were greatly deceived," she sniffed. "She was never with child. When the physician cut her, there was no bairn."

"You sliced open our Meg?" Betsy scowled.

"Aye, to save the bairn if possible: we'd done all we could for her. She was afflicted with the flux and couldn't keep anything down. And when the fever burned through her, she was too weak to fight it. She just went down. Falling like a rowan leaf in autumn."

Angry that she hadn't been sent for, Betsy failed to be fooled by Lady Douglas's grief.

"We even brought in a learned physician from Edinburgh," she whined on.

"And how many weans has this surgeon cast from his own womb?"

When Betsy began, slowly and reverently, to unwind the linen sheet, Lady Douglas shot out a hand to stop her.

"There's no need for that. The physician has already prepared her for burial."

The two women glared at each other over Meg's dead body.

Betsy narrowed her eyes. "Has he indeed? Well now, I'm going to make sure she's laid out properly. By one who loves her," retorted Betsy and went on unwinding the sheet. Seeing the ugly purple bruises blotching Meg's translucent skin, she breathed in sharply.

"That was the bloodletting," Lady Douglas said quickly. "The skin turns black and blue when it's pierced for the leeches to suck the blood. So the physician explained. Not that you'd know anything about that," she sniffed. "He learnt his skill at the College of Surgeons in Edinburgh founded by King James himself," she went on proudly. "Where the latest advances in medicine and chirurgianrie are taught and homespun remedies scorned."

"Chicanerie did you say?" Betsy asked innocently.

Lady Douglas stretched her long neck so that she could look even further down her nose at the uncouth nursemaid.

"You may be nearer the truth than you ken, for he said that Meg was so desperate for a bairn that she fooled herself into believing she was with child. It sometimes happens in barren wives. Fussing and fretting can dry up their courses and bloat the belly, duping the body like a gowk storm whirls the mind."

"Gowk storm indeed! It wasn't the want of a child that addled her wits."

Lady Douglas narrowed her eyes at the insolent nursemaid.

"And we, too, were made fools of. Meg was never robust. Had we been told the truth about her poor health, we'd never have agreed to the marriage. Perhaps it's turned out for the best. Any bairn she might have conceived would doubtless have been a weakling." With a final sniff of her long neb, Lady Douglas got up to leave. "Everyone who needs to know will be told that Meg died in childbed and that the bairn was stillborn. No more need be said."

Left alone with the wilted remains of her hapless harebell, Betsy doubted Lady Douglas's explanation. Such discoloration on a corpse could only be the result of a battering or, fortune forbid, high doses of arsenic. Not that anyone would take heed of a lowly nurse's suspicions. The crudely stitched gash in her side where Meg had been ripped open made Betsy gasp and she had to steel herself with a generous dram of *aquavitae* for the task of laying her out.

First she placed lit candles round the trestle where Meg was laid. Then, after washing the bruised body, Betsy anointed her bonnie flower with fragrant oil, keening softly all the while to keep from weeping. For no tears could be allowed to fall on the corpse or the shroud, otherwise her spirit would have no rest. There would be time enough for tears after the burial. She wrapped her lovingly in her grave clothes, her mother's oyster satin wedding dress worn by Lisbeth at Meg's proxy marriage. Uncanny it was that all three of them had worn the same dress in such different circumstances. Weird, how fortune's wheel turned.

As she took a comb to Meg's fine fair hair, it came away in clumps: another sign of arsenic poisoning. She cut off two locks, one for Elisabeth and one for herself – there would be none for Archie Douglas – covered her hair with a linen snood tied firmly under her chin to keep her jaw shut and laid her head on the bird of paradise cushion. She crossed Meg's hands, one over the other, and placed a small dish of salt on her breast to prevent the stiffening of her body. After waving a lighted candle over Meg three times, she strewed her corpse with sprigs of May blossom for her final journey. Finally, Betsy kissed Meg's icy forehead.

"Fare thee well my fairy flower," she murmured, pressing her eyelids tightly to stem the tears.

Elisabeth had been hovering outside the door, impatient to say her farewells but Betsy bundled her away and shut it firmly behind them. A woman about to give birth should never look on an unburied corpse in case the deceased's spirit claimed possession of the bairn's body. Elisabeth's eyes opened wide. So Meg's spirit hadn't yet gone to rest. She gazed about her and whispered into the air.

"Swear to me that you will stay to haunt them, Meg. Swear to me you'll never let them rest in peace."

Meg was buried in the family crypt at Hailes alongside their mother and brother. No-one from the Douglas side, not even her husband Archie, attended Meg's funeral: he was too busy arranging his nuptials to the dowager queen, Margaret Tudor.

VII

De Profundis

Ave Maria, gratia plena Dominus tecum
benedicta tu in mulieribus
et benedictus fructus ventris tui.
Prayer

St. Mary's Abbey, 8 September 1514

"And blessed is the fruit of thy womb." Prior Hepburn raised his hand over his niece's bowed head in blessing for the feast of the Virgin Mary's nativity.

No longer, Elisabeth thought sadly. Had her uncle been aware of the irony of the prayer? Is that why he had been observing her closely?

After the service, he pulled her closer to the window, tilted her chin and studied her face closely. His finger traced the blue-black shadows under her eyes and across her sunken cheeks. As he encircled her wrist with his thumb and forefinger, his dark eyebrows puckered like two black kailworms.

"You haven't been eating. You're like a skinned rabbit," he growled.

Elisabeth hurriedly pulled down her sleeve so that he wouldn't notice the weals on her arms. Biting deeply on her bottom lip until she drew blood had helped to lighten the weight of her aching heart. The little droplets of blood trickling onto her tongue tasted sweet and wersh at the same time. Cheered by the thought that bloodletting was a cure for all sorts of ills, she began making little nicks in her arm with the sharp point of the silver crucifix on her rosary. Almost at once she felt her heart lighten and her grief lessen. She continued until a filigree of purple cross-stitched scars embroidered her arms.

"You're too young to be losing your lustre, my precious pearl. You must regain your strength."

Hepburn wasn't a man who felt ready sympathy for the pain of others but seeing his niece so wretched moved him. For a fleeting moment he almost regretted lying to her. It wasn't quite true that no decent man would marry her without a tocher. With his connections it wouldn't have been so difficult to arrange a suitable match for her. He knew two or three worthy widowers and at least one notable bachelor, not in the first flush of youth perhaps, but whose scrawny arms would welcome a lithesome lass to warm their lonely beds and produce an heir or two. Luscious young flesh – virginal or not – would more than compensate for a lack of dowry for these auld lecherous greybeards. Despite her impoverished circumstances and venial past, the voluptuous Kate had been successfully married off.

94

Elisabeth's grief had numbed her to the marrow. The sharp pain that lodged like a pebble in her gullet made her want to gag when she tried to swallow. All she could chew were her fingernails, down to the quick until they were ragged and bleeding. What did she care if she wasted away? Life wasn't worth living.

With Meg's sudden death, fate had played falsely, foiling their carefully laid plans. What was to happen to the baby? What was to happen to her? Betsy had cradled her in her arms, rocking her to and fro, and when the agony became too intense to bear, had given her a potion to send her to sleep.

In the dawning hour, a surging pain seized her, as if a blazing hot poker had been plunged into her entrails. Elisabeth sat up, bent double, hugging her cramping womb. Betsy was up and about immediately, hanging a cauldron of water on a swey over the ingle, and counting out strips of linen. After setting a basin and a chamber pot by the bed she boiled up a fusion of herbs that tasted as foul as it smelled. She pressed Elisabeth's lips together to force it down and, seeing her stomach begin to heave, held out the basin.

"It's easier to thole on an empty belly," she assured her. "That's one end cleared. A good scouring out now will be easier to deal with than later."

Drained and wabbit, Elisabeth wanted only to sink back onto the pillow, but Betsy shoved the chamber pot underneath her just in time, as her bowels loosened and her waters gushed down her thighs. But still Betsy wouldn't let her lie down – breathe slowly, breathe deeply, don't lie down, stay upright, crawl about on all fours – until she could thole the birthing showers no longer. Propped on a stool, she licked the odd tasting powder Betsy sprinkled on her palm while she splayed her legs to probe between them. Tapsalteerie, she heard Betsy muttering before she sank into a stupor.

Waves of pain kept pummelling her, drawing her down further and deeper into the black, but when she tried to thrash upwards a heavy weight dragged her back down into the churning water. Pushing with all her might, she strained to rid herself of the burden until it burst from her womb, splitting her in two.

Slumped on the floor, she looked up to see Betsy dangling the gory bundle by the legs, its upside down head, slick with blood and fluid, swaying back and forth. As Betsy gave it a good slap, mucous dribbled from its thrapple, splattering onto her cheek before the bairn opened up its toothless mouth to let out a piercing bawl.

Days passed in a drowsy blur, broken only when Betsy raised her head to make her drink something. When at last she surfaced, she felt hollow, her womb scooped out and her belly shrunken. No pain now, only a dull throbbing lingered between her legs where a prickly dressing scratched the tender skin.

"If you'd stappit this up yourself as I told you at the time, you wouldn't be going through this now," Betsy muttered as she changed the dressing. "And neither would I. You had me worried for your life, Lisbeth."

"Can I see my bairn now, Betsy?" she asked drowsily. "Is it a laddie as you foretold?"

"Wheesht, my lass! There's time enough for that." Betsy dabbed her brow with a cool cloth seeped in a soothing infusion of sweet-smelling herbs. As the bairn's head had torn its way through her tender flesh she'd lost a lot of blood, but an infusion of lady's mantle helped to staunch the bleeding. Fretting that she would contract the fever that often carried off newly delivered mothers, including Elisabeth's own, Betsy had added honey and birch fungus to the sphagnum moss dressing on her wound to stem any fever, and, since sleep was the best healer, had administered precisely measured doses of deadly nightshade to keep her slumbering.

"Such a bonnie wee fighter, but he wasn't sturdy enough to fight the fever that took him away." Betsy's eyes were brimming with tears. As she'd predicted, Lisbeth's bairn had been a wee laddie. "And don't fret, I baptised him with caller water. Maybe not as grand as your godson's christening, but enough to send him safely into Meg's loving arms. Don't vex, my thistledown, she'll look after him now."

Elisabeth nodded. For hadn't fate decreed that Meg would care for her son?

"So," she said, sniffing back tears, "when you christened my wee lad, Betsy, what did you cry him? Not Archie, I trow." She managed a wan smile.

"Do you really want to ken?" Betsy frowned. In her experience it was better not to dwell on it. Giving the child a name would only prolong her mourning, but the thrawn thistle nagged until she gave in.

"Well, I swithered about calling him Adam," Betsy replied, "for your ill-fated brother, and then David, being his father's son. But since he came into this world with such a blast I thought, this lad has his grandsire's lungs. Lungs fit for a preacher: at full throttle. So there you are. John it was, for your uncle, Prior John. So think of your wee soul up there with Meg, among the heavenly host. One of God's trumpeters."

St. Mary's Abbey

On her return to St. Mary's, Sister Maryoth could hardly wait to greet Elisabeth.

"I have joyous tidings for you, dear Sister." The smug smirk tweaking at the corners of her mouth almost cracked into a smile. "About your cousin Kate. You'll be pleased to hear that she is now married," Sister Maryoth declared. *"Deo Gratias.* Does that not gladden your heart in this time of woe?"

Pity the man who's yoked to that hizzie, Elisabeth thought. He'll have a hard furrow to plough. He'll need all of God's grace. Let's pray that she's hitched to a Douglas, for then they would deserve each other.

"It's a good match, considering her lowly position. Our Blessed Lord has forgiven the woman taken in sin. She has been most fortunate to snare a man of the calibre of Sir David Lindsay," Sister Maryoth rambled on.

"Sir David Lindsay?" Her ears pricked up. "But he was slain at Flodden. His name was called out. I heard it myself."

Sister Maryoth crossed herself. "Aye, Sir David did indeed perish, but that was the son of Lord Lindsay of the Byres. Kate, however, has wed the royal herald. She is now wife to Sir David Lindsay of the Mount and Garleton. Is that not a matter for great rejoicing?"

Instead, a howl of despair reverberated deep within Elisabeth's breast, unlocking the grief hidden in her heart. Alone in her cell, she wept until there were no more tears to shed and dry, ragged sobs racked her bones and heaved along her spine. And another nightmare tormented her sleep.

She was standing outside, naked and shivering in the freezing snow, looking into a cosy room where a couple cuddling in front of a blazing fire were gently rocking a cradle. Misery and longing engulfed her. When a branch blown by the wind tapped at the window, their heads whirled round. She tried to draw back into the shadows but Kate began pointing and laughing at her. And then Lindsay held up a bundle to the window, but there was no infant in the shawl, only a hideously grinning skull.

Prior Hepburn took her scrawny hand and pulled her onto his knee.

"Grief is natural but you mustn't let it crush you to the point of despair, for that is a mortal sin. Take a lesson from Sister Maryoth. She lost her dear brother in the fray, but she doesn't mope." His plump, moist lips nuzzled her ear. "Perhaps a change of air will help. How does a spell in France suit you?"

France! So she wouldn't be staying in the convent! Immediately Elisabeth felt her heart lighten.

VIII

Knight of Love

> What lord is yon (quoth she) have ye nae feill?
> Has done to us so great humanity?
> I loved him for his manly form.
> *The Testament of Cresseid*
> Robert Henryson, 15th Century

Edinburgh Castle, Spring 1516

"Faster, Da Lindsay, Faster."

Kate looked down on her husband crawling around on all fours with the child astride his back, digging in his heels and urging him to make haste. The thick clouded skies and the unceasing wind and rain had kept them indoors for days. Being cooped up in the gloomy quarters of a draughty castle all winter was becoming unbearable and the four-year-old child that Lindsay was doing his best to amuse was not their own. As Keeper to the King's Grace, Lindsay was playing nursemaid to James V, King of Scots. Playing the fool more like, Kate sneered, as he cavorted about the floor. She, too, was not only bored but tired of playing second best to James who, however, high and mighty he might be, was only a bairn.

Where was the home she'd been promised as the Lady of Garleton? Instead, she had to endure eternal flitting from castle to palace and back again, always on the move, like some common tinker's wife. And she wanted her own child, who would love her unconditionally, unlike this spoilt whelp. Not only did Lindsay spend his days attending to the needs of the child, at night he shared a room with the king, and often his bed too.

The child couldn't bear to sleep alone and would scream and scream, "Sing me a song, Lindsay. Sing me Ginkerton" until Lindsay came to him. How could she – the invisible side of an eternal triangle – conceive a child in these circumstances?

"You're tiring him," she snapped. "Forbye, it's long past his bedtime."

"Nay," the boy king screeched and poked a little pink tongue out at her. Their jealous dislike was mutual. James resented this interloper and rival for the affections of Da Lindsay who had looked after him since his birth. "Faster Da Lindsay," he cried, digging his heels in more deeply and glaring at her.

Under her breath, Kate cursed the whining monarch. Snatching up her cushion, she flounced off to be amused by the ladies of the court indulging in their favourite game: gossip. With a quick glance over her shoulder to make sure Lindsay wasn't looking, she stuck her tongue out at the mewling infant.

"Good day, Lady Katherine," the ladies chorused.

No longer a spurned paramour, but the wife of the royal herald, Kate was welcome in their inner circle, though not for her sewing skills but her singing voice.

"Give us a song," they demanded.

Placing her cushion on a stool, Kate gave her instructions to the lute player. With spring in the air, a love song seemed appropriate – but not, she warned, one of his more ribald refrains. With a smirk and a wink, he began strumming a tune.

With the marriage of Margaret Tudor and her "Anguish", as she now called her consort, unravelling, and both lovebirds repenting having tied the knot so hastily, the ladies had plenty to prattle about. While Margaret had fled to her brother's court in London, stopping off in Northumberland to give birth to a daughter, her "Anguish" was finding solace in the arms of another – the mysterious dark Lady of Traquair.

"While the queen's away, Bell the Cat's grandson will play," Lady Crawford warbled. "But not with any of the court ladies – he wouldn't dare. Jane Stewart never leaves her eyrie at Traquair." With a knowing nod she lowered her voice to say. "It's rumoured that she's carrying his bairn and I tell you that, if Her Grace ever finds out, she'll be even more loath to make her peace with him. Were I the queen, I wouldn't have reeled in Cheeping Archie so soon," she continued. "I would have made the most of my freedom before buckling myself to another. Better to wait and see what other fish the sea may cast up. Such as the Duke of Albany," she sighed. "He's a brave looking man, is he not?"

Lady Lennox sniffed. "With royal blood in his veins, John Stewart would have made a better mate for our queen. And she would not have lost the regency."

By the terms of James IV's will, Margaret Tudor was to have been appointed tutrix to her son during her widowhood, but the Scottish council argued that her marriage to Angus rendered that condition invalid. They then stripped her of her authority and appointed Albany, the French bred grandson of James II, as regent in her stead.

"Never mind the queen, I'd fain be tethered to the duke myself."

"Aye, and they say his wife in France is wasting away and may not be long for this world," Lady Lennox scowled.

"So there may be a chance for me, then?" Lady Crawford smirked.

"Familiar tale, is it not? Though here, on our doorstep, Archie Douglas's young wife has already departed this life, setting him free to marry the queen. Very chancy for him, was it not?" Isobel Kennedy dared to suggest.

"Chancy for him: unchancy for her, poor lass. Uncanny you might say. Though it is rumoured that, such was her infatuation with Angus, the queen herself had a hand in his wife's last ailment." Lady Crawford winked at the other ladies as she waited for her rival's reaction.

"The queen you say? His own mother more like," Lady Lennox snapped as she took the bait. "Thon Elisabeth Drummond with her long neck is as ruthless as a swan when it comes to protecting her young. She'll do anything to advance her own." She resented the way the queen's new mother-in-law strutted about the court, puffed up with pride. Adding salt to her stew, she lowered her voice to whisper, "Even stoop to sorcery. They say she gave her son a powder to fall in love with the queen."

"Well, it's already worn off. And now he's found it's a puddock he's wed, not a princess." The ladies tittered.

At that moment Jinty Douglas came whizzing into the sewing room, arms whirling wildly, her wayward eyes rolling. "The beautiful knight is on his way," she squealed and then, just as quickly dashed out again.

"At least she's not still mourning her sister-in-law and spreading doom and gloom with tales of her ghost haunting Tantallon," Lady Lennox remarked.

"Lady Douglas will need all her arts to find a mate for squinty-eyed Jinty," the beautiful Isobel Kennedy sneered.

"I wouldn't be too hasty in mocking the lass," Lady Crawford said. "She may be fey but her kind often attract men who think wandering eyes mean wanton wiles."

"Well, she's taken a girlish fancy to *Mon Seigneur de la Beautie*."

"The French knight is far too …" The ladies of the court sniggered, waiting for Lady Crawford to elucidate. Sophisticated? Handsome? "Well-endowed for a maiden like her."

Jinty's announcement not only made Kate's song miss a beat, but also her heart. For she, too, was secretly smitten with the beautiful knight. Unwilling to leave his sick wife and travel to that dreich land he'd never known, the Duke of Albany had sent an envoy in his stead. Renowned throughout Europe as a tournament champion, Antoine D'Arcie, Sieur de la Bastie, had set all hearts a-flutter, young and old. Strikingly handsome with blonde flowing locks, *Mon Seigneur de la Beautie* as they called him, stood out amongst the shorn, ruddy-haired Scots.

He has learnt the secrets of love from a master in the orient, the ladies whispered excitedly, and kens how to pleasure a woman until she screams for mercy. Unlike their lords and masters who were only fit for a clumsy fumble in the dark, hurling between their thighs and huffing and puffing till it was all over. For them. Fingers fluttered to mouths as the ladies gasped in feigned horror at this deliciously wicked rumour while shiver of barely containable excitement made their skin tingle. Compared to his father's splendid court, that of the toddler king was deadly dull and dreary, they bemoaned but Antoine's arrival promised to add oriental spice to life.

While the ladies of the court vied with each other for the attention of the beautiful knight and darted jealous barbs at anyone he seemed to favour, D'Arcie cast his gaze randomly over them all, which, instead of seeming fair, caused even more friction. The ladies nit-picked his every move, his every glance. How long he had spoken to this one, how long he had looked at that one, whether or not he had bowed to one or kissed the hand of another and so on. No matter how much they squabbled over these details, each lady believed in her heart that she was the one he preferred: none more so than Kate.

The Queen of the May was the rôle Kate coveted during the Beltane festival but being married disqualified her.

"It isn't fair," Kate whined, "Isobel Kennedy is no chaste maiden."

"But she is unwed," Lindsay replied. Despite her constant pestering, he refused to use his influence as master of revels to favour his own wife. *That,* he affirmed, wouldn't be fair. She must content herself with being a lady-in-waiting. Kate, however, wasn't content to play second best yet again and was determined to outshine the forritsome Isobel.

Flamboyant in scarlet, the colour that had first attracted royal attention, Kate smouldered alongside the virginal white of the icy May Queen. Snide comments and asides rippled among the ladies, but Kate was deaf to them all. When the procession of combatants passed, led by the French knight in his gleaming white armour, she deftly tossed her glove to Antoine who, with a mischievous wink, pinned it to his tunic. Now that he was her champion and she his tournament paramour, she didn't care a jot for their criticism. Let them say what they like. Words are but wind, but dunts are the devil. How she was tempted to poke her tongue out at them all.

Later that evening, at the banquet in honour of the champions, Lindsay spent most of his time chasing the over-excited heir to the throne round the hall, playing tig and hide-and-seek among the legs of the dancers and diners who dared not show their irritation. Not even when his squeals threatened to drown out Kate's song.

"Glad is my heart with you, sweet heart, to rest," she trilled.

"For my heart is in thrall to your heart,
Until I have no heart contrary to your heart's will."

The significant glances that Kate threw were not, however, in the direction of her husband. When at last the toddler king flung himself onto the floor, girning with exhaustion, Lindsay gathered him up and took his royal majesty off to bed. Kate was not yet ready to leave: at least not with Lindsay.

In her bedchamber, Kate spent some time warming herself by the ingle. Goose flesh was never a pretty sight, and even less pleasurable to the touch. Throwing a cloak over her shoulders, she slipped out into the corridor. From behind some closed doors, drunken snores could be heard and, from others, the tell-tale rhythmical motion of creaking beds. Kate crept along the dimly lit passageways, as if pulled by an invisible thread.

Slumped across the doorway, the guard snuffled and snored, an empty flagon of ale by his side. Kate stepped over him, lifted the latch and quietly slipped into the chamber. It was pitch dark, no candles burned. The curtains of the four-poster bed were drawn. He must have retired for the night.

She was about to leave when something flashed past her ear and thudded into the heavy wooden door. She tried to move but her cloak was pinned firmly to the door by a dagger. One rough hand grabbed her arms, forcing them above her head while the other groped her all over. Antoine's blue eyes bored into hers.

"My lady Katherine?" He let out a deep breath as he released her. "Forgive me, I have many enemies in this court and must be on my guard at all times. You have mistaken your chamber? Allow me to escort you back. One moment. A taper to help light your way." As he pulled the dagger out of the door to free her cloak, she grabbed hold of his wrist.

"No, mistake, my lord," Kate whispered, pressing her back against the door. "It is indeed you I seek."

"I am most flattered, my lady. How may I serve you?" As he bowed, his unbuttoned shirt fell open exposing his muscular torso, naked down to the top of his unlaced breeches She gave a little gasp and shrugged her shoulder, shedding her cloak to the floor. She licked her lips.

"May I congratulate my champion on his victory in the field today."

He returned the compliment with a sweeping bow and then, taking her hand, he lightly brushed it with his lips. At this slight caress, a crimson flush passed over her creamy skin and her flesh craved to feel those lips searching out her every neuk and cranny.

"As my lord and champion, you may now claim your prize. I ..." She hesitated. "I have come to offer you my favours."

"I am honoured indeed, *ma dame*."

Slowly she undid the drawstring of her nightgown and let it slip from her shoulders. Shaking back her golden hair, she drew the gown over her breasts down towards the curve of her hips, stopping just beneath her rounded belly to gather it modestly above the sensuous mount of Venus.

"It is more than a kiss on the hand that I offer." Her voice had lowered to a hoarse whisper.

"My lady, you are too kind, but ..." As Antoine put up a warning hand, Kate began to panic.

"You are my champion. You have won my favours. I am yours. Take me." Then, more urgently, "Please."

Antoine hesitated. As a tournament champion, he was forever being accosted by women willing to throw themselves at his feet and, being a perfect gentle knight, he had no desire to disappoint. Even other men looked upon his amorous conquests as just rewards for his courage and skill. Only the brave deserved the fair.

"*Ma dame*, you are most beautiful but I cannot deceive your husband. I am a chevalier and will not breach my code of honour."

As he bent down to pick up the cloak to cover her nakedness, she lunged towards him, entwining her arms round his neck, her fingers gently stroking his skin.

"Do not trouble about my husband. He doesn't trouble about me. He has his own bedfellow. Don't worry. He'll never know. Nor care." For he spends more time in his young master's bed than he does in mine, she wanted to add.

Clasping her arms firmly round his neck, she rubbed her breasts against his naked chest.

"But I cannot deceive him." Prising her hands from his neck, he strove to be firm but gentle. "I implore you, *ma dame*. It is not honourable."

Fear again gripped her. If it were discovered that she'd been spurned by the white knight, she'd be a laughing stock. Unseen eyes and ears were everywhere, spying. Someone would have spotted her coming to his room. And taken note of her leaving again almost immediately.

"Forgive me, my lord. I see you are indeed most honourable. It is all written here."

With light fingertips she traced the weals and scars interlaced on his torso, evidence of the many injuries he'd been dealt in battle and combat, down towards the thick tuft of hair peeking out from beneath his breeches. As she caressed his navel, he stiffened and, seizing the opportunity, she knelt down quickly and nuzzled her face against his groin. He clutched at her hair and for a moment she thought he was about to pull her up, but no, he was drawing her head forward, encouraging her.

Smiling to herself, she ran her tongue over her lips, moistening them in readiness. The experienced King James had taught her many secrets of the bedchamber and this one never failed to please. With her skilful tongue flicking and squirming like the subtle serpent, she licked and sucked until she heard him gasp with surprise but mostly pleasure.

IX

Auvergne

And saw this written upon a wall
Of what estate man that thou be
Obey and thank thy God of all.
The Abbey Walk
Robert Henryson, 15th Century

Auvergne, France, 1515

What was she expecting – the full-throated crooning of cooing doves in a dovecot? Instead, the refectory of the Convent of *Nôtre Dame des Miracles* reverberated with the trilling and warbling of birds of paradise, mute by day but coming into full-throated song by night. Exotic in their winged headdresses, the sisters flitted around the convent, speaking only when necessary, a rule relaxed for the evening meal when they twittered and chirruped non-stop.

Her head dirling, Elisabeth turned to the novice sister who had taken her under her wing. Amidst all the squawking, Sister Agnes never raised her voice as she strove to explain the elaborate pecking order to her. Thanks to the Auld Alliance, however, they had found words their languages shared, though the pronunciation differed. When Sister Agnes had proffered *une tasse du vin*, Elisabeth had beamed in recognition since a tassie in Scots was also a goblet for wine while an ashet, a large plate for serving food, *une assiette*. On feast days they also shared *gigot de mouton*, a joint of mutton.

When some crumbs of bread fell onto her lap, Elisabeth brushed them off. She didn't want to spoil her new habit nor stain her immaculately spotless linen. She stroked the creamy, fine-spun lambs-wool, marvelling at its softness. All the habits of this order seemed softer and cleaner, Elisabeth thought. On her arrival, her first duty had been to bathe. While the maids filled an enormous tub, Sister Agnes had added handfuls of exotic smelling herbs to the steaming water. After Elisabeth had stripped off her coarse brown novice's habit and unwashed linen – grubby and stale after her journey – Agnes handed her a cloth sprinkled with a strong smelling oil – *lavande,* she explained – that dissolved the grime and softened her skin.

Wrapping Elisabeth in soft cotton *toile* to dry after her long soak in the tub Sister Agnes couldn't help but notice the scars on her scrawny arms. With a knowing nod, she had smeared them with a soothing balm before shooing her out to the garden. The southern sun would bring some colour into her chalk-white Scottish complexion and a stroll among the fragrant beds of *lavande* would help to lift her mournful melancholy.

If dour Sister Maryoth had been sour vinegar, douce Sister Agnes was a heart-warming cordial, though she rarely smiled. Her main responsibility was the convent physic garden and, over the years, she had acquired a great knowledge of herbs and their various properties and uses, both culinary and medicinal. Healing was her vocation and, in order to restore this pale, melancholic Scots girl to health, she plied her with invigorating tonics and piled her plate with tempting morsels of meats, fruits and vegetables. As she went about her chores, Elisabeth trailed behind her like a feckless fledgling, to be fed and watered at regular intervals.

When the bell rang to signal the end of the evening meal, the sisters filed out of the refectory for compline. The routine at the convent was more austere than at St. Mary's, adhering more strictly to the daily order of offices, but Elisabeth and Sister Agnes were excused the evening service. Instead, they made their way to the scriptorium. At this time of the day, when the writing desks were empty after the day's work, they were assured peace and quiet. When Elisabeth had confessed that she couldn't read her precious *Book of Hours,* Sister Agnes had been surprised. Never mind that the French order believed in educating their nuns, surely it was essential for a future prioress to be literate?

"Sister Maryoth says that I'm a wild child and incapable of learning. Forbye my aunt has been prioress many a year and she is unlettered."

"How then can she attend to her affairs? How can she know whether or not she is being deceived?"

"My aunt is too lazy to care. Forbye, Sister Maryoth does all the scrieving."

Sister Agnes frowned. "Then she is not her own mistress but in thrall to this secretary. If you remain unlettered you, too, will be at the mercy of those who have these skills. Especially those men who use the powerful tool of learning to pursue their own ends and to hold sway over others."

Sister Agnes now took out the small book hidden in the pocket of her habit. They had started studying *The City of Ladies*, not only because it was printed plainly in French – unlike the laborious Latin calligraphy of the *Book of Hours* – but because it contained more truth than many pronouncements from the pulpit. Also, the author was a woman. Christine de Pisan had been educated by her father, a Venetian lawyer invited as astrologer to the French court. When her French husband died during an epidemic, leaving her with three young children, she took up her pen to earn her living.

Lamenting that so many men condemned the entire feminine sex as monstrosities of nature, De Pisan concluded that this must be true. Even learned scholars and clerics seemed to agree that God had formed a vile creature in creating woman, though she questioned how such a worthy artisan could have deigned to make such an evil and abominable work.

"But she takes comfort from the fact that, as creatures of suffering, we're able to overcome the trials and tribulations that life throws at us," Sister Agnes explained. "And she gives many examples of how much-maligned women have triumphed over these prejudices."

Pondering these remarkable women, De Pisan concluded that God wasn't to blame, but men for fabricating false assumptions. Since women are weaker in body, they must be feeble in mind, too, and should be kept in childlike ignorance so as not to overtax their simpler minds. By these claims they sought to justify withholding education from women but there was a darker intention behind them: denying women the opportunity to read and discover all the lies written about them.

"Innocence might be a virtue, but ignorance certainly is not," Sister Agnes said. "Now you understand why men hold education in such high esteem. If you can't read, you can't form your own opinions and must only accept what you're told. So, now let us prove that women's minds are no weaker than those of men."

Elisabeth watched enthralled as Sister Agnes formed letters of the alphabet into words. This double-edged process of reading and writing filled her with wonder. That marks on parchment could communicate in such a way was a powerful kind of magic. Reading more of this visionary book inspired Elisabeth to make a solemn vow.

"When I become prioress, I shall build my own City of Ladies where justice and reason and righteousness will prevail."

For a fleeting moment, a ghost of a smile flitted over Sister Agnes's face, and just as quickly vanished.

X

The Papingo

Eagles flee alane, but sheep herd the gither.

Proverb

Auvergne, Easter 1516

The gown was exquisite. Fashioned out of the palest pink satin, the overskirt trimmed with finest Flanders lace and the bodice encrusted with tiny seed pearls, it shimmered like fairy wings. Elisabeth gazed at it with longing.

"Take it away. I will not wear it," she said.

"But it is a gift from your uncle. He is coming to visit you today and wishes you to wear it," the seamstress pleaded. This was one of her most fabulous creations. Was it not exquisite? Was it not the most expensive fabric? See the invisible stitching? But no matter how much she cajoled her, Elisabeth refused even to try it on.

As soon as Hepburn arrived the hapless seamstress flapped and flustered around him to explain that it wasn't her fault. That she'd done her best to dress the young mademoiselle. That the gown fitted perfectly and, with a frantic look at the prior's furrowed brow, that it would have to be paid for even if it wasn't worn.

"Stop skittering around and get out of here." Hepburn swished her away like an irritating fly. Then he glared at his stubborn niece still in her habit and wimple.

"If I were a bride about to be wed, I'd be proud to wear this," Elisabeth simpered innocently, "but am I not a bride of Christ? Have I not taken a vow of poverty?"

"And one of obedience," Hepburn blurted, struggling to control his rising anger. Knowing how thrawn she could be, he drew breath to calm himself. "Perhaps it's time to educate you in the ways of the world, my dear."

Elisabeth raised her eyebrows, unsure what kind of lesson to expect. He drew up a chair for her to sit down.

"Tonight you are to meet a very important person," Hepburn began. "We have been invited to the court of the Duke of Albany. As you know, he was appointed Regent of Scotland following Margaret Tudor's marriage to your erstwhile brother-in-law, Archie Douglas. The Scottish lairds were so infuriated by this untimely and unwise union that they appointed John Stewart regent in her place.

"With royal blood in his veins, the duke is more likely to keep some semblance of order among our quarrelsome lairds. That is all to the good. However, a strong hand is also needed to steer Church affairs. As you know, dearest Lisbeth, I have been managing the archbishopric of St. Andrews, for James IV's bastard son …"

Elisabeth looked puzzled. "But Alexander was only sixteen, too young, surely to be a cleric, never mind hold such an important position."

Hepburn smiled at her naïveté. "He was only appointed lay commendator for the vast revenues to be gleaned. James looked after his bastards."

"But wasn't he killed at Flodden?"

Hepburn nodded. "Aye, and that means the position of archbishop is vacant. And, my dear niece, since I have already done so much – why I've even founded a college, St.Leonard's, where I'm building up an extensive library," he added proudly, "wouldn't you agree that the post should be mine by rights?"

Elisabeth shrugged. "Since you've already been elected by the cathedral chapter, why of course, dear uncle. Is that why you've come to France? For the duke's approval?"

Hepburn shook his head wearily. "Unfortunately the post – or should I say the benefices that go with it – has attracted some competition. Even the pope's nephew has thrown his hat into the ring but since he has no intention of setting foot on Scottish soil, he is no real threat. Bishop Forman has little support and is therefore of little account. But Provost Gavin Douglas, who covets the position, has objected, arguing that my election is unlawful. And he has the combined clout of his nephew Angus and the queen."

Archie Douglas again: what a thorn in the side he'd been to their family. Elisabeth sighed. But what had that to do with her having to don an elaborate gown?

Hepburn leant forward and took her hands in his. "In order to compete with him, my dearest Lisbeth, I, too need patronage. That is why I have come to France – to gain the duke's favour. Since his wife's younger sister is married to Lorenzo de Medici, Albany should have some influence with the pope."

While Elisabeth's head reeled with all the complicated relationships and political machinations, Hepburn became dewy eyed. For, once he had secured the archbishopric, he dreamt of the day when a cardinal's hat would be placed on his head. So far he'd had little success in petitioning the regent but, knowing that he nurtured a soft spot for chaste young virgins, Hepburn had designed this eye-catching gown for his niece's presentation to the influential Duke of Albany.

"My dear lass, all I'm asking is that you wear this gown on this one occasion. If you're to press my case to the duke, you'll need to catch his bonny blue een. This is how the world works. You must wear it. Well?"

Following the example of the ladies in *The City of Ladies* who would endure torture and death rather than betray their principles, Elisabeth had intended to stand her ground. After all, she was a nun, not a doll to be dressed up and dangled on display, but she feared that if she continued to refuse her furious uncle would force the gown on her himself – not a thought to relish. But then if she could do something to spite Archie Douglas …

Elisabeth nodded. "If it is your desire for the duke to tak tent of me, uncle, then I shall make sure he will."

"That's the way of it, lass. I knew you'd see sense," Hepburn's heavy-jowled face relaxed into a smile and he chooked her under the chin. "And mind and ask for the archbishop's mitre for me."

Château de la Tour

Entering the elegantly turreted *Château de la Tour*, the Duke of Albany's palace, Elisabeth stopped to look more closely at an engraving on the lintel above the main door. The thistle and *fleur-de-lys* not only symbolised the Auld Alliance between nations but between the Scottish and French branches of the Stewart family. In the stone-pillared entrance gallery, she had paused to admire the life-sized paintings of Stewart knights and Stuart *chevaliers* at war when a herald thudded his ceremonial staff on the flagstones.

A grand procession was making its way along the gallery. The ladies in wide hooped gowns seemed to be gliding along; their magnificent bosoms, garnished with glittering gems, jutting before them as imposing as the prow of James IV's legendary ship, the *Great Michael*. Promenading behind them the gentlemen – in embroidered capes of every hue from azure to vermilion draped over vibrant satin shirts frilled and ruffled in snow-white lace – were no less dazzling.

Shrinking back into a neuk, Elisabeth was startled by a raucous shriek. Turning round, she bumped into a gilded cage, sending a multi-hued bird rocking back and forth wildly on its swing. She put her nose to the bars. Was this a bird of paradise, like the one embroidered on Meg's cushion?

A liveried footman tottered over on his high heels and eased a tit-bit through the bars of the cage. The bird took the morsel in its beak and then passed it to its claw, to peck off tiny pieces, like a perjink lady nibbling at a dainty. Fixing its bead-like eye on its benefactor, the bird squawked, *Merci!* The courtiers clapped their kid-gloved hands and clucked their tongues in admiration at this wondrous creature.

At the tail of the procession Hepburn appeared, puffing and panting, his high colour even ruddier than usual. He glared at Elisabeth.

"What did I ask of you?" he hissed, but before she could reply, the herald called them into the duke's presence chamber.

All eyes turned towards the odd couple traversing the grand reception hall. The prior's magnificent robes of heavy brocade, richly threaded through with gold and silver, were given nods of approval but short gasps of surprise greeted his niece. The courtiers rolled their eyes in disbelief at her garb. For this splendid occasion,

Elisabeth had retrieved her coarse brown novice's habit, simply adorned by a rosary dangling from her waist and a crude wooden crucifix. No one, not even a holy nun would dream of turning up at court in such humble attire.

Les Écossais! Ah! That would explain it. How quaint! How simple! How barbaric! A plain dunnock in the midst of all those exotic peacocks, Elisabeth certainly stood out.

"Isn't this what you wanted, uncle? For me to make my mark?" she whispered, as suppressed titters followed their progress up the hall.

"You're making a mockery of us," Hepburn growled, struggling to restrain his anger. As they approached the ducal dais, he strained to smooth his twisted face into a smile.

Several attendants were standing behind the duke's throne but one particular popinjay flashed to Elisabeth's attention. Never mind the sumptuous royal blue velvet doublet slashed with silver, nor the immaculate white lace frothing at his throat and wrists – though that must be the bane of any washerwoman to keep clean – nor the exquisite sapphire brooch pinned to his velvet bonnet. No, what fascinated Elisabeth – and made her want to giggle – was the brightly coloured peacock feather curling upwards and outwards from the fop's bonnet and waving ridiculously in the air every time he moved his head.

As instructed, Elisabeth made a deep curtsey to the duke. Interested to see what had impressed his court, Albany leant forward to study *les Écossais* and then, to everyone's surprise, he stood up. He shrugged open his velvet, ermine-trimmed cloak, freeing his arm, and then offered his manicured hand to Elisabeth. Inviting her on to the dais, Albany scrutinised this plain specimen: her clear complexion unsullied by powder or paint, her high forehead – a feature much envied by those fashionable ladies who had to shave their brow – emphasised by the severe cut of the wimple. To this nobleman, jaded with the excesses of the French Renaissance court, Elisabeth's lack of affectation was refreshing.

"Eh bien, votre niece! Elle est très charmante."

Prior Hepburn's great barrel chest heaved with relief and then puffed up with pride. At a signal from the duke, the plumed dandy came forward to hear his command. As the feather on his bonnet bobbed up and down, Elisabeth suppressed a giggle.

"Bonnie feathers make bonnie birds," she quipped in an aside to her uncle.

"Aye, and gude claes open a' doors," the dandy responded in her native Scots, "though an exception has been made in your case, it would seem," he adding, scanning her dowdy garb with disapproval. "His Grace, the duke, would like to give you a gift. Anything you ask, as a token of his esteem and as a souvenir of your visit to France. Say but the word."

The crowd of courtiers leaned forward, straining to hear what she would ask for. Who, in her favoured position, wouldn't ask for a precious jewel? A ring or a brooch, perhaps? Confident that he knew the answer Hepburn looked around, smugly smirking at those who'd so recently been mocking them. Elisabeth considered for a moment.

"Je désirais une… poule," she replied, unsure of the correct word.

It was now the dandy's turn to look surprised. *"Une poule? Un coq?"*

"Nay, not a cockerel. Not a hen either, but …" she said, searching for the word. "A popinjay."

"A popinjay? You have in mind a papingo? You ken that's a parrot, don't you?" The dandy was bewildered.

"Like the bird in the courtyard," she explained. "That can talk."

That more than anything else, she'd decided, would be a fitting reminder of her visit to the French court. With the hint of a smile on his lips, but a definite gleam of amusement in his eyes, the dandy nodded, causing the peacock feather to twitch again.

Word immediately buzzed round the hall that the nun had desired *une paroquet! Quelle horreur! Quel dommage!* What a wasted opportunity! The nun was too *naïve* for words.

"Mais, bien sûr." Her choice impressed the duke, especially since humility wasn't a quality he'd associated with the Scots: at least not in those he'd come across. Her wish would be granted, but she must also choose something of greater value.

"Go on. Ask him now," Hepburn almost yelled in her ear.

No, that was it. She would remain true to her vow of poverty, she replied with a simpering smile that would put Sister Maryoth to shame.

At the banquet that evening, Elisabeth was seated in place of honour at the high table beside the regent. He was interested to hear her views about the country and the people he'd inherited, both being quite foreign to him. The dandy constantly fluttered around the regent ready to swoop down to interpret for them. With Sister Agnes's tuition, Elisabeth's French had greatly improved, and his services were rarely required.

Seated further down the table, marginally above the salt, Hepburn was in no mood for polite conversation or even the exquisite food. His anger-induced bile was sticking in his craw and spoiling his appetite. How could she have missed her chance! A popinjay! What good was a talking bird! You probably couldn't even eat it! Was his niece trying to make a bauchle out of him?

The French courtiers watched in alarm and distaste as the stout, bearded Scotsman speared the tastiest morsels with his fearsome-looking dirk and quaffed copious tassies of blood red claret. No amount of drink could mellow Hepburn's temper, however. When the time came to take their leave, he watched expectantly as the duke kissed Elisabeth's hand and said, *"Adieu, ma chère papingo."* Knowing his niece, she may be waiting until the last minute before making her petition but Elisabeth only smiled in response.

"Why did you fail to grasp the thistle, lass," her uncle hissed as they left the court. "It was right there, in your hand, but you let it go. You say you've taken a vow of poverty but you've also taken one of obedience, mind. To me."

"Nay, uncle, it was neither the time nor the place to petition the duke for your archbishop's mitre. He wouldn't have looked kindly on it. He wanted to give *me* a gift, not you. To flaunt his generosity to one of his own folk in front of his courtiers."

"Hmm," Hepburn replied, dumbfounded for once. His pawkie-witted niece hadn't been wasting her time in France. She was turning out to be as cunning as any Vatican emissary.

She yawned, quite worn out with all the excitement. "Don't fash, uncle, when the time is ripe I shall put in a good word for you," she said with a smile, leaving her uncle open-mouthed and flummoxed yet again.

Convent de Nôtre Dame des Miracles

Elaborately winged heads poked out of the windows on all sides of the cloister to watch the foppish French courtier mince across the courtyard, balancing a multi-hued parrot perched on one arm and swinging a cage in his other hand. Fascinated by the peacock plume in the dandy's bonnet, the bird strained at the chain round its leg in an attempt to attack it.

"David Beaton at your service," he announced, holding the bird at arm's length as he tried to bow.

"She's taken a scunner to your bonnet. Either because she sees it as a rival, or because she has simple tastes in fashion," Elisabeth quipped.

"Like you," he laughed. "Not many would dare to grace duke's presence in a nun's garb. I was surprised you weren't laughed out of court. Your conceit is to be admired. And how do you jalouse the bird is female? The male of the species has more colourful plumage, does it not?"

Elisabeth tilted her head to study the parrot. Its main body feathers were emerald green with flashes of iridescent red, while the wings were a deep sapphire blue. In contrast, its head was golden yellow and the soft breast down was speckled through with topaz and amber. Not one jewel but many embellished this exotic bird of paradise.

"Well, what have you to say for yourself? Which are you? Lad or lass?"

The parrot fluttered its wings and stretched its neck to screech loudly.

"Wheesht! Wheesht!!" Elisabeth cried, covering her ears. "I would fain have had a bird that could talk, not a wailing banshee."

The parrot stopped and cocked one yellow gimlet eye at her intently. "Shee ... " it tried to whistle, "Whee ... whee ... sh ... "

"Well, that's a start."

"She's after a treat for her performance," Beaton explained as the little parrot pecked sharply at her sleeve.

"Ah! So you admit it's a she," Elisabeth laughed triumphantly.

"Or a eunuch – only a larbar or a woman could be so shrill. But once she's been trained, she'll make a perfect pet. Like all of your sex, she needs a strong hand. Your uncle clearly needs to be firmer with you if you are to become a great lady one day."

"And if I do, I'll stand no cheek from a Frenchified page boy such as you."

The corners of his mouth twitched, warping his wry, sarcastic smile to a peeved frown. "You may jest, but as the fifth son of a humble Fife laird I have to make my own way in the world. Unlike you, my dear sister."

Not so humble that his father couldn't afford to send him to the universities of Glasgow and St. Andrews and then to Orleans to finish his education. A tongue fluent in French and an eye for fashion had endeared him to the French *haute monde*, in particular the Duke of Albany, who had taken him into his service as interpreter and diplomat.

Beaton had already sought information about Elisabeth, the future prioress of the richly endowed St. Mary's Abbey, one of the wealthiest in Scotland. As prioress, she would have control, not only of the lands and tenancies but also of the great benefices they bestowed.

"I would consider myself blessed if given such an opportunity," he sighed. "To marry for silver may be one remedy, but what highborn lady would wed a lad with no prospects? A career in the church would be another, but cold-hearted celibacy wouldn't suit my hot-blooded humour, I fear."

He leaned towards her too closely and whispered, "Nor you, I wager, my lusty prioress-in-waiting."

XI

Rivals

> Evil words cut more than swords.
>
> Proverb

Auvergne, 1518

"What's this I hear?" Bishop Hepburn wheezed, breaking off his flow of speech to catch his breath. "I trust these rumours about you and that pompous peacock are unfounded."

He'd just returned from a short visit to Scotland where he'd had important matters to settle: matters that had clearly affected his digestion. Squirming in his chair and cradling his paunch he glared at Elisabeth.

"All this rich French food is spoiling my stomach," he complained, "and now I hear this bruit about you and Beaton. As if I didn't have enough to worry about. Thon treacherous scoundrel, Hume, has been plotting behind everyone's back. He's tricked me out of the archiepiscopal title." He let out a bilious belch.

Elisabeth listened sympathetically to her uncle's gripes. While Hepburn had been petitioning the duke to sanction his election by the cathedral chapter, Hume, the wily lord chamberlain, had proclaimed the Papal Bull in favour of Andrew Forman at the cross of Edinburgh.

"But if you've been elected fairly and squarely, uncle, then surely you can appeal to the pope?"

Hepburn shook his head. "Though it sticks in my craw that Hume has trounced me, I dare not oppose Pope Leo's decision and risk excommunication. By way of a sop they have offered me Forman's former post, the bishopric of Moray." His beetle brows furrowed as he murmured, "Hardly adequate compensation for losing the biggest prize. They will live to regret insulting me thus."

While in Scotland he'd already begun his revenge campaign by bullying the weak, frail Forman into giving up the revenues of the see in his favour. He was now planning his next move. On Forman's death – in the not too distant future given his poor health – Hepburn intended to make sure that he would be appointed Archbishop of St. Andrews.

While his French physician had told him to eat less and only plain fare, it was difficult for Hepburn to curb the voracious appetite of a lifetime. Besides, no amount of food could satisfy the gnawing emptiness in his belly. Now he took out his frustration on his niece.

"While I've been suffering in my sickbed, you've been billing and cooing with thon fancy-feathered young fop. A nobody who has to live by his wits. I might have

114

known he was up to something. The whole court is buzzing with clash of you two."

He'd been ordered to rest but how could he with this scandal going on? No wonder his heart was galumphing wildly.

"Calm yourself, uncle," Elisabeth now said. "You mustn't get upset. Shall I ask them to bring you a soothing tisane? With mint for your stomach's sake?"

"Tisane! The devil take your tisanes! A strong cognac is what I need."

Well-accustomed to her uncle's fickle humour – full of blame and bombast one minute and apologising the next – Elisabeth waited for the storm to subside.

"Believe me, my dear lass, his intentions are in no way honourable. Davie Beaton has a reputation as a gallant. Thinks he's cock of the walk crowing over his dunghill. Even nuns are fair game to him. Plucking your maidenhood would be a triumph. Another feather in his foppish cap."

It was nothing but idle gossip, she assured him. Why shouldn't compatriots abroad meet to converse in their own language? And Beaton had an endless fund of amusing stories about the personalities and conspiracies at the French court that he dared not share with anyone else.

"Not only is he out to sully your good name, he wants to discredit me with the duke. Don't be fooled by his glib-tongue and swankie clothes. Davie Beaton is a sleekit tod."

Since his mastery of the French language was negligible, Hepburn had to rely on him as interpreter in his dealings with the duke. Behind his back, however, the miniature Machiavelli had been using his privileged relationship to petition on behalf of his uncle, Chancellor of Scotland and Archbishop of Glasgow, James Beaton.

"Aye poking his meddlesome nose into affairs that don't concern him. How dare his uncle try to compete against me! As for that young fop, strutting like a crow in the gutter! How dare he have the barefaced cheek to seduce my niece! I swear I'll thrash all that flumgummery out of him." Hepburn's face, livid with rage, suddenly drained, taking on an unhealthy pallor. He fell back into his chair.

"Oh, this isn't good for my heart," he gasped, thumping his chest with one hand. "Laughing while you draw the blear over my eyes and scheme behind my back. I forbid you to see him, do you hear? Mark my words: yon Davie Beaton will come to a bad end. The likes of him always do."

While it was true that a *frisson* had developed between her and Davie Beaton, it was the result of a contest of wills rather than physical attraction, at least on Elisabeth's part. In their flyting, with each striving to triumph over the other and neither yielding, they had become rivals more than friends. Their first serious clash had occurred when Beaton had scoffed at her lessons with Sister Agnes.

"Lasses who take to learning lose what the French cry their *naïveté,* their charming *simplicité,* and soon become tiresome."

Elisabeth had bristled. "You mean they learn not to be taken in by your wiles and become bold enough to answer back. Or is it that you consider my feminine mind too feeble for such study?"

"Ladies of your standing don't need to bother themselves with such lowly occupations as scrieving. And, as future prioress, you'll have no need to concern yourself with letters and suchlike. Other people can do that for you."

"Like a man, you mean? Then such reasoning only serves to strengthen my resolve."

They'd crossed swords again on discovering that their ambitious uncles were competing for the post of primate of all Scotland.

"My uncle has been dealt with unjustly. He sought his election by peaceful means. Unlike Angus, he wouldn't use a force of men to elect a man of God," Elisabeth stated.

"Unjustly! By peaceful means! You're not as worldly-wise as you think, Elisabeth," Beaton sneered. "See how your own uncle has managed to deceive you with his artful tongue! But you cannot be blamed for that. Hepburn is well-kent as a man of subtle mind who hides his malicious intent behind crafty eloquence. Let me enlighten your gullible feminine mind. Your sainted uncle is as conniving as his consecrated colleagues when it comes to achieving a position of power. And there are always two sides to any story. Clearly he has omitted to tell you how he laid siege to St. Andrews Castle to oust the Douglas faction?"

How she would love to wipe that smug sneer from his thick lips.

"Oh aye. Weary of waiting for parliament or the pope to make up their minds, Angus occupied the castle and installed his uncle, Provost Gavin Douglas, poet and translator of Virgil's *Aeneid* into Scots. But, as an educated lady, I'm sure you already knew that, and no doubt, may even have read it." He smirked. Without giving her a chance to answer – that she did, for Lindsay had spoken about the makar, but she hadn't – Beaton was rattling on:

"Prior Hepburn, however, wasn't one to see his prize being snatched from under his very nose. And what do you think he did? Use his glib tongue to coax Archie Douglas into handing the castle back to him?"

Elisabeth recoiled as Beaton thrust his face into hers.

"Nay, he used it to call up an even greater force and attacked not only the castle but the town of St. Andrews itself, slaughtering and sparing no mercy for the townsfolk – not only men but women and children. He then cast his fere and foe, Provost Douglas, into the sea tower."

Elisabeth folded her arms defensively. "The Hepburns are a noble family, one of the foremost in our land," she maintained, irritated at Beaton for this version of events. Though aware of her uncle's self-seeking ambitions and herself a victim of his despotic rule, she wouldn't allow anyone else to criticise him. It had been drummed into her to defend any member of her family, no matter their faults: *Keep Tryst*.

"Of that I have no doubt. I admire your loyalty and I trow you will respect mine. Let's declare *touché*." He'd then taken his leave, with an exaggerated bow and sweeping flourish of his feather bonnet.

"Wheesht! Wheesht! Haud yer wheesht!"

What was all the bruit about? Elisabeth thought as she ran along to her cell after the midday meal. Papingo, as she named her little parrot, was squawking in alarm. Where was her elderly chaperone? She was trying to soothe the bird when a noise made her turn round. Sleekit Beaton had slipped past the old nun and hidden himself in her cell. He closed the door behind him and then tiptoed over to deal with Papingo.

"Let's silence yon clapper-din before she rouses the whole convent," he said and wrapped the coverlet round the birdcage. Taking the darkness for night, the parrot tucked her little head under her wing and fell asleep.

"I'd have thought with all your learning, that you'd have taught her to say something more challenging? But then your wee Papingo is a lassie after all," he added with his infuriating, sardonic grin.

"How did you get in? My uncle has forbidden you to see me."

"Unlike you, Elisabeth, who fails to be moved by this humble and contrite heart, your sisters are more merciful," he whimpered. He placed his hand on his chest and pulled a ridiculously pitiful face. "This may be our last meeting," he whined, "Ever. I'm being sent back to Scotland and I cannot leave with this ill-feeling between us. Forgive me if I've angered you but I'm here to make my peace afore I go."

"Had you donned sackcloth and sprinkled your curly hair with ashes I might have been gulled. For a vain peacock like you, that would indeed be a sacrifice." In vain, she tried to smother a smirk, for his withering look suggested that she'd touched a sore spot. She had never known a man who fussed so much with his appearance and never missed a chance to tease him about his wardrobe as extensive and elaborate as that of any fine lady.

Indeed, his figure and bearing were more feminine than masculine. Though his features were pleasant enough, they were not what she considered handsome, being too rounded, too feminine for her taste, with soft, chubby cheeks, full lips like a lassie and plump fingers. His thickset thighs and calves may signify virility but were not, in her view, enhanced by obscenely tight hose.

And there was a smell about him, a sweet, cloying odour, unpleasant to her nose. When he became excited or aroused, his skin oozed an oily film which, when mingled with the potent scents he lavished on his flesh, produced a stale, slightly putrid tang. By his reek shall you know him, and Beaton reeked of smugness and self-satisfaction and an appetite for the good life. He would grow into a fat, pompous libertine if he weren't careful.

"Please, I beseech you, cruel damsel, punish me no more." He knelt down on one knee and placed his palms together in a gesture of appeal.

"Must I leave, starved of your affection, without having tasted one tiny morsel of tenderness from your lips?"

When he dropped his eyelids and peeked coquettishly from under his long eyelashes she gave a startled gasp. Kate! That's who his mannerisms reminded her of. That's why she was taking such a scunner against him. With rounded, imploring eyes, he tried to take hold of her hand but she thrust them into the folds of her habit to avoid his greasy grip. To a man like Beaton, brought up in a French court, conducting affairs of the heart was as natural as political intrigue, but Elisabeth was ill at ease with the sophisticated rituals of courtly love. She cleared her throat before asking, "Why are you going back to Scotland?"

"I'll tell you, cold-hearted maiden. After a kiss." He puckered his rosy-red chubby lips in readiness as he moved in close.

Instinctively Elisabeth shrank back from that smell, that cloying, oily scent that would quench any passion he might try to arouse.

"Will you never take no for an answer, Davie Beaton? I'm a nun, mind."

"But against your will. Have you not confessed as much? A spirited lass like you should not be locked away denying men's eyes the pleasures of your youth and beauty. Why should we not succumb to our true natures?"

"Mine does not include a desire to yield to you, Davie Beaton. For you're the devil's man: in thrall to Auld Hornie himself. Even Satan would give up if he found the door steekit against him. Now behave yourself." As she shoved him firmly in the chest, he took the opportunity to grab hold of her hands.

"Aye, but the devil also bides his day. Which I trow will be now. Come on, let's have no more tittle-tattle when I am ready for a tussle," he chided.

Elisabeth wrenched free and tucked her hands firmly under her oxters. "*Et ne nos inducas in tentationem ...*" she pronounced, her mouth set tight.

"You realise, cruel lady, that I may be going to my death," Beaton moaned as he wiped his slimy brow with an embroidered linen handkerchief.

Beaton was not jesting. He truly feared for his life. When, after a short sojourn in Scotland, the Duke of Albany had returned to France, leaving Antoine D'Arcie, his first lieutenant, in his stead, trouble had immediately broken out among the rival factions. Then, when D'Arcie was ambushed and brutally murdered, the regency council implored the duke to return to impose order. Wary of the wayward Scots, the cautious regent was sending Beaton ahead as his scout to ascertain the seriousness of the problem and whether or not his presence was essential.

"Are you unmoved that we may never see each other again? For you, that may not be important but for me … This may be our last ever meeting." There was every possibility that, as the duke's ambassador, he would share D'Arcie's fate. The prospect of cold steel on his neck may have chilled his belly but unexpectedly warmed his loins.

"Is there really no chance of kindling a spark?"

"You're being too hasty Davie," Elisabeth replied, irritated and impatient with this performance. "As we Scots say: slow fires make sweet meat."

"Ah! So there is hope!" he cried, pouncing on her. A firm thrust from Elisabeth upset his balance and he toppled against the birdcage, dislodging the cover and waking the parrot.

"Wheesht! Wheesht! Haud yer wheesht!" Papingo shrieked in alarm.

Steps could be heard running along the corridor and the cell door flew open.

Beaton cringed. "Oh my good Lord. It's the Lamb of God: *Agnus Dei. Miserere nobis.*"

The usually benign Sister Agnes was shaking with anger. Behind her, the elderly nun assigned as Elisabeth's chaperone, hung her head sheepishly and tried to hide the *bonbon* bulging in her cheek. As penance for her lapse in duty, she'd now have to surrender the rest of the *confits* Beaton had given her to sweeten his way into Elisabeth's cell.

"Don't be alarmed, Sister," Beaton said, turning on the charm. "I am here to seek advice from our dear sister for my dearest sister." His younger sister Katherine yearned to take the veil, just as well since she'd have no dowry, and he was making enquiries about the regime at St. Mary's Abbey. "As long as her delicate mind was not overtaxed with learning," he said, with a sidelong glance at Elisabeth, "it should suit her very well." Then, raising his hand in benediction he took his leave. "*Pax vobiscum*"

"*Et cum spiritu tuo,*" the elderly nun responded from force of habit, before swiftly swallowing the sinfully sweet *bonbon*. Sister Agnes glared at Beaton, her suspicious eyes following him to the end of the corridor where he turned to give them all a cheeky, cheery wave.

XII

Prioress Elect

Veni, Sancte Spiritus,
Et tui amoris in eis ignem accende.
Prayer

St. Mary's Abbey, 1521

Sister Maryoth placed a coin on each sightless eye and covered the bloated, brosie face of the prioress with a linen cloth. Prioress Janet Hepburn's final agony was over. Sister Maryoth had watched with blank impassive eyes as the prioress grappled for every breath, her grossly overweight body swelling up until fit to burst. There was little Maryoth could do to relieve her suffering, she convinced herself. After all, who was she to meddle in divine punishment for all those years of self-indulgence? When the prioress gasped her last breath and gave up her soul for judgment Maryoth, following St. Paul's instructions, did not lament. She said a prayer for the dead and thanked God.

The funeral had to be conducted swiftly for fear of rapid decomposition, Sister Maryoth had explained to the sisters who twittered about the unseemly haste and, she had added under her breath, proof if any were needed that Prioress Janet was no saint. Now she shepherded the twenty-one sisters into the Chapter House to organise the election of a new prioress.

"We must wait until Bishop Hepburn arrives, for he'll advise us what to do," Sister Katherine Beaton objected.

Sister Maryoth's lips tightened. She mistrusted this recently ordained nun, whose enthusiasm, coming perilously close to zealotry, she'd tried to curb.

"*Bishop* Hepburn," she said through clenched teeth, "won't be giving us advice, but orders. He'll not be asking us whom we favour: neither will he call on the Holy Spirit to guide us. He'll appoint whom *he* wishes. And we all ken who that will be. We don't need him to tell us what to do. We can decide for ourselves."

"Then we should wait for the instructions from the Archbishop of St. Andrews."

"We have no need of the archbishop's authority, either. We can elect our own prioress," Sister Maryoth affirmed. "It is our prerogative, our right."

Uneasy and uncomprehending, the sisters whispered and muttered amongst themselves.

"It's all enscribed here," she said tapping her forefinger on a large leather-bound tome. Sister Maryoth had read all the documents pertaining to the nomination and been apprised of the election procedures, a claim which none of them could either make or refute.

"Our new prioress shall be elected *Per viam Spiritus Sancti*," she explained. "As the Holy Spirit, in the guise of a dove descended on the apostles, filling their souls with grace and knowledge, so shall we pray for him to come down among us to kindle our hearts. Then, with one voice, we shall name the successor to our dearly departed sister. Our decision, sanctified by the Holy Ghost, will then be sanctioned by Archbishop Forman."

Could they? Would he? Although the illiterate nuns could not dispute the rules as stated by Sister Maryoth, there was no memory of a prioress ever having been elected. Since the inauguration of the abbey, the prioress had always been appointed – and she had always been a Hepburn. It was no easy matter to persuade these subservient women to take matters into their own hands and act without male authorisation. Fearing to frighten them off, she appealed to an even higher authority.

"Sisters! Mind whom we serve! We are brides of Christ, chosen to love and serve him in this world. Do we not strive to be worthy of his love? Almighty God himself is showing us the way forward by giving us the chance to choose our spiritual leader. One who can guide us back to the path of righteousness. Have we not pledged vows of chastity, obedience and poverty? Would you not sooner elect your own prioress? One who has served and prayed with you for many years? One who follows faithfully the teachings of Christ Our Lord? Do not let this chalice pass us by."

Wimpled heads nodded. It was true. Dame Janet had not led what could be called a holy life, whereas Sister Maryoth had all the right credentials. Well-bred – she was the daughter of William Hay, the Baron of Yester – and well-educated – she knew her letters, unlike the late illiterate prioress. Her nightlong vigils, prostrate on the stone cold chapel floor testified to her piety and her capacity for suffering. Severe and unsmiling, her emotions veiled beneath a solemn mask, she personified sanctimony.

And there was one more argument in her favour: her age. Mindful that the position should go to someone older, wiser and in their middle years, the Cistercian Statutes stated that no-one under the age of thirty could be appointed prioress. Sister Maryoth was forty-two-years-old, she reminded them, while Elisabeth was not yet four and twenty. Would they dare to disobey canon law? She challenged Sister Katherine.

To settle matters once and for all, Maryoth took the irksome novice aside to mention the unmentionable: the rumours about Elisabeth's legitimacy, which if proved to be true, would mean that she could not possibly be elected.

"*If* proved to be true," Sister Katherine retorted, instinctively taking Elisabeth's side for, although she had never met her, her brother David spoke well of her. "Besides," she went on, "there is no denying the fact that Dame Janet and, more importantly, Bishop John had intended their niece, Elisabeth, to succeed her. By defying them, the sisters fear that they risk severe reprisals: facing the infernal wrath of Bishop Hepburn in the here and now and being cursed to hell by the ghost of the dearly departed prioress from the hereafter."

Superstitious nonsense, Sister Maryoth hissed under her breath. To allay their anxiety, however, she served up some strong cordials usually reserved to reinvigorate those who'd been fasting but now needed to lubricate the mysterious workings of the Holy Spirit.

Once fortified, the nuns knelt in front of the Black Madonna, where Sister Maryoth led a recitation of the rosary: the Glorious Mysteries which appealed to the Holy Ghost for inspiration, would be right and fitting, she decided. After the *Gloria* in the third decade, one of the sisters sprang up to announce that, Glory be to God indeed, a tongue of flame was blazing through her breast. Her cheeks flushed with ecstasy, she raised her arms to heaven to rejoice that the Paraclete had chosen her among many to convey his message.

These pearls of divine wisdom, however, were lost among the cries from those who, not to be outdone, claimed that they, too, had been filled with the Holy Spirit. Elbowing each other out of the way, they scrambled to prostrate themselves in front of the Black Madonna.

Sister Maryoth hadn't planned for this mass hysteria. Only her accomplice, selected for her loyalty to Maryoth, was to be blessed with the divine message. Struggling to make herself heard above the clamour, the chosen one bellowed that the Holy Spirit had consecrated Sister Maryoth as their sister superior and mother of their flock. Following her lead, the nuns meekly agreed to bleat with one voice.

Amid traditional protestations of humility and mild resistance, the newly elected prioress was seated on the elaborately carved ceremonial chair. To the accompaniment of the thanksgiving hymn, *Te Deum*, the nuns bore Prioress Maryoth up the aisle. Stopping in front of the Black Madonna, she draped her rosary beads round the Virgin's hand as a token of her gratitude. Now that she'd been elected *Per viam Spiritus Sancti*, no-one could gainsay her victory. While the other nuns knelt before Sister Maryoth to pledge their allegiance, Sister Katherine, who'd kept a clear head by refusing the cordials, slipped out of the chapel.

XIII

Prioress Appointed

Te Deum laudamus
Hymn

St. Andrews, 1521

High up in the crow's nest, the lookout yelled that St.Andrews was in sight. Impatient to see her homeland again, Elisabeth stretched out over the prow of the galley as it ploughed the chilly grey waters, while Sister Agnes clung, white knuckled, to the side-rail, hoping that the salt spray tingling her greenish-white face would whip some healthy colour into it. The ginger root she was struggling to suck was doing little to quell her sickness.

Though the coastline was a faint smudge, barely visible through the damp, swirling fog, Agnes could hear a bell ringing to guide them in towards the shore. Gradually tall spires, towers and pinnacles emerged out of the ghostly mist and then the huge walls of the castle of St.Andrews appeared.

"You don't regret coming, do you?" Elisabeth asked, sniffing the air hungrily for familiar smells, blown by the offshore wind. Agnes shook her head. However seasick or homesick she was feeling, it was as nothing compared to the desolation she would have felt at being left behind.

Convent de Nôtre Dame des Miracles

Sister Agnes watched in silent misery as Elisabeth bustled about her cell preparing to leave the convent.

"Have I really been here for seven years? My goodness. *Seven long years were gone and past,*" Elisabeth recited. "True Thomas was spirited away by the Fairy Queen to Elfland, and when he returned home no-one recognised him." She broke off abruptly, becoming wistful. "But then he recognised no-one, either."

"That will not happen to you," Sister Agnes comforted her.

"Why not? I'm not the same as when I arrived here. I've changed. I've grown up. And thanks to you, *ma chère* Agnes, I have learnt so much. Why, I can read, write and count. Without your help, I'd never have felt able to take on such a responsible position as prioress."

While she prattled on, busy with her packing, an odd sound made her look round. Sister Agnes was quaking from head to toe, large teardrops distorting her placid face.

"I ... I'll never ever see you again," she blurted, through trembling lips. "There is nobody else in the whole world I care for. May God forgive me for my selfishness."

The serene, self-possessed Sister Agnes was crumpling under the weight of her grief, which, despite all her prayers, wouldn't lift. She'd never intended to reveal her feelings — sinful in the eyes of their order — and had prayed for guidance, but watching Elisabeth gather up her belongings was more than she could bear. Startled by the intensity of her emotion, Elisabeth put her arms around her to calm her. Agnes clung to her tightly, her whole body heaving in distress while the parrot shrieked her commiserations.

"Wheesht! Wheesht! Haud yer wheesht!"

St.Andrews

They'd been about to embark when word reached Hepburn that, not only had Janet's funeral already taken place but, more significantly, the election for the new prioress.

"How dare they take matters into their own hands! How dare they elect someone without my permission!" was Bishop Hepburn's unceasing refrain throughout the voyage.

Incandescent that yet another post had been snatched from the noble Hepburn family, he'd ordered their first stop in Scotland to be St.Andrews: he wanted words with the archbishop. However much the mild-mannered Forman may have been a powerless pawn manipulated by the bishops and knights on the ecclesiastical chessboard, what he'd done was unforgivable and Hepburn was unforgiving. The archbishop owed him a favour and he would see to it that Elisabeth received her rightful inheritance

While Haddington had its fair share of religious establishments, the *raison d'être* of St.Andrews, the seat of the Roman Catholic Church in Scotland, was clearly ecclesiastical administration. Nearly everyone they passed along the noisy, bustling streets was dressed in some form of clerical garb: friars, monks, nuns and guards in arch-episcopal uniform, all rushing about in the service of the Lord.

"At least we're not as out of place here, as I was at the French Court."

Pleased to be anywhere with her soulmate, Sister Agnes managed a smile at Elisabeth's remark. Never in her most fervent prayers did she imagine that the French convent would let her go, but Elisabeth's wish was her uncle's command. If his beloved niece needed to have Sister Agnes by her side then he would arrange it. And so the French abbess gratefully accepted a suitable *dot*, or dowry, in compensation for the loss of their dear sister.

Archbishop Forman, whose health had never been robust, had been ailing for some time. Enshrouded in a thick woollen blanket, a scarf wound round his head, the ascetic archbishop shrank at the prospect of confrontation with the burly Hepburn.

"I'm here to ensure that my niece is appointed Prioress of St.Mary's," Hepburn demanded brusquely, unable to bring himself to address Forman with due deference.

"The post is already filled," the archbishop answered, his weak voice muffled by the scarf tied under his chin. "The sisters of the abbey are quite within their right to elect their own prioress and have already elected their successor."

"Well, you'll have to overrule it."

"But I've already given them my blessing," Forman squeaked in alarm. His head poked out of his scarf like a tortoise emerging from its shell.

"Has the Papal Bull been sent to the Vatican yet?"

Forman's head waggled clumsily from side to side. Thank goodness, Hepburn thought. For then it would have been more difficult to have the decision retracted: difficult, but not impossible.

"But your niece is too young to take on such a responsible position."

"Too young! Why, I was appointed prior when I was but sixteen. My niece will soon have completed her twenty-fourth year."

"That is still six years below the canonical age for such a promotion."

"Such rules, as you well know, are not canon law and can be altered to take account of the circumstances," Hepburn retorted. "My niece is a Hepburn and is perfectly capable of discharging the duties required of her station. I myself have overseen her schooling."

"Indeed." Forman shrank into himself, drawing in his scrawny neck before mumbling, "but another question has been raised, that she was not born of lawful bed ... "

Hepburn leaned over him. "By Maryoth Hay, perchance, and her brother the Wizard of Yester?" he growled, breathing heavily into Forman's face. "If you refuse, I shall petition Rome who will grant a dispensation for her defect of age and, if required, will clear up the matter of my niece's legitimacy." The large sum he was willing to donate to the papal coffers should take care of both.

Forman slumped even further down in his chair. The wasting disease he'd been suffering from for many years had worsened and he sensed that his end was near. Soon he would depart this vale of tears, this land of scheming scoundrels where he, a dutiful cleric, had striven all his life to uphold canon law. In a country of near pagans, that was often a thankless task. Why had Christ promised that the meek would inherit the earth? He, for one, didn't want it and spent his final days in prayer, preparing his soul to meet his Maker. He glanced down at his liver-spotted hands. May God forgive me this one last act, he muttered, for he had no strength left to stand up to a bully like John Hepburn.

St. Mary's Abbey

Bishop Hepburn was reading through the abbey's accounts when he felt the air in the scriptorium turn chilly. Sister Maryoth with her power to slip into a room like a spectre had materialised at his side.

"I have come to inform you that I intend to appeal to the highest authority," she said. Her manner was no longer submissive but challenging, her gaze no longer lowered but forthright. "Your niece has no right to be appointed prioress. Apart from the issues of her age and dubious birth, I know for a fact that she's no virgin," Maryoth stated, her voice shrill.

"Indeed." Hepburn narrowed his intense blue eyes and glowered at her. "Let's take that last point first. Did you not swear to silence? Do you now intend to break that oath?"

"If necessary." Sister Maryoth's thin lips clamped together.

"I see." Hepburn lowered his head and began sifting through the documents. "Of course I have no power to prevent you, Sister, but before you do …" He paused to find what he was looking for, "would you mind clearing up a few discrepancies that appear to have crept into the financial records?"

Sister Maryoth's face paled and she began trembling.

Hepburn held up the sheaf of papers and waved it at her. "Had you been elected prioress, all this may not have come to light. Is that what you were hoping? A reliable and trustworthy witness – I am not at liberty to say who – has alerted me to certain malpractices. For example, cartloads of grain and other produce have been seen to leave the abbey every week, bound for the estate of Yester, but no payment seems to have been recorded. Not only that, but the figures in the accounts do not seem to add up. I suspect that substantial sums of missing funds have been finding their way into the coffers of your nephew. What do you say to that, Maryoth?"

Nothing. Instead she lowered her eyes in her customary attitude of humility.

Hepburn's eyes narrowed. "Did you know that the late king James – may God rest his soul – denounced Lord John Hay of Yester, the Wizard of Goblin Ha', for practising the black arts? And that this worshipper of Satan has been using his share of the abbey finances to squander and indulge his wicked ways. Tsk. Tsk. Not a good family connection for a holy nun, never mind a prioress."

Sister Maryoth crossed herself continuously and kissed the crucifix on her rosary as Hepburn spat out these allegations.

"May the Virgin protect me! It was not my idea! I mean, I had no idea … It was my nephew who …" she trailed off.

"Whether you had any idea or not, Sister, the fact still remains that serious misconduct has taken place. Let's say that your nephew bewitched you, that you fell under his evil influence, but that does not expiate your guilt. God did not excuse Adam when he exiled him with Eve from the Garden of Eden. Now I think about it, banishment seems to be the most appropriate punishment. That's it. To a closed order, where you shall take a vow of silence to gag your clacking tongue."

Bishop Hepburn leaned across the pulpit to address the sisterhood assembled in the chapel.

"Sisters of St.Mary's, be sure your sins will find you out. In the past few weeks you have been sheltering the arch-demon Satan in your midst. The Prince of Darkness has been warping your minds and twisting your reason."

The bishop's accusation sent shudders up and down the spines of the susceptible sisters and the fear of hell into their ignorant souls. Auld Nick, Auld Hornie was real to them, a figure forever omnipresent, ready to jump out on the unwary, grab them with his horny claws and haul them down to the fiery depths of hell.

"You all believed that the Holy Ghost descended into your souls that day when you elected Sister Maryoth as prioress but you were deceived. Deceived by the arch-demon himself who, in the same way he tempted Eve in the Garden of Eden, whispered into Sister Maryoth's ear and lured her into giving you a potion that would cloud your reason. While she has been tainted by the serpent's subtle tongue, you, my dear sisters in Christ, are likewise guilty of sin: for choosing such a one for your prioress who will lead you down the fiery path to hell. And you all know the punishment for serving Satan: Thou shalt not suffer a witch to live. Burning at the stake is the only way to purge this accursed coven."

The bishop stretched out across the pulpit to point an accusing finger at them all in turn. Gasps and sobs broke out among the nuns who threw themselves onto their knees, beating their breasts and begging for mercy. Only Sister Katherine, observing from the back of the chapel, seemed unaffected by the frenzy but terror, rather than divine revelation, was now striking the soul of Sister Maryoth's chosen messenger. When she fainted, falling forwards and hitting her skull against the flagstones with a crack, Elisabeth dashed up to the pulpit.

"Uncle!" she hissed. "You cannot do this! You cannot punish all of them. Punish Sister Maryoth if you care, but leave the rest in peace."

As she stood before him, those fern green eyes flashing, his angry scowl softened. He put both hands on her shoulders and turned her round to present her to the cowering sisterhood.

"Behold, how your rightful prioress harbours no resentment but pleads for mercy to be shown to you sinners. Be mindful that Our Holy Father, Pope Leo X himself has confirmed her appointment by papal decree and will brook no defiance. It is now your duty to accept her with the humility and obedience that befit your vocation."

Then, his lips grazing her ear, he whispered, "Your shrewdness does you credit, my precious jewel. The nuns will now be forever grateful to you for saving their lives. And always remember: the best tool for keeping order is the rule of fear."

XIV

Consecration

"Ah sweet, are ye a worldly creature.
Or heavenly thing in likeness of nature?"
The King's Quair, James I, 15th Century

St. Mary's Abbey, 1521

"I'm the Earl of Bothwell and you are my lieges. You will do my bidding."

The assembled group of choirboys glowered suspiciously at the lad in the plush blue velvet breeches and feathered cap, standing on the top step to lord it over them. They'd been warned to be in best voice for a very important visitor but it was not, they grumbled, this cocky little fop.

"No, we'll no. No, we'll no," they yelled back in unison.

As he waved his miniature bejewelled sword in his right hand, the young earl wiped away a snotter from his perpetually running nose on his left sleeve.

"My uncle, the bishop, will have your bellies slit and your guts torn out if you disobey," he whinged, before his bottom lip began to tremble.

Sniffing out weakness, one of the choirboys dashed forward to yank off his lordship's cap and ran off with it. Stamping his foot in a fit of pique, the earl pointed his sword at another of the boys and ordered him to retrieve it.

"You're the lord with the sword. Fetch it yourself."

While the bonnet was pitched from one boy to another, the earl leapt up and down like a flea trying to catch it. On the sidelines, a stocky dark-haired lad in a black soutane watched and waited till the boy waving the trophy scampered past him. Swiftly extending his foot, he tripped up the boy, snatched the cap and held it aloft, challenging all comers. Meanwhile, the peevish Earl of Bothwell had slumped to the ground, sniffling and snivelling that he had a stitch in his side. The stocky lad knelt beside him and crammed the hat on his head, but he couldn't stick the fallen feather back on.

"Well done."

The lad scrambled from his knees to behold a magnificent creature in a cream coloured robe and immaculate white winged headdress. He stood transfixed. None other than the Queen of Heaven. The Mother of God, every inch a queen and nothing at all like the crude Black Madonna in the chapel, was gazing down on him. Chained to her wrist, an exotic multi-coloured bird of paradise fluttered its wings and pecked at her sleeve. Overcome by awe and wonder, he was torn between kneeling down to worship at her feet or running off to hide behind Betsy's voluminous skirts. Instead he blurted, "*All hail thou mighty Queen of Heaven! For thy peer on earth I never did see!*"

A beatific beam lit up her face as she took up the refrain:

"*Oh no, no, no, Thomas*", she said, "*That name does not belong to me*."

"Lisbeth! My Lisbeth has come at last!" Betsy was hirpling across the courtyard as fast as her rickety legs could carry her. She hurled herself at the Fairy Queen and hugged her tightly, laughing and crying at the same time. Peeved at not being shown due deference, Patrick, Earl of Bothwell, tugged at Betsy's skirt, demanding to be presented to the lady.

Through jaundiced eyes Prioress Janet had doted on her golden-haired angel, ruining his appetite with sweetmeats and spoiling his temper by filling him with a high conceit of himself. Earl of Bothwell he may be, but he was a thin, ingle-backit child, with stooped shoulders and an unhealthy pallor, his weak lungs aye wheezing and coughing. Try as she might, Betsy could not muster up any fondness for this orphan bairn, abandoned by a mother who, as Dame Janet herself had predicted, lowped the dyke, adding two more husbands to her tally.

"What's that bird?" he bawled, pointing with his sword.

"This is a parakeet. I call her my Papingo."

Patrick drew back as the parakeet tapped her beak irritably against the sharp weapon.

So he was right, the stocky lad marvelled. She must indeed be the Queen of Heaven, for wasn't the Paraclete another name for the Holy Ghost? Unsure how to behave in the company of such divine dignitaries, he hung back until Betsy pushed him forward.

"And do you mind your godson? John, greet your godmother."

Knox was spellbound. The Queen of Heaven was his godmother? The Mother of God was his godmother?

Clamping his gawping mouth shut, Knox began to fidget nervously, wishing that he had some kind of offering to give her. When he thrust out the bedraggled feather, she took it from him with a twinkling smile and squeezed his hand gently. He gave a little start. Her soft, smooth hands were a world away from Betsy's, rough and calloused from endless daily chores.

And she smelt heavenly. Not the camphoric stink of unclean clothes or the stale sweat of unwashed bodies, but fresh and fragrant. Betsy didn't believe in bathing too frequently – once a year in spring after wintering in smoky rooms was often enough – otherwise precious oils were washed from the skin, leaving you prey to any number of dreaded diseases. The heavenly vision crouched down, still holding his hand.

"I'll wager that it was Betsy who taught you the *Ballad of True Thomas*."

He nodded. To his surprise she leant over and skimmed his cheek lightly with her lips. His hand flew up, as if scalded. Betsy was generous with hugs but, as far as he could remember, she'd never kissed him. He blushed from the tips of his toes to the top of his scalp. Like the Queen of Fairy in the ballad, his godmother had gained his eternal loyalty with a kiss. At that moment he vowed to be her faithful servant, forever and ever. *Amen.*

Knox's first task for the prioress was to serve as altar boy at her inauguration Mass, celebrated by Bishop Hepburn. Now dottered and dithering, he kept losing concentration and stumbled his way through the service, but Knox kept a keen eye on the frail bishop's every move in case he spilt the sacred communion wine or wafers. He was ringing the *Sanctus* bell to signal silence when a commotion broke out at the back of the chapel. Some of the nuns were leaping up and down and hooching as if in a reel. Only Sister Agnes remained on her knees gazing steadfastly heavenwards.

Alarmed by the sea of waving hands, a multi-coloured bird was wheeling and diving and, in her distress, dropping little white plops of gloop everywhere. The nuns twisted and turned to avoid having their immaculate white wimples and cream habits splattered.

"Someone get that devil's bird out of here," Bishop Hepburn croaked.

Reluctant to descend into the turmoil below, the parrot landed on a rafter to roost. Knox rushed down from the altar and tried to calm the nuns.

"Wheesht! Will you all haud your wheesht! You're only scaring it."

On hearing the one phrase comprehensible to her, Papingo cocked her ear and gracefully descended to land on his head. Even though its sharp talons scraped his scalp Knox dared not move and waited for Elisabeth to inch forward, slowly so as not to startle the bird. As she grasped the parrot's claw and tied it to her wrist with her rosary beads, it stretched out to peck at something. A shiny trinket on the Black Madonna's finger had caught its gimlet eye.

"No treats for you, naughty Papingo," Elisabeth chided, tapping it on the beak.

"I found that in the vestry," John said, "I thought I'd put it there in case the owner came back."

Peering at it more closely, the prioress gave a little start. "And so she has, John," she said thoughtfully, slipping it into her pocket. "So she has."

Sniggering behind his hand, Earl Patrick observed the mayhem from the back of the chapel. His practical joke had turned out even better than he'd planned. The nuns" habits beshitten with bird's droppings was a bonus. It was even more amusing than the time he'd released mice into the chapel to scuttle about and become entangled in their long skirts. Because he was the Earl of Bothwell, the nuns dared not complain but had to tolerate and even forgive the silly pranks he played on them. That would show them, for Patrick had been deeply offended by Bishop John's remarks.

"What mealy-mouthed milksop have we here? Never mind Hepburn blood, is there any blood running in him at all?"

Patrick had winced as Bishop John pinched his pallid cheeks to redden them and pushed back his shoulders to straighten his back.

"God forbid that his mother was carrying a spineless Stewart when she married Adam. Let's see if he kens his scripture."

Patrick also attended St.Mary's Church school but, whenever the dominie asked him a question, he turned with glaikit eyes and slack jaw to Knox who answered promptly and correctly for him. Far from feeling ashamed, dull-witted Patrick considered book learning beneath his lordly dignity. That was for the likes of common lads such as Knox.

"So, John not only protects you from bullying by the other lads, but he speaks for you too? Hepburns are doughty fighters. You'll have to learn to wag your own tongue and bare your own knuckles, my lad."

Being in the company of indulgent women was clearly spoiling his nephew's nature and so, to strengthen and straighten his backbone, he would be sent to St.Andrews Priory. His uncle and namesake, Prior Patrick, who had taken over the bishop's former post, would supervise his studies. While ridiculing his noble-born nephew, Hepburn had praised the orphan Knox who could recite the whole of the Mass in Latin, both the antiphons and responses, useful when the parish priest forgot his words, or was too befuddled by communion wine to remember. Or both.

"Betsy may have brought my godson into this world, but I breathed the spirit of life into him," Elisabeth reminded her uncle.

"Aye, and I remember baptising him in the name of the Holy Spirit. A thrice blessed lad indeed," the bishop wheezed.

When their mother died a few years ago, John's older brother, William, had been apprenticed to a sea merchant in Prestonpans. Betsy had laid claim to John as Elisabeth's godson, taking him to Hailes as a playmate for the abandoned Earl Patrick. His future, however, was uncertain. When the bishop proposed a post in his episcopal guard, Elisabeth wasn't keen. Such intelligence should not be wasted in soldiery.

"You are right, my jewel. We need lads like him. He has the makings of a churchman. A parish priest perhaps."

Elisabeth, however, had higher ambitions for her godson. With Bishop Hepburn's patronage, Knox would be assured not only a place at the local grammar school, but at St.Andrews University. And she would do all in her power to ensure that he rose to become at least a bishop, if not an archbishop.

XV

Last Rites

> The state of man does change and vary,
> Now sound, now sick, now blyth, now sary
> Now dansand merry, now like to dee:
> *Timor mortis conturbat me.*
> *Lament for the Makars*
> William Dunbar, 15th–16th Century

Timor mortis conturbat me.
Lament for the Makars
William Dunbar, 15th–16th Century

St. Andrews, 1522

John Hepburn eased himself onto his bony elbows and, though his sight was failing, his faded blue eyes gleamed with anticipation.

"Has the envoy arrived yet?" he croaked.

This same question he had been asking endlessly, day after day. His nephew, Prior Patrick, shook his head. Bishop John had suffered another seizure and his condition was rapidly deteriorating. Like the drapes and folds of his elaborate vestments, his skin now hung loosely on him. Most of his teeth had fallen out causing his jowls, tinged with episcopal purple, to collapse. The fleshy, lascivious lips had withered and were now puckered with the permanent indignation of slighted worth. Wisps of silvery hair straggled from beneath his biretta. His body was covered in stinking bedsores that refused to heal.

Even as he lay on his deathbed, Hepburn had not lost hope of securing the long-coveted title. Now that Andrew Forman had died, he eagerly awaited the papal emissary with the Bull declaring him primate of Scotland.

The bishop cast an undisguised look of contempt at his nephew and barely deigned to speak to him. A stout young man with the same heavy, Hepburn jowls, but with a slackness about the mouth which bore the marks of a life well-lived, Prior Patrick was altogether a weaker character who lacked the Hepburn drive and ambition. Had it been a mistake to send the young earl to be educated by this wastrel?

"Where is Lisbeth? Bring me my precious pearl and get out of my sight!"

"Don't fret, uncle, I'm here," Elisabeth said. Seeing her proud uncle so decrepit and infirm, with only the hope of the primacy keeping him alive, tore at her heart.

His gnarled hands groped for her, pulling her down towards him. The voice that had boomed throughout chapels, churches and cathedrals had become hoarse and faint. His foul breath stank and, as tactfully as she could, Elisabeth covered her nose and mouth with a fine cambric handkerchief.

Bishop Hepburn – whose personal motto *Ad vitam* adorned the walls of St. Leonard's College that he'd helped to found – was scared stiff of death, or more truthfully, of hell and eternal damnation. As insurance against such a fate, he'd undergone the last rites several times to guarantee absolution for every sinful act knowingly or unknowingly committed, confessed and unconfessed.

"Father. Let me hear you say it. Father," he whispered gruffly into her ear as she leant over him.

"As you wish. Father." Elisabeth complied, assuming that, in his delirium, he was confusing her with his confessor.

"May God in his infinite mercy forgive me, a poor sinner. I wasn't strong enough to resist the temptations of the flesh. Afflicted by the same weaknesses as other men. Och, women are indeed the very devil," he rasped. The more his breathing became laboured, the tighter his knobbly fingers grasped her hand. He pulled her in closer.

"I can't take this lie to the grave with me," he wheezed. "When I said you were ill-begotten, that you were the fruit of your mother's adultery, that was true. But what I said about your father, that wasn't true – apart being a butter-lippit blackguard." Hepburn attempted a smile. "But he didn't die in a border foray." When he paused to inhale deeply a rattle sounded deep in his throat. "He lives still. For you see, your father … is me."

Despite his foul breath, Elisabeth leant in more closely. Had she heard him right?

"I don't understand, uncle. What are you saying?"

"My dearest Lisbeth, *I* am your father." His rheumy eyes sought hers, beseeching her forgiveness.

"My father?" She stared at him in disbelief. "But if you are my father – then who is my mother?"

"Oh, never fear, you are your mother's daughter. How I worshipped her! To my dying day, I'll never forgive my brother. When his first wife died, he was given the choice of the Earl of Huntly's two daughters; whichever would best please him. Everyone assumed he'd take the elder sister, Katherine Gordon. That would have been the right and proper thing to do. But … but …" he choked back tears, "he chose Margaret. He stole her from under my nose. Out of sheer spite."

His knotted hands began to knead the blanket as he became more and more agitated. "Since you can never wed, said he, I'll have Margaret, for she's bonnier and daintier than her sister. Though she may have been forced to marry Patrick, it was me she truly loved. And you weren't ill-begotten, my precious pearl, but love-begotten."

Elisabeth dabbed at the tears flowing down the deep furrowed lines of his face. Sniffling he went on. "But Patrick paid her scant attention. Too busy with the conspiracies and intrigues that may have gained him an earldom but lost her douce, warm heart. While he was swaggering about France and Spain and all the airts, I did my best to comfort Margaret, my most precious pearl. However profane our love may have been in the eyes of the Church, for us it was sacred."

His watery eyes narrowed and, for a second, flashed intensely blue. "Then when your birth ripped my beloved Margaret from me, I blamed you. I couldn't bear to set eyes on you, but when I did, I was stunned. You are indeed your mother's daughter. You have her ferny green eyes, with hazel tints that flicker and glint in the sunlight, and yon bonnie russet hair. I may have lost my dearest love but I've gained you, my precious jewel." He squeezed her hand. "And you are mine. You are," he rasped, "you are my daughter. In whom I am well pleased," he finally managed to declare, a faint smile flitting across his ravished features.

Elisabeth frowned. A band of pain clamped her forehead as she struggled to grasp the significance of this revelation. Her uncle was her father. The prioress was a bishop's daughter. Her head began to dirl with it all.

"My own daughter! Prioress of St. Mary's! And when I am archbishop – nay, cardinal – you and I shall have all of Fife and the Lothians under our control. What a formidable pair we shall be! We shall show those conniving Beatons!"

Gripped by a searing pain in his chest, he collapsed back onto his pillows.

The men in full regalia who arrived at St. Andrews Priory were not the escort of the long-awaited Papal Nuncio bringing news of Hepburn's appointment, but the arch-episcopal guard – headed by David Beaton whose drab clerical garb was enlivened by a conical-shaped hat with green tassels. Greeting him at the main door of the priory – before he had the chance to force his way into the bishop's bedchamber – Elisabeth had to quash a mischievous urge to flick his silly tassels. Instead she invited him into the bishop's antechamber and offered him some wine.

"So you survived certain death at the hands of the Scottish lairds?" she asked.

"As you see," Beaton replied and raised his goblet. "And now, my lady prioress, let's congratulate each other on our new appointments."

"*You* have a new appointment?"

"Aye. I've left the Duke of Albany's service and now act as private secretary to my uncle, James Beaton."

This surprised Elisabeth. "But why give up such an important position?"

Beaton tapped the side of his nose. With his instinct for self-preservation he could see great changes ahead. Albany's intermittent government was not proving to be successful. Whenever he visited Scotland, stability reigned, only to be followed by chaos and anarchy whenever he departed. Besides, the time was fast approaching when the duke may be forced to give up the regency.

"And, since he has resisted Margaret Tudor's charms ..."

"What? Elisabeth snorted. "The puddock princess tried to seduce him?"

"Oh aye, on his visits here they spent many hours closeted together and not only to discuss politics. As his secretary, I should ken. I suspect she may have been seeking his support to divorce Angus and may even have made him a proposal of marriage. But the duke is not so daft. He has no intention of staying in Scotland and as soon as he goes there will be a right old tug-o'-war between her and Angus for control of the young king. For, when he reaches his twelfth birthday in April 1524, James can be declared of age to rule.

"So, since Albany's heart is not here in Scotland, I have decided it would be best to leave his service now. I intend to assist my uncle who, like me, does have our country's best interests at heart," Davie Beaton added.

"Indeed," Elisabeth replied while thinking that Beaton's own ambitious interests would be nearer his heart.

"And, to that end, I come with a message for your uncle."

"Good news, I hope. My ... my uncle ..." Elisabeth hesitated as she considered her newly informed relationship, "is very ill. May I ken what that may be so as to forewarn him?"

"My commission is to deliver the message to Bishop Hepburn himself," Beaton replied. The rivalry between them was still as strong as ever and he was clearly set on winning this round. Taken aback by his high-handed manner, Elisabeth searched Beaton's eyes for the twinkle that would indicate he was only teasing, but she was met by a stern, humourless glare.

Beaton drained his goblet and slammed it down on the table. When he tried to push past her, she stood firm.

"From the smug look on your face I jalouse that you're not going to tell him what he desperately wants to hear. My ..." again she had to stop and think, "My uncle is dying. For pity's sake, let him die in peace. Let him die in hope. Be merciful, Davie."

"He who lives on hope dies fasting. Your family loyalty is praiseworthy, Lisbeth, but I, too, must fulfil my duty. As the arch-episcopal emissary, I have full authority to command you to stand aside," he said with his self-important sneer.

Elisabeth stared back, grim-faced and unsmiling. How tempted she was to slap the birkie's flabby, well-fed face. Or knock that jaunty hat off his swollen head. She was ordered to wait outside while he informed Hepburn that the post of Archbishop of St.Andrews had been given to James Beaton.

Only once the deed was done did Beaton crinkle up his eyes and give her an insolent wink.

"It would seem that my uncle has won this particular race."

Beaton's brusque communication crushed John Hepburn, squeezing the last vestiges of vibrancy out of him: his violet eyes dimmed and sank into their sockets. As Elisabeth mopped the beads of sweat from his brow she tried to console him.

"There is some hope," she said softly. "Your nephew, Prior Patrick, may one day gain the position you coveted."

"Patrick? Never. No that one," he snarled in a moment of stark lucidity. "That ill-begotten, fushionless nephew of mine has only risen because of me. He lacks ambition. There is no fire in his blood, no hunger for power. He craves only a full belly and a filled bed." Spittle drooled from the corners of his mouth.

"If only you'd been born a man, Elisabeth, you'd have had the smeddum to fulfil my ambition." Seeking her hand again, he lay still to catch his breath. His eyes moistened with tears as he whispered, "It's a pity about your bairn. That he …" Hepburn broke off. "That he failed to thrive. The Lord only kens but my grandson might have been a worthy successor to me."

Sitting by his bedside, listening to Hepburn's rasping breath as he slowly ebbed away, Elisabeth fought back tears. That he might, she thought, and then said, "Aye, but our godson has the makings of becoming a great bishop one day."

Hepburn's blue eyes flickered for a moment.

"I mind the day I baptised the lad," he gasped, "John Knox. May my blessing be upon him."

"And I shall make sure that he follows in your footsteps," she gulped before adding, "Father."

Hepburn had held fast on to Elisabeth's hand until he breathed his last. No sooner had she wiped his damp, chilling brow than Prior Patrick pushed her aside. She must go to her chamber now and stay there until after the funeral: she would have no say in the arrangements. Since it was not the custom for women to attend funerals – even a queen was excluded from her royal husband's requiem – Elisabeth had no choice. Birth was women's labour: death, it seemed, was man's domain.

On the eve of the funeral, while Prior Patrick entertained the invited dignitaries, Elisabeth defied his orders and sneaked into St.Andrews Cathedral to pay her last respects. Hepburn's open coffin lay on a bier surrounded by lit candles. His corpse was dressed in lavish vestments of episcopal purple and a crucifix placed between his hands, but his bishop's ring was missing from his finger. Certain that his clerical cronies – after feasting on the elaborate funeral meats – would appoint him Bishop of Moray in his uncle's place, Prior Patrick had already taken possession of this symbol of office.

Elisabeth pulled up a stool next to the coffin and massaged her bruised hand. Hepburn, she reflected, had been a difficult, exasperating man: like God the Father himself, he was often unfair and unjust. Domineering and dictatorial, he demanded obedience and subservience and few dared to oppose him. But, then, being disappointed in love had determined his life. Although it had not been his choice, he had funnelled all his frustrated desire, all his thwarted passion into a career in the Church.

No doubt Hepburn's life had shaped his character: she was beginning to understand and even appreciate his rage and resentment. Besides, was her life not following a similar path? Forsaken in love, forced into a priory — she truly was her father's daughter, she thought ruefully. So, if Hepburn had been able to forgive her — not only for her mother's death but for her youthful rebellion and misdemeanours — then she, too, would find it in her heart to forgive him his trespasses.

Hearing footsteps on the flagstones, Elisabeth whirled round to see Betsy trailing Earl Patrick behind her and John Knox tugging her eagerly forward. Catching sight of his godmother, John broke free and dashed up to tell her all about his first sea crossing: how his brave brother, William had sailed them across from Aberlady and how he hadn't been sick once. Not like Earl Patrick who had puked all the way.

"Tsk. Tsk," Betsy scolded. "No telling tales, Johnnie, and certainly not in a holy place."

Abashed, John hung his head and said sorry to Patrick who had slumped down onto the flagstones. Betsy propped him up against a pillar and wiped his ghostly white face.

"Oh Betsy! Thank goodness you're here." Elisabeth collapsed into the comforting arms of her nurse and sobbed her heart out.

"Come on now," Betsy said as she gathered her orphans round her. "A good night's sleep will do us all some good."

Later, when the lads were tucked up together in a truckle bed and Betsy had mulled some spiced wine, she explained how Prior Patrick had ordered her to bring the young earl as head of the clan to attend their uncle's funeral. On her own initiative, she had also brought John. After all, as Bishop Hepburn's godson he should be entitled to serve at the requiem Mass. Elisabeth agreed. Surely Patrick could not object to that.

She cradled the tassie of spiced wine, still too hot to drink, and said, "To think how often I taunted Kate for being a gowk and all the time it was me that was the cuckoo in the nest." She glanced sideways at her nurse. "You knew, Betsy, didn't you? Why did you never tell me?"

Betsy added a few drops of *aquavitae* to fortify her wine. "Aye, I did ken but I said nothing. For one thing, it wasn't my place to do so and, for another, why should I bother? It might only have caused you grief. Families are never simple. They're all taigled up and tapsalteerie. After all, your sister Joanna was your father's daughter by his first wife, Joanna Douglas, and your ill-begotten sister-in-law Nancy had the king's bairn. One way or another you're all gowks."

Elisabeth laughed. She'd forgotten about her sister Joanna who, being more than fifteen years older and married in 1506 to Lord Seton, she hardly knew. Widowed by Flodden, Joanna had vowed to set up a Dominican convent in Edinburgh, which she intended to enter when her son came of age.

"Aye, it's true what they say," Betsy was chuckling. "In the great scheme of things, what does it matter who your parents are? Forbye, some things are better left unsaid." She took a long draft of fortified wine and then added, "Till the time is right."

The Miraculous Cure

The vices of the evil will fall on their heads.
The City of Ladies
Christine de Pisan, 14th–15th Century

St. Mary's Abbey, 1523

David Beaton's hooded eyes surveyed her chamber, noting the books on her shelves before alighting on the pomanders filled with sweet-smelling herbs that perfumed the air.

"True to his name, Father Dudgeon is in high dudgeon." His lips attempted a wry smile but his eyes remained wary. "He has made several complaints to the archbishop about the changes you're making at the abbey. I warn you, Lisbeth, he will stab you in the back if you continue to pay him no heed."

Her aunt had always deferred to him, the parish priest had whined, but then Dame Janet had known her place. This niece of hers with her learning and that nun from France with her foreign ways did not bestow on him the respect that was his due.

Before Elisabeth could stop him, Beaton had picked a small book from the shelf and was flicking through it.

"The fact that you are teaching your sisters their letters … "

"Let him not suffer the sin of envy. Tell him he would be most welcome to attend my lessons."

"When they should be spending time in more spiritual pursuits of prayer and contemplation."

The exasperating way that Beaton smacked his plump lips in an indulgent smile infuriated her. She snatched *The City of Ladies* from him, hoping that he hadn't had time to read any of it. She didn't want him to have further grounds for complaint.

"So he agrees with you, Davie Beaton? That schooling women is about as useful as polishing the inside of a chamber pot?"

"I wouldn't put it quite so crudely. In some cases, I admit, it may be beneficial. In your position as prioress, I concede it may be to your advantage to be literate."

And the way he looked down his nose to examine his meticulously manicured fingernails grated on her nerves.

"And your own sister, Katherine, is one of our more eager and able pupils, you'll be pleased to know."

"Venerable virtues, I'm sure, but too much learning may blight her spiritual vocation."

"You have a gey low opinion of women's abilities, Davie Beaton," she retorted, "yet you gladly lend an ear to the haverings of Father Dudgeon who can hardly spell his own name. Just because he's an ordained priest, I have to respect him and let him stand in judgement over me." She had to struggle to keep her seething resentment at this unlearned cleric's superiority from boiling over.

"That is another of his complaints. He's taken a tirrivee because you've dismissed him as your confessor."

"You ken fine the reason. Our reverend father is a drunkard and a sot who would sell his soul for a drink," Elisabeth retaliated. "By inventing sins to blab about to his drinking cronies, he's betraying the sanctity of the confessional. Why, you should be persecuting him, not me. What stories he spins about us, I can jalouse. Doubtless he also tells you that we're running a whorehouse?"

"Now you come to mention it," Beaton said with a smirk, before proceeding to polish his immaculately filed fingernails on his sleeve.

The whorehouse at the Abbey of St.Mary's was steadily earning a reputation as a refuge for women. In Dame Janet's time wealthy patronesses had been welcomed, providing a substantial source of income for the abbey: devout virgins and widows seeking a spiritual retreat from the world, worthy matrons, worn-out and weary after years of childbearing, craving rest and recuperation. The poor, meanwhile, had been given alms and sent on their way and the sick directed to the infirmary run by the Friars of St.Laurence. Neither Dame Janet nor Sister Maryoth had suffered scrofulous scavengers and scroungers cluttering up her priory.

Now that Sister Maryoth had been exiled to the cloistered Abbey of Coldingham, the new prioress and her sisters were free to show more Christian charity. Mindful of their dream to establish a City of Ladies, they turned away no-one and every day more and more women came to the abbey seeking sanctuary. Not only beggars, but abused, downtrodden women; whores, diseased and sodden with drink, wives maltreated by their husbands, despoiled daughters thrown out by their families, shrunken old crones and destitute widows, poor witless souls cried after in the street as witches. The list, it seemed, was endless.

It had begun in a small way with Sister Agnes dispensing medications and ointments made from the herbs and plants she grew in the kitchen garden. She had set up an apothecary in one of the outhouses where she worked alongside Betsy who not only had a wide knowledge of native herb-lore, but an uncanny talent for diagnosis. She would peer into the sufferer's eyes, examining the whites and the pupils for tell-tale signs, inspect the pallor of the skin and sniff the breath to determine their ailment. How they could attend patiently to those ragged scraps of humanity when the sight and stench of their suppurating sores and scabs made her stomach heave, was a miracle in itself to Elisabeth.

But it was another miracle that had set Father Dudgeon's teeth on edge. Greatly aggrieved that a miraculous cure had taken place without his knowledge or approval, he had warned Beaton that the nuns must be witches, consorting with Beelzebub.

"Aye, he seems to think this is a coven, not a convent," Elisabeth sneered. "Come and see for yourself what magic spells and potions our carlin is cooking up."

Swirling mists of pungent-smelling steam from simmering pots and pans made Beaton's eyes smart as he examined the rows of meticulously labelled jars and flasks and phials. Selecting a small pot Beaton lifted the lid and sniffed.

"Ugh! What on God's earth is this?" His nose wrinkled in disgust. "I know! Such a foul-smelling ointment can only be the elixir of eternal youth! Many a lady would sell her soul for this!"

He chortled gaily at his little jest while Sister Agnes earnestly explained that the unguent, prepared from burdock, goose grass, red dock and garlic, was to treat the lepers at the hospice of the friars of St.Laurence.

"Thon disgusting stench would be enough to drive out the disease."

"Sadly, nothing can cure that dreadful ailment," Agnes continued gravely, "but it helps to relieve the pain. Besides, the poor souls believe that it keeps away the evil eye."

Beaton's eyes gleamed on hearing this snippet.

"Ah, not only lepers believe in the evil eye, I've been told. Is it true that you place herbs in your undergarments to fend off evil spirits?"

"A posy of cinquefoil helps to stifle foul smells in the same way that we sprinkle lavender oil on these." She pointed to a row of dried herbs and heather tied in bunches. "As for evil spirits ..." She shrugged. "For some people, the belief that their illness has been caused by a malevolent spirit is very strong."

"But that is just superstitious nonsense," Beaton scoffed.

"Who is to say they are wrong? Do we not believe in the power of Satan who is evil incarnate? And do you, as custodian of the relics of St.Andrew, not urge your flock to venerate them and pray to the saint for help?

"Yes, but..." Beaton seemed stumped for a moment before replying. "We must distinguish between spells which stem from sorcery and miracles which occur through divine intervention."

Sister Agnes stiffened as she guessed at his intention.

"No miracle has taken place here."

Though many would disagree. When a woman with deformed growths on her neck had come begging for a cure, Betsy's remedy had been to hang the leaves of the noble figwort round her neck as a charm to ward off the scrofula. Mindful that there was often an element of truth in these old cantrips, Sister Agnes had crushed the tubers of the plant to make a poultice and applied it to the woman's neck. Gradually her skin began to knit together until it was healed.

"A miracle! A miracle!" the ecstatic patient declared.

With Sister Agnes hailed as a saint, queues of lepers and sufferers of scrofula were soon queuing outside the apothecary to kiss the hem of her robe. Tortured with embarrassment, Agnes implored them to seek help at St. Laurence, but they howled their refusal.

"For we are sure to die in the infirmary, if not of the sickness we have, then of the wasting disease, or the pox. The friars there skirp at us women. To them we are the damned. They wouldn't even pray for our wicked souls."

While most of the women had sat down in the courtyard, refusing to move, a few had slipped into the chapel to demand the sanctuary of a holy place. Sister Agnes gazed with pity on the swarm of wretched women.

"We must do something for them. We must build our own hospice."

"Who will look after them all?" Certainly not those nuns who had entered the convent for a life free from such worldly and womanly cares as nursing the sick. Neither their vows nor their vocation demanded such sacrifice. The idea unsettled Elisabeth. "And how will it be paid for?" The sick and destitute were already a constant drain on their resources, a seeping sore of human decomposition.

"God shall provide," Sister Katherine affirmed with the confidence of the righteous. "Does He not help those who help themselves? And that is what the women shall do. In return for their bed and board, we shall teach them to look after each other."

"And show them that clean water works better than holy water to cure many ills," Agnes added.

Elisabeth laughed. "Such faith: such hope: such charity. But how could I be such a scatter-wit? Now that you're a saint, Agnes, you're the one to work miracles."

Vanity would also contribute to charity. Ladies of the court would empty their purses and sell, if not their souls, then at least their gems, for the secret of eternal youth. Persuaded to lay aside her censure for a good cause, Agnes set to work blending creams and lotions to preserve and prolong beauty while Betsy made up receipts for exotic elixirs and philtres to enhance their jaded love lives. In return, these grateful ladies rewarded the abbey generously. Just how generously Father Dudgeon was eager to know.

"So *that* explains why he is so annoyed," Elisabeth exclaimed, as she led Beaton from the apothecary. "Not because he isn't receiving due respect: but because he isn't receiving any financial due. Is that what is required to keep his mouth shut?"

Beaton shot her a look of shocked disapproval.

"Tut, tut! How can you suspect your parish priest of avarice? Surely we servants of the Church should share and share alike in our dealings with Mammon. I, for one, am more than willing to turn a blind eye to your activities here in return for a small recompense." The devilish glint in his eyes betrayed his innocent expression.

"I'm sure Sister Agnes will be able to concoct something appropriate for you. A bitter purgative for your swollen pride, perhaps, or a salve for your conscience," she retorted. Either of which she'd be more than happy to administer.

"Your new confessor will require more than some balm to grease his palm," Beaton smirked, "for I am honoured to be given that rôle."

"What? You? Our confessor?" Elisabeth was beginning to regret her hasty dismissal of Father Dudgeon. The devil they knew was preferable to Beaton.

"That's impossible, Davie Beaton. You haven't taken Major Orders."

He scowled at her. "But I am to be appointed Abbot of Arbroath. And I will be ordained." He drummed his chin with his fingers and waggled his head. "In due course, in due course. Until then I would like you to look upon me as your guardian. Without the guidance and support of your late uncle, you and your sisters need a spiritual and temporal adviser to champion your cause. Gratis, of course. And don't be losing sleep over the secrets of your confessions," he waggled his forefinger cheekily, "I'm sure there will be no mortal sin worthy of hellfire. Not a sin worth a damn."

XVII

A Case of Courtly Love

Open rebuke is better than secret love.
Proverbs 27:5

St. Mary's Abbey, Autumn 1525

The Edinburgh lawyers were dragging their heels dealing with the claims that Lord John Hay of Yester was pursuing against the abbey. How long had it been now? How many months, if not years? Of the two actions he had brought, the first – to prohibit the cutting of peats on his land – was unjust, since it violated a right bestowed on the abbey centuries ago by their founder, Countess Ada, and the second – to prohibit the passing of any carts or animals within a mile of his land – was malicious, since it would curtail access to their sheep granges and also mean a longer and therefore more expensive journey to deliver goods to the abbey.

"He's doing it out of revenge," Sister Katherine maintained. "Ever since that business with his aunt, Sister Maryoth, he's been harassing us."

Elisabeth nodded. With a mind as astute as her brother's, Katherine had quickly learnt to read and write and was proving to be invaluable in helping her to manage the abbey's affairs. Now, as they sat side-by-side in the scriptorium, the prioress placed her hand on Katherine's sleeve.

"It was thanks to you that their cheating was uncovered."

Sister Katherine moved her arm away. "When I saw what they were up to, I couldn't simply close my eyes. I only did what was right. And now I'm beginning to think that either our lawyers are in the pockets of Hay or they are too frightened to contest such a fiercesome opponent."

It was rumoured that Lord Hay, like his notorious ancestor Hugo de Gifford, the original Wizard of Goblin Ha', could summon dark forces. There was indeed the mark of Satan about him, with his full black beard and eyes that blazed like diabolic beacons whenever his will was challenged – which Elisabeth had dared to do.

Moreover, Hay was married to Elizabeth Douglas, sister of Angus who, as Beaton had predicted, was winning the struggle for the regency. A rotating council for control of the king had been set up but, now that it was time for Angus to hand James over, he was refusing to do so. A demon in his own right, many might consider, Angus would doubtless take his brother-in-law's part.

"If Bishop Hepburn were still alive, Hay wouldn't be pursuing us so forcefully for such petty causes," Katherine said. "He assumes we're weak women. Since the lackadaisical Edinburgh lawyers seem afraid to raise the hackles of the Wizard and

Angus, perhaps now is time to call on our self-appointed champion and test his mettle."

Elisabeth agreed. While Davie Beaton was attending the court in Edinburgh to defend a case brought against his patron, Lord Ogilvie, they would ask him to look into the affair.

Abbot Beaton returned from the city a man transfigured. His robes tailored in the French style hung loosely from his leaner body, his hawkish eyes had lost their predatory look and his whole being radiated happiness and joy. Elisabeth was curious.

"Have we beaten the curse of Sister Maryoth? Or has the Wizard of Goblin Ha" put a spell on you?"

To her surprise Beaton threw up his arms and twirled round her chamber on tiptoe like a giddy girl. "A lesser man I may be in body but a greater one in heart! What I have lost in flesh I have gained in spirit! The most wonderful thing has happened to me! You are the first to know. I am in love!"

Again? She knew Beaton of old and his weakness for a pretty face.

"You've been beglamoured," Elisabeth taunted. "Or else you've secretly been taking one of Agnes's love philtres."

"Really in love this time," he sighed. "Truly. Madly. Deeply. However," he lowered his voice to a conspiratorial whisper, "not a word of this to Katherine. She won't approve."

Lady Marion Ogilvie had stood in court with her head held high, refusing to be intimidated by her great-nephew's lawyers. She knew their opinion of this maiden aunt, this thorn in their side. A child of her father's fourth marriage, left dowerless on his death, she should be grateful to Lord Ogilvie for deigning to grant her a place in his household.

Lady Marion, however, was no compliant spinster aunt, grateful for any crumb left over from her master's table. She was a mature woman, nearing thirty, who'd been brought up by her mother to manage her own affairs and now she was defending her right to recover the value of her father's livestock requisitioned by her great-nephew. When his lawyers argued that he needed to recoup the costs of her bed and board, she reminded them that she was a lord's daughter, not a common lodger, and being granted grace and favour should mean just that. Would any of them divest a distressed gentlewoman of their own kin of her lawful legacy or ask her to pay for her keep?

A bonnie fighter, David Beaton thought, as she stood opposite him in court, her face flushed, her intelligent eyes flashing to defend her rights. His heart swooped and soared at recognising a kindred spirit who, like him, was striving against the odds to make her own way in the world. So bedazzled was Beaton by the doughty aunt, that he was willing to flout her nephew's wishes and find in her favour. His patron, Lord Ogilvie, would not be pleased but Beaton cared not a jot.

Before leaving Edinburgh he was thrilled to find that he'd not only met his soulmate but his bedfellow, a woman whose passion could match his. For, though her nephew's lawyers poked fun at her by saying her tinderbox must be dry, once lit, Lady Marion instantly burst into flame. At her age there was little time for virginal coyness. Her feistiness, her age and lack of a dowry had doubtless put many a suitor off, but not Beaton.

"She is a fine woman of noble birth whom I love and respect with all my heart," he sighed, clearly spellbound with admiration.

"And from what you say, she is learned too," Elisabeth couldn't resist pointing out.

Beaton shrugged. "*Touché.* Her mother made sure of that, for she knew she'd have to struggle in life. Hard-headed highlander that she is, Marion isn't vexed by the opinion of others and, since she doesn't trouble with ceremony, we've already pledged our troth to each other. For the present, our handfasting is sufficient."

At this mention of handfasting, Elisabeth felt her heart wrenching and her womb clenching. She turned away to hide her discomfort and regain her self-control.

"But what will the archbishop say? And your sister? What will Katherine say?"

"As long as I'm discreet, my uncle will turn a blind eye. My beloved Marion will become Mistress of Ethie Castle in Angus. No more grace and favour for her. And she's even agreed to take on my two bairns! On condition there will be no more. At least from any other mistress." His eyes twinkled mischievously. "As for Katherine, well, I am sure that once she meets Marion she, too, will be smitten."

If she consented to meet her, for Katherine was as rigid in her morals as her brother was flexible in his.

"And what of our little crusade against Lord Hay? Has that come to naught?" she enquired. "Or did you lose your head as well as your heart in the Edinburgh court?"

"The Wizard of Goblin Ha" won't be casting his evil eye on you again. The case has been dropped. At the behest of Angus himself."

Elisabeth bridled at the mention of his name but Beaton raised a cautionary hand. Despite being in the throes of an acrimonious divorce from Margaret Tudor, who now wanted to marry her groomsman, Henry Stewart, a younger son of Lord Avondale and a distant cousin of her deceased husband, Archie Douglas had shown some sympathy for her case.

"To think I traded white spun gold for brazen brass, a delicate Scots harebell for a coarse English drab. What a fool I was! She must have bewitched me with one of her love philtres, the witch. That I could have mistaken a puddock for a princess," the morose Angus had muttered. "And Hay is lording it over St. Mary's is he? He may be my brother-in-law but John Hay is a conniving rogue, as curly and crooked as Auld Clootie's horns. Let him dare meddle with the Hepburns and he meddles with me," he growled and ordered Hay to desist from pursuing his case forthwith.

When Beaton thanked him, Angus had replied, "Small recompense, small recompense."

"What do you think he meant by that?"

Elisabeth sighed and shook her head. Was it possible that the treacherous Archie might be feeling remorse for Meg's untimely death?

"Ah, well. *Requiescat in pace* to that case," Beaton said, giving her a mock blessing.

"Aye," she murmured, "and *Requiescat in pace*, my dearest sister Meg."

PART THREE

I

The Complaint

> After that I the lang winters nicht
> Had lyne waking, in to my bed, alone,
> Through heavy thocht, that no way sleep I micht
> Remembering of divers things gone.
>
> *The Complaint*
> Sir David Lindsay, 16ᵗʰ Century

Garleton Castle, December 1527

The goose feather quill kept slipping from his chilled fingers and the ink, crushed and pounded from oak gallnuts, had frozen in its pot. Galling indeed, and while these bile blisters might reflect his bitter mood, where was the use in registering his resentment in rhyme? Lindsay threw down his quill and pulled his Yuletide gift from Margaret Tudor more tightly round him. The expensive cloak of dark red velvet, trimmed with fox fur, was a peace offering to show that the queen mother bore him no ill feeling.

Waddling across to the casement window of the oratory where he wrote, he peeked out. The dark clouds louring in the moonless January sky threatened snow. With a shiver he turned towards the ingle to rake together the last dying embers. The wind howled in the chimneybreast. Another sleepless night.

The wine he'd drunk at supper had put him to sleep at first but then he'd woken up, wakerife and unrested, in the early hours of the morning. A feeling of deep unease crushed him. Where was he going? What was the point of his life? He'd soon be approaching his fortieth year. Two score already. One score more and ten of his span left. Why did the pace of life speed up as he grew older? Like climbing a hill – a long, trauchlesome scramble to the top, followed by a decline as swift as Lisbeth's high-spirited tumble down the brae.

Since James's birth, on the twelfth of April 1512, he'd never left the monarch's side. Ever the faithful servant, Lindsay had carried the infant to his coronation at Stirling, had soothed him through nights of painful teething, had bathed and dressed his skinned knees. But, worried that he had become too close to her son, the queen mother had dismissed Lindsay from royal service. She had given his position of master usher to Andrew Stewart, a distant cousin of James IV, and whose brother, Henry, so gossipmongers whispered, had replaced Angus in her bedchamber.

Palace of Holyrood

It had saddened Lindsay to leave the palace that James IV had built for his Tudor bride. With a lump in his throat, Lindsay had been packing up his books and manuscripts, pens and parchments, when the young James had lumbered in, armed to the hilt with the various hunting gifts his English uncle, Henry VIII, had sent him. One of them was not to the twelve-year-old King of Scots satisfaction, however.

"And I've requested an English buckler," he declared, screwing up his nose at the miniature sword dangling from one finger. "One fit for a man and not a toy for a boy."

Disappointed, Lindsay shook his head. What of his singing and dancing? Had he forgotten those skills, so delighting the visiting English ambassador that he'd given good report to his uncle Henry? Lindsay's remarks fell on deaf ears. As his personal wappinschaw clearly demonstrated, weapons of war were more to the young monarch's taste than the arts, a taste being encouraged by his new guardians. Had they all forgotten that it was his father's zealous devotion to the cult of chivalry that had been his undoing?

"And poetry? What about the songs and verses I sang to you?"

"The Earl of Angus's brother is to take charge of my schooling now and he says that poetry is for lovelorn milksops."

"Indeed. And by learning the honourable George Douglas of Pittendreich doesn't mean Latin, Greek and Grammar, but wine, women and wastreling."

For protesting too much, Lindsay had been banished to his lands at Garleton, leaving the Douglas faction free to abuse power for their own profit and advancement. Now there would be no-one to give the young monarch good advice.

Imprudently, like witless fools,
They took that young Prince from the schools.

But what was the use of penning a *Complaint* if it was never read?

Stamping his feet in cold and frustration, Lindsay trampled on his fallen quill and groaned. Was it a sign that he should give up his task? As he examined his broken quill, a loud banging from below disturbed him: the metal knocker was clanging insistently against the oak door. Opening the shutter slightly, he peeked out to see a man at the main door, clapping his arms vigorously against his chest. One of Angus's men, Lindsay assumed, and was about to warn the doorkeeper not to open up at such a late hour. But then, he reconsidered, if the regent had wanted rid of him, he wouldn't have sent one solitary brigand with his sword sheathed.

"The Master of Hailes has sent me," the man cupped his hands to call up to the window. Melting snow dripped from the messenger's boots as he delivered his warning.

Angus was on the rampage. Constant challenges to his authority were trying the regent's patience and he was now marauding his way through the land, dinging down anyone who opposed him. Already the Earl of Lennox had been slain for attempting to abduct the king and David Beaton flung in prison for his part in the conspiracy. Closer to home, Bolton Castle had been burnt to the ground, on suspicion that the Master of Hailes was harbouring rebels.

Now Angus was setting his sights on Lindsay. In her divorce petition, Margaret Tudor, was claiming that James IV was still alive and had not been slain at Flodden. The tale at the time about four mysterious horsemen carrying the king off the field was true, she insisted, and James was on pilgrimage to the Holy Land, doing penance for his sins. However fanciful her grounds might be, Angus feared that if they were divorced, he would lose the regency and guardianship of the young king would be entrusted to someone else.

"And so Angus thinks I might be a possible candidate? I should be flattered but I'd rather not cross swords with such a formidable foe as Archie Douglas," Lindsay said. "And what about you, Harry Cockburn? Are you a rebel?"

Though now broad shouldered and bearded, Harry's distinctive red hair, long and straggly and tied untidily at the neck with a piece of hempen string, betrayed him. After fleeing the abbey watchmen, he'd joined a band of border reivers, charged with keeping order in Liddesdale, though changing sides depending on whoever paid them. Now he was in the pay of John Hepburn, Master of Hailes.

"A rebel?" Harry frowned as he thought about this. Then he broke into a wide grin displaying broken, blackened teeth. "That I am, Sir David, for I'm aye the king's loyal subject. And Angus is intent on redding out his enemies. That's why ..." He broke off at the sound of drumming hooves in the courtyard. When they heard raised voices and doors being kicked open, Harry drew his sword and melted into the shadows.

As he rushed downstairs, Lindsay's way was barred by a scruffy looking soldier.

"I'm captain of the royal guard," he bawled by way of greeting.

Indeed? Noting the shabby canvas jerkin and lack of any insignia, Lindsay doubted it — or standards were slipping at the royal palace.

"Make yourself ready, Sir David," he commanded. "His Grace has called for you."

"His Grace?" Lindsay queried.

"Aye. King James himself commands you to come at once."

The slight movement of the captain's hand towards the hilt of his sword alerted Lindsay. There should be no need for coercion if it were true.

Happit in his royal velvet cloak, he was bundled out into the murky, mucky January night. The biting wind tore at his face as they rode down the hill towards Aberlady, but when they turned right instead of left, his fears were confirmed. So, they were travelling eastwards along the coast and not westwards towards Edinburgh and the king. Above the gale, he could hear waves pounding against the cliffs – Tantallon crags, no doubt. With a sudden whack, the rider next to him slapped the flank of his horse.

"His horse is affrighted. I'll go after him," a voice yelled.

Lindsay galloped towards the cliff edge pursued by the rider who grabbed hold of the spooked horse's bridle to slow it down.

"Lowp off when I tell you," Harry ordered. "Now!"

Again he spanked the horse's flanks and, as it reared up, Lindsay was thrown off. His knees buckled under as he hit the ground and he tumbled over, rolling dangerously close to the rocky escarpment.

"He's tumbled over the cliff," he heard Harry's voice shouting above the gale. "Shall I go after him?"

"Nay, leave him to the crags and gulls. Saves us the trouble. But go after his mount; that's of mair worth."

Lindsay crawled on his hands and knees, groping his way along the cliff. The driving rain had turned to sleet and, with his head and face wrapped in the hood of his cloak, he could only see a few inches in front of him. Divots had softened his fall and stopped him from plunging over the edge but if he lost his footing he'd fall to his death. Finding a narrow ledge he contorted himself into the cramped space to wait.

Out of the mist she drifted slowly towards him, her face a hazy blur until she came near. Kate? Her smile changed to bewildered sadness before gradually fading. Lisbeth! He jolted himself awake.

He strained to raise himself up but dampness had seeped through every bone and sinew. To ease the cramps in his creaking joints, he rubbed his arms and legs vigorously and then cocooned himself tightly in his cloak. After a while he began to feel pleasantly drowsy. To sleep was all he desired and to dream of his beloved Lisbeth, but he couldn't conjure her face up from the fog of his memory:

What was her name? She answered courteously.

"Dame Remembrance," she said, "called I am."

II

The Clerk's Play

> John come kiss me noo,
> John come kiss me by and by
> And make no more ado.
> *Song,* Traditional

Haddington, Yuletide 1528

"Cross my palm with silver, young master, and I'll tell your fate."

The young gypsy lass stood, legs astride, blocking his path, her dark eyes fixed on him with a bold stare. She held out a grimy hand from under a garishly coloured shawl. When Knox tried to push past her, she grabbed hold of his elbow.

"Cross my palm, young master," she wheedled.

"Begone, wretched carlin. I'll have no dealings with spae wives and witches," the indignant cleric replied, trying to shake her off. "How can you see what the future holds for me in the palm of my hand? Only The Lord God Almighty kens our destiny."

"The devil swarbit on you, for it is bad luck to spurn one of our folk." Her black eyes flashed with anger. "There's no fleeing from fate." As he tried to brush her aside she slipped the shawl down to bare a nut-brown shoulder and winked at him. "And mark this, young sir, our paths will cross again afore the day is out."

Knox was staring after her, bemused, when a guildsman ran up to him, shouting, "Master Knox! Master Knox! Come at once."

Outside the abbey a protracted argument about the order of precedence was delaying the Christ's Mass procession. By long-standing tradition and a regular payment, the bakers had always marched immediately behind the clerics carrying the Black Madonna. While the masons and the wrights were arguing for a change, the bakers were digging in their heels.

The baillie was beyond making a sensible judgement. Befuddled from too much mulled ale, he swayed back and forth trying to gather his wits and recall which side had given him the biggest bribe. The whole procession had now come to a standstill and the guildsmen were looking to Master Knox for the way forward.

A friar who'd been following the wranglings with interest, hobbled over on a crutch. He took the flummoxed cleric aside and whispered in his ear. Knox listened attentively, nodded and then turned to address the thrawn guildsmen.

"Here's what must be done, brothers. This is a religious procession, is it no?"

There was no disputing that.

"In which you must all take part as brethren?"

Again heads nodded.

"No one guild being above any other?"

That was more controversial, especially to the bakers.

"Then you shall process together in oxters, as brothers."

Knox then linked up a member of each guild so that a mason, a wright, a smith and a hammerman walked in line, arm in arm. All except the disgruntled bakers, who stood their ground, threatening to withdraw altogether if they weren't given precedence. The friar again hobbled forward, to address them himself this time. Recognising the habit of the Observantine Friars of St.Francis who had the reputation of being highly trained in canon law, the guildsmen listened to him.

"Hark at my words! For the offence of refusing to take part in a holy procession the parish priest will impose a penalty of forty shillings sterling."

A blow at their pockets changed the minds of the bakers who agreed to process – on condition that they linked up only with their own. In that case, the friar insisted, they'd have to march at the back behind the others. Finally setting out, the procession trudged towards the marketplace where a convoy of carts was forming a circle.

"Make way for the Clerk's Play! Make way for the Clerk's Play!"

The crowd surged forward, jostling each other for a better view. To resurrect some Christian significance from the pagan Yule festivities, the Church encouraged the local trade guilds to put on Biblical tableaux under the direction of the clergy. These clerk's plays were performed as early as possible in the day – before too much drink paralysed the masqueraders and stupefied the audience.

This year, instead of the usual dumb shows – silent, unmoving tableaux – Knox had written scripts for the players to perform. He'd spent hours translating Gospel texts into the vernacular for the common folk to understand more easily. Rehearsals had been shambolic since few of the guildsmen could read and could only memorise their lines by constant repetition.

A blast of a trumpet signalled the start of the Guild of Wheelwrights' contribution: the Annunciation. Toiling to flap his makeshift wings, the Archangel Gabriel lumbered gracelessly in front of the kneeling Virgin who clasped her hands to her heart in wonder.

"Hail Mary, do not be afeart," Gabriel boomed.

"Of course she's afeart. What lass wouldn't take fright at a muckle hooded craw such as thon?"

Paying the heckler no heed, Gabriel went on, "Behold, the Lord is with thee. Blessed art thou among women for thou art chosen to bear the Son of God."

"How can this be?" Mary piped up. Well past the first flush of youth, the wheelwright's wife squeaked her lines in a high-pitched voice to suggest *virgo intacta*.

"Surely you ken by now, mistress? If your guid man cannot kittle you up, there's one here that will!" the heckler jeered.

Undaunted, Gabriel continued with his speech in the singsong intonation he considered appropriate to the script: "The Holy Ghost will come down to bless your womb with his holy rod."

"The Holy Ghost's holy rod!" the heckler hollered. "Shouldn't Joseph the wood-wright be the one to bore his shaft into her dook-hole?" The rabble hooted and waggled their fingers in obscene gestures.

Knox leapt onto the makeshift stage and yelled, "Enough of this mockery! Bedone with this blasphemy! You're making a bauchle of the Holy Scripture. I warn you. Take heed of the Word of the Lord, lest your immortal souls be damned to the flames of hell."

"Master Knox seems fair put out, poor lad. Look at him lowping up and down like a freshly caught finnock. Johnnie, my lad, don't be such a marfeast," the heckler shouted back. "Spare the preaching for Sunday Mass. For at Yuletide, the Abbot of Unreason and the Monk of Misrule hold court! Let the devil take us till the auld year's wede awa'!"

Then, casting off their rôles and ditching their badly rehearsed lines, the players began improvising, responding to the hecklers with increasingly lewd wisecracks.

Despairing of the mob's profanity, Knox abandoned the Annunciation to attend the Nativity. A more respectful audience – mostly women – were cooing and clucking over the chubby little infant in the crib. But the boisterous rabble was running amok and no mercy was spared for the newly delivered mother of Christ.

"Hark at her: mild as mead. And whose wean is she nursing in her arms? The father could be one of any number. And, mark my words, it's no the angel Gabriel."

Meanwhile, the despot Herod's cruel order to slaughter all babes under two years old had infuriated his audience who were bombarding him with food scraps. Herod's rage at being duped by the Three Wise Men was as nothing compared to Knox's wrath. In a voice hoarse with fury, he railed at them until something slimy and wet smacking the side of his face silenced him. He jumped off the cart, his blue eyes blazing and fists flailing ready to take on whoever had thrown the haddock. The jeering revellers grabbed his arms and spun him round till his head was birling.

"Jocky Knox, high on the cnocks,
Maun take the knocks.
Jocky Knox – you're unco sma',
Are you going awa" to tell your ma?
Jocky Knox – who's your ma?
Nay, whore's your ma!
Your ma's your holy sister!
Where's your ma, your holy ma?

In behind the priory wa',
In the whorehoose,
Of the lemand Lamp o' Lothian!"

They pushed and pulled him, hither and thither, towting and taunting until he tripped and fell on the greasy cobbles. He was in danger of being trampled underfoot when he was grabbed by the collar and pulled clear of the mockrife mob. The friar set him on his feet and then turned back to tackle his tormentors, letting fly with his crutch and whacking whoever got in his way.

Knox took refuge in the vennel where he leant against the wall to catch his breath. Out of the shadows staggered the gypsy girl who'd clearly been spending her earnings in the tavern. Her shawl, having slipped even further down from her shoulders, was now tied loosely round her waist. The lace on her thin cotton blouse had come undone, revealing one pink nipple that poked out provocatively, with the other threatening to do so. Just a touch and it, too, would pop out.

"Did I no tell you we'd meet again? Come on, Johnnie lad," she slurred. "Let's see what the future holds. It can do you no harm. What's for you will no go by you."

A slattern, he told himself in an effort to control the feelings she stirred, slovenly and unclean. These "light" women, hussies of easy virtue and loose morals were the butt of smutty jokes by the grammar school lads curious about tail-toddle, though he tried not to listen to their smickering for he was to be a priest. He had to keep his mind and body clean and dared not be tempted by sins of the flesh. Forbye, his godmother had drummed it into him to respect women.

But sluts such as this gypsy spaewife were of a different order. Heathens, unbelievers who traded in superstitions and sold their bodies for drink were beneath contempt. Yet he couldn't take his eyes off her naked breasts. What harm would it do to hear her prophecy? No more dangerous than listening to Betsy. And wasn't unreason the rule at Yule? Stricken numb he couldn't push her away when she took hold of his elbow.

With a furtive glance to check that no-one was watching, he let himself be led further into the vennel. The hand that stroked his palm was ingrained with dirt, the fingernails embedded with filth. Her unkempt, oily hair stank of wood smoke. Her skirt, high-kiltit to the knee, revealed bare legs streaked with the ordure of the street. She was wild and wanton. A pagan. A heathen. But she had lustrous cherry lips, licked moist by her tongue and deep, dark, lustful eyes. As if bewitched, he let his right hand be caressed by the seductress.

"This palm tells who you are, but yours is gey difficult to read. I see you can be a bit trauchlesome and quick to take offence. You can be standfray and thrawn when it suits. Aye, you are indeed a true Taurus. The horned bull."

"Ha!" he scoffed, "There you are mistaken. The ale has bleared your second sight.

I was born on St. Andrew's feast day. Under the sign of Sagittarius."

Scraping her greasy hair out of her eyes, she squinted at him sceptically. "Nay," she insisted, "the palm never lies. Those born beneath the Archer are flichty and fickle but a Taurus is stockit and steady, bull-horned and thrawn. Like you are. And it's all here, scrievit on your palm. Are you sure you're your mother's bairn?"

The mob's ignorant jeers, questioning his maternity, he'd always shrugged off as a common enough insult, but her chuckling insinuation struck a nerve. Knox snatched his hand away.

"Well then, let's see what lies afore you."

Quick as lightning she'd grasped his left hand and was tracing the lines on his palm. "I see a long life, but not without its troubles. You will thole great pain which will skaith your health."

The soft tickling of her hand was sending exquisite shivers up his spine: he could hardly take in what she was saying.

"Ach, but this is of more note. Look, see where this line severs."

Unwillingly, Knox tore his eyes away from the fleshy mounds of her breasts and glanced at the line she was etching on his palm.

"I foresee two great loves in your life but you'll have to choose between them. It will be a great wrench from one to another. What'ere you decide, once you've chosen, there will be no going back. You're a man of strong character. That I can see clearly."

As she stared at him, her dark, knowing eyes seemed to penetrate his soul.

"Ha! But you can't see that I'm a prelate! I can never marry, and I'll have no doings with women."

"Women? Did I speak of women? There can be other loves in a man's life, apart from quines." The fortune-teller smiled enigmatically, squeezing his hand. "But if you cross my hand with mair silver, I'll show how a wench can take you to paradise. Here. On earth. In this very vennel," she murmured, slipping her blouse down to expose the other brown-ringed nipple.

As she tweaked and twiddled her teat, making it ripe for the sucking, Knox gawped, painfully aware of a throbbing in his loins. Then, when she threw her head back and flicked out her tongue, his body moved forward of its own volition.

"Master Knox! What are you doing up here Strumpet's Close? Unyoke thon cow-clink and come quick. While you've been fyking, your friar friend's been flayed alive."

A crowd had gathered round the friar lying face down, kissing the causey indeed. As Knox pulled back his cowl, the blood from his matted hair dribbled onto the icy cobbles, freezing into tiny red rubies.

"Fetch a cart," he shouted to the contrite-looking guildsmen, "and take him to the abbey infirmary. At once."

159

III

Resurrection

Because I see thy spirit, without measure,
So sore perturbit by melancholy,
Causing thy corps to wax cauld and dry
Therefore get up, and gang anone with me.

The Dream
Sir David Lindsay, 16th Century

St.Mary's Abbey, January 1528

"No men are to be admitted here: dead or alive. You, more than anyone, should ken the rules, John. Take him away to the friars at St.Laurence. They take in all and sundry. Let them bring him back to life, if they will, or bury him if necessary."

As Knox opened his mouth to protest, Sister Katherine turned on her heels and clattered off across the courtyard. Whenever the prioress went to Edinburgh, the stern Sister Katherine was in charge and there was no gainsaying her. The prioress was visiting her sister at the convent of St.Catherine of Siena, which, now that her son had come of age, Lady Joanna was free to enter. Impressed by the "City of Ladies" at St.Mary's she, too, wanted to establish a hospice and sought Elisabeth's advice.

"He saved me from the rabble," Knox explained to Sister Agnes who had lingered behind. "And now he needs my help. We cannot send him away."

Sister Agnes loosened the top of the friar's habit to ease his breathing and put her ear to his chest to listen for a heartbeat. As she fumbled with the lacing, her fingers got tangled up in a cord round his neck. A holy scapular she assumed, with its intricate knot symbolising some Celtic saint, perhaps.

"Take him in," Sister Agnes said, "and don't worry about Sister Katherine. I'll speak to her."

The friar looked out of place in the women's infirmary. The bed was too small for him and his feet dangled over the edge. Agnes was fearful of bending his legs, one of which must be lame since he'd been using a crutch. Running her fingers over his chest, she detected a few broken ribs. His face was badly bruised, his eyes swollen and cheekbone probably cracked. Agnes was more worried about the head injuries that might affect his sight, or worse still, the delicate workings of the brain.

It was strange, she thought as she parted his hair, that it hadn't been tonsured, but perhaps that wasn't the custom in his particular order of friars. Gently she applied poultices of knitbone to reduce the swelling and comfrey leaves to ease the bruising, and then swathed his head in a bandage.

"How is he?" Knox's anxiety was mixed with feelings of guilt and shame for being the cause of the friar's injuries. If he hadn't loitered with the gypsy girl, he might have been able to come to his aid earlier.

"He hasn't opened his eyes yet. I fear that if he doesn't come round soon then ..."

"Then what?" Knox yelped.

"Then it could be that he never will. It's hard to say how badly he's been injured."

"When will we know?"

"The next four and twenty are the reckoning hours. Watch over him with care. And pray," Sister Agnes added as she went off to rest, leaving Knox to keep vigil.

Crouched on a stool by the bedside, he sponged the friar's parched lips with weak ale, all the while keeping alert for the slightest change: the flickering of an eyelid, the movement of a finger, a change in his breathing. Under his breath he kept reciting a simple prayer: Please God, let him live – and I vow never again to tangle with a lass. In the early hours, before matins, Sister Katherine passed on her rounds. After one look at the lolling head and grey face, she sent John to fetch the priest.

"We've done what we can for his body. He's in God's hands now. For the sake of his immortal soul, he should be given the last rites."

Father Dudgeon lay like a streekit corpse on his cot where he'd collapsed, fully clothed, to sleep off the excesses of his Yuletide spree. A few drops of cold water splashed onto his face weren't enough to revive him. "Extreme measures for Extreme Unction," Knox muttered as he emptied a whole bucket to resurrect him.

Sister Katherine's nose twitched as she caught the smell of drink on the priest's boozy breath. Since he could hardly say his own name, never mind administer the last sacrament, Knox had to guide his shaking hand to anoint the friar's eyes, ears, nostrils, mouth and hands – the five portals through which sin could pass. Sister Katherine scowled as the dithering priest dribbled the holy oils all over the bedsheets and clumsily tried to cram the sacred host between the dying man's lips.

As Father Dudgeon slurred the sacred words of the prayer of consolation for the dying, she fretted that they wouldn't be valid. Would his garbled rendition guarantee three years" indulgence from the torments of purgatory or would it be seized upon by the demon, *Titivallus*, and carted off to hell to be registered as a sin? Just in case, she nudged John and asked him to recite the *De Profundis*, the powerful prayer that struck fear and awe into the soul but also made the flesh creep.

"*Out of the depths I have cried to thee, O Lord. Lord, hear my voice ...*"

"So, my time has come," a feeble voice grumbled from the depths of the pillows. His eyelids fluttered before slowly opening. In the pearly light of dawn, the candles were guttering, the smell of incense and oils pervaded the room and, in the dim light, a winged angel hovered before him.

"Gabriel," he managed to say and sank back again.

"He speaks." Sister Katherine blessed herself, *"Deo Gratias."*

Knox chortled. "He thinks he's already in heaven."

"He'll need to make a contrite confession first." As Father Dudgeon swayed over him, the patient again stirred.

"As long as I'm not in purgatory: that's the last place I'd wish to be. Hell would be preferable to an eternity of uncertainty."

Knox suppressed a snigger. "Have no fear. You're still among the quick, not the dead."

The patient nodded and smiled weakly. Sister Agnes's fears that his mental faculties might be impaired were proving to be unfounded. In spite of his frailty, the friar was revealing a dark sense of humour, a good sign that his spark of life would not be easily extinguished.

Sticking out his tongue, the friar followed the blessed wafer, wavering in the priest's trembling hand until it landed between his teeth. Sister Katherine shook her head. That such a man be allowed to handle the sacred Body of Christ, without having slept off his debauchery, was a disgrace. But if the friar could keep down the Eucharist without heaving it up, then he would survive. Knox tilted forward his bandaged head so that he could take a sip of the consecrated wine.

"Ah that's good. I can feel the blood of life seeping back into me."

Meanwhile, to ensure that no drop of Christ's blood remained to be defiled by the unsanctified and to cure his own dirling head, Father Dudgeon was draining the chalice to the dregs.

IV

Purification

> Take manly courage and leave thine insolence,
> And use counsel of noble dame Prudence
> Found thee firmly on faith and fortitude.
>
> *The Dream*
> Sir David Lindsay, 16th Century

St. Mary's Abbey, Candlemas 1528

"Why is John not at St. Andrews?" Sister Agnes asked, as they left the chapel after early Mass. "Has there been an outbreak of some disease?"

"My brother would say so," Sister Katherine replied, pursing her lips. "A serious rash of heresy which, on this feast of Our Blessed Virgin's Purification, he plans to clear up."

Beaton had, indeed, dispersed the students to all the airts, sending them home until he'd eradicated the perfidious ideas circulating at the university.

"Well, at least he can continue his studies with Friar Lazarus. He seems a knowledgeable and skilful tutor."

Sister Katherine bit her tongue. Though she'd given in to Sister Agnes's cajoling and allowed him to stay until he recovered, she was wary of the time John spent with the convalescing friar.

As Friar Lazarus stumped along on his crutch on his daily walk, Knox shuffled wearily behind. He was cold, tired and out of temper. The freezing hail whipped his cheeks and then melted down his neck. He pulled his felt scholar's cap down round his ears and blew on his chilblained fingers before tucking them under his oxters. He'd been up long before daybreak to serve at Mass for the nuns in the chapel, afterwards crossing the bridge to join the congregation at St. Mary's Parish Church.

As a chorister at St. Andrews Cathedral, sitting in the choir stalls in front of the rood screen, he was separated from the riff-raff but, standing with the lay folk in the body of the kirk, he'd been taken aback by their constant yatter. Only when the *Sanctus* bell rang to signal the raising of the Holy Eucharist did they fall silent.

Friar Lazarus cast a sideways glance at the lad who kept rubbing his eyes, bleary from lack of sleep and yawning.

"Come, enough rambling in the chilly wind for today."

While Knox glaised his hands by the fire in the guest's chamber – a comfort not allowed in his own tiny cell – the friar poured some wine into a skillet, stirred in cinnamon and cloves and set it to heat gently on the embers. Even the rich, spicy smell was warming enough.

"You could try pissing on your mouls, John. They say that cures the itch."

Knox quickly drew his hands away and cupped them round the tassie that the friar held out. Chilblains were the scholar's scourge. Too cold and the fingers couldn't hold a quill, too hot and the fiery mouls throbbed beyond forbearance.

"Why do we have services in Latin that the lay folk cannot understand? Who can blame them for blethering behind the back of a drunken, unlearned priest who barely understands it himself, since he's learned it all by rote. Parrot fashion. The prioress's parakeet has more understanding of the Bible than Father Dudgeon. His sermons are all: Thou shalt not do this; Thou shalt not do that, with no explanation of Holy Scripture. Is it any wonder that the folk have contempt for the clergy? They drag themselves to Mass, not from any sense of devotion, but for fear of hell and eternal damnation."

The friar smiled sympathetically at this fourteen-year-old lad, full of youthful enthusiasm and proselytising zeal. Those ever-vigilant dark blue een, the far-seeing eyes of a prophet, smouldered when his dander was up. No wonder he was tired; kept awake at night by his righteous indignation.

"Then it is the clergy who are in need of reform," Friar Lazarus suggested. "Teach them first and then we can teach the faithful."

"My tutor John Mair would agree with you. But he says that the Church fathers have no interest in doing so but strive to keep the mystery to themselves."

Too late Knox's hand flew to his lips. He shouldn't have mentioned Mair who was one of those being persecuted by Beaton for his sacrilegious teachings, but to his astonishment, the friar agreed.

"Aye, he's right and not only that. Priests pilfering from the poor and friars living off the fat of the land cloistered behind high walls have become too grasping and greedy."

"Contrary to their vow of poverty, but you aren't one of them. Tell me, why did you become a Franciscan?"

Friar Lazarus mulled over the question before replying. "Because I believe in the principles of St. Francis of Assisi. He established the order so as to preach the true word to the common folk. Our order has strict rules."

"Unlike the Franciscan Friary here that they cry the lemand Lamp of Lothian." Knox's face reddened, ashamed that he may have offended him.

"Aye, you're right," the friar surprisingly agreed. "Sadly, ribaldry and debauchery are mockrife in monasteries where they are in thrall to Dame Sensual and throw out Dame Chastity. In the words of one of our makars:

> "Soon they forget to study, pray and preach,
> And think it a pain poor people for to teach."

Knox laughed and then quickly covered his mouth with his hand. Bashfully he lowered his eyes to ask "Forgive me for asking, but do you find it hard to keep this vow?"

The friar hesitated. "Aye, we all do, lad."

"For I have a confession to make," Knox mumbled, still refusing to look up.

Again the friar paused. "Confession? You may tell me what is on your mind, John, though I may not be able to give you absolution. Only your confessor can do that."

Heaven forfend that his sin could not be absolved. Knox winced as he scratched at his chilblains. "At the Yuletide fair I was accosted by a lass," he blurted.

"What lad has not been given the glad eye by a lass at a fair?" Friar Lazarus winked.

"But she was a gypsy and offered to read my palm."

"And did she tell you anything of interest? Don't fret, John. The Church, like Fortune herself, turns a blind eye when the ignorant rabble seek carnival and revelry to thole their drearisome existence."

Knox's brow furrowed as he tried to follow the friar's reasoning.

"But surely the future cannot already be set down? If, as the Church says, we have free will, then we must work out our own fate."

"Ah, the age-old dilemma that so unsettled St. Augustine has been bothering the Church for centuries," the Friar nodded. "And since they cannot solve it, they decry it as heresy."

When blood oozed from his itchy chilblains, the friar leaned forward and tapped him on the fingers. Grimacing, Knox shoved his hands under his oxters.

"But I jalouse that it is neither the Augustinian heresy nor the Church's stance on fortune-telling that is troubling you, John." The friar's eyes twinkled. "Did the gypsy lass offer to stroke more than your palm?"

The lad's reddened eyelids blinked uncontrollably and he blushed to the roots of his hair. How could he confess to the unchaste thoughts about the half-naked gypsy girl with her black flirting eyes and flaunting ruby lips that buzzed in his brain? Even now he twitched uncomfortably as he felt his pistle harden at the thought of her provocative breasts and the brown buds of her nipples. A sheen of sweat glistened on his forehead.

Until recently, chastity had just been a word for one of the vows he'd have to take as a cleric. He'd foreseen no difficulties being forbidden to marry for he had no desire to procreate. His destiny was to live by the spirit. Yet now his body was betraying him and he was unable to control these perturbing, physical sensations aroused by the gypsy girl. The first inklings of lust, he suspected, and therefore sinful.

Friar Lazarus leant closer and whispered confidentially. "You've been taught, I'm sure, that chastity symbolises purity and that celibacy enables the clergy to devote all their time and energy to Christ's ministry. But Luther believes there is no need for clerics to remain chaste."

Knox leapt from his seat as if scalded. Even to utter the heretic's name was blasphemous. He glanced nervously around, fearing that they might have been overheard.

"Nowhere in his teaching does Christ mention celibacy and Luther has exposed the Church's reason behind it. Realising that its wealth was being dispersed whenever the children of clergy inherited, the Vatican forbade them to marry. Celibacy then became a convenient piece of dogma, enshrined in canon law for the enrichment of Rome."

Knox gawped at Friar Lazarus. That a cleric should suggest that the rules of the Church were not set in stone and that the Church fathers could invent articles of faith to their own advantage was not only shocking but teetered on heresy.

"In all earnest, John, until Rome changes its mind again, now is the time to decide whether or not you want to follow a religious path. Such feelings won't melt away. Not unless you are libbed like a bull-segg. Only you can decide whether you are strong enough to conquer them. But bear in mind, yon gypsy girl with her flashing eyes doesn't promise love but raw, naked lust."

Knox looked away. Whatever else might have diverted him from his spiritual path, he hadn't reckoned on this sexual power of the female to lead him astray.

"Though it may feel as if you are spitting into the wind, John, you must not give up your vocation."

V

Inquisition

Anger punishes itself.
Proverb

St.Mary's Abbey, 14 February 1528

Pacing up and down the aisle of the chapel, Abbot Beaton brandished a heavy cane aimlessly in the air with his right hand, while his left hand kept rubbing the side of his face. Damned toothache. He prided himself on being able to withstand any measure of pain, but not this constant nag. His right cheek was beginning to swell and his whole head was throbbing from not enough sleep and too much cognac, though no amount of the precious French brandy seemed to quell the maddening pain.

He took another swig from the silver flask hidden within his robes and ordered Knox to kneel, hands clasped in front, head bowed. He then grabbed at the short tuft of hair encircling the postulant's tonsure and jerked his head back, forcing him to look upon the statue of the Black Madonna.

"Before you answer my questions, you will swear to Almighty God and his Holy Mother to tell the truth."

With his thrapple constricted, Knox could only mumble the oath.

"Louder," Beaton bellowed, as much to drown out the throbbing pain in his cheek as to intimidate the penitent.

From under his dark eyebrows Knox scowled. He neither liked nor trusted this extravagantly dressed priest who, since his uncle's promotion to archbishop, was ruling the roost at St.Andrews. The Abbot of Arbroath's overweening behaviour had angered many of the students: the more so for discontinuing their studies and sending them all home.

"Look at me when you answer," Beaton now commanded and twisted his head round. "The light of the soul shines through the eyes. Let's see whether or not you are full of the darkness of evil and deceit."

He let go of his hair and stood before him, his legs apart, languorously stroking the large cane. He circled his victim slowly before asking.

"Do you believe in the one true catholic and apostolic church?" The words stumbled from his tongue thick and swollen with pain.

Knox nodded.

"Did you not hear me? You will respond as a Christian and not as a heathen donkey."

"Credo in unam sanctam catholicam et apostolicam Ecclesiam," Knox recited the words of the Creed.

"And do you believe that the teachings of Jesus Christ – as written in the Gospels – are the word of Our Lord Our God?"

"I do believe," Knox mumbled back.

"And do you believe that the doctrines of this one, true, Catholic and apostolic church founded by Christ Himself should be meddled with, by those who call themselves servants of the Lord?"

Flummoxed by the question, Knox was about to nod his head, but swiftly shook it instead. The abbot was well-kent as a wily tactician and practised inquisitor.

"You have heard of the heretic Martin Luther and his satanic Theses?"

Beaton had moved closer and was lifting his chin with the cane.

"Aye." Knox shrank back from the strong brandy fumes, "But he has been condemned as an enemy of the one true Church."

"And excommunicated. And his soul will be condemned to the eternal fires of hell. Along with those of his infernal legion," Beaton roared. "Amongst them the treacherous heretic, Patrick Hamilton."

Knox stiffened. It was one thing to condemn the German reformer, Martin Luther, as a devil's disciple. His face was unknown to him, whereas Patrick Hamilton was a popular preacher, a natural leader and inspirational teacher who cared deeply about his religion, unlike many of their jaded ecclesiastical tutors. Illicit copies of his work, *Patrick's Places*, had been circulating secretly among the students at St. Andrews. A fellow student, George Buchanan, had passed it on for him to read, but so far Knox had never dared.

"It is my duty to save you from falling under the evil spell of these reformist ideas. Heresy is like the Black Death which comes like a thief in the night, creeping stealthily under cover of darkness. Sleekit and sly, it spares no-one who is smitten."

Troubled and confused, Knox listened to Beaton with one ear while the other rang with Friar Lazarus's harangue of the clergy who were bringing the Church into disrepute. It was they who were in need of reform, not the organisation itself. Other faithful servants of the Church agreed and were calling for amputation of the infected, decaying parts to save the health of the whole. That would be fatal in Beaton's view.

The Roman Catholic Church was an indivisible body, with Christ as its head, and the clergy and congregation its various limbs: one, holy and whole. As limbs cannot be severed without damage to the body, the Church couldn't sustain the dismemberment of its hierarchy. Such a slow death, blow by blow by a few feckless priests must not be allowed to happen.

"This heretic isn't worth your loyalty," he lowered his voice to an insidious whisper, the hiss of the serpent seducing Eve. "Confess that the reformist Hamilton has poisoned your mind and corrupted your soul and you shall be forgiven and absolved. Your conscience will then be clear."

But would it? If Hamilton were found guilty, he would be burnt at the stake. Cleansing by fire the only punishment for a heretic. Knox couldn't bring himself to testify against such a gentle man who had shown nothing but Christian charity to all those he encountered.

This was taking too long. Why was the lad being so stubborn and thrawn? A stabbing pain through his jaw made Beaton flinch. He desperately needed another numbing shot of cognac. Now. Losing patience, he ordered him to bare his buttocks and bend over. By God, he would thrash a confession out of him. He drew the cane up over his shoulder and struck him several times. Knox bit his lip, drawing blood, but still he didn't cry out. A beating from Beaton would be over soon. The death of an innocent man would be branded on his soul for the rest of his days.

"See how Beelzebub has entered your soul and struck you dumb. We must unleash his power, and loosen your tongue," Beaton ranted as he drew back the cane and brought it down again and again. "And beat the disobedience out of your damned soul."

As the blood rushed to his head, Knox gazed up at the Black Madonna who swam before his eyes. *Salve Regina*, Hail, Queen of Heaven! Give me strength ... For what I am about to receive ...

"Stay your stick, David Beaton," a voice boomed from the rafters – powerful and authoritative. Startled, the abbot glanced upwards but could see no-one. Was it the voice of God rebuking him? Or that of Satan? This accursed toothache was surely unhinging him. He was about to strike the lad again when the cane was knocked from his hand.

On her return from Edinburgh, Elisabeth had been bewildered. First she'd been greeted by Sister Katherine protesting about a brother who'd been admitted to the infirmary against her better judgement and then by Betsy moaning that John was in the infirmary, put there by Sister Katherine's brother. With Betsy trailing after her, she hurried to her chamber to find Beaton helping himself from her stock of rare French cognac.

"Our lad's been battered black and blue," Betsy grumbled. "This one here has given him a fair sackful of sair bones."

Absorbed in rolling the brandy round his tongue and coating the inside of his cheek, Beaton glared back at the insolent old nurse.

"I was acting on the orders of my uncle, the archbishop," he began fixing his eyes on her. "I, for one, defer to my superiors."

Patrick Hamilton, the Abbot of Fearn, had already been brought to his attention two years ago. Suspecting him of having Lutheran sympathies, Beaton had urged his uncle to accuse him of heresy, but the archbishop was reluctant. As the son of Sir Patrick Hamilton and Catherine Stewart, a natural daughter of the Duke of Albany, Hamilton had connections with clout.

Yet that shouldn't shield him from the Vatican's investigation, he berated his uncle. No matter from whose tongue it fell, heresy was heresy and should be ripped out, before it infected the one, true Church. Being too weak and sick to argue, the archbishop washed his hands of the whole business and let his nephew deal with it.

Forewarned of Beaton's suspicions, Hamilton had fled to the continent, but his series of theological propositions setting out Luther's doctrines was being secretly circulated as *Patrick's Places*. Hamilton may have evaded Beaton's net once, but on his return to Scotland, Beaton made sure he wouldn't escape a second time. He set the Dominican Prior, Alexander Campbell, to spy on him and was, himself, gathering evidence to support the charge of heresy. He intended to make an example of him.

"Surely the testimony of your sanctimonious clype, Campbell, will suffice?" Elisabeth declared. "The word of a respected Dominican against a reviled heretic? You don't need a confession thrashed out of a fourteen-year-old lad."

Beaton patted the side of his head several times to stop his ears ringing. Had he heard correctly? Was she defying him? Her impudence was staggering.

"My godson, John, is a devout lad, who intends to dedicate himself to the Church," Elisabeth was saying.

"In which case, his first lesson will be to learn obedience. I'm disappointed that his godmother is not setting a good example."

Elisabeth arched her fine eyebrows. "I've always taught him to listen to his conscience and never be led by falsehood."

"Which is why he needs to be saved from this plague spreading like wildfire across continent. We cannot permit one pestersome priest to corrupt the minds of the young," Beaton ranted. "Our future is at stake. Before heresy becomes rife, it must be stamped out."

"Or beaten out." She smirked.

"Better still – burnt out," Beaton threatened.

A chill ran through her. "You mean to burn Hamilton? And you want John to give evidence in such a trial? I won't allow it. His testimony will not add fuel to your fire. Have the courage to be your own judge, jury and executioner, Abbot Beaton, if you are determined to be rid of Hamilton."

Beaton's eyes narrowed to slits in his puffy face.

"No-one else would dare to question me thus," he said gruffly. "And who is this meddlesome monk who ca'ed the cane from my hand with his crutch? Why is he here?"

"The friar was set upon by a drunken mob and is here to recover from his wounds."

"Indeed." Beaton turned to scowl at Betsy for her cheek in answering.

"It seems our coven has raised Friar Lazarus from the dead. With spells and cantrips, no doubt," Elisabeth added with a wry smile. But the ill-humoured Beaton failed to respond to her witty banter. His face darkened.

"Let me speak with him."

"That's not possible. He's taken a vow of silence," Betsy butted in.

"Not when he bellowed at me, he hadn't." Beaton was rubbing his cheek furiously. "He has no right to be here. I'll send him on his way. Now, this minute."

"He's not fit to leave yet," the nurse had the cheek to say.

Beaton was about to explode at her impudence when she hirpled up to him, and without begging his leave, jammed his head hard against the wall and yanked his mouth open.

"Toothache, they say, is the devil's own punishment. What have you done to deserve this?"

There was no mistaking the wicked glint in her eye but, before Beaton could reply, the old carlin had produced a tool, the like of which he'd only ever seen in the hands of a blacksmith or an inquisitor.

"It doesn't take the second sight to see that yon troublesome tooth will have to come out," she predicted. As she poked around his jaws, sending shards of pain shrieking through his skull, Beaton's head jerked backwards. "If you leave it to rot in your head, then you'll soon ken what suffering is."

A few more measures of brandy were administered before he would agree to endure her primitive surgery. Sister Agnes and his own sister, Katherine, summoned to hold him down, did so with obvious pleasure. Pushing against his chest with one hand and brandishing the instrument of torture with the other, Betsy wrenched with all her might.

"I'd rather my limbs were stretched on the rack and my bones splintered than suffer this," he screamed out.

"What better way to commemorate the martyr St. Valentine than to emulate his suffering?" Elisabeth said sweetly.

Triumphantly Betsy held up the twisted, blackened tooth for him to see.

"That is also my business," he mumbled, his mouth filling up with blood. "To pull out the rotten tooth that infects the body of the Church."

VI

Pride and Grace

Pride and grace ne'er dwelt in the one place.
Proverb

St. Mary's Abbey, 14 February 1528

"But the fatted calf has been prepared," Elisabeth's voice rang out.

Beaton's swollen face contorted into a grimace, whether a smile or scowl was unclear, but he would have to excuse himself from his customary dinner with the prioress. Betsy had stapped the cavity with some putrid smelling substance which she assured him, would eventually dull the pain.

"You are a veritable alchemist. A wizard," he'd groaned as he tried to pour his cognac into the other side of his mouth. Betsy had twitched uncomfortably.

Crawling away like a wounded animal, all he wanted to do was to lie down in a darkened room – in peace. But his sister, Katherine, had found out his bed. While his own tongue niggled away at the bloody cavity, hers nagged at his conscience.

"You'll be renouncing your concubine now that you are about to take Holy Orders," his merciless sister stated rather than asked.

Beaton closed his eyes wearily. It irked him sorely that he hadn't been born with the advantages that others took for granted. It stuck in his craw to think that he had more sense in his pinkie than all those gormless gowks who, by sheer accident of birth, wielded power. With no lands or title, he had to live by his wits and grasp the opportunities that came his way.

As his uncle's secretary, his rôle had been limited, but now that the archbishop was ailing, Beaton had ambitions to take over his post and become Lord Chancellor of the Regency Council. To do so, however, he would need to take Major Orders. As a lay abbot he could marry, but he wouldn't be considered for promotion. It galled him that whereas a king's bastard son might be legitimately appointed to the post of archbishop, Beaton had no such pedigree. He knew that there would be a price to pay for a bishop's mitre, or better still, a cardinal's hat. After all, high office demanded high sacrifices. Though he would willingly renounce matrimony for Holy Orders, he was not prepared to abandon his Lady Marion.

"My dear sister, while you're fretting over my domestic arrangements, the enemies of the Church are battering at her door at this very moment. The forces of evil are not only gathering on the continent but right here on our own doorstep, Henry's Chancellor Wolsey is seeking to swallow us up into the episcopacy of York. But the Scottish Church, the pope's special daughter, is subject only to Rome and we must keep our independence. With such formidable foes louring on the horizon, my home affairs are small salt."

Katherine listened, tight-lipped and scowling, to this tirade.

"None of this excuses you from living in sin and bringing into the world bastard bairns: What doth it profit a man if he gain the whole world ... "

"My bastard bairns, as you call them, will hold important positions in the Church one day. That way, at least, I may be assured of some family loyalty. Now, if you've come only to castigate me, I've endured enough torture for one day."

"So that's your purpose!" she spat out. "To swell episcopal sees with your own spawn!"

"I have to admit the notion of founding my own dynasty is not unappealing. Forbye, both Marion and I made our promises to each other in good faith and neither is prepared to give up the other. Since she has shown willingness to be the mother of my children and endure society's scorn for me, in return, I swear to be faithful to her and give her children my name. I have crossed my heart and promised never to let her down."

"Promises, promises, what use are your promises when you are sinning against the law of God?" Katherine thundered. "You mean to keep Lady Marion as your mistress and bear your children while you pursue a priestly path?"

"Let me remind you that I am, as yet, a lay abbot, mind, unlike thon fornicator, the Abbot of Fearn who, since he cannot abstain from fyking, challenges the celibacy rule. Hamilton seeks not to spread God's word but his own seed."

"But he has now wed," Katherine retorted.

"And has therefore broken his sacred vows. Is that not a graver sin? Whereas I have taken no vow of chastity. And since neither of us is married, neither can we be guilty of adultery. The Church my dear sister, makes rules ..." he broke off, his face contorting in pain.

Katherine snorted in disgust. Trust her brother to bend the rules to suit his own selfish purposes. From the way his puffy face was turning purple and beads of perspiration were breaking out on his forehead, she had clearly poked a festering sore.

Unlike her profligate brother, Sister Katherine had a true vocation. Of that she had no doubt. Being called by God had given her a strong sense of moral purpose and the courage to hold true to the principles and rules of the one, true Roman Catholic Church. Entering as a novice at St.Mary's, she had been eagerly looking forward to a rigid regime of discipline and self-denial in a community of like-minded and like-hearted women. Instead, Prioress Janet languished in luxurious indolence, rarely leaving her overheated chamber while the nuns cowered in fear of Sister Maryoth.

For the good of the abbey she had agreed to spy for her brother during Maryoth's reign but with the arrival of Elisabeth and Agnes and their new vision for St.Mary's, Katherine had changed sides. Now that she could read and write and, more importantly, think for herself she was less willing to be browbeaten by her brother.

"I was about to say that, when making rules, canon law takes account of the facts of life. I am a realist. You, however, are an idealist, my dear sister. The Church has need of us both. Speak not of what you don't understand. Go back to your beads, wee sister."

"I am no naïve nun. Well I ken about the wantonness and vice rife among the whoremongers and fornicators of the clergy, but I had thought my own brother would smite them down. Instead of setting an example to your weaker brethren, you are wallowing in the stinking mire yourself. I am ashamed to call you brother."

Flabbergasted by her outburst, Beaton's eyes bulged. The women of this abbey were becoming too brazen, the fault of too much learning, as he'd predicted.

"Would you rather have hedonistic heretics and rampant reformists overrun your beloved Church?" he snarled, his lips drooling flecks of bloody spittle. "Mind this. In the eyes of Rome, your despicable brother is a champion. The only man in Scotland who can slay the two-headed dragon of schism and reform and rid the country of loathsome snakes."

"How grand you've become, brother," Katherine sneered. "Not only do you compare yourself to St.George but St.Patrick as well? It's a pity that Wales already has a David as its patron, otherwise ... Nay, only Lucifer who dared to exalt himself above the law of God showed such presumption. Beware, Davie, that you are not cast down to the uttermost recesses of the fiery pit."

VII

Revelation

> "O where hae ye been, my long, long love,
> These seven long years and more?"
> "O I'm come to seek my former vows,
> That ye promised me before."
> *The Ballad of the Demon Lover,* Traditional

St. Mary's Abbey, March 1528

Elisabeth dropped her fist. She had been about to knock, but the door was slightly ajar and the lowered voices from inside made her pause. The door swung open at her touch but the two heads bent over the writing table were too engrossed to notice.

"Forgive me for disturbing you, but I have come to offer my thanks."

The two heads sprang apart. John, looking bashful, avoided her eyes, while the friar quickly slipped something up the wide sleeve of his habit. He struggled to his feet and leant against the desk. His mouth gawped open like a landed haddock and he clutched at his chest. Alarmed, John put out a hand to steady him.

"*Me thought ane lady, of portraiture perfect,*" he mumbled, "*Did salute me with benign countenance. What was her name? Dame Remembrance.*"

"Nay, I am Dame Elisabeth, prioress of this abbey."

"Dame Elisabeth? Prioress? It cannot be …" the friar tottered back against the table. The crease etched between his thick, dark eyebrows deepened. "Lisbeth? Or her ghost come to haunt me?"

His jaw had slackened leaving his mouth drooping like a drooling fool. A straggly beard sprouted from his chin and his scrawny neck poked out from the ill-fitting habit hanging loosely on him. His hair, inexpertly hacked by Agnes before bandaging his head, stood up in ridiculous tufts like Papingo's mottled crest. The lines on his face, still healing from the bruises, were testimony to the years. Years they had spent apart. For the voice, sounding so familiar, was despite its hoarseness, undeniably that of Davie Lindsay.

Elisabeth's heart skipped several beats. "I'm not the only one to have risen from the dead, Friar Lazarus," she said with a short, nervous laugh, before turning to Knox whose head was swivelling from one to the other. "I fear the friar is about to swelt, John. Run along to the apothecary and ask Sister Agnes for a tonic to revive him."

To steady his trembling knees, Lindsay leant heavily against the writing table. Elisabeth had pulled out the stool and was helping him to sit down when the manuscript hidden up his sleeve slipped onto the floor. They both lunged forward to pick it up, banging their foreheads together with a stomach-churning crunch. Sprites flashed in front of her eyes.

"Our first meeting and we've locked horns already," Lindsay quipped as he nursed the bruise on his brow. "Here you are, Lisbeth, hale and hearty: spiky as ever and as speedy to crack my neb. Even your vow to chop off my shanks has come true." He glanced at his crutch leaning against the wall.

"Do you mind the other hex I put on you?" Her brusque tone was belied by a laugh catching in her throat. "That if you ever kissed another lass you'd turn into a puddock? Is that why you're in a monk's guise?"

Lindsay beamed his crinkly, lop-sided, grin. "Frog or friar! Not so different perhaps. I should be wary of dealing with a carlin such as you."

"It serves you right. For marrying Kate."

Though her lips were dry and her tongue stuck to the roof of her dry mouth, she couldn't hold back the accusation. She inhaled deeply to quell the spasm of grief that cramped her heart.

Whenever that agonising nightmare – with Kate and Lindsay rocking her baby in a cradle – had threatened to rip her grief-stricken heart to shreds, she had resisted it with all her might. With neat, precise stitches, she had darned the frayed ends of the torn wound and then, after the last double stitch, had bitten off the end of the thread. Cleanly, with sharp teeth – the way Betsy had bitten off her bairn's umbilical cord.

And, whenever a tiny pinprick of pity had threatened to undo her hidden pocket of grief, Elisabeth had quickly stitched it back again. The darn was almost invisible and so skilfully sewn that it could never be unravelled. Never, she had assured herself, until now. Though nearing thirty, she wanted to pummel his chest like her feisty thirteen-year-old self.

"But only because I believed you were dead, Lisbeth. May God forgive me! Had I known, I would never have ... Please don't blame me," he stuttered plaintively.

"Who told you I was dead?"

Remorse and regret contorted his face. "She did. Thon nun. I did come back for you, Lisbeth. I did keep my word, but she said you'd passed on."

After Flodden, when it was feared that the infant heir to the throne would be kidnapped, or even murdered, if not by the English then by ruthless pretenders to the Scottish Crown, Lindsay had taken his young charge into hiding. Not until the late summer of 1514 had Lindsay been able to return to the abbey. On the fifteenth of August to be exact, the first anniversary of their handfasting.

"Sister Elisabeth is no longer with us," a pious looking nun had told him. She then reverentially raised her eyes to heaven before crossing herself with her rosary and kissing the tiny figure of the crucified Christ.

"Pray for her," she implored, and then, eyes blazing with fervent zeal, she went on, "Lest her soul roast forever in the fires of eternal damnation. And may we all rest in peace."

And then she had clanged the gate shut in his face, leaving him forsaken and forlorn.

VIII

Wandering Willie's Tale

I will sing to you a woeful song
Will grieve your heart full sair.
The Ballad of the Clerks of Oxenford, Traditional

St. Mary's Abbey, March 1528

Knox patted the dark inkblot seeping across the creamy parchment with a rag. Too much ink on the quill had dripped onto the page, and when he tried to dab at it, the stain spread even more. Usually his work was scrupulous but a sleepless night had left him too woolly-headed and clumsy to concentrate on the document he had to copy. Fearsome images of Patrick Hamilton, burning on his funeral pyre and his own guilt-stricken conscience had kept him awake till dawn. Could he not have done or said something to save the martyr?

He rubbed furiously at the infernal stain until he had scraped a hole in the expensive calfskin parchment. Seething with helpless frustration, he lay his head down on his arms. His hot tears splashed onto the parchment, creating more splotches and dissolving his scrupulous handwriting.

Tibbie's Tavern, Haddington

"Twas on the last day of February when the reformist, Patrick Hamilton, was tried for heresy. A snell east wind was howling around the cathedral in the city of St. Andrews that dreich and dreadful day. The Dominican Prior, Alexander Campbell, got up to present his case, crying forth as his chief witness, James Hamilton of Finnart, known as the Bastard, bribed no doubt by Abbot Beaton to denounce his ain cousin. The Bastard Finnart has sold his ain soul often enough so it's no wonder that he was ready to sell that of his kinsman and all."

Knox jostled with the rowdy crowd for a standing space at the back of the alehouse. Regular drinkers were sitting round the ingle where Wandering Willie had pride of place. For a jug of porter to wet his whistle, he was willing to tell the tale of the reformist's cruel end. The seasoned old storyteller waited till the mob had settled down before continuing.

"The Archbishop of St. Andrews, James Beaton, and his nephew, Abbot Beaton, sat surrounded by bishops, abbots and ...

"And their whores and limmers, no doubt," a heckler shouted.

"Foutering away while the holy man burns," another added.

177

"Aye, the Beatons are namely for their whore-mongering."

"Not only the Beatons – all the high heid yins of the Church," the heckler mocked and then began chanting:

> "The Monks o" Melrose supped good kail
> On Fridays when they fasted
> They never wanted beef or ale
> As long as their neighbours lasted."

As the crowd took up the chorus, Willie thumped down his empty tankard, spat onto the sawdust and turned away to gaze sulkily into the flames.

"Wheesht, wheesht!" Tibbie the alewife bawled. "Steek your gabs! Let Willie tell his story. There'll be nae mair ale for any of you until he's finished."

She slapped another foaming tankard down in front of Willie to slake his drouth and chivvy him out of his glunders. There was silence in the tavern while he took his time slurping it. Only after wiping his lips, was he ready to go on.

"Sentence was passed. Patrick Hamilton was to be burned at the stake. Unmovit, the reformist bowed his head and accepted his fate for he wouldn't recant of his sins for awe of the fire. Nay, he'd rather burn speedily in their fire for heeding his conscience than burn forever in the fires of hell for no heeding it."

The tavern chorus hummed in assent.

"They were no slouches when it came to the bigging up of the stake. All kinds of kindling – bundles of faggots, sticks – had been gathered at the gates of St. Salvator's College. When they led Hamilton out, he took off his coat and gave it to his servant. It was just like his master, he wept, to have such forethought for others and no think of himself. He was aye giving to the poor and needy."

His audience, too, became tearful, snivelling and slavering into their tankards.

"Thereupon he was thirled firmly to the stob with ropes and bindings. If you've ever seen a burning you'll ken that oftimes the merciful smoke chokes its victim long afore the body goes up like a blazing torch. But in the gale howling from the sea, the fire wouldn't spark and neither would the damp powder strike. When at last the flames did take hold, they only skrimpled the martyr's left hand and the side of his face, for the rain kept smooring the fire. Hamilton had to thole his agony for six hours."

Willie paused for dramatic effect and to take a swig of ale. "Six … long … hours he was tormented, as many hours as Christ Our Lord did dree on the cross. All the while Prior Campbell taunted him with cries of: Convert heretic! And goaded him to recite the *Salve Regina*. But the raging heat had melted Hamilton's tongue to the roof of his mouth and he couldn't speak. He lifted up three blackened fingers. Whether in blessing or cursing, who can say."

In a corner of the tavern, Knox had hunkered down on the floor, hugging his knees tightly to stop himself from fainting. He dug his nails into his arms and forced himself to listen to Wandering Willie's grisly description.

"Mercifully, at long last, the fire became fierce enough to end this burning of flesh and bone, the like of which has never before been seen within the realm of Scotland and, God willing, never again."

While the superstitious listeners touched the wood of the trestles or settles, the more religious ones signed themselves with the cross.

"As the flames scorched the young martyr, Davie Beaton's eyes glowed like the coals of hell," Wandering Willie went on, "and no wonder. He's becoming namely as a butcher of heretics. The University of Louvain, no less, has praised his uncle, the archbishop, for his zeal in defending the one, true faith and thanked him for purging the Church of an infidel. Yet, for Friar Campbell who taunted him in his last agony, there would be no such thanks. He died a few days later. Of a stroke, some say. Of despair say others. Whether by the hand of God or Auld Nick – who rightly kens?"

Was the mild-mannered Hamilton a heretic or a martyr? A fool or a saint? A foolish saint or a heretical martyr? This dilemma was torturing Knox for it raised a more burning question: that of his own bravery. Would he be ready to die for his convictions? And, if so, would he have the courage to climb so heroically to the stake?

So stricken was he with such thoughts that he didn't hear the prioress come into the scriptorium and glance over his shoulder. Hunching over his desk, he curled his arm protectively round the smudged document.

"It's only a blot, John. I'll get you another parchment."

"Oh, that it were as easy to restore a man to life," he mumbled, his dark blue eyes glistening with unwept tears.

"So that's what's upsetting you. Do not fret, John. Patrick Hamilton died because he was mistaken in his beliefs. Satan had so possessed the heretic's soul that he would never have recanted."

"Would a man give up his life for a falsehood?" he growled.

She tried to pat him on the shoulder but he shrugged off her hand. As a woman she would have little understanding of theological issues.

"Friar Lazarus says there are many who share Hamilton's views. Friar Lazarus says they are not heretics but seekers after truth." His expression hardened, his blue eyes resolute.

Elisabeth frowned. "Friar Lazarus says all this? Has he been filling your head with heresy? Then you'd be better to speak to Abbot Beaton."

"Abbot Beaton." Knox sneered. "Thon champion of the Church is doing more harm than good. Do you ken what they're saying about him? That if he burns any more martyrs, then he'd better burn them in deep cellars. For the reek of Master Patrick Hamilton has infected as many as it blew upon."

Alarmed at the vehemence in his voice, Elisabeth crouched down beside him and placed her hand on his. Unable to resist her soft touch, Knox let her uncurl his tightly clenched fist. As her cool fingertips stroked his tingling chilblains, he flinched in exquisite pain.

"No wonder you're crabbit, John. These mouls are so red and inflamed that they would try the patience of a saint – or even a martyr," she teased, giving his hand an affectionate squeeze. "I'll ask Sister Agnes to make up a soothing ointment – and how about a sweet cordial to take away the itch?"

Unable to meet her eyes full of tender concern, he kept his head bowed. Gently she brushed a stray lock of hair from his clammy brow and then murmured, her sweet breath caressing his cheek, "I'm only trying to do what is best for you, John. I have no wish to see you consumed by the fiery flames of heresy."

IX

Birdsong

> Of her courage, she would, without my lore,
> Sing like the merle, and craw like to the cock,
> Pew like the glad and chant like the laverock.
>
> *The Testament of the Papingo*
> Sir David Lindsay, 16th Century

St. Mary's Abbey, May 1528

Singing to her Papingo whenever she was troubled was Elisabeth's remedy to lighten her heavy heart. The way the bird would cock its head in rapt attention and then try to mimic her made her laugh. And she'd had plenty to concern her recently, not least her godson's youthful rebellion. As a lad, John had shown such promise, such enthusiasm, but since he'd been attending St. Salvator's College in St. Andrews, he had become thrawn and secretive.

Though worried that he was being led astray by the reformist teachings of his tutors, Elisabeth did not wish to clype on him, for that would only inflame Beaton's persecuting zeal. Once John left university she might be able to dissuade him from this dangerous path, but then Friar Lazarus had come onto the scene to sabotage her plan. When the disgruntled Papingo squawked to gain her attention, began to sing a verse from the Ballad of True Thomas:

> "The fig and also the wine-berry,
> The nightingales lying on their nest …"

But she before she could finish the lines, another voice chirped up:

> "The popinjays fast about gang fly,
> And thrushes sing would have no rest."

Startled, she whirled round to see Lindsay leaning on his crutch in the doorway. He had knocked, he maintained, but she had been too absorbed to hear him. No doubt her voice of a songbird had drowned out all other sound, he said, a wide grin splitting his face.

"Which one?" Elisabeth queried, sensing a jest, for she would be the first to admit she could not hold a tune. "The linnet? The mavis? Or the song thrush perhaps?"

"I was thinking more the storm cock, or the rawky crow. Or even your squawking Papingo," Lindsay teased

"Wheesht, wheesht! Haud yer wheesht!" the bird screeched at her name being taken in vain.

Well, for such a jibe Elisabeth would have slammed the door on him but, with a deft manoeuvre of his crutches, Lindsay sidled in and closed it firmly behind him.

"At least my pretty popinjay brightens up my dull life and cheers my spirits too," Elisabeth retorted, raising her eyebrows. "Which is more than can be said for you, Davie Lindsay."

"Still throwing out barbs, my prickly thistle."

"And *your* tongue is still as sharp and spiky. The years have not lent it sweetness. Nor has your time at court taught you the art of fulsome praise." There was so much more to say but she tightened her lips so as not to spit out the bitter resentment she was feeling.

"I was never one for the lickspittle, as you well ken. I only give praise where it is due. If it pleases you, I shall earn my keep and pen a fitting eulogy for a lady fair."

Lodged between the crutch and the oxter of his left arm, Lindsay was carrying a parchment which he was now trying to pull out with his right hand. Elisabeth watched him struggle but she would not invite him to sit down. Let him wriggle. He placed the parchment on her desk, unrolling it clumsily with one hand. Then, producing a quill from his pocket, he waved it with a dramatic flourish.

"Or perhaps a hymn or a psalm would be more fitting for my lady prioress?" he asked in the obsequious tones of a crawling clerk.

Elisabeth tucked her hands into the sleeves of her habit and tried not to laugh. His glib tongue would not win her round.

"God forbid!" she exclaimed, "I have never been one for praying and chanting. Forbye, my head is too full of taxes and teinds, and rents and dues nowadays."

"Taxes and teinds! What a woman of affairs you have become, Lisbeth."

"I had no option. And see what a good wife I would have made, if you hadn't deserted me." There she had said it.

Seeing the reproach in her eyes, he beat his breast contritely. "*Mea culpa.*"

"As good as Kate, even though I cannot sing so sweet," she added.

Lindsay's shoulders sagged. "The years haven't softened your temper, Lisbeth."

"Nay, on the contrary, they have taught me to harden my heart. And it's high time you left here." She gripped her elbows more tightly and glared at him. "Our cosy wee hencoop needs no cockerel to ruffle our feathers. Nor does my godson need to listen to any more from your forked tongue."

The crinkly corners of his mouth drooped. "Have mercy, Lisbeth. I am not long snatched from the jowls of death. You surely don't want to cast me back. I wouldn't like to be on the end of Sister Agnes's tongue if that were to happen."

Painstakingly over the years, Elisabeth had polished her heart to a kernel as smooth and hardened as that of the St. John's nut so that now his pleas failed to crack its surface but slid off painlessly.

"But Lisbeth, you must let me explain." His voice dropped to barely audible whisper. "You're the only one I have ever loved. Will you believe me?"

Lindsay leant his crutches against the wall and limped towards her. He was about to place his hands on her shoulders when the latch rattled and the door opened. Armed with a bucket of water and some rags for the weekly cleaning of the parrot's cage, Sister Agnes stood in the doorway and narrowed her eyes suspiciously. The way the two of them were standing stockstill, their arms straight down by their sides, like stooks in a cornfield, unsettled her.

X

Extreme Unction

The ladies of France may wail and mourn,
May wail and mourn full sair,
For the bonny Beaut's long fair locks
They'll ne'er see waving mair.
Ballad of the Death of la Beauté, Traditional

Craigmillar Castle, 1517

The plague was filling the kirkyards of Edinburgh. While the townsfolk were confined within the city walls to prevent the disease spreading, the court had moved from the castle of Edinburgh to Craigmillar, situated on higher ground in the southeast of the city, beyond the filth and stench of the narrow streets and wynds. The young king had to be protected from the botch at all costs, especially since the sudden death of his younger brother. Rumours that the infant Alexander had been poisoned by the Duke of Albany to secure his place as next in line to the throne were as rife as the plague. Since he was now the one and only legitimate heir, James V was all the more precious for that, and Lindsay had to be all the more vigilant.

As a safeguard against disease, many of the ladies believed *aquavitae* to be beneficial. Sipping small doses or adding it to wine not only strengthened the blood but lightened the melancholic humour of those disturbed by unpleasant thoughts of pestilence and death. *Aquavitae* also brought a bright sparkle to the eyes and a healthy flush to the cheeks, or so Kate justified her daily medication.

But Lindsay had been too preoccupied with the king's health to consider that something else may have contributed to Kate's merry mood: what he had to tell her would smoor her high spirits. Trembling with anger, he sank heavily into a chair and leant forward, head in hands, to keep from lashing out.

"What ails thee?" Kate hopped from one foot to the other, her hands fluttering helplessly in alarm. Had he come down with the botch that had broken out in the city? She was wary of touching him lest she herself became infected. "Shall I send for the apothecary?"

He shook his head more violently. "Of all people! I can't believe it! The most valiant knight in Christendom, the knight of beauty and truth ..." he stammered, choking on his words.

His tear-drenched eyes flashed with fury. Kate had never seen Lindsay so angry and upset before. As the court jester, the clown, it was his business to amuse people, make them laugh. So he had found out about her affair with the beautiful knight, Antoine

D'Arcie. Castle walls had ears. No secrets could be kept in the close confines of the court. Who had told him? The jealous and spiteful Isobel Kennedy, no doubt. Or the fickle, faithless Nancy Stewart, perhaps?

"Who ... who dealt the fatal blow?" Kate asked, trying to keep her voice calm but, as she poured some wine from the flagon, her hand was trembling.

Lindsay got to his feet. "I thought you could tell me that," he hissed and whacked the pewter goblet flying out of her hand.

His dear friend and honourable knight had been brutally murdered – in cold blood by thon coward, Hume of Wedderburn, and his tribe of ruthless reivers. Hell-raising outlaws who, it was said, never even flinched when slaying their king at Flodden.

Kate cowered as he came towards her with flailing arms, but he only grabbed her by the shoulders. Had she told anyone of Antoine's plans? His voice was low and menacing. She shook her head and looked longingly at the pitcher on the table. Even a sip of wine would steady her shaking hands.

"Nay," he yelled, so forcefully that she jolted. His fingers dug into her flesh as he forced her to listen.

As soon as the Duke of Albany returned to France, leaving Antoine D'Arcie as lieutenant governor of Scotland in his absence, trouble had broken out in the Debatable Lands. After rounding up the treacherous Humes of Wedderburn, D'Arcie sentenced them to hang and then ordered their heads to be impaled on spikes outside the Tolbooth prison for all to see and take heed.

"It was only what those brigands deserved, but do you know what their henchmen did then? Look at me," he growled, holding her fast by the arm. She flinched. "Look at me and listen to the full horror of your deed." Lindsay's ashen face, contorted into an ugly grimace, was unbearable to behold.

Antoine had been billeting secretly at Dunbar Castle when he'd been alerted to a skirmish, only to find it was all over when he got there. On the way to another alleged incident, he and his men were ambushed by a gang led by one of Hume's sons seeking vengeance against the interfering Frenchman. The so-called skirmish was a decoy, a cowardly trick to lure him from hiding. How did they know he was at the castle?

"Who told them?" Lindsay glared at her. "Only a handful of people knew and you, being his lady fair, were one of them."

Knowing that the day must come when he'd find out, Kate had thoroughly rehearsed her excuses to justify her infidelity but now, being confronted in this way, she could only blurt them out. That she was not to blame, that he didn't care about her, that his neglect had forced her to find comfort in the arms of another. And it wasn't her fault that Antoine had been ambushed. She'd been tricked. By that whore, Nancy Stewart, who'd betrayed Adam's memory by marrying that rogue, Alexander Hume, in unseemly haste.

At first Nancy had feigned innocent curiosity about Kate's affair with Antoine, flattering her vanity, saying how lucky she was to have ensnared the heart of such a champion before asking seemingly innocent questions: Where was he? When would she be seeing him again? Puffed up with smug superiority, Kate had taken pleasure in making Nancy jealous: sweet revenge on the dudron who had stolen Adam from under her nose.

"He that speaks the things he shouldn't, will hear the things he wouldn't," Lindsay growled his voice loaded with contempt. "Shall I tell you the story of his untimely murder? The tragedy of your brave knight?"

He pushed her roughly onto a chair and knelt before her.

"Thrown into disarray, D'Arcie's company scattered, leaving him to be chased by the horde through the bogs and marshes of the Merse. Well acquainted with their own border country, the reivers hounded Antoine and his beautiful white charger into a swamp."

"Oh no!" Kate cried out. "Did he drown in the mire?"

"Nay, that would have been a merciful ending compared to what he had to thole." Lindsay inhaled deeply before continuing. "D'Arcie put up a brave fight. But one single man against many – even such a valiant knight against a gang of cowardly blackguards – was hopeless. They overpowered him, taking turns to pierce him through and through. They tore out his noble heart and hacked through his entrails. And then …" his voice began to break as he strove to fight back tears, "as if those tortures were not enough, what did those fiends do? They hacked off his head with a sword. While he was still alive."

"Oh, may the Lord have mercy on his soul!" Kate crossed herself. Visualising the body she had so lovingly caressed being ripped apart, his blood gushing from mortal wounds, was more than she could bear. Her hands flew up to her face but Lindsay wrenched them away. Then, when she tried to cover her ears to drown out his pitiless tale, he slapped them down, for she must hear the final insult.

"After his fiendish henchmen had plaited your beautiful knight's long hair into a golden wreath, thon wolf in wedder skins, Hume of Wedderburn, rode off with Antoine's head tied to his saddle. Bumping and jolting it all through the borderlands, to the town of Duns, he then stuck it on a spear for all to see. That's the justice of your border reivers," he snarled angrily into her face. "And all because you couldn't keep your wanton tongue between your teeth."

Kate put a hand to her throat. She feared she would faint if she didn't get some air – or, better still, a reviving drink – but Lindsay was prolonging the torture.

"Thon rogues had been tried in the highest court of the land and found guilty of treason, the punishment being their life. Whereas Antoine was given no trial but was hunted down like a beast and torn apart, limb from limb."

Dumbstruck, Kate could only shake her head. With a look of utmost disgust, Lindsay got to his feet and shoved her chair away with such force that she fell onto the floor.

"That's the way," he sneered, looking down on her, "and while you're on your knees you can pray to the Lord for forgiveness."

Forsaken by Lindsay and grieving for Antoine, Kate sought solace more and more in *aquavitae* but its beneficial effects began to dwindle. The water of life gladdened her heart less and less and shrivelled her brain more and more. Cursed with constant visions and doited from lack of sleep, Kate staggered through the corridors of Craigmillar, plaiting and unplaiting her braids of golden hair and wailing the ancient dirge of the three ravens picking at the eyes of a new-slain knight:

"She lifted up his bloody head
And kissed his wounds that were so red."

When she became feverish and her face and arms broke out in a rash, it was feared that Kate had fallen victim to the Black Death. For the young king's safety, she was banished from the castle to suffer the cruel treatment inflicted on those suspected of carrying the plague. Imprisoned in a cage in a field some distance away, with food and water to last a few days, Kate was left to her fate.

No-one from the court was allowed to go near, especially not the king's trusted tutor. For several long, lonely days and nights Kate cowered in the corner of her cage, open to the wind and rain. When no tell-tale swellings or black blisters appeared on her body, the royal physicians, after much anguished deliberation, allowed her back into the castle.

Her cruel quarantine had done nothing to cure her grief or guilt, however. Accursed Kate could not be at peace as she clawed at the rash on her skin and cried out in delirium that devils with whiplash tails and forked tongues were crawling all over her, jabbing her, tormenting her. Bloodletting was the only remedy the physician could recommend.

Kate's crazed eyes stared in horror at the tiny demons sucking her life-blood: corbies picking at her blue een. She had to be tied to the bed with linen bandages to stop her plucking off the leeches clinging to her skin. When her eyes had sunk deep in her shrunken face and life seeped from her wasted frame, the priest was called to give her the last sacrament. With shining eyes, she grasped the crucifix with both hands, kissing it over and over again. The demons were fleeing her body, she was sure. Her soul felt lighter. Bring more holy relics, she pleaded, believing that only their miraculous healing powers could cure her.

Though loath to pander to such superstition, Lindsay gave in because, if nothing else, the blessed trinkets pacified her. He watched helplessly as the rosy-cheeked Kate withered away to a skeleton, with a sacred scapular round her neck, the wishbone of an obscure saint in her hands and holy water dabbed on her lips.

St.Mary's Abbey, May 1528

Chased out of the prioress's chamber by Sister Agnes for the weekly cage cleaning, Elisabeth and Lindsay had taken refuge in the walled garden. They sat down on a bench strewn with wild cherry blossom and admired Agnes's *potagerie* with its neatly trimmed lavender bushes and regular lines of planted seedlings. Elisabeth shivered, the light spring breeze chilling her as much as Lindsay's gloomy account of Kate's demise.

"If Kate didn't die of the plague, was it the sweating disease, perhaps, or, God forbid, leprosy?"

"If truth be told, Kate died of the pox," Lindsay stated glumly and ran his free hand across his face, as if wiping away a bad memory. The physician had confided that this new affliction, becoming more common among courtiers, induced just such demonic delusions.

"The pox? But that is a disease of ...debauchery and ... degeneracy."

Lindsay nodded. It was not a pleasant tale. The knight in shining armour had blighted those he laid siege to with the French disease. Kate died for love – but not for love of Lindsay – then again, neither had he loved her. He had felt a responsibility towards her: after all, it was he who had led her to the king's bed. King James was generous with his quines but he'd made no provision for her before he died. Out of a sense of duty, Lindsay had given her a home but not his heart. Perhaps if he'd been able to give Kate a child, her life would not have turned out so tragic.

"Everyone's life is tragic. All human lives end in tragedy." Elisabeth fell quiet. Had fate turned widdershins on Kate for casting curses on herself and Meg?

"But you and I are fortunate, Lisbeth. We've been given a second chance." Lindsay twisted round to face her. "We risk flying in the face of Fortune if we fling it away."

He put his hand on her arm but she wriggled free and stood up. She didn't want to be wooed by his honeyed words.

"Remember our handfasting, Lisbeth?" he said quietly. "When we swore to be true to each other until death? Thon night – as brief as a fire-flaucht – when we loved each other? If we can snatch that back again, then ..."

"Then what Davie?" Her voice was sharp and edgy. "We are no longer the same as we were then. We've grown older. We've changed."

"Only on the outside, Lisbeth. You may be dressed in a nun's habit and I may wear a monk's robe, but that's not who we are. We're only playing these parts." He raised himself up on his crutch to stand closer to her. "For though the years may have left their mark on my body, in my very soul, deep in my heart, I'm the same man who loved ... nay ... " he faltered, "who still ... loves you."

Elisabeth shook her head. What was the point of declaring his love now? It was too late. The pocket of grief, so fastidiously sewn together, must not be ripped apart. She couldn't risk the life she'd carved for herself. In order to hold fast, to *endure fort*, she imagined her heart as the polished kernel of the St. John's nut: her charm against witches. Or wizards.

"Forgive me, Lisbeth, if I am disrupting your quiet life." The corners of Lindsay's mouth crinkled.

She threw her head back and laughed. "For one thing my life is anything but quiet. Whoever thinks of a convent as a place of peace and quiet contemplation need only stay here for four and twenty hours. And for another, you disrupted my life years ago − at the Tournament of the Wild Knight and the Black Lady. Making my head giddy and my heart thump with your birling."

Lindsay's eyes twinkled. "And your bold proposal that day captured my heart forever. I am not whole without you, Lisbeth. Like the lame man in the Scripture, I need faith in your love to heal me so that I can throw away this."

As he raised himself up, the crutch fell from under his oxter and clattered against the bench. He gripped her shoulders with both hands and held her at arm's length, studying her face closely to read her thoughts.

XI

The Tragedy of the Papingo

Who climbs too high, perforce his feet maun fail.
The Tragedy of the Papingo
Sir David Lindsay, 16th Century

St. Mary's Abbey, Spring 1528

Perched on the edge of the table, Papingo cocked its head in rapt attention. As Sister Agnes cleaned out its cage, she crooned a French lullaby, but when she abruptly stopped, Papingo flapped its wings.

"Wheesht! Wheesht!" the bird shrieked, urging her to continue, but Sister Agnes was blushing with shame. Was it not sinful to use her singing voice other than to praise the Lord? But perhaps the little bird was as nostalgic for her homeland as she was. A wistful sigh fluttered from her. She mustn't feel so gloomy when she had so many blessings to count.

From the window Agnes looked down on her *potagerie* where cold east winds had shrivelled her French-grown herbs and shrubs and was pleased to see tiny green shoots peeking through the clay soil. *Deo Gratias*, the onions, so necessary for cleansing the blood and warding off the plague, were at last thrusting their way through the foreign clay. Through trial and error and listening to Betsy, it had taken her some years to learn what would survive the harsh, fickle weather. In the orchard, sheltered by high walls, the fruit trees were beginning to blossom. At least, apples, pears and plums managed to thrive in this dour climate.

Though she longed for the warmth of the nurturing southern sun, was it sinful to admit that, more than anything, she missed the food of her native land? Would that be the sin of gluttony? Agnes was astounded at the humble fare the Scots seemed to survive on. Coarse barley bread! And oats! And everything salted – beef, mutton and herring – all washed down with barmie ale. Tired of chewing her way through the tough, leathery meat, she had sent to France for herbs, spices and olive oil to disguise the taste and soften the texture, and for good wine to help digest it. In season there was plenty of fish and seafood – everything from tiny buckies and whelks to mussels and oysters – delivered fresh or "caller" from the nearby ports. As well as laying hens and geese the convent had a large dovecot and a rabbit warren for year-round meat.

All in all, the weather may be foul but the fare was almost fair, she smiled at her little *bon mot* for, when she added up all the benefits, her crosses to bear were flimsy indeed. What greater happiness and contentment could she have on this earth than to be among those she loved and who loved her?

Though of late she'd been concerned about Dame Elisabeth. Sensitive to the slightest change of mood in the prioress, Agnes had noticed that she seemed more agitated, more distracted, especially in the presence of Friar Lazarus. With his glib tongue and teasing manner, he seemed too sophisticated for a religious man. Who was he? A feigning fox in their coop, false and dissembling, ruffling their feathers as he prepared to pounce?

Banishing the thought, she bundled up the debris from the bottom of the cage and went to the window to shake out the cloth. The bird hopped up and down a couple of times, trying out its wings, before perching next to her on the sill.

"Ah, *ma petite* Papingo you have no desire to flee either, do you?" The parrot clung on to the sill with its claws for dear life. "All your creature comforts are here."

Sister Agnes leaned out to flick the cloth then suddenly drew back. As she brought her hand up to her mouth to stifle a startled gasp, her elbow knocked the little bird and propelled her into the wide blue yonder.

"*Mon Dieu!*" she shrieked, as the bird flapped its wings in a frantic effort to keep airborne. Agnes propelled herself downstairs, as fast as her long habit and heavy flannel petticoats would permit.

"John! *Venez! Vite, vite!*" she screamed.

Carrying a ladder, John struggled to keep up with Sister Agnes as she darted hither and thither. He trailed after her, leaning the ladder against one fruit tree and then another in response to her ever-changing directions.

"No, not there! Here! There she is! No, not that one! This one! *Vens, ma petite! Ici!*"

After the initial shock, the cage-bird found the giddy sensation of flight thrilling. It circled round a few times before attempting to escape over the orchard wall, but that proved too ambitious. The plump, well-fed Papingo, unused to such exercise could only flit about in short bursts and a flash of colour revealed that it had come to roost high up in the branches of a tall apple tree.

Weary from all its efforts, the parrot snuggled down for an afternoon nap, savouring the warmth of the early spring sun on its feathers. Slowly, so as not to alarm the bird, John inched his way up the ladder, but it wasn't long enough for him to reach it.

"We'll leave her be for a while," he shouted down to Sister Agnes. "She'll come down in her own good time. When she gets hungry."

"It's not *her* appetite that worries me," Sister Agnes wailed, "I fear for her safety. Papingo never leaves her cage. She's not used to flying. Her wings are not strong. She'll be caught and devoured by a hawk. Oh, what are we to do?"

He could wing her with his bow and arrow, John suggested. That would force her down, but Sister Agnes threw up her arms in horror.

"*Mon Dieu! Non! Non!* You might kill her. Glory be to God! Oh, Blessed Virgin!"

she wailed, making the sign of the cross over and over again. She'd never forgive herself for letting the bird go, but she'd been distracted. For, as she had shaken her cloth out of the window, she'd spotted Elisabeth and Friar Lazarus together by the dovecot near the boundary wall. From the way the prioress was shaking her head and the friar was gesticulating, it looked as if they were arguing. Her earlier sense of unease may not have been imaginary. And the way he suddenly, violently, laid hands on her, had made Agnes gasp.

"Oh what are we to do? What are we to do?" She wrung her hands in despair. "What will Dame Elisabeth say? She'll never forgive me."

"Agnes! Are you hurt?" Sister Katherine dashed from the infirmary. Judging from the volume of Agnes's screams, she was expecting to find someone seriously injured. Dame Elisabeth too, came running, followed by Friar Lazarus hobbling on his crutch.

"She'll come back down when she's hungry and cold," John said. Having no head for heights, he didn't offer to clamber among the branches to coax the bird down.

They all craned their necks as the fugitive fluttered its wings but then folded them again to settle down for another little snooze. Just then a brisk breeze blew up, shaking the topmost branches and ruffling the feathers of the little bird, waking it up. Displeased at being disturbed from its reverie, Papingo gave a disgruntled squawk, "Wheesht! Wheesht!"

Another blast, stronger this time, rustled the newly sprung leaves and it squawked again, more loudly, alerting birds of prey in the area. The sky darkened as a sparrow hawk glided silently towards it and hovered, poised ready to dive.

"*Mon Dieu!*" Agnes cried. Her hands clasped in despair, she stood looking upwards. While John positioned the ladder on one side of the apple tree Elisabeth was waving frantically on the other side to fend off the hawk. Stationed thus beneath the tree of knowledge, the trio of the grieving mother, the fearless Magdalene and the beloved disciple, formed a striking tableau of the Crucifixion, Lindsay reflected.

"Papingo!" Elisabeth cupped her hands to call out as the sparrow hawk finalised its position. The little parrot tried to respond with a plaintive cry of "Whee … whee … but the hawk swooped down on its prey and carried it off. Seconds later, startled by an arrow from John's bow, the hawk dropped its catch. After a pathetic attempt to flutter its broken wings, Papingo plummeted to earth. Elisabeth knelt down and carefully picked up her little pet bird. Its wings hung limply and its scrawny twigs of legs were splayed out awkwardly. Running her fingers along its tiny skeleton she could feel its bones – as fragile and frail as Meg's had been – and the appeal for help in its bead-like eyes squeezed her heart.

"I think her back and wings may be broken."

"Then it would be more merciful to put an end to her suffering and wring her neck, Lisbeth," Friar Lazarus said softly.

"*Mais non, impossible!*" Meek, mild Agnes bristled at his cruel suggestion. "We must do what we can to help her." She glared at him angrily. Besides, how dare he address the prioress so boldly?

Elisabeth cradled the bird in her hands, cooing to it like a baby. Papingo gave a final shudder before its head sagged limply to one side. Elisabeth let out a plaintive little moan, and with a look of utter misery, turned to Friar Lazarus. Without a second thought, he drew her in towards him with his free arm.

"Wheesht, wheesht," the friar murmured, ill-chosen words which set her off into further paroxysms of weeping.

Agnes could hardly believe her eyes. How dare he be so familiar with the prioress! Was he indeed a friar? Noticing his untonsured head she had wondered but then, if not a friar, who was this interloper? Why had he come here? To take the prioress away from the convent? From her? Instead of wrenching away from the friar's insolent embrace Elisabeth had flopped shamelessly into his arms. Seeing their two bodies in such an intimate clinch, Agnes whimpered in pain, for an intense pang of jealousy, as sharp as one of John's arrows, had pierced her to the very core. Hearing Agnes's stifled sobs, Elisabeth disentangled herself and rushed over.

"Don't torture yourself, dearest Agnes. Our *petite* Papingo was getting old. But at least she had her moment of freedom. Flying in the sunshine. Who knows what happiness she found in her last moments?"

How sweet Elisabeth's embrace should have been but Agnes shrank from those arms so recently entwining the friar. Her eyes welled up with tears. That it was her elbow that had nudged the Papingo, first into liberty and then into eternity, was unbearable enough but now, as she examined her conscience, she decided that the fall of the Papingo was a fable, a parable even. A warning and a punishment for her sins: self-pity, complacency, but most of all for jealousy and wicked thoughts. As she turned away in agony Sister Katherine's usually callous eyes gazed at her with pity.

John wrapped the Papingo in a square of linen and, with all due ceremony, buried it in a deep hole in the orchard where its little corpse would be safe from disinterment by foxes and other wild animals.

"*Adieu, ma chère* Papingo! *Requiescat in pace*," Sister Agnes wailed while Betsy shook her head, wondering what all the fuss was about.

"A burial for a bird! Whoever heard the like? What a waste of a plump-breastit chookie! Why don't we just put it in the pot? It would earn its keep at last."

XII

Best Laid Schemes

> Marriage, by my opinion, is better religion
> As to be Friar or Nun.
> *Ane Satire of the Three Estates*
> Sir David Lindsay, 16th Century

St. Mary's Abbey, 2 September 1528

Betsy plonked her well-cushioned bottom on the rosewood kist to take the weight of her arthritic legs and wiped away the tears rolling down her cheeks.

"Here was me thinking that I was one of them that had lived long enough to see the most." Her shoulders were shaking with laughter. "Who'd have thought it? And now you plan to run away together? To gang o'er the marsh as you yearned to do all those long years ago. I'm not sure whether to laugh or greet."

Neither was Elisabeth, so taigled up and tapsalteerie were her feelings.

"Betsy, it's no jape. I truly believed I'd smoored my feelings but now ... " She slid her hand into the deep pocket of her habit to make sure the velvet pouch was still there.

"I feel as if I've been awakened from a long sleep, Betsy, and now being in love ... Why, every scrap of you comes alive. It consumes your whole being, stirs your blood ..."

"And boils your brain," Betsy scoffed. "Look at you. As skittish as a sappie-headed kitty."

And so she was. After leaving Papingo's tiny grave, Elisabeth had shown Lindsay the secret passage from the chapel to her chamber where she would meet him that evening. First she had taken off her wimple and shaken out her hair confined beneath the skull-fitting coif. Contrary to convent vows, she had let it grow – her little rebellion – and then set about grooming it to its former glory. After a great deal of brushing with long, hard strokes she was pleased to see the shine returning to her copper mane. Stripping off her nun's robes, she'd dressed in the only gown belonging to Dame Janet that fitted her – of blood-red satin.

Then she dug out the velvet pouch, buried at the bottom of the kist, where she'd hidden the king's ring. Weird it was that her Papingo's beady eye had spotted it glinting on the Black Madonna's finger. Even weirder that it had been John who had hung it on the statue after finding it in the vestry where it had lain hidden all these years. Fortune's wheel had come full circle.

When Lindsay arrived later that evening, she closed the door of her chamber and slid the bolt home. From round his neck he unwound the lover's knot he'd worn since their handfasting and placed it gently round hers. As Elisabeth stuttered to explain how Sister Maryoth had frizzled her own knot in a candle flame, Lindsay had gently quietened her with a kiss. It was of no matter, he whispered. In their hearts they had kept tryst, kept faith.

Forgetting the torment of their own personal purgatory – the years spent apart – they were whirled back in time to the dizzy headiness of their young love to recreate their brief spell of happiness. Then, as they lay together, drifting in a drowsy limbo of love, they renewed their vows, pledging to be together. Forever.

Betsy heaved a great sigh and shook her head.

"I mind fine the day of your handfasting when you thought you'd cheated fate, but the signs bode no good and a lot of water has flowed under the brig long since. Forbye, the pair of you are gey old to go flitting round Europe like a couple of cooing-doves. Where will you live? How will you live? Lisbeth, my lass, have you thought this through?" Betsy's voice kept breaking with emotion. Struggling to stem tears, she twisted her apron round her fingers. "You'll never come back here again. We'll never see you again. And I'll no live long enough to see you again on this earth," Betsy predicted. She wiped her teary eyes with the corner of the apron.

"But, Betsy, I'd never dream of leaving you behind. You'll come with us."

"Ha!" she cackled, showing a gummy mouth. "And what would an old crone like me want with traipsing about foreign countries where they don't speak my tongue? Forbye, I'm too lang in the fang to learn new-fangled ways."

"Nay, that's not true," Elisabeth contradicted, at the same time noticing how tired and worn-out Betsy looked. How had she lost so many teeth? Since when had she become so breathless and wheezy as she hobbled about her chores?

"And what will you tell your holy sisters? That you're about to run off with a man?"

"I'll tell that I'm going to Rome. On a pilgrimage. To pray."

Betsy raised her eyebrows. "To flyte with the pope more like. And who'll look after the abbey while you're gallivanting across the continent?"

Elisabeth had thought it all through: Agnes would continue to run the apothecary and the hospice and Katherine would be in charge of day-to-day affairs.

"Oh aye, and that will please Davie Beaton."

No doubt Beaton would rub his podgy hands in glee and gloat on hearing that his sister was in control of St. Mary's – with all the monies pertaining to it – but Elisabeth had faith in Katherine's ability to slap down her brother's greedy paws.

"And what about young John? He'll be bereft. He worships you. You're more than just a godmother to him," Betsy faltered. "Will you leave him to the mercy of Beaton?"

"Why, no! He'll come with us. To study in Rome. In the very heart of the Vatican."

"Aye, but is that what he would want?" Betsy looked doubtful.

Elisabeth groaned. "I don't even know what *I* want. Oh, Betsy, what should I do?"

She began worrying at her hangnails, reverting to the bad habit a French education had stamped out, but when Betsy reached out to smack her down, she swiftly thrust her hands into her pockets. Turning aside, Elisabeth withdrew the velvet pouch and quickly slipped the king's ring onto her finger. Kneeling down in front of her old nurse, she held out her left palm.

"Read my future, Betsy. Tell me what lies ahead."

"What's that you have there?" Seeing the ring Betsy frowned. "You're not needing my counsel. It looks as if you've already made up your mind."

Elisabeth gave a nervous laugh. "Aye, and it's a tight fit. It'll need some softened wax to twist it off again. But, tell me Betsy, have I chosen right?"

The old nurse heaved a sorrowful sigh. "Why ask me? What do you want to do? Open up your heart and ask yourself honestly. For that's what will lead you."

"I don't know, Betsy," Elisabeth shook her head. Hadn't she just torn open the pocket of grief to allow love in once more? But was that what she wanted? "When I was a lass, I was so sure that all I wanted in life was to wed Davie Lindsay. That was my wish, do you mind, Betsy?"

"Aye, and your wish was granted," she murmured, lightly stroking Elisabeth's palm, "when you were handfasted. And Meg's wish, too, came true, for she found the peace and quiet she craved while Kate was willing to sell her soul to become one of the highest ladies in the land."

"Aye, but Meg had no wish to die, nor did Kate desire to be a discarded mistress and an unloved wife."

"Did I not warn you all to be wary what you wished for?"

Elisabeth sprang up, hugging the velvet pouch to her heart. "So where's the use of wishing if everything that is to be, will be? But I'll not be a plaything of fate. I shall take charge of my own destiny. I'd fain be free of responsibilities. To cast off wimples and rosaries and live with my love – wouldn't that be paradise?"

"Life on earth is never paradise," Betsy said quietly as she stared into the fire burning low in the grate. Elisabeth followed her gaze and knelt down to rest her head in the comfort of Betsy's lap.

"There's aye something to gar you grue in this life, my thistledown," Betsy whispered. "And at the door, a shoogly stone waiting to stammle you."

XIII

The Return of the King

> "What help," quoth she, "would that I ordain
> To bring thee unto thy heart's desire?"
> *The King's Quair,* James I, 15th Century

St. Mary's Abbey, 3 September 1528

The stealing sands of the hourglass numbered the hours of Lindsay's absence. Where was he? They had much to discuss. What Betsy had told her might change their plans. Anxious and impatient, Elisabeth slid back the tapestry in front of the hidden door of the garderobe, stepped inside and put her ear to the panel to listen for his footsteps. Dame Janet's secret passage to the chapel had proved to be useful for their clandestine trysts.

"The king is free! Long live the king!"

Startled by the shout from the courtyard, she rushed to the window to see John helping Patrick Hepburn to dismount. With a dismissive wave of his hand, the Fair Earl then strutted self-importantly across the abbey courtyard. As she hirpled her crooked way towards him, Betsy was swiftly overtaken by Friar Lazarus.

He tugged at the earl's dust-covered doublet. "What's that you say? The king is free?"

"Aye." The sixteen-year-old Earl of Bothwell replied, with a look of disdain at the monk. "He's escaped the clutches of Archie Douglas and he's on his way here."

That was the good news, Patrick declared. The bad news was that preparations were being made for war and he'd been ordered to organise the muster at the abbey fields before the arrival of King James himself – this very Monday. Patrick was about to swagger off when he was stopped again.

"My lord, do you mind me? Do you mind your old nurse?" Tearful at seeing her wee laddie again, Betsy flung her arms round him. Self-conscious and fearful that his men would think him a milksop for being a hen-wife's darling, he tried to prise her arms from around his neck. When Knox, appreciating his embarrassment, tried to drag her off she grabbed them both in a sturdy clinch, squeezing them for dear life. For such a small woman, Betsy was surprisingly strong.

"My two wee laddies. My bonnie blue-eyed bairns. Here you both are. The pair of you together."

Anyone seeing them for the first time would have assumed that the lanky, fair-haired Patrick, with his rounded shoulders and pale consumptive skin, was the cleric and that stocky John Knox, with his thick dark hair and ruddy complexion must be the soldier. Bothwell gave his childhood companion a curt nod of thanks before disentangling himself from Betsy's embrace. He was on the king's business and had important, grown-up matters to deal with.

The Palace of Haddington

To avoid being detained by the palace guards, the friar waved his hand in an exaggerated blessing over any he encountered for they would be unwilling to hinder a holy man doing his sacred duty. In the royal chamber the young monarch, arms outstretched in the crucifixion pose, was being tortured by seamstresses jabbing him with pins. Still a martyr to fashion, then, Lindsay mused.

James had grown taller and lankier since he'd last seen him, but there was an edgy restlessness about him, a result, no doubt, of being kept a virtual prisoner all these years. His pale eyes were no longer innocent but hardened with distrust. Years of court intrigue and being played as a pawn had made him suspicious but, on assuming command, he was quickly learning to play the imperious king.

"I have no wish to confess." As James waved the friar away impatiently, pins tinkled to the floor. The friar bent down to pick one up and held it up.

"So, I'm not even worth a pin to you, sire?" The friar then placed his right hand on his heart and began reciting:
> "When thou was young I bore thee in mine arm
> Full tenderly, till thou begouth to gang,
> And in thy bed oft happit thee full warm
> With lute in hand, syne, sweetly to thee sang."

James's brow furrowed as he delved deep into his memory and then his eyes opened wide with childlike wonder.

"Da Lindsay! Is that you!" He kicked away rolls of silks and satins to throw his arms round his old tutor's neck. Lindsay winced at the pinpricks but the easily shed tears pained him more. Though overjoyed to see his young master again, he was saddened to see that James hadn't cast off that fatal weakness of Stewarts – a tendency to be maudlin and sentimental.

Watching him grow up, Lindsay had feared that the young monarch was more alike in temperament to his grandfather, the ill-fated James III, than his father. When Archie Douglas took over his education, Lindsay despaired that James's weak nature would make him easy prey for the rapacious regent to manipulate him for his own ends. In his exile, he worried that all the hard work he'd put into the king's upbringing may have been ruined and now, meeting him again, it looked as if his fears had not been groundless.

Arms fluttering in excitement, James gabbled about how he himself had planned his own escape, how he'd dressed himself as a groom to dupe the guards at Falkland, how he'd ridden to Stirling and claimed the Great Seal. From his account it would seem that he alone had engineered his flight. Lindsay's heart sank.

"Now I am king, I shall no longer be ordered about. I am the one who gives the orders." James's mouth ached from the satisfied smile stamped on his face since his escape.

"Strip off that shapeless sackcloth at once, Davie! Not only does it not become you, but it offends the royal eyes. What will Jessie say? I'll have her make up a tabard of the finest brocade for my Snowdon Herald," said James. "You are friar no longer. I hereby command you to return to my service. And I shall dispatch you to the royal courts of Europe to herald my accession. Forthwith."

XIV

The Lollard Oath

He was a constant Catholic
All Lollard he hated and heretic.
Chronicle of Scotland
Andrew of Wyntoun, 14th–15th Century

St. Mary's Abbey, 1529

"John, please tell me, why will you not take the oath?"

Elisabeth tried to keep her temper as she followed Knox into the vestry where he was tidying up after morning Mass. He was being infuriatingly obstinate by refusing to answer her question. He continued folding the linen altar cloths and arranging them in neat piles, his usually forthright eyes downcast, avoiding her gaze. He seemed to have become so gloomy and morose lately, nervous and edgy, but then he was growing into manhood; already fifteen, with tufts of hair sprouting from his chin and clusters of pimples dotted about his face. As he turned to put away the cruets in the cupboard, she picked up the gold-lined chalice to admire the intricate engraving. He spun round.

"Put that down. It's consecrated," he said, his voice rising from a low growl to a high-pitched shriek. He snatched it from her hand and held it close to his chest. "It's a sacrilege for a woman to touch the sacred vessels."

"Only when you've taken holy orders will I take orders from you, John," she retorted, startled by his rudeness. "And afore that can happen, you must take the oath."

"What in heaven's name is Lollardy?" Elisabeth had enquired of Beaton. "It sounds like some kind of wasting disease."

"In a way," the abbot had replied, "but it is the worst kind of disease, even more odious than the French pox. While that may disfigure the body, Lollardy is an insidious heresy that damages the soul. The Lollards, or Babblers as they are sometimes called for the nonsense they babble, believe only what's written in the Bible. Since they also deny the authority of the pope and condemn our whole ecclesiastical structure, you can understand how dangerous their ideas could be.

"So, since the Declaration of 1416, all students must swear on oath to defend the Church against the insult of the Lollards and resist with all their power whosoever adheres to their sect. We thought they'd all been wiped out, but they are rearing their ugly heads again in the form of Luther and his ilk on the Continent. I had thought that the examples of Patrick Hamilton and Henry Forrest would serve as a warning, but enemies of the faith, such as John Mair and thon blackest of Black Friars, Thomas Williams, continue to sow evil heresies in the minds of our impressionable youths. Perhaps the time has come for sterner measures."

Since all of these misguided students couldn't be excommunicated, Beaton was putting pressure on their families to make them change their minds. If not, he would be prepared to overlook their youthful rebellion in exchange for a contribution to the university purse but, for those students intent on a career in the Church, taking the oath was mandatory.

So far Knox had been an outstanding scholar at St. Andrews and testimonials from his tutors reported that he had a promising future. However, before he would be allowed to graduate, he'd have to take the oath or face excommunication. As Knox's godmother, the prioress was responsible for his spiritual education and, if she wanted him to follow a clerical career, she must ensure that he took the oath.

Chasing Knox round the vestry as he tidied up, Elisabeth tried to reason with him.

"You're jeopardising your future, John. Abbot Beaton says …"

"Thon so-called priest has a concubine and a wheen of bastard bairns!" Knox spluttered angrily. "Abbot Beaton has as much conscience as a border reiver, flouting the rules and stealing from the Church. A bully, who slashes and burns his way through the truth of Christ's teaching. Have no fear, his time will soon be over."

"The abbot has his faults, I have to admit, but …" Her sentence tailed off. But what? What virtues could she point out to this youth seething with impotent rage? Defender of a Church the lad held in such low esteem?

"Friar Lazarus says …"

"Neither can you always believe what Friar Lazarus tells you," Elisabeth retorted.

"When is he coming back?" Knox suddenly demanded. His angry stare as he pressed for the truth pierced her heart.

"I don't know if he will be coming back." Elisabeth's eyes flashed with impatience. "Unlike his biblical namesake, I doubt he'll be rising from the dead."

"Aye, he will. He never bade me farewell. And he wouldn't leave without doing so." His brow creased as his look of stubborn determination modified to one of doubt. "Has Beaton arrested him? Is he going to burn him, too?"

His obvious concern and affection for the friar touched Elisabeth and, she was surprised to admit, stirred a pang of jealousy. She shook her head.

"Well, then, I need to speak to him," Knox said and glared at her, his lips tightly compressed.

Elisabeth fain would speak to him, too, but she hadn't seen Lindsay since the day he'd suddenly rode off with King James. Without bidding her farewell, either. Only a letter in which he poured forth his guilt at having broken his solemn promise – not to her, but to the late James IV, for failing to take care of his precious son and heir. Stalked by unseen vipers lurking in the undergrowth, plotting and conspiring to wrest power from him, the young king was vulnerable, but fate had blessed Lindsay with a second chance to rescue him. Only he could counsel and shield him from faithless friends and hostile foes.

This had infuriated her. Had Lindsay forgotten that they, too, had been given a second chance? Twice she'd been willing to elope with him, and twice he'd let her down. Forever destined to be the faithful courtier, Davie Lindsay would always put the king's will first. He hadn't even mentioned John in his letter. Had he abandoned him, too?

"You can talk to me, John."

Knox turned away. "You're a woman. You cannot understand."

He was loath to tell her he was thinking about joining the Franciscans, the only religious order that vowed to be true to the teachings of Christ. Like Friar Lazarus, he'd become a travelling preacher and reach out to the common folk.

"You disappoint me, John. Is that what those larbars are filling your head with? Turning you into one of those men who justify their scorn for women by insisting that we, weak-willed daughters of Eve, are lax and immoral and full of vice?"

Knox shot her an angry look. "They're no larbars."

"Why, then, do they closet themselves in a university with only other men and young lads? I'll tell you why. Because these impotent men are afeart of women," she scoffed. "Jealous and scared of what they dare to cry monstrosities of nature."

Knox shifted uneasily because there was truth in what she was saying.

"Consider this, John. Who stood by Christ in his hour of need? Not his cowardly apostles who denied him before running away, but his holy Mother and Mary Magdalene. And why did he appear first of all to Mary Magdalene after his Resurrection, rather than to his disciple Peter?"

Knox bowed his head and bit his lip. Because, his colleagues jeered, though he dared not tell her, in this way the news of his Resurrection would be spread the sooner. For Christ knew that a woman wouldn't be able to keep her mouth shut.

"And because Christ held women in such high regard, your cowardly scholars attack us out of jealousy. For they ken fine that our minds are as strong as our hearts, yet we have to thole their lies and conceits. You say that you want to be true to Christ's teaching, well that's one truth you can bellow from the pulpit."

Taking his bowed head as a sign of his submission, she dragged him from the vestry and into the chapel where she shoved him in front of the statue of the Black Madonna.

"Consider the Blessed Virgin, chosen by the Lord God himself to bear his only Son. Blessed is the womb that bore him and the breasts which he sucked."

Knox flushed as she unashamedly touched on those parts of the female body that set them apart from men and which set his colleagues smirking and sniggering with guilty embarrassment. Though they claimed that women were feeble creatures, this didn't ring true with Knox. They underestimated the mysterious powers a woman had either to kindle strong desires in a man, or to reduce him to an impotent larbar. His face burned as he reflected that beneath the nun's habit lurked a woman's body. In an effort to purge his impure thoughts, he tried to think of her as pure as the Virgin: unsullied, immaculate.

"I fear your mind is being poisoned, John. Take heed of Patrick Hamilton's tortuous death," she appealed to him. "If you will not take the oath against Lollardy, will you give me, your godmother, your word that you will forsake all heresy and that you will be forever true to your faith?"

He squirmed uncomfortably, unwilling even to look on the silly, simpering face of the Black Madonna.

"For that is the Hepburn motto: *Keep Tryst*. For my sake, swear on your life in front the Blessed Mother and her beloved Son that you will keep the faith."

"I swear," Knox said, keeping his voice low and solemn while crossing his fingers behind his back, "that I will: *Keep Tryst*."

Underneath the sweet scent of her French lavender oil he could sense her womanly smell and, when she kissed him gently on the forehead, his knees quivered.

"John, please don't consider us as monstrous creatures. It is my wish that, one day, you will be our herald and trumpet to the world the worth of women."

PART FOUR

I

Raggle Taggle Gypsy

> As soon as they saw her weel-favoured face
> They cast a glamour o'er her.
> *The Ballad of the Gypsy Laddie,* Traditional

Haddington, 1 May 1531

"All that lassies lack from head to heel," the tinker bellowed as he stepped out in front of him. "A bonnie wee fairing for your jo!"

Stumbling his way through the streets of Haddington bustling for the Beltane festivities, Knox cursed the chapman billies and tinkers raucously peddling their wares. The cacophonous din from pipers, minstrels and songsters all competing to be heard, hammered his reeling brain. Up ahead, Patrick and his cronies were lowping and jigging their way from stall to stall; knocking down pins at roly-poly, flinging the dice and losing on games of chance. Unlike them, he had no head for drinking bouts, nor was he in any mood to celebrate. Beaton had refused to register his graduation until he'd taken the Lollard oath and that he'd never do. Grabbing hold of a post, he leant his birling head against it to steady it.

"Beware of the bear, laddie!" the handler bawled. "For he'll drive you berserk."

Opening his dizzy eyes, Knox stared in alarm at the mangy brown bear being tethered to the stake beside him. The beast yelped in pain as its handler yanked at the chain, rubbing the iron collar against its raw inflamed neck. Tufts of mangy fur sprouted through patches of bare skin, covered in seeping sores, which never had a chance to heal. In his maudlin mood, tears of pity for the beast sprung to his eyes and Knox leaned over to stroke it. But misunderstanding his gesture, the maltreated beast gaunted toothless jaws and lashed out with its great paw.

"Bruin's no a dancing bear but you can teach him if you have a mind to, my bonnie lad," the handler grinned. "That's sure to draw a crowd."

Already a small gang had gathered with brutal bulldogs and mastiffs straining at the leash. Unable to watch the bear being baited, Knox pushed his way past the jesters and buffoons waving their jingling sticks, tumblers and rope-climbers turning head over heels, and causey–paikers hawking their favours. Every so often the cry: Stop thief! rang out as picky-fingered pursepikes weaved in and out amongst the crowd, helping themselves from the pockets of those too muddle-headed with drink to notice or care.

Then, catching sight of the Fair Earl's shock of blonde hair, he staggered over towards him. In a quiet corner of the marketplace, Bothwell and his companions were taunting a lass pinned up against the wall. As dark-skinned as the Black Madonna, the swarthy gypsy lass gawped, bleary-eyed with drink at her tormentors. Her naked belly, big with child, swelled over the top of her skirt and from under her bodice.

"This gypsy besom tried to cheat us," Bothwell slurred as he took a swig from a pewter flask.

"Aye, she's been demanding silver for reading palms," burly Patrick sneered, "when everyone kens you can't sell spaecraft. That's robbery. Forbye, look how much this hizzie has pilfered."

Burly Patrick and fat Patrick were two of the many bastard sons of the dissolute Patrick Hepburn who had succeeded his uncle John as Bishop of Moray and who, confusingly and vaingloriously, called all his offspring, after himself. The pair were sharing out coins she'd hidden in the pocket sewn inside her skirt.

"I'm no purse-pike. And I never ask for payment. Folk give freely for the good luck I bring," the gypsy lass retorted.

"And we'll take freely the favours you'll give," the earl jeered, thrusting his face into hers. When a gob of spittle landed on the earl's velvet jacket, fat Patrick grabbed her by the wrists. "This filthy wee trollop needs to be taught a lesson."

"Let her go," Knox barked. "Can you not see she's far gone with child?"

"Meaning she's been well ploughed. It's best to work a mare when she's in foal." The fat one licked his leering lips. Brought up by their dissolute uncle, a lecherous pervert with nearly twenty bastard sons, the Patricks had carnal knowledge well beyond their years. As he thrust his hand between her legs, Knox growled, "Leave her alone."

The gypsy lass focussed groggy eyes on him. "I ken those bonny blue een. I saw your future," she mumbled and put up two fingers. "Mind and choose aright."

"Don't think you're favoured just because she's giving you the glad eye, priestie. I'm the one to yoke her up," fat Patrick snarled.

Knox raised his fists to square up to him but a hard thump between the shoulders from behind hurled him headlong. Burly Patrick then heaved up the gypsy lass, threw her over his shoulders like a sack of oatmeal and lurched towards the river while she spewed a stream of vomit and ale down his back.

In the eerie May twilight, Knox trailed him down to the Tyne where he stopped underneath the span of the Nungate Bridge and dumped his load onto the grassy bank. After the muggy warmth of the day, an ethereal mist rose from the river, wreathing the bank and distorting everything familiar. A sudden flash of light burst in front of him and then just as suddenly dimmed. He watched it flickering and flitting hither and yon, now near, now just out of reach. The twinkling, twirling will o" the wisp was a bad omen: a malign spirit that presaged a tragedy or led the unwary to their death. While he always dispelled superstitions, Knox couldn't ignore the hairs rising on the back of his neck.

Alarmed, he turned to go, but stumbled over a boulder that gave a low, aggrieved moan as it lurched sideways. He thudded down beside the hunched form of Bothwell who thrust a flask under his nose. Through the wispy trails of mist a shape stirred under the bridge. The bare hurdies of the fat lad glimmered like pale moons in the gloaming as they heaved up and down. When, with a last gasp he collapsed on top of his victim, threatening to squash her to death, the burly one shoved him away to straddle her. Her warped cry – like a wild animal in pain – split the night air.

"Wait!" Knox yelled as he struggled to his feet.

"Don't meddle in their roistering Johnnie," Bothwell slurred. "You'll only come off worst. Here, a swig of this'll quicken your pistle."

Knox knocked the flask out of his hand and stumbled across the bumpy ground.

"Go on, priestie," the burly one dared him. "One more will no matter to her, but I wager it's the first time for you."

They had pulled her skirts up, exposing the swollen mound of her belly and the dark triangle beneath. Blood was oozing from the split between her splayed legs. Tears dribbled from beneath her closed eyes and she was breathing heavily. Knox crawled over and knelt in front of her, intending to pull down her petticoat to cover her nakedness.

Her eyelids flickered. "You, too, changeling," she burbled and puckered up swollen lips to spit at him. Stung by her words, Knox fell backwards onto his haunches.

"The devil swarbit on you all," she growled. "As for you," she panted, lifting her head to fix her dark eyes on Bothwell, "your loins will spawn devils that will bring shame on any woman they touch."

Bothwell's pale complexion tinged green as he took a gulp from the flask.

"Witch," burly Patrick muttered as he kicked her stomach.

"Carlin," the fat one growled as she rolled over hugging her belly in pain.

"Let's see if she is," the burly one said, looking round. "We need a douking stool. A plank of wood will do. If she sinks, she's the devil's own and if she floats, she isn't."

Knox shook his head to clear his befuddled wits. Was that the test for a witch? Or was it the other way round? Well, surely, with her womb so swollen, she wouldn't drown. He grabbed the flask from Bothwell.

"Sir, you are their lord. You must call off your henchmen," Knox hissed, shaking him by his humpit shoulders.

Bothwell tried to focus his sozzled eyes on him. "She's just a gypsy lass, Johnnie. A pagan. She doesn't have a soul like we do. If she is a witch, she deserves to die."

Knox half-crawled down to the riverbank where the two Patricks, having given up their search for a douking stool, had lifted the girl by the arms and legs.

"Nay!" Knox screamed out as he stumbled towards them.

"Heave ho!" They swung her once, twice and thrice before hurling her into the water. The Tyne was in full spate from the spring rains and swarms of May midges jittered above the ripples where she'd vanished.

Knox peered into the cold, greenish-brown water where he'd caught a glimmer of limbs and the sway of the black fronds of her hair undulating under the surface. He blinked to clear his vision. If he dived in, he could grab hold of her but the thought of being submerged in the dank river-water paralysed him. He stood rooted to the bank, as numb and wooden as a statue as the strong undercurrent carried her away. He wiped his clammy brow and turned to her tormentors.

"You'll hang for this!" he growled.

"And who's going to clype on us? You, priestie?"

While fat Patrick gripped him by the arms, burly Patrick punched him hard in the belly, knocking the wind out of him. Dragging his limp body by the legs they set off back down to the riverbank.

"One less priestie to mar our fun."

"Leave him be!" Bothwell struggled to his feet to block their way. "Here, take this!"

Dropping their burden to the ground with a callous thump, the two Patricks wrestled with each other for the purse of silver he'd thrown at them.

II

The Thirling of Bothwell

To the great God Omnipotent
Confess thy Sin, and sore repent,
And trust in Christ, as writes Paul,
Who shed his blood to save thy soul:
For nane can thee absolve but he,
Nor take away thy sin from thee.
Kitty's Confession
Anonymous, 16th Century

Edinburgh Castle, August 1531

As the warder unlocked the studded iron door, a sickening sour-sweet stench belched out from the cell. Knox screwed up his nose while Elisabeth covered her mouth with her wide sleeve and tried not to gag. They both hovered in the low doorway, waiting till their eyes adjusted to the dimness. A chink of light through the narrow slit in the far wall was enough to show a bedraggled figure cowering in the corner. He was curled up into a ball, his head resting on knees tucked into his chest, his feet shackled in chains. His flaxen hair was leaden grey and lank with grease and straggled untidily over his hunched shoulders.

"Get up onto your feet to greet your holy visitors."

The prisoner flinched at the warder's voice, his frightened eyes squinting in the unexpected light. As he stumbled to his feet, the stink from his soiled breeches grew sharper.

"They can't cut my head off," he snivelled, sniffing back the snot hanging from his nose. His eyelids were encrusted with pus and inflamed from hours of weeping. "I am the Earl of Bothwell," he maintained, though his voice was squeaky with fear.

"You don't seem to have learnt your lesson, Patrick. You've been charged with treason," his aunt said impatiently.

He lowered his head and howled like a fox caught in a trap. For this wasn't the first time that he'd been imprisoned for giving protection to robbers in Liddesdale. His failure to oust Angus from his coastal eyrie of Tantallon, even with the promise of the castle as a reward, was another black mark against him. Looking at him as he sat in his own mess, a midden of his own making, Elisabeth despaired of ever persuading him to take responsibility for his actions. Bothwell blew with the wind, like one of God's fools, above the common law.

211

"This is far more serious: a hanging offence. Take heed of how the reivers Johnnie Armstrong of Gilnockie and his henchmen were strung up."

"Am I to die? Don't let them hang me, Johnnie," he snivelled while Knox hunkered down beside him. "You've always stood by me. Stay with me. Don't leave me now. Hear my last confession."

Patrick's jaw slackened, his lips trembled and his eyes began to water. Please don't weep, Elisabeth begged silently. Cringing and wretched, he appeared to have none of the traits of his father – if indeed he were his father's son – or even his grandfather. The first earl, Patrick, had earned his title; the second, Adam, had given his life for his country, and now, the third earl had been found guilty of betraying his monarch.

What a great pity Adam had been slain! He'd never have allowed his son to grow into this petulant milksop, his shoulders stooped under the weight of all his perceived grievances. But, however much her nephew deserved punishment, however much he'd weakened the Hepburn line, she couldn't allow it to die out.

With this lofty end in mind, Elisabeth knelt before King James to plead for his life.

"Whatever Patrick may have done, I beg Your Grace to grant him mercy."

"I've shown great forbearance with your nephew, Dame Prioress, but the Fair Earl has overstepped himself with this."

James unclenched his fist and thrust a missive into her hands. She quickly scanned it, shaking her head in disbelief as she read how Bothwell was offering to bring six thousand commoners and one thousand gentlemen to the service of Henry VIII, should the English monarch wish to invade Scotland.

"There must be some mistake."

"No mistake." James jabbed his finger at the foot of the document. "There, do you see?"

There was no doubting the distinctive flourish of the Snowdon Herald's signature.

"He sent me this missive or I wouldn't have believed it otherwise. Bothwell was one of the three lords I trusted to sit upon my secret council. But Davie Lindsay is my eyes and ears at the English court. Would that he were here now for I am surrounded by traitors. Who am I to trust?"

The king's breaking voice sounded tetchy and insecure, as if he were on the verge of tears. And then he began to pad about restlessly, nervously stroking his wispy beard as if willing it to grow more profusely for a lush growth would be a visible sign of manhood, a symbol of strength to all challengers. Another young lad with too much responsibility. Not yet twenty years of age but with all the worries and concerns of the kingdom on his narrow shoulders. A puppet king, manipulated by the lairds for their own ends. Elisabeth could not but feel sorry for him, but would he feel the same for Patrick?

212

"Your Grace may take into account the earl's youth. And the fact that he lost his father at a young age," she began, hoping to evoke some fellow feeling for an orphan.

"He wasn't the only one," James snapped.

"But the Fair Earl was then abandoned by his mother when she took another spouse."

"Aye, as I was too. But chancy for him, he didn't have Angus as his stepfather: a mishanter and milygant, in league with Auld Nick himself. Are you saying that Bothwell has fallen under his evil spell?"

More likely beglamoured by gold, Elisabeth thought. Patrick's peerie heid, easily swivelled by the promise of money, made him easy prey.

But these were not just glib, toom-tongued words. James truly believed that Angus had learnt the black arts from his mother and knew how to cast cantrips to bewitch his allies and curses to menace his foes. To forestall this he'd asked Beaton to use his powers to excommunicate him but the abbot had no authority to do so. Instead, he'd issued a decree denying anyone of the name Douglas, their tenants included, the holy sacraments.

Being refused baptism, matrimony and Christian burial, however, was having less effect on the heathen Douglas tribe than the cancellation of their grazing rights on the vast Church lands and being refused access to the monastic mills to grind their grain. Spiritual deprivation might have little effect on their immortal souls, but leaving their unharvested grain to rot in the fields and imposing increased tithes and payments, would starve out the Douglas clan.

"But unlike you, the Fair Earl lacks a mother's love," Elisabeth now said. Despite Margaret Tudor's past misdemeanours, James seemed to have been genuinely fond of his mother for he had not only sanctioned her divorce from Angus but also given her new husband, Henry Stewart, the title of Lord Methven. Meanwhile Bothwell's mother, the flighty Nancy Stewart, married for the third time to Lord Robert Maxwell, had well and truly flown the coop. To Thrieve Castle in the far south west of Scotland.

Seeing James stroke his beard as he considered this, Elisabeth went on, "Forbye, neither has my loveless, luckless nephew been gifted with your wisdom or wit, sire. Nor has he been blessed with such a wise guide and prudent guardian as Sir David Lindsay."

The king's boyish face lit up at Elisabeth's words.

"Aye, indeed, my faithful tutor. Only Da Lindsay is true to me."

How she wished she could say the same. Before leaving on a diplomatic mission Lindsay had promised to take her with him. Urging her to be like her Papingo. To stretch her wings and fly off with him across the seas to far-flung places, but the Snowdon Herald had only got as far as the English court to spy for James. She'd always known that his first loyalty was to the king. Once this difficult period was over, then perhaps …

James was now frowning. "Da Lindsay, too, tries to convince me that the earl is a victim of circumstances. But what am I to do with him? If I don't execute him, my lords will think me weak." His voice rose to a petulant whine.

Sensing from James's crestfallen face that he was swithering, she hastened to say, "May I remind you that you and the earl are bonded by blood, Your Grace. You share a half-sister, Jenny."

Perhaps a sense of kinship would soften his heart. As she observed him shaping his scraggy beard into a point, she was struck by the likeness between the king and the earl: fatherless bairns with absent mothers, both lads sulky and resentful. Could the rumour that James IV had sired Patrick indeed be true?"

"*Treat ilk true baron as he were thy brother,*" she started to say, "*Which must at need thee and thy realm defend.*"

With this quotation she had the king's ear, which he inclined towards her, listening intently as she went on:

> "When suddenly one doth oppress one other,
> Let justice mixed with mercy them amend.
> If you have their hearts you have enough to spend …"

"Ha, these are Da Lindsay's words, no? He's aye scrieving lines like that for me. Never gives up advising, counselling. Aye, and complaining."

"Aye, indeed. They're from his poem, *The Tragedy of the Papingo*. The death of my pet bird inspired him to write these lines advocating mercy and I'm sure, if he were here now, Sir David would have wise advice with regard to the wanwittit earl."

"So, what would his counsel be?" James asked plaintively.

Knox sighed and heaved himself up from the dank floor of the cell. He was about to call for the warder to be let out when Bothwell yelped, "Don't go, Johnnie. Stay and tell me, what sin must I confess? What have I done wrong?"

Being urged to confess, Bothwell had, with prompting, owned up to some minor, venial sins. "Maybe I've swyved with a lassie or two but they were willing enough. And maybe I've taken the Lord's name in vain but then who doesn't?"

"And the gypsy lass. What about her?"

"Oh, aye, that still tortures me."

"Then confess. Make an act of contrition and you shall be absolved."

Bothwell gave him a blank, glaikit stare. "Confess? For doing what? I've done nothing wrong. She's to blame for all my bad luck. Didn't she put a curse on me? May she rot in hell."

Knox took a deep breath. Years of being tutored by his reprobate uncle Patrick, now Bishop of Moray, had cleansed Bothwell of any conscience. He had no concept of sin for, if he could justify any of his actions or pass on the blame, then they were not, to his mind, sinful.

"It is what you did not do, Sir Patrick. You could have stopped your kinsmen from flinging her in the river. A sin of omission is just as venial, or as mortal, as a sin of commission."

Bothwell furrowed his brow.

"I'm no scholar, Johnnie, as you well ken. I trauchled with Latin and so I cannot understand all yon flumgummery. But I wasn't to blame. I'm the one who was accursed when that heathen put her damned spell on me. Forbye, did I not save your life? And that cost me dear. A whole purseful. We're brothers in blood, now. So, since you're in my debt, you can cast out the gypsy's spell for me with your priestly blessings, Johnnie. Rid me of the evil eye that has blasted my life."

Knox sighed. The earl was as contrite as the fox in Henryson's Tale. In the Tod's confession to Friar Wolf his only regret was that he'd slain so few sweet hens. Aware that further theological discussion would be pointless, Knox instructed him to repeat after him the *Confiteor* in Latin.

What could be done with a penitent who showed neither understanding nor remorse for his sins? Knox reflected as he made his way towards the king's stables. Should he have absolved Patrick after his empty act of contrition? But then how many of his congregation were ever truly sorry for their sins? When Knox had finally said, *Et dimissis peccatis tuis,* Bothwell seemed reassured that these magic words would exorcise his demons. Was that all they were? A magic spell?

Elisabeth was more satisfied with her morning's work. After they had picked up their horses and they were riding down the Lawnmarket she said, "Dame Fortune has smiled on the Fair Earl. King James has shown mercy. He is to bide in Edinburgh Castle as his ward." Only after she'd agreed to pay a substantial bond as guarantee of his good behaviour. "And when he comes of age, he'll be married. If we can find a suitable wife," she added with a sigh, feeling sympathy in advance for the woman doomed to marital thirling with Patrick.

"Earl Patrick has aye been pompous and vain but his nature has been further spoilt by his uncle," Knox said grimly.

Glancing at his face, stern as a judge, Elisabeth was pleasantly surprised at his readiness to forgive human failings. Justice mixed with mercy: Lindsay's influence hadn't been totally harmful. Knox would make a good notary apostolic, she decided, and that would help further his career in the Church.

They had reached Holyrood Park where they would set their palfreys to canter, when Knox snarled, "Wantonness has weakened the earl's wits. That well-knit lecher and whoremonger, the Bishop of Moray, has taught him to value gold over goodness and the flesh over the spirit. But never fear. His like will burn in the flames of hell," he spat out angrily.

Or perhaps not, Elisabeth reconsidered.

III

The Royal Hunt

"Away, away, thou traitor strang!
Out of my sight soon may'st thou be!
I granted never a traitor's life,
And now I'll not begin with thee."
The Ballad of Johnnie Armstrong, Traditional

Meggetland, August 1531

The royal hunting party had left Traquair House at daybreak and ridden through the Ettrick Forest with little success. Cursing the thieving poachers, the Master of Hounds was calling in his pack of fallow hounds and buckhounds scampering among the underbrush on the scent of deer.

"The men will be moaning," Margaret Erskine whined. "They loathe losing the chance to smear themselves with stag's blood after the gralloching. Doubtless they'll be after the blood of the poachers."

The king's favourite mistress had shaved her hairline to emphasise her fashionably plucked eyebrows and raising them usually suggested criticism, Elisabeth had noticed. Those eyebrows had arched on being told who would be joining the royal hunt. A prioress indeed! Shouldn't she be praying in her cloister? And then again – on scrutinising the tight-fitting jacket and the specially made leather breeches which enabled Elisabeth to ride astride a saddle. Now their haughty elevation implied that it was *her* fault that the royal chase was being deprived of game, not only because the lands belonged to Bothwell but because the Hepburns had been laggard in routing the reivers in the Meggetdale and may even be in league with them.

"The Fair Earl was lucky not to lose his head, only his freedom. He should be grateful to His Grace for showing mercy," Lady Margaret declared.

Elisabeth held her tongue, resisting the temptation to answer back. If that was the price to pay for being invited to hunt with the royal party, it was worth it. To be back in the saddle galloping across open ground, breathing in the sharp, crisp moorland air was exhilarating and made her feel alive. And if it meant feigning fawning gratitude, then so be it. Besides, she preferred hawking on the wild open moorland to hunting with hounds in the deep, dark confines of the forest with the continual threat of ambush.

Gradually the trees began to thin out to scrubland where black cattle, grazing among the whins, scattered as the riders trotted by. By mid-morning they were galloping across wide, rounded swelling hills clothed in purple heather and brown bracken and strewn with lichen-covered rocks. Their horses flew over the drystane, dividing dykes and splashed through sparkling burns that tumbled down mossy banks into black pools. High above the hawks circled then hurtled down at great speed to snatch their prey – blue hares and rabbits.

They stopped at midday beside a burn for the horses to drink the peaty water and for Margaret Erskine to rest. Though she was heavily pregnant with the king's bairn, she had insisted on joining the hunt to keep in check the king's roving eye and wandering shanks. Taking after his father, James V had a fancy for disguising himself as a beggar to traverse the land. Crying himself the Gaberlunzie Man, he would seek shelter in hovels where young maidens would take pity on him. How many bastards he may have sired from his roving, Margaret didn't know, but she was making sure that hers would be acknowledged as having royal blood.

With her right hand, Elisabeth shielded her eyes against the sun, held out her left arm encased in a leather gauntlet, scanned the sky and waited. In a flash, her favourite peregrine falcon alighted on her wrist. Its hard yellow eyes fixed her with a look so akin to her Papingo that it made her heart jolt. She covered those piercing eyes with a hood and cautiously transferred the falcon to a perch. A falcon is an eagle's prey, she thought as she positioned herself on a rug near enough the ladies of the court to hearken to their gossip.

"She's still a Douglas. And with those skellie eyes what's to stop her casting a hex on His Grace? Or withering my womb with her evil eye?"

Elisabeth pursed her lips. They were tearing to pieces Jinty Douglas whose husband Lord Glamis, a friend and supporter of King James had died suddenly. Jinty had been accused of poisoning him, though why she should murder her beloved husband was never explained. Elisabeth wouldn't be surprised if the malicious Margaret Erskine herself were behind the rumours. She could hold her silence no longer.

"But the charges against her were dropped, were they not?" she dared to point out.

Beneath the arched eyebrows, Lady Margaret's eyes smouldered with spite. Though she was the king's favourite mistress, the title she coveted was queen, but while she was still wed to Sir Robert Douglas of Lochleven that could never happen. It made more sense for her husband to be poisoned, leaving her free to marry the king, Elisabeth thought. While the position of queen consort was vacant, Margaret regarded any unwed lady of rank with jealous suspicion, and Jinty, a young widow with a rare kind of glamour, was now a potential rival.

"The trial collapsed because the jurors failed to appear. And, pray tell me, why? Because they were bribed to do so. No doubt by Angus himself, to save his own sister. Thon Douglases will do anything to gain power. Who's to say that Angus isn't now plotting to put his sister Jinty on the throne? That she poisoned her husband so she'd be free to wed His Grace? And that, with thon squinty eyes, she uses witchcraft to beguile men?"

Meddlesome minx, Elisabeth thought. Had she conveniently forgotten that she herself was married to a Douglas? Jinty may have kept her skin this time but clearly she wasn't out of the woods yet, with Lady Erskine ruffling a whaup in the nest. Just then, the horn signalled the start of the hunt.

They would soon be within sight of Caerlanrig, Lady Margaret announced. Where Johnnie Armstrong and forty of his men had been executed without trial on the king's orders. Hempen ropes had been slung over branches of trees, nooses placed round their necks and their horses shooed from under them. Tales were told that, since then, the trees had withered and never flourished again, leaving the site abandoned and godless. Despite the warmth of the day and the heat worked up by the hunt, Elisabeth shivered. Not from dread of catching a glimpse of shrivelled corpses dangling from wind-twisted hawthorns but in sympathy for the ghosts of those who, having been promised safe conduct, were unjustly jettisoned into the next world.

"That's how His Grace deals with his enemies," Lady Margaret declared proudly, with a warning glance at Elisabeth. "No quarter given."

On the way to Melrose they crossed over the Eildon Hills where Thomas the Rhymer had descended into Fairyland. Elisabeth hummed the ballad to herself quietly while she cantered along, wondering which of the hillocks might be the fabled fairy mound.

> He heard the trampling of a steed,
> He saw the flash of armour flee
> And he beheld a gallant knight
> Come riding down by the Eildon tree.

They were about to crest the hill when a scout reported sighting a small group of horsemen making its way along Tweed valley. An English raiding party, perhaps? Or marauding border reivers? They reined in their horses and waited for the order to flee but, after being identified, the horsemen were taken to report to King James. There followed a brief discussion and then the riders, a weary band of Scots returning from the English court, fell in beside the hunters.

"Have you come all this way to blow your horn for the hunt, Lyon Herald?"

Lindsay stopped rubbing his stubbly cheeks, streaked with dust and grime from the long journey, to stare at her in surprise.

"What are you doing here, Lis … Dame Prioress?"

"You didn't recognise me in my new riding gear. A gift from King James himself. Specially made for me by the finest seamstress in the land …"

He looked abashed, Elisabeth thought, and so he should. She couldn't resist a smug smile as she went on, "The king's wardrobe mistress, no less."

Lindsay reined his horse round and, as they rode side by side, she prattled on merrily.

"Only the best cloth for the hunting-coat and the supplest of leather for my breeches. Though I drew the line at any plumage." She put up a hand to her velvet bonnet, recalling the sight of Beaton's ridiculous feathered *chapeau*. "Forbye, I'm a prioress, not a lady of fashion."

Nor was the Mistress of the King's Wardrobe, Jessie Douglas. And never would be for she was plain, she'd said sadly, her long face drooping even more. "I may be a fine seamstress, but I'd fain be bonnie."

And no amount of bathing her face in the dew on a May morning would get rid of the scarring from smallpox. In vain she'd tried every auld wives" remedy.

"If I were bonnie and not an old scrag of mutton," Jessie went on wistfully, "my good man might not find me tiresome."

She twisted her fingers nervously then dropped her voice to a confidential whisper. "Dame Prioress, is it true that there is a sister at the abbey who can work miraculous cures? That she has found the elixir of beauty?"

So the court ladies had reported when they extolled the virtues of Sister Agnes's remedies. What a surprise that would be for her husband when he came back! In gratitude for her painstakingly precise tailoring, Elisabeth had given the glaikit seamstress some of Agnes's salves, which she slapped on her plook-ridden skin religiously, morning and night. To little avail – apart from giving her some hope.

Elisabeth brought her horse to a halt and wheeled it round.

"Do you see those hills over yonder?"

Lindsay's gaze followed her gloved hand pointing at the purple-misted Eildons.

"Yon is where Thomas the Rhymer disappeared for seven long years, forsaking his loved ones to bide with the Queen of Fairyland. He came back with two gifts. One was the gift of prophecy: and the other, a tongue that could never lie. Since I doubt you have the second sight, Davie, will you now tell me the truth?"

IV

Twice-Marrit Lindsay

> "Away wi your former vows," she says
> For they will breed but strife;
> Away wi your former vows," she says,
> "For I am become a wife."
> *The Ballad of the Demon Lover,* Traditional

Stirling Castle, 1521

"Da Lindsay, you shall wed Nurse Marion," the boy king decreed. "You'll be my father and Marion will be my mother. And then you can both look after me."

"If she were willing, I would consider it an honour to take Nurse Marion as my wife." Lindsay winked at her behind the young monarch's back as he sat on his hunkers to survey his army of toy soldiers lined up across the floor. "If she'll have me."

"Me? Your wife? I'm o'er auld to marry," she hooted in reply. A stout, motherly woman in her early fifties with an easy-going, kindly nature, Marion Douglas had been the king's nursemaid since his birth. "Davie Lindsay needs a younger and bonnier lass, no an old wizened crone like me."

"I'd rather have you any day than some of those painted floozies that decorate the court."

"You're aye the gentleman, Davie Lindsay. I can see that it would take more than a pretty face to turn your head. Now, my kinswoman, Janet that we cry Jessie, would make him a good wife, Your Grace."

The boy king's expression was serious as he contemplated this.

"She may no be bonnie but she's no flibbertigibbet either. She's a couthy, canty lass, steady and hardworking. And there would be no harm in marrying one of us." Marion cast Lindsay a meaningful glance.

It was no secret that, as soon as Regent Albany returned to France, Angus would attempt to seize power to prevent his estranged wife, Margaret Tudor, holding the reins for her son. Nor did Angus hide the fact that he was jealous of Lindsay's influence over the young monarch and wanted rid of him. Being married to a Douglas might mean a stay of execution for Lindsay.

Jessie Douglas came from an impoverished scion of the family but her legendary skill with a needle had earned her a place at court as seamstress. Not only could she sew a fine seam, with the tiniest stitches invisible to the naked eye but she had a way of cutting cloth to drape so elegantly that it veiled defects of figure.

While her skills were much sought after, she herself was not. With neither beauty nor dowry, Jessie expected to go to her grave an old maid, and so a proposal of marriage from the king's own gentleman usher and tutor was most unexpected and most welcome. Flushed and flustered as a young maiden, she accepted, and when, in honour of their marriage, James elevated her to Mistress of the King's Wardrobe, she was overjoyed. Despite reaching the dizzy pinnacle of her career, Jessie remained a douce, simple soul who resisted all her husband's efforts to teach her to read and write.

"Such learning is not for the likes of me! A gowk with no head for letters."

Yet, Lindsay would point out, she could measure up to within a twelfth of an inch, calculate exactly how many yards were needed for a garment and judge the quality of a cloth by its weight, but it made no difference. His praise made her blush with embarrassment and tilt her head to one side with a coy smile. She was quite content to listen to Lindsay reading out his poems while she plied her needle.

While her meekness may be commendable, it hindered her from being able to gainsay the young monarch. His royal wish was her command and his first, on coming of age at twelve years old, had been to burn all his childhood clothes. Those practical woollen garments of grey, russet and black were far too drab and mundane for a monarch, he had decided. While James jigged and reeled about the bonfire, screeching encouragement, Lindsay looked on aghast as his wife flung them onto the flames.

Not even given away to the poor, he complained. Though learning humility was beginning to seem a lost cause, then at least James might have acquired the virtue of charity. Instead, Jessie was pandering to his vanity, turning the monarch into a manikin by choosing the most sumptuous fabrics and extravagant trimmings for his new clothes; breeches of crimson satin, doublets of plush velvet, bonnets trimmed with outrageous plumes, robes of cloth of gold embroidered with pearls and encrusted with precious stones. James V had inherited his Tudor mother's love of finery.

"Forbye, he's the king. It's his right to be clad in the best," Jessie said to excuse him.

"But not to be pricking and prinning himself like a pensie princess."

In vain Lindsay grumbled, shaking his head as James strutted about proudly showing off each new lavish costume: with rings on his fingers and bells on his toes.

When Lindsay was dismissed from court along with all the other members of James's childhood entourage, Jessie was spared. Not for being a Douglas, though that was the whisper, but because of her sewing skills. Keeping the vain boy king amused with clothes of wondrous splendour and extravagance, left Angus free to pursue his political joukerie-pawkery.

After listening to his tale, Elisabeth looked at him askance. And did the twice-marrit Lindsay – thrice-marrit if he counted their handfasting – ever intend to tell her that he had taken yet another wife? she enquired.

"Lisbeth, you must believe me. I never meant to mislead you. We haven't lived as man and wife for years. It's hardly a marriage. While Jessie may be my wife in law, she has never been my soulmate." He frowned, the lines on his face deepening to accentuate his look of utter dejection.

"You've been most ill-fated in your selection of wives, Davie Lindsay. It makes me question your taste in women."

As they trotted along, he held the reins in one hand and began to count his fingers on the other, enumerating the various grounds he had for an annulment. There had been no issue from their marriage that, if truth be told, had never been consummated. They had been separated for several years. And most importantly, if their handfasting were acknowledged, then he was already married – to Elisabeth.

"At least we have a witness in Betsy. And King James will show favour. Then you can accompany me to foreign courts."

She gazed ahead, blinking rapidly to clear the tears that threatened to mist up her eyes.

"Oh, Davie, what a buttery-lippit hunker-slider you've proved to be. Your poet's tongue can beglamour with all kinds of dreams and fancies."

She brought her horse to a halt and then turned in the saddle to glare at him.

"Whatever tales you spin me, you must tell John the truth. For some reason he reveres you – or at least he's put Friar Lazarus on a pedestal. Forbye, his ambition is to become a Franciscan, like the blessed friar."

Lindsay's face twisted in pain, wounded by the scoffing sarcasm he knew he deserved.

"Lest I forget, take this." She tore off her gauntlet and pulled the ring from her finger. "Put this ring back on your finger where it belongs. You'll aye be the king's man, Davie Lindsay."

Pressing the ring into his palm, she spurred on her horse and rode off to join Margaret Erskine's entourage.

V

The Pardoner's Tale

> My patent pardons you may see
> Come from the Khan of Tartary
> Well sealed with oyster-shells;
> Though ye have nae contrition
> Ye shall have full remission
> With help of books and bells.
>
> *Ane Satire of the Three Estates*
> Sir David Lindsay, 16th Century

Haddington, 1536

Knox left the courtroom in a foul temper. At the age of twenty-three, with Prioress Elisabeth's intercession, he'd at last been ordained a priest by the Bishop of Dunblane. But, with Beaton's intervention, he suspected, he'd not been assigned a parish. Instead, the prioress had suggested that he train to become a notary apostolic, a position that would appeal to his innate sense of justice. While the legal work veered from the boring and mundane – drawing up and witnessing documents, dealing with disputes between neighbours – it was court duty that roused his blood.

Today Knox had faced yet another flagrant flouting of the law. A blacksmith who had lent his neighbour a horse that had then drowned in a quarry was seeking compensation. Totally bewildered by the Latin legal terms, the illiterate blacksmith had failed to pay his court fees on time and was being forced to pay "sentence-silver." When he'd dared to challenge this unfair verdict, Knox had been overruled. Now, as he made his way back to the abbey, he strove to curb his anger at this latest example of injustice.

A fine drizzle was falling, mingling with the dung and muck chucked onto the street and leaving the cobblestones dangerously slippery. Unaware that her stylish petticoat tails were leaving a snail's trail through the sludge at her back, an elegantly clad young woman had hitched up the front of her skirt to avoid the swill. These young kitties would never forfeit fashion for forethought: they'd rather be dead. Knox shook his head in disapproval. This new French style that was literally sweeping the streets had inspired at least one poet to ridicule the folly of it. What were the rude verses that were going round?

> I ken ane man who swore great oaths
> How he did lift ane kittock's clothes
> And would have done, I know nocht what,
> But soon remeid of love he got.

He thocht nae shame to make it witten,
How her side tail was all beschitten.

When she turned and winked at him, Knox fled across the market square. He had
to push his way through a rabble of drink-fuelled young bucks whose entertainment
consisted of tossing bawbees into the gutter and jeering at the miserable beggars
scrabbling for them. In the midst of this heaving mass of desperate poor, a scrawny
lad and scraggy lass were being trod on and kicked as they grappled for a groat.
When at last the lad grasped a coin, a heavy boot ground down to crush his fingers,
but he wouldn't let go.

Knox waded in to pull the lad and lass from the scrum and thrust some coins into
their skinned hands. While wiping down his mud-splashed hose he noticed the look
of cold fear erasing the gratitude on their shrunken faces. The other beggars were
skulking round them with darkly envious glances. As soon as he left they would
ambush the miserable mites.

In the abbey kitchen, Sister Agnes gazed with pity at the two winsome waifs
ladling broth into their mouths. Tattered rags hung from their skeletal bodies and
stinking mud splattered their barefooted legs. Clarty streaks ran down the lass's
hollow cheeks as she licked her bowl clean while her brother's hungry eyes pleaded
silently for more.

"I'll go and find some warm clothes for them to wear home."

"They have no home to go to," Knox replied. "Neither mother nor father, nor
even a merciful church father. They've walked all the way from Tranent. Father
Cadell should be black affronted."

Hardly was their father cold in his bed when the buttery-lippit corbie had flapped
down to get his claws into the corpse-present: his coat, the quilt and his best cow.
When their mother, a wretched widow, died not long after, the predatory priest had
returned to take the other cow, condemning these bairns to destitution and beggary.

"Hanging by the neck is the penalty for a paltry thief, but there is no such
punishment for the grasping clergy who besiege the beds of the dying to extort
bequests for themselves or the Vatican on pain of hellfire," Knox snarled. "The
bishops have thumbed their noses at the king's request to forbid the exaction of the
corpse-present as a death-due to the Church."

While Knox railed against their plight, struggling to suppress his pent-up fury,
Sister Agnes could only reply, "The poor, as Christ said, will always be with us, John."

"Aye, but that need not mean that the very people who should be showing them
charity, the clergy, should trample them further into the dirt with their greedy
trotters. Where's the justice in that?"

"Don't worry, John, they will be called to account on the Day of Judgement."

That was not soon enough for Knox who stomped off to Tibbie's Tavern to sluice out the anger rising in his gullet. Inside, a crowd had gathered round a trestle laden with knick-knacks, a tinker's stall, he assumed, until he caught sight of Father Cadell presiding over it.

"Ah Master Knox, have you come here to seek out an indulgence? The pardoner here has sacred relics that will lessen your soul's stay in purgatory."

"It is you who would fear eternal damnation, Father Cadell. For devouring a widow's house and stealing from two orphan bairns."

The priest held out his arms in supplication. "Is the law sinful? You cannot accuse me of theft. I only ever take what is my due: Render unto Caesar, saith the Lord."

Knox took a deep breath to control his anger. It was true. Since the Church connived in the parish priest's greed, there was nothing he could do, not even as notary apostolic, to bring him to account. And if the shameless priest could stand behind a stall, brazenly selling false promises to poor, guileless folk, then he had no conscience.

Just then a skirmish broke out behind him. A hired man in ragged nicky tams was shouting and waving a shard of bone in the face of a man dressed in a long black coat and a wide-brimmed hat.

"My cattle are all dead!" the hind was screaming. "This bone of St. Bride that you said would cure them is of no use. I gave you my last groat for this shard of shit! Give me my money back!"

The man in black shook his head, the smile on his lips patronising. "Nay, nay! I cannot give you back your money, for it will break the sacred contract. But I tell you what I'll do. I'll bless it again. Free. Gratis. *Deo Gratias.*" He took out a phial of holy water and sprinkled it over the bone. "And this time your pardon will last a thousand years."

"A thousand years? I'll no live that long. I crave no pardon. I want my last groat back."

The pardoner chuckled as if at a secret joke before addressing the crowd who had gathered round the disaffected hind.

"Take heed while I explain." Which he did, slowly and deliberately, as if speaking to a dullard or a simpleton. "When you die and are condemned to purgatory, say for a thousand years, then you'll be able to redeem this pardon and go forthwith to Paradise."

"Not till I die? Not till then? And what if the good Lord condemns me for more than a thousand years?" the hind asked.

"In that case your stay there will be cut short by that time."

"But what if I end up in hell? How shall I redeem my pardon then?"

When the pardoner raised his eyes and extended his arms as if to say, O Lord, grant me patience, Knox grabbed one of his arms.

"Give him back his money," he snarled. His blue eyes flashed with barely controllable anger. "Your kind are nothing but blood-sucking leeches. Even the most sleekit tinker bearing tawdry wares is more honest than you. Swindling honest, simple folk into parting with money for a bogus promise. Hanging, drawing and quartering is too good for cozeners such as you."

The pardoner feigned an ingratiating smile as he shrugged off Knox's grasp. "I see that you're a man of the Church. My work is sanctioned by no less an authority than the Vatican itself," he started to protest, "as Father Cadell will verify."

Knox clenched his fists, digging his nails hard into the palms of his hands to stop himself from hitting out at the sacrilegious scoundrel.

"Peddling dead men's bones for pardons. Pious defrauding of the faithful with the false promise that: *as soon as the coin in the coffer rings, so the soul from purgatory springs,*" he trilled with undisguised sarcasm. "These so-called indulgences are just another ruse to fill the papal treasure house. Why do you line the pudgy paunches of Romish cardinals when the bellies of our own folk are squashed flat against their spines?"

Knox cast a scornful eye over the table where the charlatan had laid his god-forsaken gew-gaws and then, filling his lungs, he heaved it up and tipped it over. In a frenzy of anger, he trampled on the so-called relics; crushing bones of martyred saints, scattering splinters of the True Cross and smashing to smithereens phials of the Virgin Mary's blood which splattered the floor with ruby-red tears.

Blinded with rage, he stumbled outside and was struggling to control his temper when someone grabbed him by the arm.

"Well done, John," Friar Lazarus said with a smile. "Well done."

VI

Ordeal by Fire

Thou shalt not suffer a witch to live.
Exodus XXII:18

Edinburgh, July 1537

"I hear they are preparing a pyre on castle hill," Joanna said.

From the window of her sister's chamber in St.Catherine's Convent, situated on high ground to the south, Elisabeth had a panoramic view of the city dominated by Edinburgh Castle squatting like a toad on a rock.

"For a reformist martyr?" Elisabeth asked.

Joanna gave her a stern look. "Nay, not for any *heretic*," she said spitting out the hateful word.

Now that both sisters were mother superiors of convents they should have more in common, Elisabeth thought. However, the severe black habit of the Dominican Order matched Joanna's stricter, more orthodox views – her support of the campaign by the Archbishop of St.Andrews and his nephew, David Beaton, to burn out heresy, for example – whereas Elisabeth's cream-coloured Cistercian robes reflected her more tolerant outlook. Again the difference was manifest in the way they ran their convents. The refuge of St.Mary's welcomed hopeless cases – fallen women, wretches wasted with *aquavitae* – while St.Catherine's "City of Ladies" preferred pious penitents and paupers with a prospect of salvation.

"A witch," Joanna stated.

"So some poor lass, then," Elisabeth said sadly.

"Poor lass or not, one of the Douglas tribe has been found guilty of conspiring to kill the king. Lady Glamis that was, Lady Campbell that is, or Jinty Douglas as she's better kent."

At the gate of Edinburgh Castle, a grisly, blood-spattered head impaled on a stake brought Elisabeth up sharp. This gruesome caricature of its owner had belonged to the Master of Forbes, a guard informed her. The skull of Jinty's son-in-law leered at her like the one in her nightmares. She hurried on past and into the castle.

Elisabeth had come to plead for mercy for Jinty but, on requesting an audience with King James, she was confronted by his mistress, Margaret Erskine. His Grace had gone hunting, she informed her with an insincere smile, and the prioress need not wait for his return: for one thing he would be gone for several days and for another he would be deaf to any defence of a Douglas.

"If that is indeed so, Lady Douglas, then you, too, must be cautious."

Margaret Erskine's lips compressed and her high drawn eyebrows fused as she glared at Elisabeth. "My husband has aye been a faithful friend to His Grace."

So faithful a friend was the gallant Douglas of Lochleven that he'd turned a blind eye to his wife's unfaithfulness, Elisabeth thought.

Besides, Margaret Erskine had continued, the prioress's intercession would be futile for Jinty's servants had already confessed that her family had been plotting with Angus to organise a coup. And hadn't her churlish brother George threatened to tear the young king in two when he'd tried to escape his gaolers? James had never forgiven this terrible show of *lèse-majesté*.

More seriously, Jinty, her husband and her young son had been found guilty of conspiracy to poison the king. His Grace could not turn a blind eye to high treason, Lady Margaret said haughtily and reminded her of the fate of the reiver, Johnnie Armstrong of Gilnockie, hanged from a tree in Liddesdale.

"And tomorrow I'm to be burnt on the pyre …"

With creaking knees and feeling all of her thirty-five years, Elisabeth crouched down on the floor beside Jinty chained to the wall of her cell. Her jailer stood near the door, watchful that nothing passed between them.

She moistened her lips with her tongue, then gazed skellie-eyed at Elisabeth who tried to focus on the gap between her eyebrows. The disconcerting cast in her eyes, more pronounced in her grey, grief-stricken face, gave Jinty a fey, demented look.

"… as a witch." She chewed the dry, cracked skin of her bottom lip until she drew blood. "But there may still be hope," Jinty went on. "If I throw myself on the king's mercy, perhaps he will show clemency. He must." Her voice rose to a desperate squeal. "I'm the mother of young bairns. If he will not pardon Campbell or me, for the love of Christ, will he not spare Johnnie! Oh, my poor bairn!"

She rocked to and fro, tortured by the image of her sixteen-year-old son being hanged, drawn and quartered. With a cry of anguish she bent over to cradle her womb. It would be no comfort to tell her that all the confessions had been extracted by torture, Elisabeth decided. Knowing that her son's youthful bones had been broken and mangled on the rack, his flesh ruptured and screws driven through his thumbs, would be more than a mother could bear.

"They say I poisoned my own dear husband! And now that jury of craven henchmen has found me guilty of plotting to poison the king himself!"

Aided and abetted by the Earl of Huntly. Whether or not he lusted after Jinty, whose skellie eyes seemed to inflame passion in men, he definitely lusted after her lands. In order to lay his hands on the Glamis estate, he'd bribed witnesses to give false evidence as well as the jury to deliver a guilty verdict.

"They cry me a witch. They say I have the sleekit eyes of a grimalkin. That I learnt my powers at my mother's knee." As she laboured to breathe, her speech became jerky, coming in short spurts.

Though Jinty and her family were undoubtedly martyrs in the bitter feud between Angus and James, Elisabeth suspected that they might also be victims of Margaret Erskine's bitterness. The pope's refusal to grant her a divorce had quashed her twin ambitions – to become queen and to legitimise her son – and then, further stoking her black-affronted fury, King James had gone off to France in chase of a royal bride.

Pale and frail with feverish eyes, Princess Madeleine, the delicate daughter of Francis I, had to be carried off the boat at the port of Leith. The two bright spots on her porcelain cheeks – tiny ripe cherries and a sign of good health, James affirmed – had spread rapidly, like sparks from a bonfire inflaming her whole body. When the damp, smoky air of Auld Reikie finally stifled the last of the breath in her weakened lungs, James was inconsolable, tearing his hair out, beating fists against his breast in grief.

Thon witch, Jinty Douglas, must have put a hex on her, the rumour went round. Wasn't her own sister wed to the Wizard of Goblin Ha'? Hadn't her mother been knacky in the black arts? Lest James turn a glad eye on her, Margaret Erskine was dripping poisonous tittle-tattle into his ear, Elisabeth suspected and, in his misery, he believed her. Someone had to be blamed for his misfortune. Since the other Douglas sisters were too well-connected to be persecuted, Jinty was to be the scapegoat. Her blood sacrifice would serve as a warning to Angus.

There was a faint chance that the flichtersome James might have a last minute change of heart. The monarch's capricious behaviour, veering from the weepy sentimentality of the Stewarts one minute to the harsh brutality of the Tudors the next, was evident in his reaction to his beloved queen's death. No sooner had Madeleine's body been shrouded in her wedding dress and nuptial bells tolled as funeral knells than James dispatched the two Davids, Beaton and Lindsay, to France to negotiate for the twenty-one-year-old widow of the Duke of Longueville.

If only Lindsay were here to intercede – the king would listen to him, surely – but, in his absence, Elisabeth could only hope that gralloching a few deer might drain his bloodlust enough for James to grant mercy to Jinty.

"And I am to be executed!" Jinty cried. "Not by a swift blow of the axe or a sudden jerk of the rope, but cleansed by fire so that not one single hair on my head remains to sully God's earth."

She gazed up at the iron-barred window where a glimpse of sky could be seen.

"Oh, Lisbeth, how I wish they'd fling me off the topmost tower of Tantallon! Do you mind the time we stood there together? I'd rather be dashed to my death against the rocks than my flesh roasted and my blood slowly broiled." She leant her cheek against her knees and closed her eyes. "And then, while my body plummets into the depths below, my soul will be lifted high above the waves, up into the heavens."

Her body shook with the sobbing spasms juddering along her spine. Elisabeth put out her arms to console her, but the jailer chided her.

"No touching," he barked, for he had orders to make sure that the prisoner had no chance to take her own life or to be given any help to do so.

"As a sister of mercy it is my duty to comfort the afflicted," Elisabeth pleaded, "and to pray with her. Would you deny her that consolation in her last hours?"

The jailer shrugged his shoulders. Prayers could do no harm: nor any good, for a hellbent carlin such as yon.

Hugging her tightly, Elisabeth could feel Jinty's heart flip-flapping wildly like a scary doo fluttering to break free from its cage. As her sobs quietened down to pitiful whimpers Jinty whispered, "Soon I shall be able to beg Meg's forgiveness. Dame Fortune is punishing me, Lisbeth. My soul has never been easy not since …" She trailed off, her voice fading. "Meg's death hangs heavy on me."

"Meg's death was tragic but you were not to blame. It wasn't your fault."

If anyone, Elisabeth held Angus responsible and her curse at the time had been meant for him.

Jinty shook her head violently. "But it was. Mind how you and I used to have fun playing tig together at Tantallon? Well, I was playing hunt the gowk with the maids. We were chasing each other round and round when I saw Meg standing at the top of the stairs. She must be feeling better, I thought. She was smiling. She must want to join in. So I threw the veil over her and shouted: Hunt the gowk! But she was so frail that she toppled over and tumbled down and down."

Jinty had hovered on the top step of the staircase watching helplessly as Meg's arms flailed at the air in a futile attempt to fly. She pressed her eyelids tightly with her manacled fists, as if trying to gouge the memory from her skellie eye.

"Perhaps I am evil," Jinty sobbed, breaking the silence. "Perhaps I deserve to die."

"Nay," Elisabeth replied, shaking her head. "And neither did Meg."

Outside the dungeon, a messenger bade Elisabeth follow him – to see the king she assumed. In spite of Margaret Erskine's meddling, perhaps James would hear her mercy plea. She was shown into a chamber, lit by many candles and heated by a coal fire burning in the grate. Though it was past midsummer, the warmth of the July sun hardly penetrated the thick stone walls of Edinburgh Castle.

"Take a seat, Dame Prioress." The voice, high-pitched with an English twang, was not that of the king but his mother, Margaret Tudor.

Seated at a writing desk, the squat figure was no longer the princess praised by poets as being *most pleasant and preclare*. If she ever had been, for Elisabeth hadn't believed it then when she first set eyes on her at the Tournament of the Wild Knight. Now, in late middle age, the Tudor Rose had lost her bloom. A bout of smallpox had scarred her complexion leaving it pockmarked and sallow and a French hood concealed her once luxuriant flaxen hair. Her face had become puffy, threatening to obscure her small, froglike eyes – eyes that still flashed fiercely when aroused. Elizabeth's impression of the innocent English bride all those years ago was reinforced. At nearly fifty-years-old, the royal princess had transformed into a puddock.

The queen mother put down her pen. "I hear you've come to plead for Jinty Douglas. Don't look so surprised, Prioress, I know everything that goes on in this godforsaken castle. Despite everything, I am still the queen mother and retain my own loyal retinue."

And still the proud Tudor princess, Elisabeth thought.

"But Margaret Erskine will have the last word in this sorry case. Whatever arts that shameless harlot uses to keep my son in thrall, I dread to imagine. Like his father before him, my son James has a string of mistresses but this wily wanton is getting too bold. She has what you Scots call a guid conceit of herself," the queen mother said, trying to mimic a Scots accent. "But as she wangles her way to the throne, *she* is the witch, I wager, not hapless Jinty."

"But Lady Margaret is already married to Douglas of Lochleven," Elisabeth said. "And His Grace's ambassadors are at this moment negotiating for a French bride."

"There's many a slip betwixt cup and lip. And divorces can be as bought as easily as fish at the market nowadays – and smell just as high. That wasn't the case in my day. I would have done anything to break free from Angus. Nothing but anguish he gave me," she whined, her voice rising to a resentful wail. "I should have bided my time and married Albany. He was very fond of me." Her froggy eyes misted up at the memory. "But his French manners were too sophisticated to put up with our boorish, uncouth Scots. And so he left, more's the pity, leaving us all at the mercy of Angus."

Had she been called to the royal presence only to hear Margaret Tudor's confession? Elisabeth wondered. Or would she be offering to support her mercy plea?

"Sadly I can do nothing to help Jinty." The queen mother was shaking her head. "I have no influence over my son any more. He has surrounded himself with fools, not least my Lord Muffin," she gave a contemptuous snort. "My nickname for my errant husband," she explained, "the noble Lord Methven who has tired of me and taken a younger mistress. And they say that women are weak, inconstant creatures! Hmmph. Like all the men in my life, Henry Stewart is proving to be false and fickle."

She picked up her pen and waved it. "To that end I've petitioned the pope for a divorce and I'm now writing to my brother Henry the heretic to see if that hypocrite can help me. But I fear that he has created himself the Supreme Head of the Church in England only to justify his own divorce." She gave a snort of contempt and then her expression softened to one of self-pity. "All I crave now is to be free of men and their machinations," she whimpered. "You see, Dame Prioress, I envy your reclusive life of peace and tranquillity. My life has not been a bed of roses, but strewn with thorns and thistles," the Tudor Rose whined. "My health is not good and I may not have many years left. St.Mary's has a reputation for being a haven for distressed gentlewomen. I mean to enter your City of Ladies."

Not if I can help it, Elisabeth thought, taken aback by this royal command. Then, recovering her self-composure, she said, "If and when your divorce is granted, Your Grace, then by all means you will be at liberty to seek out the destiny you deserve. But perhaps the regime at St.Catherine's, here, in Edinburgh would better suit your royal temperament."

The mood among the spectators at the execution was subdued, Elisabeth sensed. Any sporadic jeers and heckles, mainly from drunken youths, were swiftly shooshed into silence.

"That might be your own mother up there," a matron scolded, deeply affected that a mother of poor bairns should be sent to such a cruel death. "And that might be you up there." She pointed up at the tower where Jinty's second husband, Archibald Campbell, and her son John, the Master of Glamis, had been dragged from their dungeon to watch her die.

As Jinty was led to the pyre, her fey eyes, pools of black ink in her sunken face, had a vacant look and she seemed unaware of the tarred barrels and oiled faggots being piled around her. Her squint eye rolled in its socket, seeming to search out the crowd, but her good eye was directed upwards, beyond the parapet where her husband and son were being forced to watch. She'd been locked in the darkest dungeon for weeks, poor lass, the rumour ran through the crowd, so that her blinded eyes could hardly see.

Thank goodness, Elisabeth sighed. Under the watchful eyes of the jailer she'd been unable to pass on the phial of belladonna she'd smuggled in for Jinty but, at first light, she'd waylaid the priest on his way to give the condemned prisoner the last rites. The bejewelled silver casket contained a communion wafer, freshly made that morning by the nuns of St.Catherine's Convent, she explained, already blessed with Christ's blood by the archbishop himself. And, of course, the reverend father could keep the casket for his pains.

The holy wafer had indeed been anointed – with enough drops of the drug to numb Jinty's senses and dull the pain – and, if she remembered Elisabeth's instructions to inhale deeply when the first smoke scorched her lungs, she would suffocate long before the flames consumed her. Judging by her vacant expression, Jinty had managed to take the drug.

As she was being tethered to the stake, the executioner, his head eerily shrouded in a hood, knelt to beg her forgiveness. Jinty blinked and gave a cursory nod. And then, before putting the noose round her neck, he asked if she wanted a hood to cover her eyes.

"To play hunt the gowk?" she replied, a fey smile playing on her lips, and shook her head. The executioner turned one last time to the captain of the castle guard who bowed his head. There would be no reprieve. As the hangman pulled on the rope to fasten her head to the stake, Elisabeth prayed that he would be merciful and throttle her. Jinty gazed skywards to where her spirit would be soon soaring, up and away into Meg's forgiving arms.

The reprieve for Jinty's husband and son came the next day: too late for Campbell. The night before, while lowering himself down from the castle, his escape rope ran out and he fell to his death. His body was dashed to pieces against the volcanic rocks, freeing his spirit to join his jinxed Jinty.

VII

Dramatic Interlude

Famous people, tak tent and ye shall see
The Three Estates of this nation
Come to the Court with a strange gravity;
Therefore I make you supplication
To keep silence and be patient, I pray you.
Ane Satire of the Three Estates
Sir David Lindsay, 16th Century

Linlithgow Palace, 6 January 1540

The two mistresses stood together, eyeing each other with sidelong looks, as they waited for the royal procession. When Margaret Erskine extended her short neck as far as she could above the ermine collar of her gown and adjusted the necklace of Scottish seed pearls to show them off, Marion Ogilvie looked askance. The flesh of her rival's ample bosom, mottled blue with the cold, did not display this expensive gift from the king to best advantage. With a shudder, she pulled her own fox fur collar more tightly round her neck, for even the finest Flemish and French tapestries covering the bare stone walls and windows failed to keep out draughts in the Great Hall. To retain heat, the fourteen small apertures in the high window in the eastern wall had been glazed so as to keep the richly painted ceiling illuminated.

"Those are bonnie." Lady Marion pointed to the French hangings she knew to be part of Queen Marie's dowry.

"Not as fine as the ones His Grace has commissioned for Stirling Castle. All to his own design, they depict the hunting and capture of a unicorn," Lady Margaret boasted. "Since he hasn't stinted on gold and silver thread, they sparkle and shimmer like illuminated manuscripts in the candlelight. And here, under His Grace's direction, our own guildsmen have carved all the woodwork." Indicating the intricate intertwining of the crown, thistle and *fleur-de-lys,* she added, "Even the French craftsmen cannot match that."

"That's as may be, but is the Great Hall not over-vaunting?"

"In what way, my lady Marion?" Elisabeth had already circled the hall to admire the tapestries before coming to join the two matrons.

"Well, these pillars and porticoes may suit a grand palace in Rome with its warm climate but they make a Scottish castle such as this far too cool and draughty. Though some may beg to differ," Lady Marion remarked, looking pointedly at Margaret Erskine.

But the royal concubine's attention was drawn elsewhere. Her eyes had narrowed beneath the arched eyebrows and were darting a look of such malevolence that Elisabeth was startled. Was this the powerful evil eye that had wrought so much havoc on Jinty and her family? She followed her gaze towards James Hamilton who was dashing about as if his life depended on it – which it probably did.

For failing to persuade Pope Paul III to grant Margaret Erskine a divorce, this erstwhile minion of the king had fallen out of royal favour. The royal mistress had seen to that. She would never forgive the Bastard of Finnart, as she insisted on calling him, for robbing her of the crown. Let him rush hither and yon in a desperate bid to wean himself back into favour, but she would make it her business to ensure that he did not.

Lady Margaret crooked her finger to summon the Bastard. In a loud, commanding voice she demanded to know whether the waterways and drains had been checked. Also, had the chimneys stopped reeking? And what about the *pièce de resistance,* she snorted in parody of a French accent, would it be flowing freely with French claret?

Finnart frowned. Overseeing the building programme started by James IV, now carried on by his son to impress his French queen, was a thankless task. While Falkland Palace was being refurbished for his private pleasure, Linlithgow was to be the setting for grander, public entertainment. The *pièce de resistance,* the courtyard fountain, was being decorated in the classical style, with all manner of ornate carvings, including naked musicians, but those idle masons had downed tools. The stone was too hard to work with, they complained and were demanding more money to finish it. Finnart jaloused that, forewarned of his weak position, those mowdieworts, the masons, were holding him to ransom. There were many who would rejoice to see him fail.

"There may be no whimsical whinstane whistlers but at least there'll be warm-blooded, well-wetted pipers playing in the gallery for your entertainment. And a banquet fit for a Queen Real."

The royal mistress glowered at this jibe. On the king's orders, the rarest delicacies had been kept back from the Yuletide tables to be served up on Twelfth Night; goose, swan, peacock, sturgeon and porpoise would surely satisfy the greediest of pudding fillers and titillate the pickiest of palates, as well as impress his French bride. At the blast of the trumpet, the chattering courtiers fell silent. As the heavy oak doors creaked open to admit the royal procession, a young lad broke free and scampered over to show off his new plaidie to his mother.

"Jamie!" She hissed. "Get yourself back there! Mind who you are!"

Margaret Erskine shooed her son away. At her insistence James Stewart was always to be included in any formal ceremonies. A bastard he might be but this trophy of her womb was his father's eldest son with a royal birthright, never mind what anyone said. The ill-begotten lad pouted and grudgingly slung the plaidie over his shoulder. The queen mother would have been affronted at the royal mistress's audacity to flaunt her bastard at court, Elisabeth thought, but Margaret Tudor was ill with the palsy and not expected to live.

Frolicking beside the procession, waving his stick and bell, the court jester, Cacaphatie, teased the royal party, even daring to mock King James himself in his multi-hued highland garb, specially made for him by Jessie Douglas. James, however, took it in good humour for it drew attention to his intent to "daunt the isles" and challenge the authority of the rebellious highland chiefs.

Catching Elisabeth's eye, the king asked her to sit with Queen Marie. Being able to converse fluently in French, she'd become not only an invaluable counsellor to the queen, guiding her through the mire of Scottish affairs, but a valuable confidante and friend. Elisabeth settled her on an upholstered chair, plumping up soft cushions at her back and resting her swollen ankles on a footstool. One of the first to learn of her pregnancy, Elisabeth had offered the services of Sister Agnes and Betsy in her confinement. Pleased to have the experienced Scots midwife as a buffer against the self-important physicians as well as the French-speaking sister for spiritual comfort, Queen Marie had gratefully accepted. Besides, she felt comfortable in the company of nuns.

Before being married off to Louis, *Duc de Longueville*, she'd shared the ascetic life with her grandmother who had retired to the convent of the Poor Clares. Now she sat with her arms folded protectively over her swollen belly, trying to rein in her resentment at hearing the gurgling laugh of her husband's mistress as she gushed her praises of his exquisite taste and generous patronage. Sadly, David Lindsay's reproving reminder of the marriage vow in his wedding speech – to forsake all others – had fallen on deaf ears.

"Oh that I could have stayed with my dear grandmother in the convent but my family had greater ambitions," the queen whispered. "A woman is merely a pawn in men's affairs and, I have to admit, the prospect of being bundled off to Scotland and abandoning my three-year-old son did not fill me with joy. My compatriots warned me that Scotland was a country of wild savages with a primitive culture and even more inclement weather. It is little wonder that poor Princess Madeleine perished here."

"And are we, Your Grace?" Elisabeth enquired.

The queen smiled before responding tactfully. "Compared with the English – no. At times I give thanks that I wed the King of Scots and not that Bluebeard, Henry of England. Just imagine! When he expressed interest in having *une grande dame* like me, I let it be known that, though I may be big in person, my neck is far too small!" She trilled, patting her throat. "I thank God for my lucky escape and pray that the Scots do not follow the English custom of beheading their queen.

"Nevertheless, though I keep my head, I do not have my husband's heart," she lamented, her gaiety changing to sadness. "He is fond of me, as he is of his pet dogs, but I know he does not love me as he adored the Princess Madeleine," she declared.

"That was *une alliance d'amour*. I still remember how his eyes sparkled when he first beheld her. *Fou d'amour*, we all agreed. But then, I must confess, I do not love him the way I loved my dearly departed Louis, or my son. *Mais, malgré tout*, I have fulfilled my duty," she said, patting her protruding stomach. "Though it is not easy when I know he is still warm from the embraces of his mistress."

Margaret Erskine must have sensed her resentful glance, for her head swivelled round and she darted a malevolent glower at the two women that so alarmed Elisabeth that she leant forward to shield the royal womb from her green-eyed jealousy. Just then the jester leapt before the queen, jiggling his bell and pointing his stick at her.

"What grows in its neuk and swells up under the firm grasp of a cocky young bride?" he said with an impudent leer.

While the queen coloured and turned away, Margaret Erskine let out a gleeful screech at his bawdy riddle, loudly whispering the answer in the king's ear.

Meanwhile, Beaton came sauntering down the hall, cricking his craig to look upwards, before seating himself beside his mistress. Resplendent in cardinal red velvet, with an enormous bejewelled crucifix dangling on a gold chain round his neck, the flamboyant cock robin overshadowed his dowdy female, dressed modestly in russet silk.

"Where are the carvings that His Grace has commissioned?" he asked. "Thon likenesses of well-kent figures of our time? Mine will doubtless be among them."

Lady Marion patted his arm. "For one thing, thon whittled heads are to be raised to the rafters at the Great Hall in Stirling Castle, not here. And for another it would take a muckle block of oak and a wheen of paint to render your grand visage, Beaton o' the *Ceann Mhòr*," she quipped.

He looked askance and feigned offence. No kind words then from his lady fair whose Scotch love could be relied upon to cut him down to size.

"With your lacerating tongue you rival Cacaphatie," Beaton retorted. "Or even the makar himself. No doubt Lindsay will present us with some seasonal anarchy. A witty Epiphany from his well-inked quill," he said with a smirk.

A flourish of trumpets heralded the start of the spectacle and the audience hushed as a cloaked figure stepped on to the dais. Pulling down his hood, the character introduced himself as Diligence the narrator, who would relate how the Vices who held King Humanity in their evil grip at his court were at last overcome and driven out by the Virtues.

"Saints and sinners alike, tak tent to me," he bellowed. When he announced that the Yuletide reign of misrule was now over, disgruntled jeers and hisses broke out among the spectators who'd been expecting the anarchic Abbot of Unreason and his unruly mob. They were in the mood for entertainment, not a sermon, and certainly not the morality play this was turning out to be. The comely figures of King Humanity's dissolute courtiers, Wantonness, Placebo and Solace in various states of undress, appeared to appease the audience. But appreciative whistles greeted the entrance of Dame Sensuality who shimmered onto the dais, swaying sensuous curves discernible through her gossamer gown.

At first the flame gold hair and the knowing smile playing on the luscious lips of this Dame of Vice, made Elisabeth sit up. That can never be Nancy. Her brother Adam's widow would now be in her mid-fifties, she calculated. No, since it couldn't be Nancy, it must be her daughter Jenny, now wed to Lord Fleming. La Fleming, as they cried the king's half sister, oozed with the same kind of voluptuous desire and promises of sensual pleasure as her mother. As this lusty lady and her maidens took centre stage, King Humanity's adviser, the virtuous Good Counsel, was hustled out.

"*Qu'est-ce que dire?*" the queen whispered, her eyebrows furrowed in confusion. "They speak too quickly for me."

It wasn't only the fast-spoken language that prevented her from enjoying the spectacle: the sight of plump Margaret Erskine, wobbling in paroxysms of glee at the king's side and hugging their son in her copious lap, grieved her. Well acquainted with the agony of being the short side of an unequal triangle, never to be foremost in your lover's heart, Elisabeth sympathised At this very moment, behind the scenes, Jessie Douglas would be fussing with costumes and acting as Lindsay's helpmate. She sat up and straightened her back to concentrate on the play.

Dame Sensuality had moved on from the first estate – the court of King Humanity – and was now seducing the Abbot and Friars of the spiritual estate. Driven out of the monastery, one of the Virtues, Chastity, in a long white flowing robe was appealing to Dame Prioress for sanctuary in her convent, but the Prioress, who was learning to dance a *pavane* with the Abbot, shunned her, saying:

"Pass hind, Madame, by Christ you come nocht here!
You are contrary to my complexioun.
Gan seek lodgins at some auld monk or friar
Perchance they will be your protection."

Saying so, the rôle-playing Prioress pulled off her wimple and shook out her hair and then lifted up her habit to reveal a kirtle of red silk. While the audience howled with laughter, nudging each other and exchanging knowing glances, the real-life prioress blushed with embarrassed indignation. "The flighty nun" was no better than a common cow-clink, they whispered behind her back. Elisabeth knew that her habit of following the king's hunt, an unorthodox figure in her flapping nun's robes, had earned her this nickname but there was no need for Lindsay to reinforce it. None of the three estates was spared his merciless satire but surely he could have forewarned her that she, too, would be ridiculed.

Stricken by this cruel caricature, her mouth dry, Elisabeth could no longer summarise for the queen. As she squirmed uncomfortably in her seat, swithering whether to flee, she felt a sympathetic pat on her hand. Queen Marie tilted her head slightly before raising her chin to stare proudly ahead and lifting the corners of her lips into a strained smile. Aware of being dubbed the "French mare" – a *sobriquet,* if not started by Margaret Erskine, then certainly not silenced by the spiteful mistress – the queen was showing Elisabeth her way of coping with derision: *Endure Fort.*

After a short interlude for refreshments, the play began with a warning blast from the character of Divine Correction dressed in unremitting black. Without his uttering a word, his stern countenance was enough to silence the mocking laughter from the spectators, now even more inebriated.

"I am an judge richt potent and severe," he cried, his bass voice resounding throughout the Great Hall. Imperious and mighty in his robes, he glared at the audience and waved an admonitory finger at them all, while accusing them of every possible vice. No estate was spared his censure. Courtiers were arraigned for their shameful wickedness, the lords for selfishness, the burgesses for greed, the Church for immorality and sensuality and the monarch for lethargy.

As the Three Estates, blindly led by their Vices, entered walking backwards, he raged at them. With their backsides foremost, how could they know where they were going? Commanding them to turn and face King Humanity, he bellowed,

"Get up, Sir King! Ye have sleepit enough into the arms of Lady Sensual."

While the audience gasped at his audacity, Margaret Erskine drew her high brows into a frown of displeasure that deepened as Divine Correction continued his tirade. He reminded King Humanity of one of the lessons of Sodom and Gomorrah: how King Sardanapall spored his lust among fair ladies for so long that he was overthrown by rebellious lieges. Although the actor was heavily disguised, Elisabeth recognised the candid blue eyes glinting above the theatrical bushy black beard.

Now he thundered:

> "I have power great princes to down thring
> That lives contrair the Majesty Divine
> Against the truth which plainly does malign
> Repent they nocht I put them to ruin."

Unnerved by how vehemently he spoke these ominous words, Queen Marie clutched her belly with one hand and gripped Elisabeth's arm with the other.

> "I will begin at thee, which is the head,
> And make on thee first reformation."

But Divine Correction's warning had also startled Elisabeth. Lindsay had trained him well, too well perhaps, in his rôle as avenging angel. For John Knox was not play acting, she feared, but meant every word he uttered.

VIII

Indictment

> Then Patience says, "Be not aghast:
> Haud Hope and Truth within thee fast
> And let Fortune work forth her rage
> Whom that no reason may assuage."
> *Meditation in Winter*
> William Dunbar, 15th–16th Century

St. Mary's Abbey, June 1541

"He's been waiting for you coming home, as fidgety as a fiend in the inferno," Betsy said as she helped Elisabeth off with her riding cloak. "Says it's important, but won't tell me what it is." She gave the cloak a good, hard shake. "I've told him to wait until you've had your supper or caught your breath at least but he says he can't put it off."

Worn out after a fifteen-mile ride from Edinburgh, Elisabeth's only desire was to fall asleep in her soft feather bed. Instead she flopped down onto the settle and closed her eyes.

"Let's put him out of his misery. I'll hear what he has to say."

After placing a cushion behind Lisbeth's wimpled head and a pitcher of weak ale on the table, Betsy folded her arms and glowered. "And then you'll have your supper," she stated and hirpled off to the kitchen.

As Knox gazed down at the prioress, her care-worn face smeared with dust and grime, a sharp pain stabbed at his heart: *Stabat Mater dolorosa*. The lustre may be fading from the radiant Queen of Heaven but her innate beauty was still intact. In those few moments of contemplation her face was impressed upon his memory, as that of Christ had been embossed forever on Veronica's veil. Loath though he was to add to her sorrows, the document he was holding was so inflammatory it seemed to scorch his fingers. The accusation should be doused at once.

"While you were away this came."

"You are the notary, John. Surely you can deal with it," she said, keeping her eyes firmly shut.

"It concerns you personally, Dame Elisabeth. It appears to be an indictment."

"An indictment?" Her eyes flew open and she raised her head from the cushion. "Who has served this on me?"

Knox quickly scanned the parchment. "One John Hay, 3rd Lord of Yester."

"Lord Hay! The Wizard of Goblin Ha'! How dare he! No doubt he's acting out of spite because of the case he lost against me years ago. That devil incarnate would haggle the breeks off a beggar. Why, he even sued his own grandmother."

It was true. When Hay had reneged on an agreement to manage her estates, his grandmother, Lady Belton, had obtained a decree appointing her other son, his uncle, as factor. Not to be outdone, Hay had declared that she was illegally occupying Belton Castle. From the goodness of his heart, however, he would allow her to stay there if she allowed him to continue to factor the lands. The wrangling dragged on for years and, while the Wizard seemed to thrive on it, his grandmother finally gave up her broken spirit.

"He haunts the courts like a demented demon. Do you ken he sued the Earl of Arran for pulling down eighty yards of a boundary dyke! Eighty yards! Forbye, a man who would pursue his own grandmother to an early grave for the sake of a groat is not to be trusted."

"But what does he hope to gain by this?" Knox frowned.

"Thon miserable lickpenny would fley a louse for its skin to sew a purse for his scrimped savings. Hay covets lands at Nunraw bestowed on the abbey by Countess Ada. I jalouse the warlock has conjured this up out of thin air to blackmail me, hoping that, in return for his silence, I will hand over the lands to him. Burn it."

With an impatient sigh, she rested her head again and closed her eyes. Knox picked up another document from amongst those spread on the table. This one was no less damning. He pulled up a stool and sat down to steady the tension in his shaky legs.

"There is also statement from his aunt who claims to have been a witness at the time."

Elisabeth blinked. "His aunt? Who might that be?"

"It would appear that a certain Sister Maryoth Hay was once a nun here. Do you remember her?"

Remember her? How Elisabeth wished she could forget her. So that's where all this was coming from. She sat up and rubbed her eyes. There could be no rest for her now.

"Sister Maryoth and her brother have borne malice towards me ever since I was appointed prioress in her stead. No doubt thon warlock is kindling his clyping aunt's grudges to fan the flames of his case against me."

Knox waited until she'd settled down. "She swears by Almighty God and His Holy Mother, that," he paused to take a deep breath before reading from the witness statement, "the accused, Elisabeth Hepburn, has not preserved a wholly unstained character these many years. Namely, that her unseemly conduct and past misdemeanours render her unfit to be a prioress of the Church."

"This is nothing more than clash and clatter," Elisabeth sneered. "The vindictive tittle-tattle of a serpent so full of venom and hate for me that it has poisoned her soul and shrivelled her senses."

"More seriously," Knox began, but his tongue kept sticking to the roof of his dry mouth. And when a fit of coughing couldn't clear his constricted throat, she poured him a tassie of weak ale. With a nod of gratitude, he drained it before carrying on, "More seriously, Sister Maryoth claims that the child you were carrying, the result of this liaison, was done away with in murderous fashion."

Knox looked up to see that the prioress had slipped from the settle and was now standing over him, eyes blazing in her ashen face. He shifted nervously from one buttock to the other.

"What malicious slander is this? What precisely is the accusation?"

Knox gripped the parchment with trembling hands and began to read. "On the Second Day of June in the Year of Our Lord 1541, this Indictment to be served on one Elisabeth Hepburn, Prioress of St.Mary's Abbey," he broke off, "an accusation of ..." Again he hesitated, swallowing hard before he could continue, "Carnal Dalliance." In his rush to finish reading, his voice had ascended from a sombre bass to a high-pitched squeak.

"Carnal dalliance? Is that what they cry it? Fyking in other words!" the accused spluttered. "And who, if anyone, is cited as my partner in this crime of carnal dalliance?"

The intensity of her stare was causing beads of prickly sweat to break out on his forehead. Knox moistened his dry lips before pronouncing, "One Harry Cockburn, brother of Patrick Cockburn of Newbigging." He kept his head down, his eyes fixed on the document, for he could not face her. The idea of his prioress engaged in the act of carnal dalliance was making him feel uncomfortable, even queasy. After a brief, unbearable silence, she suddenly burst out laughing.

"Harry Cockburn, you say? Harry Cockburn indeed!" Still shaking with laughter, Elisabeth picked up the witness statement. "Here's what we do with this festering filth from that old witch, that accursed crone." She held it up by the corner as if it were soiled. "Purification by fire." Despite her creaking knees, she knelt down and placed it on the glowing embers of the log fire.

Knox didn't try to stop her. Once flickers of flame had licked its edges, she slowly fed in the rest of the indictment. In silence they watched the black ink of the parchment gradually turn grey, the corners slowly curl up and the remains finally shrivel into a heap of ash.

"There," Elisabeth said, wiping her hands as she rose from her knees. "There's an end to that. Harry Cockburn indeed," she snorted. She crossed to the cupboard and took out a bottle of French cognac to pour them each a generous dram. She took a long swig and, this time, as her head touched the cushion, her starched wimple slipped askew. "Who do they take me for?" she said, her laugh heavy with scorn. "The Abbess of Unreason?"

Sipping his cognac, Knox seemed uneasy: he didn't share her joke, rather his frown deepened.

"I fear it may not be the end," he began tentatively. "Lord Hay has sent copies of

243

these papers to the diocesan commissioners in St. Andrews. The board plan to discuss it when they attend the half-yearly session here at the abbey next week. Abbot Beaton is coming with them. He is taking a personal interest in the case."

"Indeed? Then we can rest easy. Davie Beaton and I may be auld enemies but we're also auld friends. He'll make sure this scurrilous scandal is scrapped."

Knox squirmed on his stool. "Perhaps. But if so, then why has his uncle, Archbishop Beaton, granted Sister Maryoth a special dispensation to break her silence? She is prepared to give testimony."

Coldingham Priory, April 1541

"What do you want with me?" Her voice, brittle from lack of use, cracked through the grille in the cell door. "And speak up," Sister Maryoth demanded, cupping her good ear with her hand. "Who did you say you were?"

"John Knox. Notary apostolic. I've come to enscribe your testimony."

"Nay," she shrieked loudly in the way of deaf people. "Parchments can be burned, or torn up or lost, perchance. My testimony shall come from my own tongue. I will trust no-one with it, far less the godson of the prioress. Oh, aye, my memory hasn't deserted me yet. You may not remember me, Johnnie Knox, but I mind you."

She tapped a bony finger against the grille for him to come closer but her rancid breath made him turn his face away. "Carnal dalliance is venial compared to the gross sins committed by that woman. Their dallying had been going on for some time. I should know. I kept close watch on them. Let her say that Harry Cockburn snatched her from the abbey and then violated her, but I tell you, I saw her jump up behind him of her own free will and ride off with him for three days and three, long, nights."

She broke off, wheezing with the excitement of telling her tale. After years of incarceration in a closed order – at John Hepburn's insistence so as to gag her errant tongue – she was now being given the chance to break her silence and she wasn't going to waste it.

"And when she came back she was heavy with sin and heavier still with child. She will deny it, but I saw her swelling belly with my own eyes. She left the abbey to have her bairn and, for all I know, thon pagan, Betsy Learmont, slaughtered the innocent to protect the reputation of that Jezebel. I was sworn to silence, but I did so, not on the Holy Bible, but a book of fancy pictures," she spat in contempt. "My time in this vale of tears is nearly up and I cannot go to my Maker without seeing justice done to that whore of Babylon."

Listening to these slurs on the prioress's reputation, the easily riled Knox had to clench his teeth to keep his temper. "If what you say is true, Sister, then Harry

Cockburn would have been charged with …" he had to pause to draw breath, since the scurrilous words were searing his tongue. "Abduction and ravishment."

Sister Maryoth cackled in glee. "He was never found." She had made sure of that – plying the old watchmen with strong drink and setting Harry off on a horse from the abbey stables. "While *she* escaped her punishment," she said bitterly.

A cloistered life of prayer and abstinence had clearly not filled her heart with peace and love but addled the wizened old crone's wits.

"You may think I'm doited, but I tell you my mind is as clear as my conscience. But what about hers?"

When, once again, her skeletal finger dunted against the grating, Knox had to fight a strong urge to grab hold of if it, twisting it until it cracked. Instead, he took a deep breath before attempting to reason with her.

"If what you say is true, Sister, then why not leave the prioress to divine retribution? Is it not written: Vengeance is mine, sayeth the Lord? Like us all, she will have to stand before Almighty God to be judged and punished."

"It's not vengeance I demand, but justice," she cried, rattling the grille with both hands. "Forbye, when she's sent to hell, I shall not be there to see her suffer!"

Knox winced before taking another tack. If she would not listen to reason, perhaps an appeal to her better feelings would melt her hardened heart. "Did not Our Lord, Jesus Christ exhort us to turn the other cheek?" he reminded her. "Let he who is without sin cast the first stone."

Sister Maryoth puckered her thin, withered lips up to the grating and rasped.

"Turn the other cheek? Show mercy to a shameless sinner? By Christ's sacred blood, I'm prepared to cast the first stone. If it's the last thing I do. Only then will I rest in peace."

St. Mary's Abbey, 12 June 1541

When Beaton arrived in full cardinal pomp, Elisabeth looked him up and down, noting his four-neukit cap and voluminous scarlet cape of watered silk trimmed with ermine that needed to be supported by a trainbearer, an acolyte in a pure white lace surplice.

"An avenging angel come to give judgement, Davie. You may have gained the long-coveted cardinal's hat, but I think your peacock-feathered bonnet suited you better."

With a huffy harrumph Beaton, now a fully-fledged Prince of the Church, straightened his biretta and dangled his podgy hand adorned with the cardinal's ring for her to kiss: like a remorseful collie dog offering its paw, seeking forgiveness. For she was infuriated that he'd taken the indictment seriously enough to bring to court.

As *Legatus a latere* to the Vatican, he could easily have used the papal plenary powers to trample it underfoot. To squash it, by hook or by cardinal's crook.

Sadly he couldn't do so, he'd explained, for he would be accused of turning a blind eye to a serious case of veniality. Furthermore, a bride of Christ, especially a prioress, like Caesar's wife, should be above suspicion. However, he did hint that Hay might be prepared to drop the case in return for the lands of Nunraw.

Elisabeth was unyielding. "Since you, not only as cardinal but as self-appointed champion, are not willing to defend my honour, I shall have to contest this case to clear my name. And, if anyone should be charged with carnal dalliance, it should be you, Davie Beaton."

With a curt bow he replied, "Let battle commence."

Lord Hay had mustered a formidable force. In the front line, the two independent commissioners were flanked on one side by the prosecuting notary and his team, and on the other by a detachment of notaries apostolic for the defence and their scribes. The preliminary bout opened with a request from the plaintiff to hear the case in private, behind closed doors, but Lord Hay objected and threatened to appeal to the Archbishop of St.Andrews.

Claiming superior authority as cardinal, Beaton immediately overruled it. If nothing else, the abbey's champion would ensure that the lady's honour would not be subject to public scrutiny. Nor would she be called to give evidence before the other party cited in the indictment.

It had taken four men to haul Harry Cockburn out of the alehouse where he spent most of his time and money carousing with his cronies. Now an aging, battle-scarred border reiver gone to seed, his burly frame swayed unsteadily in front of the bench, yawning and clawing at the beasties that were gnawing at his nether parts. Though coarsened with war and bleary-eyed with drink, the fright at seeing the assembled might of the Roman Catholic Church went some way to sober him up.

Fear was replaced by bewilderment when the charge of "carnal dalliance" with Prioress Elisabeth Hepburn was read out. His legs buckled underneath him and he clung on to the back of a chair for support. Carlin dancing? Dancing with witches? That would be serious. Folk were burnt for less.

"Or to put it more simply, that you have lain with the prioress," one of the commissioners helpfully explained.

"Lain with the prioress?" Harry's red-flecked eyes narrowed as he tried to concentrate. "What sort of carlin would I need to be to have done that? Auld Clootie himself couldn't lowp o'er yon nunnery wall. Though the monks o" Mains might manage it." When his inane, black-toothed grin was answered by scowls, sweat broke out on his forehead, for he may well be digging his own grave – if not lighting his own funeral pyre.

"No cursing and no calumny in court," the prosecutor reprimanded him. "We're speaking of the time before she became prioress and you were employed as a stable lad at the abbey."

"That was auld lang syne." Harry rubbed the sweat running into his eyes with a clarty hand. "I cannot mind what I did yesterday, never mind when I was a lad." Again he pulled an idiotic grin.

"Answer the question or you'll be put in the stocks for contempt. Is the person with whom you have been accused of committing said carnal dalliance present in this court?"

Clearly confused, Harry was clawing his scalp and rubbing his dirt-streaked face as he scanned the courtroom. Just then, Elisabeth, who had been sitting with her head bowed, looked up and beamed an encouraging smile. Lady Lisbeth. Harry blinked a few times to clear his bleary eyes. From deep within his drink-sozzled brain a memory surfaced and with it a promise that never, as long as he lived, would he ever betray Lady Lisbeth.

"Aye, I think so, but no I didn't …"

"Which is it?"

Lord Hay tugged at the prosecutor's sleeve. "You may have to use more persuasive means to extract a confession from him," he said in a whisper loud enough for Harry to hear. "A night in the dungeon would not go amiss with …" He mimed twisting the thumbscrews.

Harry's eyes bulged in terror at the threat of the pilliewinks. He clung to the back of the chair to steady the quaking in his knees that rapidly spread upwards until his whole body was trembling. Whether the waggling of his head was voluntary or involuntary; whether he was nodding or shaking it, Elisabeth couldn't tell. She braced herself for what he might say.

"It wasn't me. I never touched her. Maybe I did try to kiss her – for yon Sister Maryoth told me she was keen on me – but Lady Lisbeth was having none of it. Aye, I did ride with her but only to take her to Hailes … to her brother …"

As he began gibbering incoherently, Elisabeth clasped her hands tightly together in silent prayer. Please stop, Harry. Don't say any more.

"I need to piss," he whimpered, hopping nervously from one foot to the other.

"Well, piss in your breeks," the prosecutor grumbled. Which Harry did, letting the stream run down his legs to form a puddle on the flagstones. The sour smell, mingling with his sweat and rancid body odour, wafted towards those on the bench who pinched their nostrils.

Knox stepped forward to object – the prosecutor's question was clearly confusing the witness. Then, with the court's permission he asked, "Harry Cockburn, you only have to answer one question. Have you ever lain with Dame Elisabeth Hepburn? Aye or nay."

"Naaay!" Harry's long drawn-out wail deafened the court.

"That was not a denial but the braying of a donkey," Lord Hay protested. Beaton, however, swiftly overruled him and signalled to the guards who heaved Harry out of the chamber, dragging his feet along the flagstones.

Tap-tapping her walking cane before her, Sister Maryoth shuffled into the courtroom. Now in her late sixties, she was shrunken and shrivelled from years of fasting and denial of the flesh. Though cataracts veiled her eyes, rendering images fuzzy and blurred, her sense of smell wasn't impaired. As she was led to her place, she sniffed the air, screwing up her nose in disgust.

"Is this a courtroom or a pigsty you have brought me to? Hogs on the bench with their swinish snouts in the trough," she muttered.

When informed that Harry Cockburn had denied the accusation of carnal dalliance, her withered lips tightened.

"He would. The Jezebel beglamoured him."

"Are you now accusing the prioress of witchcraft?" Knox asked.

She crinkled up her cloudy eyes to peer round the room before pointing her cane at Elisabeth. "All I ken is that she learnt weirdly ways at her heathen nurse's knee."

When Knox called Sister Katherine as his first witness, Beaton immediately raised an objection. Because she was not even at the abbey when the events on trial took place, her testimony was not relevant. Because her evidence would shed light on the character and disposition of the accuser and would dispute the validity of the indictment, Knox argued, she should be heard.

The acid malice in Beaton's withering look unsettled him momentarily, but he would not be intimidated. Nor would he yield to his demand. Before the trial, the cardinal had taken Knox aside to hint that, if the case against the prioress were proven, he'd be well rewarded. Not only would he overlook his refusal to take the oath and award him his degree, but would assign him a lucrative parish.

Though Beaton cited the main benefit of her dismissal as being the end of her monstrous regime, Knox was not deceived. The end of Hepburn reign at the abbey would leave the cardinal free to exercise his right to appoint her successor and, by filling the vacancy with one of his cronies, he would then gain control of the abbey's considerable finances. Instead of defending the prioress, Beaton was scheming behind her back. That this Judas had been prepared to sacrifice her to cram pieces of gold into his fat paws only stoked Knox's contempt for the cardinal.

While the commissioners listened with considerable interest to Sister Katherine's testimony, Beaton couldn't decide who had angered him more; Knox – for calling on his own sister as witness, thereby signalling his defiance – or Katherine, for agreeing to testify. Coldly and dispassionately, she described the scene at the election for the new prioress when the intoxicated sisters had been asked to pray for inspiration from the Holy Ghost.

"May I suggest," Knox was saying, "that the potion was hexed and that it wasn't the Holy Ghost but Satan himself who was called down to inflame their minds."

Then, when asked if Lord Hay had been a frequent visitor to the abbey, Katherine nodded. "Aye, and he always left with a laden cart or two."

Again, Hay leapt up to object, but once again was ordered to sit back down.

"Weighed down with goods and monies misappropriated by his sister which he then misused to indulge his necromancy," Knox declared. "The Wizard of Goblin Ha', as Lord Hay has become known and not without reason, was accused of practising sorcery and cavorting among the legions of Lucifer. His sister Maryoth was banished from St. Mary's, not only for unlawful election, but for swindling the abbey finances."

Turning to the commissioners" bench, Knox continued. "I contend that it is the plaintiff's intention to besmirch the good character of the prioress and bring about her dismissal, not only to wreak personal revenge, but to arrange for the lands at Nunraw to be awarded in compensation to her nephew. In doing so she has concocted this story to dishonour the prioress. However, the question now arises: if the plaintiff's own reputation is morally corrupt, can the court trust her testimony?"

Realising that the trial was turning against her, Sister Maryoth uttered a strangled squeal.

"What about the bairn! That wanton had an ill-begotten bairn! I saw her swollen womb with my own eyes! Then she got rid of it! She's a murderess!"

When the commissioners looked baffled by this disclosure, Beaton called Knox over. Why had this been withheld? he demanded to know. If it were true, such an outcome would be undeniable proof of the crime of carnal dalliance. Indeed, Knox agreed, and begged permission to call another witness.

Over the years Betsy's hirpling gait had worsened as both hips had become rickety. Leaning heavily on a crutch, she limped into the courtroom, stopping for a moment in front of the old nun before taking a seat directly opposite her. Sister Maryoth's milky eyes blinked in terror and a chill ran through her bones. She fumbled for her beads and began mumbling prayers.

"Aye, Dame Elisabeth did indeed bring a wean into this world," Betsy began, sending a *frisson* throughout the court, "when she helped me deliver it. After a lengthy struggle, the bairn had no strength left to take his first breath. When Dame Elisabeth here blew life into his weak lungs, the mother asked her to stand as godmother. I mind it as if it was yesterday. For the bairn she gave life to was you, John Knox. Aye, and you wouldn't be here today if it wasn't for the prioress," she said, waggling her head at him. "But auld age doesn't come alone and, if it's no the body, then it's the mind that weakens. I'm thinking that Sister Maryoth's brain may be wasted and her memories all taigled up."

There was silence as the court digested this information. Positioning himself in front of Sister Maryoth, Knox asked, his voice low and threatening, "How do you respond to this, Sister? Or has the grimalkin got your tongue?"

She had indeed been struck dumb, not only by the evil eye of that heathen, Betsy Learmont, but the ghost of Bishop Hepburn, whose voice – deep and resonant enough to fill a cathedral – rumbled like distant thunder in her deaf ears. But when Knox leant forward, those piercing blue eyes speared into her very soul, seeking vengeance for breaking her sacred word. She squirmed in her seat, jerking her legs and sending her stick clattering onto the tiles. Bending down to retrieve her cane to fend off the fiend, her head began to whirl. She opened her mouth to speak but her face had drooped into a one-sided grin. No words came from her lolling tongue, only slavering drool as she slumped sideways.

The men in the court gawped in helpless horror while Betsy and Elisabeth rushed to Maryoth's aid.

"Is she dead?" Elisabeth asked.

Betsy shook her head. "Nay, there's life in the auld bird yet, but I fear she's been blastit. Struck by what we cry the apoplexy," she explained. "She might live for a while but her tongue will never clatter again."

As Lord Hay scooped up his aunt's crumpled body and carried her away, Betsy squeezed Elisabeth's arm and whispered in her hear. "That will teach her to cry me a witch."

When the commissioners dismissed the case, Elisabeth gave her nurse a grateful hug. Though found not guilty, Harry still had to be cleared of any accusation or suspicion of carnal dalliance with Elisabeth, Prioress of Haddington. Willingly he agreed to purging by oath rather than purging by ordeal. Repeating incomprehensible words was preferable to being locked in the stocks and pelted with keech or whatever muck the mob would fling at him.

The verdict did not please Beaton, however. "Two fools in one house is a couple o'er many," he remarked through gritted teeth. "And I jalouse there may be yet another who thinks himself smart."

From the black glowering looks that Beaton hurled at him, Knox knew that his future in the Roman Church was doomed. His defiance had tolled the death knell in their troubled relationship.

IX

St. John's Vigil

> See, I have this day set thee over the nations and
> over the kingdoms, to root out and
> to pull down and to destroy.
> *Jeremiah* I:10

Haddington, 23 June 1541

Dark figures were whooping and whirling in and out of the shadows cast by the huge bonfire burning on the bank of the Tyne. On this, "the merriest of nights", the mob were celebrating Midsummer as they had always done, by flagrantly flouting the Church's attempt to usurp the pagan festival with their own feast day – the Vigil of St. John the Baptist. He hurried towards the Nungate Bridge, stopping for a moment at the spot where the gypsy girl had cursed them all.

When her drowned body had been washed up at the weir further down the river, Knox gawped along with the other ghouls. He should have come forward, perhaps, but when it was presumed she'd fallen drunk into the river, he decided to say nothing. Nor had he said anything at the time to prevent her brutal murder. Should he have confessed? For a sin of omission was just as venial as a wicked deed. Though the gypsy girl's blood had long since been washed away, he fretted that it tainted his soul with mortal sin, like an inkblot seeping into a parchment. Head down, whipped by the lash of conscience, he scurried up the ramp of the bridge when he heard his name being called.

"Hey! It's Johnnie Knox!"

"Are you going awa?"

Others took up the refrain, their raucous voices jarring in the still, midnight air.

"To tell your ma?"

"Who's your ma?"

"Naw – whore's your ma!"

"Your ma's your holy sister."

"Where's your ma, your holy ma?"

"In behind the priory wa."

"In the hoor-hoose."

Knox hurried on. Nuns and priests would aye be the butt of jokes even so these jibes at the prioress wounded him. The recent indictment against her for carnal dalliance, even though disproved, had further stoked the fire of innuendo against her. And Lindsay's cruel and public mockery of her in his *Satire* hadn't helped.

Knox had been distraught when Friar Lazarus disappeared but he understood his reason: a friar with his reformist beliefs would not be safe from Beaton's persecution. He was taken by surprise when, outside Tibbie's Tavern, he had literally bumped into the friar who had invited him to meet a good friend of his.

At Garleton Castle, Friar Lazarus had left John to wait in the oratory while he sought out his friend. The summer sun streaming through the stained-glass window lit up the shelves of books, many of them poetry, but Knox was surprised to see laid out on the table works by reformers such as Luther, Melancthon and Erasmus. Who would dare to read such prohibited books?

"I see you're admiring my collection."

Knox looked up in surprise and took a moment to recognise Friar Lazarus, his monk's habit having been swapped for the ceremonial tabard of the Lyon Herald.

"Forgive me for deceiving you, but I had to do it, John," he explained. "At the time I feared for my life."

Lindsay had been on the point of freezing to death on the cliffs near Tantallon that January night in 1526, when he'd been arrested by Angus's men posing as the royal guard. After Harry Cockburn had left him on the cliff-top, he'd come back and taken him to the Franciscan Friary in Haddington. Disguised as a friar he'd avoided recognition and arrest until King James seized power and recalled him into his service as ambassador. During his travels on the continent he'd met many reformist sympathisers and had managed to smuggle in these inflammatory works. For no-one – not even Beaton – would dare challenge the king's trusted envoy, the Lyon Herald.

"I've seen exciting new dramatic forms that have inspired me to write a play criticising corruption in the Church. Not a blundering charge with the heavy-handed cudgel," he explained, seeing Knox's horrified face, "but swift, stinging cuts with the sharp rapier of satire. Folly, not reason, John, is the governing principle of the makar's world. The conceit centres round a satirical parliament of bishops, knights and burgesses, to where the Poor Man brings his complaints. I have a rôle in mind for you, John, if you are willing to take part in the performance at court."

Far from disappointing Knox, the transfiguration of the monk into the makar had given him new heart, and he'd readily agreed. The scathing criticism couched in poetic imagery of Sir David Lindsay's, *Ane Satire of the Three Estates,* should certainly make them sit up and take heed, though Knox was uneasy with his cruel condemnation of Prioress Elisabeth.

"*Mea culpa,*" Lindsay had beat his breast, "but only because I deem it a sin against nature for women to be closeted away, imprisoned behind the walls of a nunnery. They should be wives and mothers. Nor, for that matter, should priests remain celibate."

"No doubt the cardinal and most of his bishops agree with you," Knox scoffed, "but the hierarchy will only change the rules again when it suits them."

"But they will have to. There is change afoot, but small steps at a time, John, for long strides risk leaving the faithful too far behind."

But now Knox was disillusioned. Nothing would change the minds of those gross ignorant sloths: the glimmer of hope kindled by Lindsay's play had been extinguished. Though it had stirred King James into issuing a decree for the Scripture to be translated into the vernacular, the bishops had immediately objected, a meaningless protest since few people could read anyway.

As he fled the pagan rabble over the bridge, Knox remembered that crossing water was one of the defences against evil spirits. Some superstitions were as deeply ingrained in him as Catholic doctrine. In the abbey chapel he knelt down to pray for guidance but almost immediately leapt up again. This was not how the Lord should be worshipped, subserviently on the knees, mindlessly mumbling incomprehensible litanies. He settled on a bench at the back of the chapel, as far away from the altar and the tabernacle lamp as possible, and bowed his head to examine his conscience.

There was no future for him in the Church of Rome. He'd hammered the final nail in the coffin. Not even the prioress would be able to save him from Beaton's flames of persecution. Knox's heart constricted. She was the only reason he hadn't already left the priesthood. He was beholden to her for everything – his upbringing, his schooling, even his very existence, for had she not breathed life into his failing lungs?

Let them mock her, but she was one of the few heads of a religious house who used the benefices of the abbey for the common good to support the apothecary and infirmary. Though the prioress struggled to understand his theological concerns, she'd tried to channel his rebellion and listened to his dream of establishing a school for the sons of the poor. Not without criticism, however.

"Only the sons?" she'd asked, one eyebrow raised.

"Forbye, you already have a school for girls here."

"Aye, for the daughters of those brave gentry who do not fear that straining their brains will make them unbiddable and unbeddable. A school for poor lasses would be of more worth – like Isabelle. What would have become of that wee orphan if you hadn't brought her here? She'd have ended up a strumpet on the streets but she's fortunate that Sister Agnes has taken her under her wing and is not only teaching her the mysteries of the alphabet but the secrets of the physic garden."

Schooling for girls was not a matter that concerned him when he was preoccupied with preparing lessons for the sons of local lairds who'd hired him as tutor at the small village school of Samuelston. While giving her permission, the prioress had requested that, in return, he serve as priest at the Chapel of St. Nicholas. That was what pained him. He'd have to disobey her, for he could no longer, in all conscience, serve such a corrupt organisation as the Roman Church.

He wouldn't celebrate Mass again, not the next day, not ever. How could he? With its incense, bells, and extravagant vestments, holy Mass was nothing more than an elaborate ceremonial, a smoke screen designed to mystify the faithful. And to insist that, at the Eucharist, the bread and wine was transformed into Christ's body and blood to be devoured by the worshippers, reeked of paganism. As for baptising newborn babes in arms who had no inkling of the solemn pledge being made on their behalf – that was plain dishonest. Better to wait until they were of an age to decide for themselves.

That thought made him sit up straight on the bench: he was nearly thirty years old. The same age as John the Baptist and Christ had been when they started out on their ministries. Neither of them had baulked at leaving home. The time had come for him to follow his conscience.

Striding down the aisle he shook his fist at every plaster saint and graven image, cosily ensconced in its niche. Idolatry. The worship of false gods. Only when he stopped at the statue of the Black Madonna draped with offerings from the destitute and desperate did he remember the promise he'd made to Elisabeth: *Keep Tryst*. Could an oath made to a false idol with his fingers crossed be binding? He would indeed keep faith. By keeping true to his own conscience.

"You no longer have any hold over me. I refuse to prostrate myself in front of you." He lowered his voice and sneered. "Look at you! Bedecked with baubles like the whore of Babylon."

He stripped off the rags and trinkets and tossed them onto the floor. Indulging in prayers and offerings to the saints was no different from believing in spells and incantations to the gods. He wagged his finger in front of her face as blank and unfeeling as the plank of wood she was carved from.

"Never again will I worship a graven image. May God strike me down if I do!"

And for good measure he tugged at the rosary beads dangling from her hand, hung there by some misguided soul. The Black Madonna teetered for a moment on her pedestal before crashing face down onto the flagstones. With a woeful crack her right arm splintered and sent her infant flying across the aisle. On the way out he passed the Missal still open at the Order of Mass for the Vigil of St. John the Precursor. He was about to smite the book from the lectern when the words from Jeremias caught his eye:

The word of the Lord came to me, and his message was: I claimed thee for My own before ever I fashioned thee in thy mother's womb; before ever thou camest to the birth, I set thee apart for Myself I have a prophet's errand for thee among the nations.

And with that the Lord put out his hand and touched me on the mouth.

X

The Madness of King James

Bewailing in my chamber thus alone,
Despaired of all joy and remedy
Worn out with thought and woebegone.
The King's Quair, James I, 15th Century

St.Mary's Abbey, July 1541

"Where is Agnes? Is she not with you?"

With alarm in her voice and distress etched on her face, Sister Katherine greeted Elisabeth who was struggling to dismount.

"I, too, would wish Agnes were with me. And Betsy for that matter," she replied archly, rather peeved at receiving no warm words of welcome after her long absence. "What would I give for one of Betsy's remedies to soothe this pounding in my head and Agnes's healing hands to ease my aching back," she groaned, leaning back and forth to stretch her spine, "but the queen has the greater need. Do not fret. Agnes is well and you will see her soon enough."

"Surely you didn't ride all the way from Stirling?" Sister Katherine shook her head in disapproval.

"Aye, and my creaking old bones are also showing their displeasure. But think of Agnes's pain. Our pitiable pilgrim is at this moment tramping her way to Musselburgh with King James. To the shrine of Our Lady of Loretto, where he means to pray for peace in the realm and his own wits, and the queen, the health and strength to bear another heir."

His queen had already given birth to two sons. The French doctors and apothecaries officially in attendance had condescended to let the French speaking Sister Agnes and Betsy the Scots skeily wife do the messy work while they pontificated about how the royal sons should be cared for.

When Prince James, a fine thriving child until his wet nurse's breasts ran dry, mewled and whined at the breast of the new one, Betsy suggested that her milk may be too sour and was upsetting the infant's digestion. Only when the queen threatened to feed him herself was another one brought in.

During her next pregnancy, when the queen became very heavy and lethargic, Betsy shook her head as the learned French physicians prescribed daily purging that left her even more drained. Delivering him after a long travail, Betsy was troubled to see that the listless newborn's skin was an unhealthy yellow pallor. The archbishop was immediately called to baptise Prince Robert. Their twofold joy, however, changed to twofold grief when the prince died within hours, followed a few days later by the heir, Prince James.

"Having released them from the womb, we are now to bury them in the tomb," Betsy lamented. What other ways would fortune find to skelp their unfortunate queen?

Rumours abounded that they'd been poisoned by ruthless enemies, but Betsy blamed overzealous French doctors. Tripping over themselves to show off their high-flown ideas —to justify their high fees, no doubt — they ended up falling flat on their faces. All theory and no practice was their problem; barking orders without getting blood on their hands. If only they had let her and Agnes get on with it, the bairns might have survived.

Queen Marie sat bolt upright in bed as her bed-curtains were suddenly drawn back and a tall figure loomed in the darkness. Not her lady of the chamber, then. And since her husband rarely visited her at night, preferring his current favourite, Oliver, as bedfellow, probably not the king. Ever since infancy James had had a fear of sleeping alone and it had become one of his minion's duties to share his bed, Lindsay had explained in response to the queen's query. Was this not done in France where the word *mignon* arose? Besides, bedsharing to keep warm wasn't uncommon in this cold climate. An interloper then. As she let out a scream, the figure began hopping up and down by her bedside reciting:

"And sometime, like a feind transfigured,
And sometime, like the grisly ghaist of Gye,
In diverse forms oft times disfigurate
And sometime, disguised full pleasantly."

The madman was tearing wildly at his hair and beating his chest.

"It has come true!" he shrieked. "My nightmare has come true! The grisly ghost of Gye is none other than James Hamilton. The Bastard has cut off my two arms. Slain my two bairns," he wailed and loomed in closer, his mad eyes rolling with terror. "And he shall come back for my head. For me. Oh, what have I done? What have I done?"

"Wheesht, wheesht!" The queen tried hushing him in the Scots way to quieten him. "There is no sin that cannot be forgiven and absolved. Besides, we are young enough to have more children."

Saying that, she pulled back the bedcovers and tried to persuade him into her bed but James waggled his head.

"Nay, there will be no more children. We are undone. The evil eye is upon us."

For the Stewart curse was falling heavily on him. Had not his father, James IV, been slain at Flodden for killing his own father, James III? And now he too, was guilty of beheading his minion and kinsman, James Hamilton. He should never have listened to his lords of council who had urged him to convict the Bastard of plotting to assassinate him. Was it even true? He didn't know what to believe any more. There were too many whispering voices, too many conspiracies. He could trust no-one.

And the recent death of his beloved mother, Margaret Tudor, had left him ridden with guilt not only for thwarting her divorce and desire to enter a nunnery but for taking her husband's side. Methven was turning out to be just as sleekit and self-seeking as the rest of his lairds.

Now James was being tormented with the Stewart jinx when the greatest glee was followed by the deepest gloom. After a bout of high spirits when he hardly slept, he would lie listless, heavy-lidded and hollow-eyed for days. His mind, already raddled with fear and mistrust of everyone around him, was becoming more and more unhinged. During his descent into the depths of despair, the king accused the queen of adultery, his lords of treason and his courtiers of cheerfulness.

"What am I to do?" Queen Marie wailed. "He accuses me of being the cardinal's mistress."

Elisabeth shook her head. "He should close his lugs to all that clatter and clack about the Carnal Cardinal and his myriad mistresses. Havers and nonsense. Tell him that any woman, no matter who she was, even you, Your Grace, would have to vie with Lady Marion Ogilvie."

Even his faithful tutor and life-long mentor, Lindsay felt the lash of his tongue but, stooped with sorrow and grey-faced with his own grief, he let his master's outbursts wash over him. His wife, Jessie, had been suffering from a vigorous tumour in the breast and, since nothing could be done to halt the spread of the canker, it was now ravaging her body.

Agnes and Betsy racked their brains for ways to help both patients. With Jessie's condition being a matter of time, they could only prescribe pain relief, mostly in the form of a powerful drug, but they disagreed about how much hemlock should be dispensed.

"Such large doses as you propose could prove fatal," Agnes argued.

Betsy sighed. "Isn't the canker doing that anyway? And so much more slowly and painfully. Jessie doesn't deserve to die in such distress."

They also disagreed about the treatment for their royal patient. Betsy was not only sceptical about the expensive receipts that Agnes had ordered from France, but her own more homely remedies. Neither, she believed, would prove effective.

"Potions and possets won't cure him," Betsy decided ruefully after observing the king closely. "His eyes are birling in his head for want of sleep and his spirits are out of kilter for he believes he is accursed by the evil eye. I fear he may not be cured till the spell has been lifted."

Elisabeth shot her an enquiring glance.

"Don't look at me." Betsy recoiled. "I'll have no truck with the black arts. Poor Jinty was burned for less."

"If, indeed, the king is possessed by an evil spirit then it must be driven out," Agnes fretted, wringing her hands in concern. "Exorcism may be the only cure."

But on finding out about their proposed cure, Lindsay startled everyone by his vehement opposition. "Nay," he roared. "There shall be no cantrips and spells to cast out any evil eye or demonic power. Betsy is right. I loathe this superstitious gobbledegook as much as she fears sorcery."

Besides, it wouldn't do to have Cardinal Beaton poking his long neb and waving his magic wand of a sceptre to gain power.

XI

Widow Ker

> All the days ordained for me were written
> in your book before one of them came to be.
> *Psalm* CXXXIX:16

Samuelston, 1542

Swirling and twirling its grotesque, tumescent tail the dragon flirted and flounced with the whore of Babylon. The harlot whipped up her scarlet petticoats as the loathsome serpent flicked its tail between her legs in a monstrous act of fornication. The dragon reared its head with the bloated bulbous face of Beaton while the whore leered at it with the face of …

Knox woke up swathed in sweat, a milky flux oozing between his legs and trickling onto the bed sheet. The whore of Babylon, the daughter of Eve, the mother of God had all transmogrified into one creature, the horror being that it had the face of the prioress. Despite studying late into the night to tire himself, this recurrent dream troubled his sleep.

He sprang out of bed as if chased by a ghoul and tore off his nightshirt. He filled the basin from the pitcher and splashed cold water on his face and onto his groin. Opening the shutter, he stood in front of the window to let the fresh morning breeze dry him. Once dressed, he cast his eyes over the lines he'd written the night before and could not help sniggering like one of his schoolboys.

> And meikle Latin he did mummle
> But I heard nocht but hummle-bummle.

What had started as a dull re-writing of the Calvin Catechism for his pupils had, when he'd given his imagination free rein, turned into a satire, a scathing parody of the clergy who used the confessional for sexual voyeurism. The rather ribald, *Kitty's Confession*, owed a large debt to Lindsay's *Satire* and would not only amuse his pupils but have a more lasting impact. Nevertheless, however amusing, his censure of the Church was as dangerous and heretical as the protestant tracts, smuggled in from the continent, which he spent long nights studying. If he were caught with these, the penalty wouldn't simply be excommunication – a fate he didn't fear – but death, which he did. His treasured copy of the forbidden, *Patrick's Places*, that had sent its author Patrick Hamilton to the pyre was hidden away.

It was true: words were more powerful than swords. This belief now fired his ambition that everyone should be taught to read so as to experience the beauty of evangelical truth in the Bible. Till then, he preached his vision from the pulpit and his sermons at Samuelston and Longniddry were gradually converting many to the reformed faith. He slipped the manuscript of *Kitty's Confession* between the covers of his copy of Lindsay's poems and went down to breakfast.

The housekeeper, Widow Ker, was a small compact woman, as plump as a dumpling yet who carried herself daintily on tiny feet as she went about her domestic chores. A safe type of woman, soft and warm, like Betsy, he remembered fondly. A maternal Martha rather than a demanding Mary Magdalen, whose comfortable presence made him feel lazy and drowsy. Following her generous figure as she bustled about, he felt his eyelids droop and a warm glow, like melted butter, seep through his veins. If she were to stroke him he would purr like a cat. How would it feel to nuzzle up to her generous warmth, bury his head in her soft bosom and be caressed by her strong hands? Feline feelings, he murmured, rousing himself from his lethargy.

Sloth might be making him smoulder like a smoored fire, but at least it was not the lust aroused by those shameless hussies of his parish who, with their brazen, forthright looks, lured their menfolk to sin. Who, in turn, stumbled shamefully to confession to receive absolution from Knox who, in his turn, felt ashamed – of the very voyeurism he denounced in *Kitty's Confession*. Such scarlet harlots, however, did not kindle any carnal desires in him. Kindred sisters of the gypsy girl, they used their charms to beguile unwary men. Nay, if truth be told, the type of woman who quickened his loins was the young, innocent maiden with downcast eyes, demure, unsullied, unknowing of the ways of men. He gave a sudden start as Widow Ker put his bowl of porridge in front of him and stood beside him with her plump arms folded.

"You should take care, young master."

He gave a start. Had she been reading his sinful thoughts? She looked around furtively before delving into the pocket of her apron. "You should be wary of leaving such as thon lying about. Some would deem it downright heretical."

"You can read, Widow Ker?" he asked, as she slapped down one of his pamphlets.

Her brother-in-law, James Ker, who had invited Knox to stay in his house, was one of those sympathetic to the idea of reform. Along with Hugh Douglas of Longniddry and John Cockburn of Ormiston, he'd hired Knox to educate their sons in the new evangelical thinking: to discuss and debate the Bible for themselves.

Widow Ker looked over her shoulder as she busied herself with washing up.

"Aye, that I can. And I can write as well. My father made sure of that. He believed that everyone should be able to read. Even women."

Her father, she confided, was a descendant of Adam Reid of Barskimming in Kyle. In the hills of Ayrshire the spirit of Lollardy was still kept alive. Evangelicals, the people of the Book, swore by the Holy Bible as their only guide and rejected the vast religious edifice of formal priestly religion that centred upon the outward temple.

Now that the synagogue of Satan, Roman Catholicism, was under threat, she wasn't afraid to share her ideas. For too long the Anti-Christ in Rome had usurped the teachings of the Saviour and warped them for his own ends. For too long her kind had been lurking in the shadows. Now was the time to abandon the darkness and light the lamp of faith.

"I mind my father telling me about how his grandsire was charged by Bishop Blackadder for denying that God is in heaven. And what did Adam Reid respond?" Widow Ker drew herself up to declaim, "Whereas I believe that God is both in heaven and on earth, you, Bishop Blackadder don't even believe that God is on this earth. Otherwise you wouldn't be playing the proud prelate and neglecting the charge of Christ when you preach the Gospel."

Her plump shoulders heaved as she wiped away tears of laughter with the hem of her apron. Widow Ker exuded the quiet confidence of one who knew she was right and therefore could do no wrong. To be one of the elect, she explained in her slow, languorous tones, was to be one of the righteous, chosen by God for salvation. For those who receive the gifts of faith and divine grace there would be no eternal damnation, even if they sinned.

"Even a mortal sin?"

"For his elect, God puts aside his wrath as judge. He that believeth in him shall not perish. As long as they forsake evil and keep true to the light."

"But how can you be sure you are one of the chosen? And how can you know that it is not Satan sowing doubts?"

"Because I have faith, Master Knox." Widow Ker raised her eyes to heaven. "As it is written: The Just shall live by faith – and faith alone. And being justified by faith, we have peace with God."

Her eyes took on a faraway look as she explained how, once the gracious gift of faith had taken root in her soul, she had experienced a sense of mystical peace and spiritual security that released her from anxiety. Her placid tranquillity was enviable to Knox as he struggled to douse the unwelcome stirrings her sensuality was arousing in him.

"Except a man be born again he cannot see the kingdom of God. Not by entering his mother's womb a second time, but through the spirit." Her words sent a slight shiver up his spine as he eyed her plump belly beneath the capacious white pinny.

"Faith is all, John. Faith alone."

XII

The King is Dead: Long Live the Queen

Ladies no way I can commend
Presumptuously which doth pretend
To use the office of ane king
Or Realms take in governing.
The Monarch
Sir David Lindsay, 16th Century

Linlithgow Palace, 27 November 1542

"And I am to have my hair cut short and wash it once a month. For greasy hair gives rise to croup and an unhealthy mother will give birth to an unhealthy son." A wry smile curled the queen's lips as she considered her mother's latest advice. She passed over the long, solicitous letter for Elisabeth to translate.

"And she seems confident that you are carrying a lad," Elisabeth noted.

"God willing, her prayers, and mine, are answered. What are your thoughts, Betsy?"

"Every land has its ain law," the humble Scots skeily-wife muttered, though she didn't agree with all the French ways. Whenever she'd tried to put in her ha'penny worth, the physicians had turned up their hoity-toity noses at her. Hell mend them, she'd thought, and then gone behind their backs to follow her instinct. But she was getting too old to put up with all their cocky chicanerie. This would be her last royal birth.

And now the grand French Duchess Antoinette was meddling – with advice that might even be the death of her daughter – for Betsy's greatest dread was that the queen would catch a chill. Let French women hack at their hair and boil their heads for all she cared, but it would be perilous for a pregnant woman to do so at any time, far less in the midst of one of the bleakest winters Betsy had ever lived through.

Great billows of immaculate white snow drifted high up against the palace walls. Wells and water-courses were frozen and not only water, but all meat and victuals had to be thawed. High in the north-west corner of Linlithgow Palace, where they were preparing the chamber for the queen's confinement, Betsy made sure the fire was stacked high with logs day and night. She wouldn't allow coals to be burned for, to her mind, there was the whiff of the devil about the reek from thon infernal black stones.

Swathed in a fur-lined cloak, Queen Marie peered intently through the thick, greenish window glass. Below, the ice-covered lochan shimmered in the last rays of the low November sun, before it disappeared over the horizon. This would be her last glimpse of daylight for a few months. She dreaded the perpetual night of the sealed chamber, the womb-like existence she'd have to endure until the birth.

262

Shuttered windows were hung with heavy curtains to blank out the light; every possible opening – every chink, crack, or keyhole – was plugged with straw and cloths to block perilous cold air from seeping in.

Cocooned like a grub in the tightly curtained four-poster bed, the queen would not be allowed to stick out an arm or even her nose in case she caught cold. Smothered in blankets, choking on the reek of tallow candles and smoke from the constantly blazing log fire, she was more likely to suffocate and precautions would be even stricter this time. With the deaths of two sons, no chances could be taken with this birth. Little wonder she longed to postpone her incarceration as long as possible.

She wiped her frosted breath from the glass pane and gazed at children screaming excitedly as they slid down the brae on their hurley-hacket, whizzing past servants dragging up sledges.

"See how the foraging worker bees bring supplies to their queen cloistered in her hive."

"The drones having done their duty," Elisabeth quipped.

Queen Marie gave a hearty laugh and rubbed her very rounded bump.

"*Oui, c'est vrai!* Oh, how you lift my spirits, my lady prioress."

"Why are you laughing?"

A draught of cold air as the door curtain swung open cut through their mirth and made them shiver. Swaying unsteadily, the king staggered over towards them.

"Why do you laugh when my heart is full of misery and foreboding? I look around for pity, where pity is none: for comfort, where no comfort is to be found. And my own dear Oliver is fled," he wailed, doubling over in pain. "Oh, Oliver is taken! Oliver is fled!"

The queen looked nervously at Elisabeth. The rout of his army by the English at Solway Moss seemed to have unhinged the monarch. His bloodshot eyes blazed at his wife. "And your accursed Cardinal Beaton is to blame for this catastrophe. Spurred on by your faithless De Guise brothers. Guisers each and every one of them, masquerading as cardinals and dukes."

After finding out that a belligerent Henry Tudor had instructed his archbishop to comb through every possible document for proof that he was their overlord, Beaton had badgered him to declare war on England. A show of force was necessary to prevent Henry from taking over Scotland. Overcome by a mysterious malaise, however, the monarch had been unable to lead his troops into battle and had sent his favourite, the young and inexperienced Oliver Sinclair in his place. Resentful of his incompetent command and reluctant to fight, his cringing lords had thrown down their weapons and surrendered.

"My lord," Queen Marie began hesitantly, "I am about to be brought to childbed. Does that not fill your heart with joy?"

Surely the imminent birth of an heir would rouse him from his deep melancholy? She leant forward to take his hand to place on her bump but he lurched backwards as if she were putting a hex on him. His eyes burned with a weird glint and his gaunt, twisted face grimaced with pain.

"How do I ken that it is my own bairn lying in your belly? Lying and false."

"My lord! Have you no faith in me?" Aghast, Queen Marie hugged her womb. "Do you suspect me of disloyalty. Do you accuse me of ..." she hesitated before daring to utter, "adultery?"

While she may have had to take care of his bastards, she knew better than to risk carrying one. Gripping his side, the king slumped down onto the settle. He grabbed a cushion and cradled it on his stomach, his tongue lolling idiotically as he rocked back and forth.

"What does it matter? Any son you bear will only become a vassal of Henry of England." A shadow of pain darkened his face.

"Stay a while and rest, my lord. You are weary. Let Betsy bring you a comforting posset."

"No more potions. No more sorcery. No more blood-letting. No more blood."

He rolled his head from side to side then sat quietly for a while, his glazed eyes staring into the middle distance. He leant forward, hunched over the cushion. "They're poisoning me," he muttered. "The Douglas witch and the Hamilton Bastard are plotting against me. From the fires of hell, spurred on by Satan himself. I can hear them whispering constantly. Conferring. Conniving. Conspiring."

Throwing aside the cushion, he stood up abruptly like a startled hare, his ears on the prick. "Here they are ..." His eyes widened. "One here," he yelped, glancing over his right shoulder, "and the other, there," glancing over his left. "By Christ's blood, they will be the death of me."

Once the queen was sealed safely in her chamber, James set off like wildfire around his kingdom to escape his demons. Lindsay kept Elisabeth informed with alarming reports which she dared not show to the queen.

The king veers from lying flat on his back to running round in a feverish frenzy. His physicians believe that an internal wound is the cause of his frequent vomiting but he resists all their attempts to investigate. He doses himself with regular swigs of cognac from his pewter flask to dull the pain in his side. He is jittery and edgy and we, his courtiers, can hardly keep up with him.

First he made us ride to Edinburgh to make an inventory of all his treasures and jewels, and then we sailed to Hallyards in Fife to consult with this treasurer. After a long conference with Sir William Kirkcaldy of Grange, James sank again into deep melancholy. The canty lady of the house endeavoured to rouse him, wishing him good cheer for the merry season of Yule about to begin. His Grace gawped at her as if she were a simpleton or a fool. "My portion of the world is short," he answered with a sneer. "Ere fifteen days are past, I will be gone from this wretched life."

I fear for his wits. Though growing weaker by the day he has given orders to set out for Falkland. I had thought it would be his desire to return to Linlithgow to be near the queen who is soon to be delivered of an heir. "You choose where you want to be," he said with the secretive smile that has become a habit now, "but this I can tell you. On Yule day, you will be masterless and the realm without a king."

Linlithgow Palace, December 1542

After braving the blizzard that had blasted their craft in the stormy waters of the Firth of Forth, the royal messengers then had to trudge knee-deep in drifting snow to Linlithgow to deliver the tragic news.

"The king, my lady, is dead."

The official statement from David Beaton, Cardinal of Scotland declared: On the fourteenth day of December in the Year of Our Lord 1542, James V of Scotland, in his thirtieth year, had passed from this world: *Requiescat in pace*. In his missive the Lord Lyon King of Arms, Sir David Lindsay, expressed his deep-felt condolences and offered his loyal services. The queen said a silent prayer and made the sign of the cross. She looked towards the cradle where her newborn infant lay quietly sleeping.

"Was he told of the birth of his daughter?"

"Aye, Your Grace."

"Had he any words for her?"

Elisabeth furtively fingered Lindsay's letter hidden up her sleeve, willing the messenger to be silent. The queen had enough to grieve her and the disturbing details of the last few hours of the king's life would only distress the new widow. No more portents, no more prophecies. The messenger hesitated before shaking his head.

"Nay, Your Grace."

Elisabeth breathed out. Coming round after many days of delirium, Lindsay wrote, James had lain motionless, a rapt expression on his face, as if listening to an inner voice. The joyous news that the queen was lighter of a child seemed to rouse him from his languor but when told he had a bonnie daughter, his spirits sank again.

"A lass! Alas a lass! It came with a lass and it will gang with a lass," he'd murmured, before falling into a dwam, his glazed eyes focussed on the world beyond. Not long before midnight, a faint smile had flitted across the king's face as if he were glad to be departing this vale of tears.

Hearing the infant cry, Betsy carefully lifted the precious bundle from the cradle and placed her in her mother's arms.

"Long live the queen," Marie de Guise whispered into the tiny buckie-shaped ear of the eight-day-old Queen of Scots as she snuggled into her mother's breast.

She'll have a sair fecht with our dour and fickle folk, Elisabeth thought sadly.

The walls of the Dolorous Chapel were covered with funereal black, buckram hangings fringed with black silk. Black velvet draped the catafalque on which the cast lead coffin would rest, covered in the cloth of state. Lindsay could feel a lump choking his thrapple. He'd never thought that in his lifetime he would witness the death of another monarch. At fifty-five, it should have been him in the coffin, not the thirty-year-old king. And then, the night before, he'd sat with his wife Jessie until she passed away.

As he watched the life-size effigy of his beloved monarch being dressed for his last state engagement in his royal robes of purple velvet lined with ermine, every stitch of which had been painfully sewn by the Mistress of the King's Wardrobe for the queen's coronation, the twice bereft Lindsay fought back tears. Despite the pain in her gnarled, misshapen fingers, the strain in her eyes weakened by years of working by candlelight and the canker devouring her, Jessie had been determined to finish the king's grave clothes herself.

Betsy had kept her going, dosing her with enough arrows of hemlock, as she called them, to deaden the pain but, when Jessie finally put down her needle, she gave Betsy a meaningful look. Now that she had fulfilled her last royal duty, Jessie surrendered to the final, fatal onslaught. While the ground was frozen, her body would remain unburied until Lindsay could take her on her last journey to Garleton. Lindsay swallowed hard. Tumbling swiftly to the foot of the hill, he may not be far behind.

To the mournful sound of trumpeters rehearsing the dolorous dirge, Cardinal Beaton strode into the chapel and shoved a parchment under Lindsay's nose. The Last Will and Testament of His Grace, James V, Beaton assured him. In the gloom, Lindsay screwed up his eyes to peer at the signature scrawled at the foot of the document.

"This doesn't look like the king's hand."

The funereal torches flickered eerily across the cardinal's inscrutable face.

"As you well ken, His Grace was in great distress before he passed away. His confused wits would affect his hand," the cardinal declared.

"Then even more reason to discount his so-called last wishes." Lindsay was pensive for a moment before saying, "As you well ken, I have been King James's closest friend and trusted confidante since the day and hour he was born. It seems very odd that His Grace didn't inform me of his intentions."

Beaton drew himself up and puffed out his barrel chest.

"His Grace confided in me during his last confession. While I was administering the sacred sacrament of Extreme Unction."

"If that is so, is it not then a sacrilege for a confessor to betray what should be known only to God?"

Beaton bristled. "Of course, that is why I beseeched the king's permission to put it in writing for him to sign. To make it a lawful document."

Lindsay quickly scanned the provisions of the Will, one of which specified a regency council for the infant queen to be set up – with the cardinal as chief governor and ruler of the council.

"I doubt whether this document is legal. I see no notary's signature as witness."

Beaton jabbed his finger at the bottom of the parchment. "See here the Great Seal. That is sufficient authorisation."

"Ah, the Great Seal," Lindsay harrumphed, "which rests in your safekeeping as chancellor. This is o'er ambitious, even for you, Beaton. The lords will not take kindly to a man of the Church o'erstepping himself. Nor will they be so easily deceived. I would advise you to destroy this."

Fearing that Lindsay would tear it up, Beaton snatched the precious document from him and narrowed his eyes.

"Tell me then, Lord Lyon, who will take charge of this godforsaken kingdom which has been malgoverned for so long? Who is capable of taking the reins? Certainly not the fey Hamilton, the most inconstant man under the sun. Now in thrall to the reformed religion, he would hand over the infant sovereign to that murderer and heretic, Henry of England."

"Perhaps now is the time to negotiate with Henry Tudor," Lindsay said wearily. "His son and heir would make a good match for our queen."

"What do you say?" As Beaton fumed, spittle spluttered from the corners of his mouth. "These words are not only treacherous, Davie Lindsay, but blasphemous. Our future is wedded to Catholic France, not Protestant England. Stay out of politics, Lyon Lindsay, and see to your dolorous duty. You have a royal funeral to arrange: I have an unruly kingdom to rule."

XIII

The Queen's Suitors

> My clear voice and courtly carolling
> Where I was wont with ladies for to sing
> Is rawk as rook, full hideous hoarse and rough.
> *The Testament of Cresseid*
> Robert Henryson, 15th Century

St. Mary's Abbey, August 1543

Elisabeth twisted round on the low stool, cricking her neck to see what he was doing. The rope tying her arms behind her back and securing her to the bedpost rubbed against her wrists.

"You'll find no money here," she grumbled. The lid of the kist was open and, while one of his henchmen flung the silk and satin gowns on to the floor, another slashed through them with his dagger in case gold or jewels were hidden in secret pockets or pouches.

"Where is it then?" Bothwell demanded.

"You receive the amount due to you as baillie of the abbey," she replied, trying to keep her voice calm, though inside she was fuming.

"One hundred pound Scots! God's troth, that is hardly enough to mend my boots!" Patrick raged and stomped his foot. "The abbey can well afford to settle on me more than that. It is richly endowed with lands and moneys."

"And it is my duty as prioress to see that it remains so and not become a pot for you to dip into whenever it pleases you. Forbye, if you choose to squander your money on drinking and gambling, rather than repair your boots, then that is your choice."

He tilted her chin upwards with the tip of his sword and glared at her.

"I am the Earl of Bothwell and your liege lord. You shall obey my orders."

"And I am a nun in thrall to no man: I answer only to God. And in return for these generous endowments we sisters pray for the souls of our patrons in perpetuity."

"Aye, and they're all on their knees in the chapel at this moment," he jeered, "paying tribute to my men."

"If any of my sisters are harmed, you will hang for it, Patrick, and you'll have to plead for mercy yourself, for I won't be doing it again."

What a traitor the Fair Earl had turned out to be: he could no more keep tryst than tell the truth. His boyhood mischief had matured into malicious self-interest and now, through his own fault, Bothwell was seriously in debt. Because of his repeated disloyalty and inconstancy, James V had eventually banished the flichty earl and confiscated his lands. Had his experiences taught him nothing?

Clearly not, for now, on the king's death, he'd deemed it safe to return and had arrived at the abbey demanding funds. Frustrated by her obstinacy, Bothwell had instructed his men to comb through the abbey, leaving nothing unturned. So that they could work unhindered, he'd then ordered them to round up the nuns and servants and imprison them in the abbey dungeon.

"And you shall join them unless you give me my due. I am the Earl of Bothwell, mind, the leading noble of the land! I cannot attend court dressed as shabby commoner."

Why, then, he need look no further than Hailes Castle where there was a kist of fine clothes belonging to his late father. Sadly, the twenty-one-year-old Adam had never had the chance to wear them out.

"Dead man's clothes! Moth-eaten and outdated! How will I win the queen dowager's hand dressed as a bogle?"

So that was his intention. She might have jaloused as much. Now that the official mourning period was over, the widowed queen mother should be thinking of taking another husband to shoulder her burden. As the foremost earl in the land, Patrick Hepburn ranked his chances very highly, and why not? Had not all his ancestors courted queens? Aye, thought Elisabeth, it was indeed a sorry trait in Hepburn men to be dintit with the king's women. And had it slipped his feeble mind that he was already married?

"Agnes Sinclair has been a devoted wife to you and mother of your two bairns."

Patrick swatted away her objection as if it were a pesky fly. That was a minor problem. As they were second cousins, he was pursuing an annulment of their marriage on the grounds of consanguinity.

"Had there been any suspicion that madness or any other serious affliction might weaken the bloodline, then you wouldn't have been allowed to marry in the first place. And your union has produced a sturdy son and a healthy daughter," Elisabeth reminded him. "Forbye, you risk raising the hackles of all those nobles who, like you, were granted a papal dispensation to marry their cousins."

Curses on the whole clamjamfrey: Bothwell didn't fear their contumely. Divorce he must in order to stand any chance against Matthew Stewart. Unmarried, with royal blood and a valid claim to the Scottish throne, Lennox was the firm favourite. He also had the backing of Cardinal Beaton who had lured him back from France with the promise of the hand of Marie de Guise, the queen dowager, and the regency of her infant daughter.

"Your brutal ill-treatment of our sisters and insolence to me will hardly win you the favour of my dear friend, the queen, who greatly values our abbey's charitable work. If you seek to raise yourself in her esteem, you'd better untie me now and release my sisters. And, if you do so with good grace, I may even smooth the path of your rough wooing," she added.

The sulky earl pondered this for a few moments, stamped a scruffy boot and then called off his men.

Linlithgow Palace

"Is the earl singing in Scots?" The queen dowager was perplexed. "For I cannot catch any of the words."

Elisabeth covered her mouth with her hand to smother a giggle. No, this mangled doggerel, delivered in a quavering falsetto punctuated with guttural catches in the throat, was the Earl of Bothwell's attempt to impress the queen with his poetic prowess in her own tongue. He'd spent hours with Sister Agnes who had done her best to teach him endearing words and phrases in French so that he might compose *verses de amour* inspired by the *Song of Roland*.

"Hark at the screeching from his thrapple. Like a peacock afflicted with rheum."

This cruel barb prompted other courtiers to erupt into unashamed jeers. The battle between two young bucks vying for the favours of a widow queen was beginning to cheer up the court in mourning. Paying no heed to their heckling, Bothwell finished his *chanson* and then bowed low to present the queen with his poetic composition, flamboyantly tied up with red ribbon and sealed with the Hepburn crest: *Keep Tryst*.

"Weigh well these verses that I write for Your Grace," he whispered, "for they express the secrets of a heart that is subject, bound and in thrall to your governance."

Graciously Queen Marie thanked him and promised to read them in private.

When Matthew Stewart took the floor, the courtiers listened in hushed and attentive silence. Newly arrived from France, the twenty-six-year-old Earl of Lennox was still a novelty at court. How would this brave peacock perform? No worse, surely, than his tuneless rival. From the first notes on the lute it was clear that Lennox was an accomplished musician and when, in his strong tenor voice, he sang the latest song from France – in perfectly pronounced French – the audience was enchanted.

Elisabeth glanced over at Patrick whose round shoulders slouched even more. Dark circles of rage flushed the Fair Earl's cheeks and his watery blue eyes were pink-rimmed with petulant tears. As soon as the musicians struck up a gavotte, Lennox was whirled onto the floor by the brazen Jenny Stewart. Despite being well married to Lord Malcolm Fleming, she was determined to shine in the reflected glory of this handsome and fashionably dressed gallant.

Not to be outdone, the gangling Bothwell shuffled clumsily into the throng and attempted to follow the steps but he kept treading on toes with his shabbily shod feet and bumping everyone with knobbly elbows. Finally cast out from the dance for having tripped up Lady Fleming, Patrick loitered on the side, gawky and gauche in the expensive ribbed velvet doublet that his handsome, broad-shouldered father had worn to great effect.

"The earl seems most disconsolate," the queen remarked.

As well he might, Elisabeth thought. Bothwell glanced up at the raised dais where she was sitting with the queen and glowered at her. If looks could kill … She knew of old that he would be blaming her for his humiliating trouncing by Lennox.

"Spare no pity for my nephew, Your Grace, for he deserves none. But take care not to cross him. He could be a dangerous enemy."

Though amused by their contest, Marie de Guise's strong head was not easily turned. However persuasive Bothwell's poetry may have been, written in his spidery scrawl it was unintelligible and, however tall and splendidly built Lennox may be, his weak chin hinted at an inner, spiritual frailty. Too vain, she pondered, too proud perhaps. Nor was she in any hurry to marry again. To do so would not only lose her the regency and control of her daughter but stir up dissent amongst her nobles. Learning from Margaret Tudor's ill-judged experience, she would devote herself to her daughter's present wellbeing and future prosperity.

In the meantime, too worldy-wise and tactful to make her true feelings known, she continued to play off her two suitors against each other. This way she could count on their loyalty – for a while, at least. Until Bothwell started boasting that the queen dowager had promised to marry him as soon as he had secured an annulment.

Crichton Castle

Furious at his foolhardiness, Elisabeth rode to Crichton where Bothwell was hiding out. Lacking the funds to pursue his suit of the queen, he had slunk away to his favourite castle to think again. The ride to the castle, amidst a bleak landscape overlooking the Tyne, was not one a woman of her age and in such wet weather should be tackling, but needs must.

Finding the earl slumped in a chair by the fire, drowning his sorrows with a flagon of wine, Elisabeth groaned. Patrick's wits were addled enough without their being sozzled. Was the thick-headed dolt wanting in wit by angering and insulting the queen in this way?

"Nothing but fair words she offers," Patrick whined. "If I don't force her hand she'll keep me dangling and give Lennox time to worm his weasely way in."

"You may think so, but if this act of bravado were construed as an attempt to abduct the dowager queen, you could be charged with high treason. And the punishment won't be a term languishing in jail but the loss of your block head."

Her threat seemed to make him stop and think about his actions.

"Aye, that's very true," he said, rubbing his scraggy beard thoughtfully. "Why should I waste time wooing the dowager when I can have her daughter? The queen herself, though but an infant, will be a much better catch."

Taken aback Elisabeth spluttered. "What? *Who climbs too high perforce he must fall.* You must rid yourself of such grand ideas, Patrick. Forbye, neither the dowager queen nor the Queen of Scots would countenance marriage to a man who has put his lawful wife away."

Cursing him for his arrogant presumption, she left him to stew in his own juice.

Hailes Castle

Deaf to all advice and blind to all the scandal, Bothwell was granted a divorce from the mother of his children. Feeling sympathy for his long-suffering wife, Elisabeth went to lend her support but Agnes seemed quite light-hearted, as if a great burden had been lifted from her shoulders. No longer thirled to the flighty earl, she was beginning a new life at Morham, lands he'd gifted to her as part of the divorce settlement.

However, while she was preparing to take her daughter with her to Morham, a few miles from Hailes, Bothwell had taken custody of his son and was sending him to the Bishop of Moray at Spynie. Elisabeth's heart sank as she considered what kind of moral and religious instruction the nine-year-old James would receive from his dissolute uncle Patrick, along with his innumerable ill-begotten offspring.

His education was to include the French language, the art of good handwriting and dancing lessons, Agnes informed her. Having scuppered his own chances of a royal marriage Bothwell clearly nurtured hope for his son. Work hard at your lessons, he'd told the young James, so as to be worthy of winning the hand of a queen.

"For a Hepburn shall sit on the throne of Scotland one day. That is our destiny."

PART FIVE

I

The Abbot of Unreason

At the end of the Holy Days called Yule,
in a most vehement frost ...
The History of the Reformation in Scotland
John Knox, 16th Century

Haddington, December 1545

"Tak tent to me while I make a proclamation! Hark at my ordinance!" the Abbot of Unreason bawled as he struggled to keep his balance on the cart. He kept tripping over his cope of office, fashioned out of canvas and embroidered with curious signs and symbols, while his mitre, made of leather and studded with tawdry trinkets of tin, kept falling from his head. But never would he think of letting go of his tankard of ale.

"Hark at *his* ordinance! *You* maun take heed of *our* ordinance, you feckless friar!" a protester shouted. Reaching up, he tugged at the hem of the cope, causing the mock abbot to wobble. His mitre fell off and the tankard flew out of his hand, splashing over the folk at the front, to cheers from the rabble at the back. The Monk of Misrule, his friar's paunch well stuffed with a cushion, waddled over to his superior with another tankard.

"This'll help to loosen your tongue."

The abbot took a grateful swig and wiped his mouth with his sleeve. "I proclaim that from henceforth ..." But his words were drowned out by the mob.

"Steek your gabs and muck out your lugs o'er there. Hear what the unholy abbot has to say," the Monk of Misrule yelled.

"Auld Nick has dryted on his tongue. Make way for one whose lips drip honeyed words."

"What din-raisin Gilmoubrand dares to make a bauchle out of the abbot?'" the Monk of Misrule challenged.

"Call me Cacaphatie, for my foul speech may offend your lugs."

Recognising their late monarch's favourite jester, the crowd cheered as he scrambled onto the cart. His choice of outfit – a woman's sark that was too tight and too short and showed off his hairy shanks, combined with his manly beard – provoked jibes and jeers questioning his gender. Jigging up and down and jingling a bell on the end of a stick, the jester began to heckle the abbot. Annoyed that his homespun wit couldn't keep up with that of the more skilled professional, the abbot attempted to pull rank on him.

"Be mindful that it is I who've been elected the Abbot of Unreason, the master of these revels, and not you. The Burgh Council themselves have decreed that I have command of the proceedings."

"Aye, but in these daft days any command is to be defied, even yours. The order of all things is tapsalteerie; the maid is to be served by the mistress, the laird must bow down to the soutar and the clergy must give ear to the laity. And all must heed the fool. Let the ranting and raving begin!" the jester bellowed.

Great cheers demonstrated unequivocally whose side the crowd were on. The Abbot of Unreason retired, but not before making rude gestures behind the fool's back.

"Aye, and about time, too. Now get on with it," a voice from the crowd shouted.

"Preen back your lugs," Cacaphatie called out. "I have made a new rule. From henceforth all prelates, clerics, monks and abbots shall have not one whore ..."

"There's nothing new about that rule," the abbot piped up triumphantly. "They do that anyway. Just take a keek in at what they cry the lemand Lamp of Lechery and you'll see the Franciscan friars with their lusty concubines."

As his brethren whooped in delight at his flyting, the abbot's face broke into a self-congratulatory smile – soon wiped away by the jester's retort.

"Nay, I say not one whore ..." Cacaphatie yelled, "but two, or three. Or more to their loins content!"

The noisy rabble roared with laughter and cried out, "Another law, another law."

"Wheesht! Have I not been elected abbot?" the deposed abbot reminded them. "Fairly and squarely? Would you listen to the jestings of a buffoon?"

"Aye they would! For now the Abbot of Unreason is using good sense to win them over. And they'll have no sense!" The jester grabbed the abbot's crosier and plonked the crudely made mitre onto his own head. "As the Right Reverend Abbot of Unreason," he called out, waving his crook, "I now ordain the First Estate to gang backwards – and widdershins round the cart."

"Gangan backwards? And widdershins? By the holy Mass, that's the way of Auld Nick himself," the usurped abbot retorted. "I'll have no dealings with the devil."

"Then you'll have to shun the demon drink! Do as you are bid or you'll be tossed into the mill-dam for a douking!"

The mill-dam? The rabble became more subdued and less cocksure, for that ill-fated spot was where the gypsy lass had been found drowned. Reluctantly, the abbot obeyed but, as he waddled backwards round the platform, he puckered his lips and a deep ruckle came from his throat. Tottering unsteadily, he turned to spit forth his retort at the jester who nimbly sidestepped the gob of spittle that splattered into the crowd.

"No more of your proclamations, Cacaphatie! Give us a song! Give us a song!"

"Fill up ma shoon with silver first and then I'll give you a song." The fool took off his shoe to be passed among the crowd. Then, waving the crook in one hand and his bell on a stick in the other, he began to sing:

"With a hey and a ho and rohumbelow,

Let some drink ale and some drink claret wine,
　　Michtie drink comforts the dull ingyne."

With this, he rubbed his groin, making lewd, suggestive movements that roused shrieks from the womenfolk. Then, as he raised his sark to unfasten his underbreeches, the crowd clamoured for more to be revealed.

"Would you look at the throng that's gathered here," he cried. "I can get no place to pish in for you all but my own shoe." Saying so, he took off his other shoe and pissed into it. "Here's something more tasty than ale. *In nomine domini*, I baptise thee," he intoned, spraying the crowd with its contents. While the first few rows ducked, two passers-by, stony-faced and sober and clad in clerical black, weren't quick enough to avoid the unsavoury shower.

Jumping into the mob to retrieve the shoe filled with coins, the jester cried out, "And now I restore to you your rightful abbot." He rammed the tawdry mitre back on the abbot's head and thrust the crooked crosier into his hand. Smarting with hurt pride, the ridiculed Abbot of Unreason caught hold of him.

"For your brazen cheek you must now kiss my arse," he grumbled before flipping up his cloak to expose his behind.

Cacaphatie screwed up his nose. "I'd rather kiss a bullock's buttocks than a bishop's behouchie," he scoffed. "And you should take heed before baring your arse. Pride gangs afore a fall." He winked conspiratorially to the crowd before landing a hefty kick on the abbot's generous hurdies. The jester then pranced off, followed by a swarm of admirers howling for more entertainment.

"So that is how I am welcomed by Haddington. Pissed on from a great height." The tall preacher calmly wiped his face, but his companion's short temper was inflamed. Shaking his fist, he called out after the jester.

"How dare you soil the garments of this holy man of God!"

He would have run after him and boxed his ears but the preacher held him back.

"I've had worse flung at me, John. Forbye, yon fool's drowned body will be washed up in Lochleven ere long." As he took off his French cap to shake it dry, Knox gawped at him. It wasn't like George Wishart to bring down curses on those who crossed him. He jammed his round velvet cap firmly back on his head and added, "But it doesn't augur well." Shivering, he wrapped his black frieze mantle more tightly round his gaunt frame. Knox led him to a stall where, despite his protests, he thrust a cup of hot, spiced ale into his white-knuckled fingers. He knew better than to believe Wishart's assertion that he never felt the cold.

"Yet there are more words of truth being spoken here in jest than in much of Catholic doctrine," Wishart remarked, blowing onto the sizzling ale. "If only we could harness the common folk's instinctive distrust of the hierarchy to topple the Church of Rome. Sadly, the popish Church knows only too well how to distract folk from engaging with Scripture and the word of God," he went on. "To check him from champing at the bit, the Vatican unbridles the humble workman to allow him to frolic with mindless merrymaking one day then brings him sharply to heel the next."

Knox heartily agreed. Hardly a week went by when there wasn't some kind of elaborate ceremonial. Every possible feast day and obscure saint's day was marked by a procession and, with pageants at *Corpus Christi* and miracle plays at *Pasche*, it was a wonder that the local craftsmen got any work done. And now the Daft Days at the tail end of the year marked the end of the Yuletide festivities. Knox was disgusted. What impression was this gallimaufry of pagan saturnalia in his hometown making on his master?

Lamentably, the infestations of the Roman Church in Haddington – one abbey, two monasteries, three churches and three chapels – were no longer houses of God but palaces of sumptuous splendour. Quantity did not signify sanctity. Was it not sinful and corrupt that so much wealth had been accumulated here and misdirected into endless erections of ecclesiastical edifices?

Now that the spiced ale had warmed their bellies, Knox tried to tempt his companion to eat something nourishing. The appetising smells from the abundant stalls selling all kinds of festive food – stuffed pies and sausages, mussel brose and howtowdie broth, mealie dumplings dripping with fat – were assailing Knox's nose. Being ravenously hungry, he wolfed down a mutton pie, the grease dribbling down his chin, while Wishart only pecked at a bannock and a sliver of cheese to satisfy his modest appetite. While admiring his master's temperate habits, Knox was finding it difficult to emulate him.

Wishart ate skimpily, often skipping meals, and could lay his head on a bed of prickly straw. The one comfort he couldn't do without was a regular bath, daily whenever possible, a habit which those who bathed once a year whether they needed to or not, found most idiosyncratic. A monk's life would have suited him, in a strict ascetic order, as long as he could indulge his weakness for frescoes. Though he disdained the ostentatious ornamentation of Scottish churches, the frescoes in Italian churches painted by local workmen had moved him greatly. So much so that, in his native parish of Fordoun, he had decorated the walls of his dwelling with his humble attempts. Knox had frowned when he saw them but said nothing. It was a small fault in a great man he decided. For, despite the adulation shown him wherever he preached, George Wishart was the least vain and least covetous man he had ever met.

He was also the most charitable. At some point during their wanderings, the long black mantle, along with other items of clothing, would be given to the poor. Everything, that is, except the precious cap he'd bought as a scholar in France and which would be difficult to replace. Faithful to the true Christian principles, Wishart desired to do good to all men and to harm no-one. Besides, knowing that his every action, every movement was being scrutinised, both by his enemies as well as his friends, he resolved to teach by example.

Leaving the Yuletide fair, the two men took the high road to Ormiston where they would lodge for the night. At the side of the tall, gangly Wishart who loped along in great strides, the shorter, stockier Knox, weighed down by the hefty sword, was struggling to keep up, but then he slowed down.

"We're being followed," he said in a low voice.

"I know." Wishart seemed unperturbed. "Those sergeants of Satan have become our constant shadows."

As Knox turned round again, the two greyfriars faded into the gloom.

"What if they try to make another attempt on your life?"

In the plague-stricken city of Dundee, a Catholic priest – at Beaton's behest Knox guessed – had attacked Wishart. When the enraged congregation began tearing the priest to pieces, Wishart bade them to stop and sheltered his assailant in his arms. Such a response was so different, so contrary, to his own, Knox reflected. He'd have been the first to rip the murderous priest limb from limb with his own bare hands. With his fiery temper he'd never be able to live up to such high standards, he feared, but then scolded himself for envying his master's cool self-possession.

"But you too are in danger," Wishart warned.

"Aye, I'm sure to be in Beaton's bad books," Knox grimaced. His lips were freezing as they trudged, heads down against the sleet.

The rumour that the cardinal had drawn up a black list of heretics whom he proposed to eliminate one by one was probably true and Knox could no longer count on his godmother to protect him. Nevertheless, since the assassination attempt, a faithful follower always carried a two-handled sword for Wishart's defence and now it was Knox's honour to be entrusted with this task. When he gripped the sword with both hands, making ready to strike, Wishart laid a steadying hand on his shoulder.

"Nay, John, I know that I shall finish my life in that bloodthirsty man's hands, but it will not be in this manner." Then, gazing wistfully ahead, he added in a sad whisper, "But it might be easier on me if it were."

II

Wise Heart

> Two women shall be grinding at the mill;
> the one shall be taken and the other left.
>
> *Matthew* XXIV:41

St.Mary's Parish Church, 15 January 1546

Every blasphemous utterance stabbed mercilessly at her heart, every sacrilegious statement wounded her soul. She longed to jab her fingers in her ears to deafen the stream of evil heresy gushing like bile from the heretic's lips.

"The Holy Scripture is the highest and, indeed, only authority for my teaching," he claimed. On and on he went, attacking every belief that she held sacred. Ransacking the holy sacraments, destroying the creed, tearing apart her beloved Church limb from limb.

She kept her head bent, forcing her beads between her fingers and burbling *Ave Marias* to drown out the blasphemous torrent flooding from the pulpit, for she feared she was committing a grave sin by her very presence. But curiosity had overcome her misgivings.

His sermon under the ancient yew tree at Ormiston had even enthused the godless beggars and indigents who traipsed to the abbey for alms. She wouldn't have had the courage to come but for Sister Katherine who was eager to hear this devil's advocate. What would her dear friend, a stern authoritarian, be making of this? When the devil incarnate in the pulpit paused for breath, Sister Agnes took the opportunity to whisper:

"He'll burn for this. If not in this world then surely in hell."

When Katherine turned her head slowly, Agnes stared at her in surprise. Despite the gloomy darkness of the church, a radiant glow shone from her friend's face. She seemed transformed. Transfigured. The harsh lines of her face had softened and the deeply etched line on her puckered brow had smoothed out. Her lips were slightly parted and her eyes dreamy. Katherine made no sign that she'd heard her friend but turned away again to gaze, enraptured, at the heretic.

"Wise Heart," she whispered. "He has come as I knew he would."

III

The Sermon on the Tyne

The voice of him that crieth in the wilderness.
Prepare ye the way of the Lord, make straight ...
a highway for our God.
Isaiah XL:3

Haddington, 16 January 1546

The windows of Lethington Tower, the home of Sir Richard Maitland, were ablaze with light and the strains of music and singing rang clearly through the frosty air to the cottage where Wishart and Knox were spending the night.

"They're wetting the head of Sir Richard's newborn," the cottager, sympathetic to their cause, explained. "Another wee laddie for the laird."

"May the Lord grant him a long and prosperous life," Wishart said. "And the freezing cold hasn't prevented his guests from attending the festivities," he added morosely, an uncharacteristic hint of peevishness in his voice: for that was the reason Knox had given to explain the sparse audience at his sermon that afternoon. A lame excuse, Knox knew, for the truly committed would struggle through hell and high water to hear him.

Why, only a few days ago, Wishart had preached to capacity in the parishes of Inveresk and Tranent, but that afternoon only a humiliating smattering of souls were dotted about the cavernous nave of St. Mary's. "Well, we can only pray that word will spread and that tomorrow the kirk will be full. Forbye, my Ayrshire friends have promised to come. They will not let me down."

Widow Ker was resting on the steps of the Nungate Bridge, struggling to get her breath back after hurrying from Samuelston. She held out a letter for Wishart. As he read it through, his melancholy face became ashen and his long thin fingers trembled.

"They're not coming," he said quietly, crumpling the letter in his fist. His eyes dulled and he breathed a huge sigh as he stared down the river where the Lamp of Lothian, the Franciscan Friary, glowed in the winter sun. A rookery of spies for Beaton, he'd been warned.

"You ken why, don't you?" Widow Ker folded her plump arms across her bosom. "They've got wind that your sympathisers at Longniddry are plotting against the cardinal and are afeart the finger will be pointed at them too. My own heart is sick sorry that my cringing countrymen have let you down. They should all be black affronted."

"So, then, I am on my own?" Wishart's long face drooped even more.

"Nay, you are not alone." Knox snatched the crumpled letter, tore it up and scattered the scraps over the bridge. For a few seconds he watched them flutter down into the river Tyne and float towards the mill-dam. He shuddered. "I will never abandon you."

"May God bless you, my faithful disciple," Wishart said softly, though his watery smile hid a deep foreboding.

Outside St.Mary's Parish Church, the Earl of Bothwell was giving orders to his troops with his customary arrogant swagger.

"No-one is allowed to enter the kirk," he proclaimed, "on pain of … On pain of death … of their immortal souls," he added hesitantly, his grasp of religious dogma as hazy as his sense of loyalty. The soldiers had been ordered to mount up so as to appear more menacing to the congregation and the breath from the snorting, whinnying horses steamed in the frosty air. "Halt!" he yelled to a group who were trying to slip past him into the church.

"Come down from your high horse, Patrick." Elisabeth drew back the hood of her cloak. "I need to speak with you in private." She beckoned for him to follow her behind a buttress, where she confronted him. "On whose orders are you prohibiting us from attending the sermon?" she asked, trying to hide the anger in her voice.

"His Eminence, the cardinal's. He forbids the folk to hear this dangerous heretic."

"And the queen mother? What are her orders?"

"The queen? Aye, well, I've been commissioned to arrest them," he boasted, puffing his chest out proudly. "As the sheriff of Lothian I have that power."

"I see." Elisabeth paused before asking, "Them, you say?"

"Aye," Bothwell replied rather sheepishly, avoiding her eyes, "Wishart and one of his disciples. But we're not to arrest them till later – after his sermon. The cardinal doesn't want the flichty mob to turn against us and bring the wrath of the people down on us. And then I've to take them to the cardinal at Elphinstone. Forthwith."

At the mention of Beaton, one from their group withdrew quickly and left.

"Patrick," Elisabeth moved in closer to whisper, "you ken I have the queen's ear. And I can tell you that all is not lost as far as future prospects are concerned. Now that Lennox is safely married to Margaret Douglas and Arran's flimsy wits are befuddled, the way is clear for you."

Hope lit up his pale blue eyes. Bothwell had lost a great deal in his fruitless contest with Lennox. Not only time, money and his reputation but also his wife, two children and, of course, the dowager queen Marie who had snubbed his advances. No wonder he was peeved, but now that his rival had flounced off to the English court and married the daughter of Margaret Tudor and Angus, he had another chance.

"You may think the queen is in glunders with you," Elisabeth continued, "but she's not at all pleased with Cardinal Beaton. She wants no more bloodshed. But if Wishart and his follower are taken to Elphinstone, Beaton will send them to the stake. And you know who his disciple is, don't you?"

Dull-witted Patrick looked down, avoiding her gaze. "John was aye a good friend to you, was he not? He always took your part when you were bullied. Whatever his beliefs may be now, he would never, ever betray a friend. And," she added confidentially, "I can assure you that Queen Marie would look kindly on you if you … took your charges to Hailes rather than to Elphinstone." She'd almost suggested that he "lose" the prisoners but stopped herself in time. Bothwell might take it ill to be reminded of his humiliation when, ordered by the king to capture Archie Douglas, he happened to "lose" him, or so he maintained. As punishment, he was flung into the dungeon at Edinburgh Castle and then, only after her appeal, was thirled as king's ward till his 21st birthday.

He shrugged his rounded shoulders. "But those are my orders."

"From the cardinal perhaps, but the queen's will surely carries greater weight."

Bothwell furrowed his brow as his slow wits considered the options. Well aware that her fickle nephew had almost bankrupted himself from his own rough wooing of Queen Marie, Elisabeth surreptitiously slipped a packet into his hand.

"Here," she said. "Perhaps this may help you make up your mind."

Inside St. Mary's Kirk, Wishart was pacing up and down behind the high altar, in and out of the shadows cast by the great pointed east window. Before preaching, he usually spent some time quietly absorbed in prayer and meditation but now he was too tense. His Lollard friends had forsaken him. Haddington had forsaken him. Had God forsaken him? Was this a sign that he was losing his gift?

Knox placed a hand on his sleeve. "Master, the time of your sermon approaches. You must calm your mind."

"And how many have braved the elements today?" Wishart replied with uncharacteristic sarcasm before ascending the pulpit.

"O Lord," he began, his voice echoing through the nave to be heard by the few intrepid souls who had sneaked past Bothwell's guards. "I've heard that in Haddington, two or three thousand people would attend one vain clerk's play, and lately I've seen for myself the multitude cheering on the Abbot of Unreason. Yet now, in all this town and parish there cannot be numbered a hundred persons to hear the messenger of the Eternal God. Men of God from Troon to Tranent have heard me gladly, but not the people of Haddington."

Gazing up at the rafters, he continued his bitter complaint, sparing no scorn. "How long shall it be that Thy holy word shall be despised, and men shall not regard their own salvation?" Then, digressing wildly from the sermon he'd prepared, Wishart began to rant and rave at his sparse congregation, warning them of the wrath to come.

At the back of the church Elisabeth looked round for Katherine who had persuaded her to attend. Wishart was a true man of God, she'd said. She'd never encountered anyone with such conviction in his beliefs and, however wrong they might think him to be they should hear his message, if only to understand the reasons why Knox had abandoned the Church. Listening to him now, Elisabeth was puzzled. Was this the man who was either revered or feared? She wasn't the only one to be perplexed.

"This is not the sermon he preached yesterday," Agnes murmured.

Underneath the pulpit, Widow Ker fidgeted uneasily on her stool. "What is he saying? Perhaps we should stop him?" she whispered to Knox. But he paid her no heed, leaning forward on the hilt of his two-handed sword, listening intently. This was more like it. This fire and brimstone sermon echoing the Old Testament prophets or even Bishop Hepburn's tirades would stiffen the sinews and stir the blood.

After an excoriating hour and a half, Wishart reached the climax of his sermon. As if infused with some supernatural force he drew himself up to his full height and, waving his lanky arms madly, he began raining curses and prophecies down on them all.

"For your contempt of God's messenger, strangers shall possess your houses, chase you from your habitations and set upon you with sword and fire," he predicted, smiting the air with his hand. "Pestilence and famine shall afflict you. And the walls of this rose-red kirk by the Tyne will be open to the skies."

Sitting upright, terrified by this tirade, Agnes whispered anxiously to Elisabeth. "He's not well, I fear."

Indeed, despite the freezing temperature of the cold stone church, his usually pale complexion was flushed and beads of sweat trickled down his brow. His fist thumped down on the hard stone of the pulpit, making Agnes squirm for the pain it must have caused him. His blazing eyes scoured the church, seeking out sinners and ingrates. Then he bowed his head to say, his voice breaking with unbearable sadness, "I am weary of the world because the world is weary of God."

Knox laid aside the sword and joined Widow Ker to push through the small group of followers who, alarmed at his performance and concerned for his wellbeing, had gathered at the foot of the pulpit. After being helped down the steps, Wishart slumped onto a bench. The sermon had exhausted him. While Knox shooed the onlookers down the aisle and Widow Ker went to fetch some water for the preacher, Elisabeth crept up quietly behind him and stood in the shadow of a pillar.

"Listen to me. Please." She spoke in an urgent whisper. "There isn't much time. Bothwell and his men have surrounded the church. You are to be arrested tonight."

Wishart listened without turning round. He nodded wearily. He didn't need to be told: he had foreseen it.

"But don't worry. You won't be taken to Beaton – I give you my word on that – but to Hailes Castle. From there you will be freed." How, she was not yet sure, but for now it was important to wrest Wishart from Beaton's clutches and gain time.

"But I have one thing to beg of you. Please don't take John with you. Order him to stay, for he won't leave your side otherwise. Please, as his godmother …" her voice trailed off and she slipped back into the shadows as Knox approached.

"Whatever will be, will be," Wishart muttered. "My travail is at an end. One is sufficient for a sacrifice. *Alas! he said and woe is me!*" he cried out and then went on:
"I trow my deed will work me woe:
Jesu! My soul commend I thee,
Wheresoever my body go!"

Alarmed by his master's haverings, Knox's voice wavered. "What are you saying? Who were you talking to?"

"Fate," Wishart replied, his eyes staring into the gloom. "Destiny. Fortune. Whatever you like to call it." He gave a long sigh. "My mother was a Learmont, did I ever tell you? A descendant of True Thomas the Rhymer. Given two gifts by the Queen of Fairyland … "

"Aye," Knox interrupted, "a tongue that never lies and the second sight."

Wishart nodded. "Though I fear my inheritance has been more of a curse."

He'd always been true to his beliefs, had never compromised, even when his life was at risk, as it surely was tonight. But it wasn't difficult to foretell his future. From the day and hour he'd turned his back on the Roman Church his destiny had been decided. But, he wondered sadly, had he had any choice? Had it all been predestined?

It was a mirk and starless night. Thick frost was beginning to settle, they could see their breath on the freezing air and, since the frozen road would be too slippery for horses, Wishart's small party prepared to set out on foot for Ormiston. When Knox appeared, wielding the two-handed sword, Wishart took him to one side.

"Nay, John, stay with your bairns. Take the lads safely back to their lodgings."

"And then I shall follow you."

Wishart nodded. "Aye, John, you shall, but promise me this:
"If thou wilt spell or tales tell,
John, thou never shall make lee:
Whereosever thou go, to frith or fell,
I pray thee speak never no ill of me."

And, kissing the mystified Knox on the cheek, he murmured, "One is sufficient for a sacrifice."

IV

Last Supper

> Moreover if thy brother shall trespass against thee,
> go and tell him his fault between thee and him alone.
>
> *Matthew* XVIII:15

Elphinstone Tower, 16 January 1546

Sister Katherine left St.Mary's Kirk to flee along the high road to Elphinstone. Faith in the truth of Wishart's preaching was giving her wings but her strength was threatening to run out. She had stopped to catch her breath when a farmer, merry after market day, offered her a lift on his cart. While she gave thanks to God for sending this guardian angel, the farmer, oblivious to her vocation – or perhaps not – carried on warbling the bawdy songs from the tavern.

At Elphinstone Tower she ignored the warnings from astounded guards and burst into the chamber where her brother was taking supper. Her breath was ragged from running in the freezing night air. Frost had formed a silvery halo round her starched wimple making her eyes glint and her cheeks glow crimson.

"Davie, you mustn't arrest Wise Heart," she blurted. "Wishart is a man of God, his wise heart full of grace and goodness."

She shook her head, spraying him with tiny flakes of melting frost. With a scowl, Beaton put down his goblet of wine and wiped the drips from his darkening face.

"Wise Heart? Is that what you cry him? Am I hearing aright? My devout sister is pleading for mercy to be shown to a heretic? Has the devil's disciple bewitched you, too?"

He stood up and, resting his knuckles on the table, he leant forward. His hooded eyes narrowed to peer intently at her flushed face. "Or have you fallen in love with him? Is that it? Well, that is further proof that he must be stopped. If Wishart's sleekit tongue can beglamour my pious sister so easily, think how he could dupe weaker minds."

"John Knox has chosen to follow him and you cannot say that he is feeble-minded," she retorted.

Beaton snorted. "That may be true, but perhaps his weakness lies in thon part which responds neither to reason nor religious conviction. Prioress Elisabeth has good cause to be concerned about his being in thrall to Wishart. There is something unhealthy in thon zealot."

"What do you mean by that?"

Slowly and significantly Beaton picked up the wishbone of the woodcock he'd been devouring and balanced it on his pinkie.

"Forbye, celibacy seems to be scant sacrifice for Knox who has never, to my knowledge, sought comfort in tail-toddle, at least with women. Which makes one jalouse that he may satisfy his base cravings by other, how shall I put it? More perverse means. A monastery would suit him better; where he can associate with those who prefer the company of men. While for women who favour their own …"

He curled the wishbone round his finger, all the while looking pointedly at his sister.

His lewd suggestion was not lost on her. "What are you saying?" Her flushed cheeks deepened to a darker shade of crimson.

"It isn't uncommon for close friendships to thrive between young men who have shunned the companionship of women. Nor indeed among women who spurn men."

Katherine's whole being was now aflame. She longed to fly at him and gorge out those scornful eyes. What was he insinuating?

"Whereas you have aye condemned me for my relationship with Marion, whom I consider my lawful wife in all but name," Beaton went on, "I have turned a blind eye to your *amitié* with the French nun. Pray, sister, where is your tolerance of human failings? Your much vaunted Christian charity?"

His words made her gasp for breath. How like her bullying brother to locate a skelf and then press on it mercilessly until it throbbed. She grabbed the wishbone and snapped it in two, letting the splinters fall to the floor.

"You are no brother to me, Davie Beaton. May you rot in hell."

Ormiston Hall

Faint with fatigue, Katherine leant against the wall outside the gates of Elphinstone Tower. The sleety rain helped to douse her burning indignation and wash away the tears smarting her cheeks but could not wipe out the humiliation she felt from her brother's sneering insinuations. How dare he pervert her innocent friendship with Agnes or taint her admiration for Wishart with his smutty suggestions! Slowly, as her feet started slipping in the slush, her back began sliding down the wall. What did she care if she sank down into the mud and never got up again? Having failed to plead for Wishart's life, she felt weary unto death.

From out of the darkness, a hand touched her elbow and a voice whispered, "Come with me, sister. I'll take you to the master."

She followed Willie Brounfield, a groom at Elphinstone, to the house in Ormiston where Wishart was lodging. A reformist sympathiser, Brounfield had been spying on Beaton and had heard about all the confrontation between brother and sister. Reaching Ormiston, Brounfield stopped underneath an enormous yew tree just outside John Cockburn's house.

"This is our cathedral," he declared. Within the canopy formed by its falling branches Wishart had held his open-air services. There was standing room for up to two hundred people, he told her proudly. Katherine laid her head against the trunk and said a silent prayer for her Wise Heart.

"Deliver me from mine enemies. O my God: defend me from them that rise up against me. Deliver me from the workers of iniquity and save me from bloody men. For lo, they lie in wait for my soul: the might are gathered against me ... "

Wishart was leading the small company in the 51st psalm when loud banging at the door interrupted their prayer. All but Wishart stiffened in their seats, fearful and alert. The arrival of the traitor Judas leading the multitude held no surprise for him and he began calmly reciting the Lord's Prayer. He was, however, caught unawares by the bedraggled nun who had pushed past Cockburn to hurl herself at his feet. With Brounfield reassuring them that, though she might be Beaton's sister, she was no spy, the small flock welcomed Sister Katherine into their midst. Widow Ker made them all shift round to give their new recruit a place by the fire to warm up and dry off.

As she glanced at their rapturous faces glowing in the firelight, charmed by Wishart's readings from the Sacred Scripture, Katherine experienced both deep joy and deep sorrow. While she was happy to be among folk who shared this new and wonderful wisdom, knowing what fate awaited their master saddened her. They kept watch until midnight when the Fair Earl surrounded the household with a troop of cavalry. Cockburn was standing his ground, refusing to surrender Wishart to him without a guarantee of his safety, when the preacher slipped past him to address his captor.

"I praise God that so honourable a knight receives me this night," he said, fixing Bothwell with his forthright gaze, "for I'm assured your honour will not permit anything to be done to me against the order of the law. Forbye, I fear less to die openly than to be murdered in secret."

Bothwell glanced shiftily from one to the other before addressing the floor. A flush of colour spread upwards from his throat to infuse his pale cheeks as he stuttered over the words he'd been rehearsing under the prioress's instruction.

"Not only shall I protect you from violence but I promise upon my honour that neither the governor nor the cardinal shall be able to harm you. I shall keep you in my own power till either I set you free or bring you back here." So saying, he was satisfied that he'd honoured his promise to his aunt.

"Don't believe him," Sister Katherine whispered. "Bothwell cannot be trusted. He sways with the wind. This Judas has been paid his thirty pieces of silver by my brother, the chief priest."

Wishart inclined his head towards her and shrugged. "My hour has come," he murmured in fatalistic tones that alarmed her. "It is written."

V

The Trial

> Greater love hath no man than this,
> that a man lay down his life for his friends.
> *John* XV:13

St.Andrews, 28 February 1546

The noise was deafening. A ceaseless booming, relentlessly pounding against the hold of the ship. Bodies unsteady on their feet battered against each other. Slop buckets rolled about, sloshing out their squalid contents and stinking the already foul air. The booming grew louder and louder. The ship must be under attack. Every time a cannonball hit the side, the ship shuddered, planks creaked and cargo exploded.

When the smell of smoke stung their nostrils, the prisoners in the hold panicked, scrambling over each other to get to a source of air. Rats were scampering up the ropes but the hatches and portholes had been closed. Some tried to knock holes through the sides. From above they could hear sailors shouting, "She's on fire," and calling for water. From out of the depths they cried, "Open the hatches! Let us out! Save our souls!" Briny seawater was seeping upwards from the bowels of the ship and lapping round their ankles. His lungs were burning. He gasped for air.

"Wake up!" A voice shouted. But as he tried to move his cramping limbs he realised he was shackled to the wall. In the perpetual darkness, he couldn't tell whether it was day or night and, despite the eternal booming and the chilling dampness in the unlit Sea Tower of St.Andrews Castle, he must have dozed off. The unexpected light from a candle thrust in his face made him blink.

"What day is it?" Wishart enquired.

A Franciscan friar stepped out from behind the warder. "The last day of February," he said.

So, the twenty-eighth day of February: an ominous date. Fourteen years to the day since Patrick Hamilton's execution. Twice seven long years. Is that why he'd dreamt of fire? And, with the waves battering his ears, hardly surprising that he dreamt of the sea. Fire and sea together, his mother would have avowed, were powerful portents of disaster. Predictably enough, he thought wryly.

He was to appear before the lord cardinal the next morning, the Franciscan, John Winram, informed him. "To give an account of the seditious and heretical doctrine you have been teaching. But beforehand, I've been asked to preach." He paused before continuing. "And I am taking as my text the parable of the sower in St.Matthew's gospel, which I am sure you well ken."

Wishart gave a slight nod of acknowledgement. The sub-prior of St. Andrews had chosen the very text he'd used in his Christmas sermon at Leith when he'd dared to liken the clergy to the thorns among which the seed of truth was sown. "And some fell among thorns and the thorns grew up and choked it and it yielded no fruit." Saying this, he scrutinised Winram's face for any sign of sympathy, but the Franciscan remained inscrutable.

St. Andrews Cathedral, 1 March 1546

On the grassy knoll in front of her brother's grand house, soldiers were piling up wood. Horror-struck, Katherine stopped abruptly: such a huge pyre would not be for roasting the fatted calf. So the Bloody Cardinal had already judged Wishart and found him guilty. Other soldiers were training the castle cannons onto the execution pyre while an armed force of one hundred men lined up to escort the prisoner on his last journey.

"Your brother must be afeart that we'll try to rescue our Wise Heart." Taking her by the hand, Widow Ker hauled her away. "Come on, there's no time to stand and gawp. We'll no get a place otherwise."

Outside the cathedral, the cardinal's men, emboldened by liberal tots of French brandy, were haranguing the large crowd of spectators seeking entry. There were no places left. The cathedral was packed. Go home.

Widow Ker nudged Katherine. "Tell them you're the cardinal's sister."

Katherine glanced down at the scruffy woollen skirt and clarty pinny, which barely skimmed her ankles. "They'd never believe me. An Anstruther fishwife is better clad than I am. Forbye, I'm ashamed to call him brother."

Widow Ker grunted and together they inched their way round the cathedral to a narrow door guarded only by a gnarled old porter who barred their way.

"Take pity on us," she moaned, "for I'm the prisoner's poor widowed mother and this is his beloved sister."

"Aye well, there's many who say it's the wrong man on trial and that Beaton will rue this day," he whinged and directed them along a dark, musty passage into the nave. High up in the chancel, the hierarchical rivals, Cardinal Beaton and Gavin Dunbar, the Archbishop of Glasgow, famous for his "monition of cursing" against the border reivers, headed the tribunal on the specially constructed grandstand.

In the pulpit, the Franciscan friar Winram began his sermon but, listening to his opening words, Katherine could hardly believe her ears. He seemed to be accusing the hierarchy of sacrilege and criticising bishops for failing to be faultless, sober-minded and holy. He even decried them as thorns among the seeds of truth. Was he not meant to be defending the Church? What would her brother, the cardinal, think of that?

Katherine stretched up on tiptoe, craning her neck, hoping to glimpse her brother's reaction, but he was too far away. Instead, Winram may have caught sight of the cardinal's disapproval for, after this defiant lob, he seemed to change tack and was now calling for heretics to be cut down. He certainly seemed to have lost courage. Head downcast he descended the pulpit where, waiting at the foot, he met Wishart. They exchanged a few words: Winram then shook his head while Wishart patted him on the shoulder.

Despite her claim to be the prisoner's widowed mother, the crowd were reluctant to let Widow Ker cut a swathe through them, until Katherine pulled back her shawl. On her head she'd squashed the French cap Wishart had gifted her on the night of his arrest. As she'd predicted, Bothwell had proved false, moving Wishart about from pillar to post in a macabre parody of Hunt the Slipper. From Hailes, the Privy Council ordered him to be taken to the Regent Governor Arran, who was then solicited by the queen mother to surrender his prisoner to the cardinal who in turn imprisoned him in St. Andrews Castle. Hovering in the shadows like a helpless guardian angel, Katherine had followed the martyr on every station of his *via dolorosa* to his final Golgotha – the place of the skull.

"Aye, that's the master's hat all right," a sympathiser stated. "He never took it off, not even in his bed. God's blessing on you ladies." With that, the crowd parted to let them through.

When Wishart knelt to pray in the pulpit, Katherine bowed her head. Instinctively she began fumbling for her rosary to join him but she'd flung her beads away with her nun's habit. She would not be lost for words, however. What better time to discard her Latin prayers and appeal directly to God in her own tongue to come to the aid of her Wise Heart?

When she raised her head again, the cardinal's secretary was standing in the opposite podium, drumming his fingers impatiently on the battery of case papers piled up in front of him. John Lauder. A powerful prosecutor: a pitiless persecutor. By force of habit she began to cross herself to ward off Satan, but stopped short on seeing Widow Ker's disapproving frown.

In a quiet, determined voice, Wishart requested permission to summarise his doctrine: so that he wouldn't be judged unjustly, he explained. Lauder's screech of derision skirled throughout the cathedral.

"If it were not lawful for you to preach without any authority of the Church, then it is certainly not lawful for you to preach now," he bawled, before going on to spit out a list of accusations:

That it was vain to build costly churches.

That the Eucharist was only common bread and wine.

That a priest saying Mass was like a fox wagging its tail.

Dear God in heaven! Katherine squirmed. He's hammering in the nails. He'll crucify him ere long.

"My lords, I did not say so. What I said was that the moving of the outward body, without the inward moving of the heart, is nothing else but the playing of an ape, and not the true serving of God."

While Wishart nimbly defended himself against all the charges with admirable self-control, Katherine couldn't stop the violent thrumming in her breast. If only she'd thought to bring a stool like some in the congregation, but then scolded herself for her weakness. She must stand firm. When Widow Ker linked a comforting arm through hers, Katherine strained to smile her thanks but her mouth was frozen in a rictus of fear. By way of consolation, Lauder, too, was finding it difficult to maintain his composure.

"You deny that there are seven sacraments?" he snarled.

Whether there were seven or eleven sacraments Wishart couldn't say since he taught only what was in Scripture.

"So neither confession nor baptism is, in your humble opinion, a sacrament?"

Since God alone could grant forgiveness and absolution, confessing our sins needed no intermediary. And as for baptism: how could an infant make a promise before God without understanding the conditions?

Ignoring these replies, Lauder continued. Did he not say that every layman was a priest and that the pope had no more power than any other man? From the grandstand the clergy greeted these accusations with howls and snorts of derision. In the body of the kirk, meanwhile, Katherine was pleased to notice many nodding heads and mouthings of agreement among the lay people.

"And you deny the existence of purgatory?"

"I have read over the Bible many, many times, and to this day I have never yet found such a term in any place of Scripture," Wishart admitted, before throwing the question back to Lauder. "Can you prove any such place?"

Lauder spluttered and spumed before spinning round to seek guidance, but no-one from the humming and hawing ranks of the highest clergy was prepared to do so.

As for the practices of fasting, not eating flesh on Friday and the use of holy water, Wishart dismissed them as sheer flummery, conjured up by the Roman Church to mystify their flock. Faith, not the routine of rituals, was the way to God.

"You must be in league with Lucifer to teach such lies – or Luther, as the wily archfiend guises himself. This Luther-Lucifer is but a scurrilous servant of Satan, spouting forth skaiths and curses on the one true Church," Lauder blustered, finally losing his temper.

If his teachings were being condemned as the work of the Evil One, then Wishart knew he was doomed. Weighed down by weariness and dejection, his shoulders drooped and he seemed to shrink into himself. He clutched the edge of the pulpit for support awaiting the next onslaught. Just then a voice from behind Katherine yelled out, "The devil cannot speak such words as yonder man speaks."

Murmurs of agreement among the lay-folk, rankled by John Lauder's abrasive manner, began to ripple through the nave and rose to a crescendo. Wishart gave a wan, grateful smile because this surge of sympathy showed that ordinary folk had come not just to gawp at the heretic, but were listening and taking heed of his defence.

And there, near the front, he could see his French cap bobbing up and down. Katherine was here. If he could convert a devout Catholic nun, Beaton's own sister, then all was not lost. From that moment he perked up. Making the most of his last chance on God's earth to preach, Wishart roundly ignored Lauder and directed his replies at the congregation. The exasperated cardinal beckoned to his prosecutor.

"Read out the remaining articles," he rasped, crooking his chubby finger at him. "And, if you cherish your life, make sure he has no chance to reply."

Sentence was to be formally pronounced after a break for dinner. Since Beaton had already passed judgment before the trial began, the tribunal of the cardinal's esteemed colleagues was free to enjoy the lavish dinner in his private chambers. They were licking their fingers and patting their well-filled paunches when the king's herald pushed past the guard.

"Ah, the post-prandial entertainment is here. The court jester has come to amuse our little gathering," Beaton quipped.

Lindsay, however, was in no mood for jests: returning from a diplomatic mission abroad, he'd just found out about the trial. Whatever judgement may have been passed on the accused, he reminded Beaton, the law demanded that Governor Arran supply a criminal judge, not a clerical one, to pronounce sentence.

Mellow with cognac, the cardinal continued to taunt. "Arran! That witless fool's authority is of no consequence. If we were to await a decision from that swithering dolt, Wishart would die a slow, lingering death in the Bottle Dungeon. This way is more merciful and he'll face Divine Judgement ere the day is out."

"You're making a grave mistake. You will only make a martyr out of Wishart. Followers will rush to his cause and instead of stamping out heresy, you'll be dealing the Church a deathblow. Do not uproot the whole tree for the sake of a few rotten branches. Whereas if you set Wishart free …"

Beaton gave him a scathing look. "Have no fear, the rantings of Luther and his loathsome lackeys cannot topple the Holy Roman Church with one thousand five hundred years of tradition and truth behind it. But why should I set free this English spy in the pay of Henry Tudor? If it were not heresy then your saintly Wishart would be on trial for treason."

"Nay!" Lindsay interjected. "You mistake him for Wishart, the Baillie of Dundee, who is indeed a spy and a traitor. Set the preacher free and events will take their natural course."

Beaton sneered. "Their natural course? You mean a reformation in Scotland paid for by English gold? Do you not see how Henry's rough wooing is laying waste to our land? An alliance with the cruel and merciless English king would be the deathblow to Scottish independence. It is far better that we ally with France and Rome."

"Mark my words. The time is ripe for reform but it must be properly directed, without bloodshed ..."

"Properly directed! Hark at the minstrel playwright! Harp and carp, Lindsay! Harp and carp! You are an idealist, Lyon Herald, forever playing the part of John the Common-Weal."

"And you, Cardinal Beaton, are a self-important pragmatist who fears not so much the rise of heresy but the loss of power: any power, however petty. Was it really worth brawling with your sainted colleague there," he pointed to Gavin Dunbar, "over who should head a procession in his own cathedral? Have you mended your crosiers yet?" Lindsay snorted, whipping up gales of laughter from the other bishops.

"I'd be wary, Beaton, in case the archbishop calls down a curse upon you. But here's a prophecy." Lindsay's tone became serious. "Mind what was said about Patrick Hamilton? That the reek of his burning would only fuel the fires of reformation, not put them out. If you burn Wishart I can predict, without a word of a lie, that your blood will be splattered next, Davie Beaton," he warned. "Now will not be too soon to start writing your obituary."

VI

Burnt Offering

For thou desirest not sacrifice;
else would I give it:
Thou delightest not in burnt offering.
Psalms LI:16

St. Andrews, 1 March 1546

The crowd was so dense that she couldn't get near the pyre, nor could she see above the jiggling heads and shoulders.

"Let me through. For pity's sake, let me through. I am his sister."

Charily at first, the onlookers stepped aside and jostled her up to the front. When he was brought out, his hands tied behind his back and an iron chain fastened round his waist, Katherine felt her knees go weak. Would she be able to thole it alone? Widow Ker was heartily sorry, but she had no stomach for the burning. If only Agnes were here. Her heart clenched as she recalled how she'd left her dear friend without saying a word. No explanation, no word of farewell for *Agnus Dei*.

A noose was hanging loosely round his neck. Perhaps they would hang him instead. That way, at least, his agony would be over sooner. Friar Winram was by his side, ready to hear his confession if he changed his mind at the last minute. Wishart had already dismissed the two friars sent by Beaton but had asked for Winram. Not to shrive his soul but to thank him for his sermon and to consider his own future.

"Do not fear the truth, friar. There is no middle way. One day you'll have to decide. And may the Holy Spirit come down on you." Before kneeling to pray, he shuffled forward to address the crowd, his eyes swiftly scanning the jumble of spectators. "Because I am about to suffer this fire for Christ's sake, do not turn against the true religion. You must keep on learning the Word of God which I have taught you."

Katherine took off the French cap and waved it frantically in the air to catch his attention. He glanced towards her and as he inclined his head, a smile flitted over his lips, for those standing next to her were staring in surprise at her shorn head.

"Behold my face," he declared, keeping his eyes fixed on her. "You shall not see me change my colour. I fear not this grim fire. Weep not for me."

Biting into her bottom lip to quell the tears, she drew blood, but Wishart remained calm, even forgiving the hooded executioners. As he kissed them on the cheek, one of them went down on his knees: his declaration, that he didn't will the death of so holy a man, provoked a chorus of *Amen* from the crowd. Nevertheless, he joined his colleague in stuffing bags of gunpowder into the pockets of the buckram coat, tying more under the condemned mans" armpits and then buckling the coat with straps.

Though every inch of her being yearned to flee from his suffering, Katherine braced herself to stand firm. When they chained him to the stake, she willed him to look her way and see that she, too, would not flinch. She would share his suffering: no matter what. When Wishart twisted his head, she followed his glance to the window where her brother, the cardinal, and his bishops were viewing their victim's final agony.

The treacherous High Priests, their plump behinds seated on cushions embroidered by nuns at the abbey – herself being one of them – were callously laughing and joking as if at a fool's play and not a tragedy. She wanted to spit. Wishart's lips were now moving in prayer, she presumed, but the rumour flashing through the crowd claimed that he'd uttered a prophecy.

"Whereas I expect to sup with my Saviour before the night is spent, he who feeds his eyes on my torments in a few days shall be hanged at the same window."

To the piercing blast of trumpets, the executioners circled the giant stook of the pyre, setting it alight at various points. A gasp ran through the crowd as the captain of St. Andrews Castle suddenly leapt up on to the scaffold. Had there been a last minute reprieve? Was he going to wrench the martyr from the stake and carry him off? But no, the captain had only braved the blaze to wish him good courage.

At first, as the flames from the kindling lapped gently at his feet, it looked as if Wishart were paddling in the shallows of a fiery sea, but then they crackled into life and spiralled upwards into a blazing tower, hungrily devouring his hose, peeling the blistering skin from his legs and sizzling through to the bone. Blood oozed from the corners of his mouth as he sank his teeth through his tongue to silence his scream of agony.

As the stench of his roasting flesh punched the pit of her stomach, Katherine gulped hard to keep from retching. Those sadists, anxious not to miss a moment of the martyr's torment, wafted away the scorching air and smoke, only backing off, choking and coughing, when the pungent reek hit their throats. With loud bangs, the bags of gunpowder began to explode, spurting blood and spewing flesh, bones and offal into the crowd. Those blood-soaked slivers splattering her cap and shawl could have burst from his liver, spleen or even – may God have mercy – his heart. His Wise Heart.

When a halo of flames encircled his blackened head, instinctively she recoiled in horror, but then steeled herself. However harrowing it was to witness the intense heat melting his skin through to the skull, transforming his features into the ghoulish grin of a neep lantern, she *would* behold his face. Only when a last blast blew his head from his shoulders, leaving it to dangle by a sinew, did her eyes close as she slumped to the ground.

VII

Murder Most Foul

As for the Cardinal, I grant
He was a man we weel could want,
and we'll forget him soon.
And yet I think that, sooth to say,
Although the loon be well away,
The deed was foully done.
The Tragedy of the Cardinal
Sir David Lindsay, 16th Century

St.Andrews, 29 May 1546

She sat in the gloom of the hovel watching the old woman simmer a concoction on the swey hanging over the fire. Acrid smoke stung her eyes and offensive smells assaulted her nose. A cluster of kittens scampered about the floor watched over by their mother, a tawny she-cat with luminous green eyes. The stouthearted Marion was, nevertheless, scared of cats and started in terror when a sooty black cat leapt onto her lap, digging its sharp claws into her flesh, fixing her with its evil eyes. An ominous sign. A shudder ran through her but she was more afraid to shoo the crone's vile creature away.

She was beginning to regret coming but the potions prescribed by Sister Agnes had run out. The wise wife had listened, head cocked to one side, eyeing her up like one of her chookies, as she read out the ingredients of the French sister's receipt.

"That's as may be, but I'll use my own home-brewed remedies, not any fancy foreign ones," the auld wife declared, and began dropping powders and dried leaves into the cauldron.

She wished the old witch would hurry. She'd left Davie propped up in bed with the promise that she wouldn't be long. He'd had another restless night, kept awake not only by stomach-wrenching pains from his bilious liver but also the nagging fear of assassination. Ever since Wishart's execution, the mood of resentment against the cardinal had intensified and plots against his life were rife. He'd stubbornly refused her suggestion of seeking refuge at their newly built castle at Melgund near Forfar. It would be safer to remain in St.Andrews Castle, which was being fortified against attack.

Clad from head to toe in black so as to move unnoticed among the clerical populace, Marion had slunk out through the postern gate at daybreak. Herring gulls swooped in and out of the skeleton of wooden scaffolding erected around the castle for the army of workmen. She passed the drawbridge where the porter, old Ambrose

Stirling was remonstrating with a group of masons about the work not being carried out fast enough for the cardinal. The labourers hung about idly chattering and loitering but straightened up when a Franciscan friar approached them.

Impatient to leave the roach-ridden hovel, Marion paid the crone the extortionate price she asked for, without any haggling, much to the old hag's surprise. Clutching the precious flask and treading cautiously so as not to slip on the cobbles, she made her way back to the castle. The din of the skirling gulls had been replaced with that of a yammering crowd gathered at the edge of the castle moat. Workmen were fleeing in panic over the drawbridge and yelling that a monstrous deed had taken place.

She hurried to join a small group of townsfolk gathering about the provost who, with his hands cupped round his mouth, shouted up at the castle.

"What have you done with my lord cardinal? Where is he? Have you slain him? We shall ne'er depart until we see him."

Alarmed by the hubbub nearer the east end of the castle, Marion darted over to a small group huddled tightly in a circle. She edged her way through, her heart battering against her ribs. A body had been tossed over the walls and was lying splayed on the strand. The back of the skull had been crushed, splattering the brains like skirlie across the sand. Marion struggled to hold back the bile that was gathering in her throat as they turned the body over. The face, smashed to smithereens, was unrecognisable.

"Nay, it's not the cardinal. It's the porter. Poor old Ambrose Stirling. Never did anybody any harm."

Hearing shouts and screams from the east blockhouse, she ran back. They were lowering something slowly down the wall of the tower. Her hand shot to her mouth. It can't be. They wouldn't. She prayed that her eyes were deceiving her. With one arm and one leg tied to a makeshift rope of the best linen sheets the naked, bloodied corpse was bumped and battered against the stone wall until it dangled in mid air. Between his legs a gaping wound was encrusted with dark purple blood where his genitals had been hacked off before being stuffed crudely between his lips.

She shoved her fist into her mouth to stifle the scream of despair that threatened to alert everyone around her. If they realised who she was, she'd be hoisted up there beside him. One of the assassins had tottered unsteadily along the ramparts and was now untying his breeches. As it dawned on the crowd what he was about to do, they began to jeer.

"Pishing is too good for the likes of him."

"Aye! Keech on him from a great height."

Waving his free hand in the air in a triumphant gesture to the cheers of some of the spectators, the desecrator of the murdered cardinal toppled backwards as he was hauled off the rampart.

"First they desecrate now they defecate. *Sic transit gloriae mundi.*"

As Marion turned round, the Franciscan friar pulled his cowl over his head and scurried away. It crossed her mind that, in this city sated with ecclesiastics, he had been the only cleric she'd seen that morning. She left the crowd yelling insults at her husband's mutilated body and slipped round to the postern gate, unsure what to do. It would be foolish to try and go in. What could she do? Her husband's murderers might turn on her, leaving eight children orphaned. Nay, she had been faithful unto death. No-one could condemn her for leaving his side now.

She was about to turn away when a young lad sidled through the gate. A velvet bonnet with a bedraggled feather bobbing at a jaunty angle was pulled down over his eyes and under his arm he was carrying a box. He hesitated for a moment, his frightened eyes darting hither and yon.

"Charlie!" She signalled to him. "Over here."

As Beaton's chamber-child, Charlie Baxter's chores included emptying the cardinal's chamber pot, tending to the fire, keeping his bed warm in winter and carrying out other menial tasks. After she'd left that morning, the lad had been about to set the fire to heat water for the cardinal's ablutions when he heard a clamour outside.

"What was that?" Startled from his doze, Beaton stumbled to the window.

"The castle has been taken," someone shouted.

Tripping over his nightclothes, Beaton hurried to the postern gate. On his orders, this exit was always kept open, not only for the free wayleave of his mistress Marion but in case he ever needed to escape. The gate, however, had been secured and a guard stationed.

Fleeing back to his chamber, he ordered the terrified Charlie to pile up kists and anything he could find against the door. Meanwhile, he hastened to conceal a casket of gold coins in the coal box and laid coals on top. When they began to ram the door Beaton took up his two-handed sword and bellowed:

"Will you spare my life?"

"It may be that we will."

"Nay," the cardinal replied. "Swear to me by God's wounds and I will open unto you."

This time there was no reply, only the sounds of mutterings and scuffling from behind the heavy oaken door. Charlie sniffed the air. Was that burning he could smell? He keeked through the keyhole: a chamber pot filled with burning coals had been placed against the door.

"Fire!" the terrified lad screamed. "Fire! They're going to burn us out!"

What may be an appropriate end for the Bloody Cardinal was not Charlie's choice of exit from this world. He scrambled over the kists and boxes, knocking them over in his haste to open the door. Beaton braced himself to confront his enemies face-to-face but cramping pains in his belly forced him to sit down. When two men rushed in, daggers drawn, he clutched his stomach and cried out,

"I am a priest! I am a priest! You will not slay me!"

"For that very reason we shall!" they laughed, slashing their daggers through his flimsy nightshirt.

"Haud your hand!" The cold-blooded murder of the porter had sickened and disgusted William Kirkcaldy of Grange who wanted no more slaughter.

"Aye, he's right," James Melville agreed. "The work and judgement of God ought to be done with greater gravity." Saying so, he forced Beaton to his knees and pointed his sword at him. "Repent of your wicked life! And of shedding the innocent blood of George Wishart that demands vengeance afore God!"

Without giving Beaton time to repent, the murderer ran his sword through his body once, twice, thrice, splattering the walls red with martyr's blood.

"Fye, fye! All is gone!" The cardinal spluttered his last words before slumping forward in the chair.

While the rest of the conspirators tumbled over each other into the room, squabbling about what to do next, Charlie swiftly retrieved the casket of gold. From behind one of the kists, his eye caught sight of a bonnie velvet bonnet with a fine feather. Picking it up, he crept out of the chamber.

"Good lad, Charlie." While the lad adjusted the bonnet on his head, Lady Marion took the casket from him and tucked it under her cloak. "This will help us on our way to Melgund Castle. No good can be done here."

VIII

Armistice

Wherefore I counsel everyilk christened king
With in his realm mak reformation
And suffer no more rebels for to ring
Above Christ's true congregation.
The Tragedy of the Cardinal
Sir David Lindsay, 16th Century

St.Andrews, 16 December 1546

A light snow was beginning to fall and the December light was already fading as Lindsay crossed the drawbridge to St.Andrews Castle for the second time that day. Once again a trumpet heralded the arrival of the Lord Lyon King of Arms, but this time the Castilians, as they called themselves, agreed to speak with the messenger. Passing through the courtyard, he had to make his way through piles of rubble from buildings bombarded by the governor's artillery.

As usual, Arran had been at a loss what to do when his eleven-year-old son, kidnapped by Beaton to secure his father's loyalty, was being held for ransom by the Castilians. James was dear to him. He had high hopes of marrying him to the young Queen of Scots. He'd swithered between starving them out – but he feared for his son's life – and blowing them out, but he hadn't enough guns. One of his dafter ideas had been to hew a passage through the solid rock to rescue him. In the end he'd ordered a cannon to be discharged sporadically to remind them of his presence.

The courtyard was littered with snow-covered humps. Could they not at least shovel up their dead and store them away until the frozen ground thawed? At his approaching footsteps, some of the corpses roused from their slumber and tried to struggle to their feet: so, not dead then, but dead drunk. The ragged urchins rummaging among the rubble and poking around the debris and detritus were skinny, undernourished and sickly looking. Lindsay sniffed deeply at the posy of dried cinquefoil Elisabeth had thrust into his hand. It would help to ward off infection from the deadly sickness raging through the garrison. He was hoping, too, that the freezing temperature would kill off the plague.

"Is the cold skrinking your cockles? I can warm them up for you." The thin, pinched face of the woman accosting him was covered in suppurating pustules. "Whatever it pleases you to give, kind sir, I'll take."

"But I won't take what you'll give me," he muttered, waving her away.

"Anything," she pleaded, trying to link her arm in his, unwilling to let him go for, as a visitor coming from the outside, this well-fed, well-dressed gentleman must have something. Lindsay brushed her off, striding out at a pace too fast for her half-starved body to keep up with him.

It was a difficult mission. The deadlock had to be broken. On the one hand, Marie de Guise was anxious to send for French help but Arran was unwilling. Never decisive at the best of times, twa-fangelt Arran swithered and dithered, relying on others to make his decisions for him. Then Sir David Lindsay of the Mount would be the man to negotiate with the Castilians, advised the gentry of Fife, the very gentlemen behind the murder of Beaton. Lindsay was not only an experienced diplomat but known to be sympathetic to their cause. Despite this, the Castilians had been in no hurry to grant him admission to the castle.

"We're expecting Henry of England to send aid at any moment," William Kirkcaldy explained.

"You may have a long wait. The English king is bloated and cunt-bitten from the pox and is in no state to help," Lindsay informed them, not daring to divulge Henry's exasperated comment that what always swayed the skittish Scots was the sum of gold on offer. In that case, they would only surrender on certain conditions, the first of which surprised him.

"You're demanding a papal dispensation for the murderers of Beaton? Why?" Lindsay was bemused.

John Leslie dropped his eyes. "We fear for our immortal souls," he said. "For if we die in a state of mortal sin, we will go straight to hell."

Lindsay snorted in disbelief. "But you are followers of the reformed faith, are you not? Evangelicals such as you do not recognise the authority of the pope and answer only to Almighty God Himself. Surely only He has the power to pardon you?"

Leslie shifted uncomfortably. Like most uneducated laymen whose beliefs were based on a mixture of superstition and hearsay, he barely understood Roman Catholic dogma far less the arguments of the new, reformed faith.

"We also demand a pardon from the governor. And his assurance that we will be allowed to go free," Kirkcaldy stated.

"And unpunished," Leslie added.

Lindsay could see the strain of the long siege in their gaunt, haggard faces and the desperation in their eyes. It was clear that they were floundering in a mire of their own making and were looking to him to pull them out. They should be willing to barter.

"The pope will not grant absolution while the body of the cardinal lies unburied," he claimed.

If it were up to him, Beaton's mutilated corpse, which had lain in a lead-lined vat of salted water at the bottom of the infamous Bottle Dungeon in the Sea Tower, could languish there, unblessed and unburied, until Judgement Day, but he would keep his promise to Elisabeth.

Distraught that, until a requiem Mass had been said, there could be no eternal rest for the soul of her beloved Davie, Lady Marion had beseeched Queen Marie to intercede and arrange for a Christian burial. Only then could she, too, rest in peace. The queen, too, was bereft. She'd not only lost her husband to an early death but now her trusted counsellor had been savagely slaughtered. Since she had no influence over the Castilians, she'd sought advice from Elisabeth who, in turn, had appealed to Lindsay.

"Whatever else he may have done in his life, he was a good father to his bairns," Elisabeth stated, "and Lady Marion was eternally grateful that he'd given her a life as mistress of her own household when no-one else would have her. And he was a faithful spouse, Aye, it's true," she added in response to his sceptical look, "for ever since their first, fateful meeting, Beaton never looked with lustful eyes at any other woman. Rumours grew wings and lies long legs where Davie Beaton was concerned. How dare they decry him as a butcher of hundreds when he was guilty of only seven executions? Why, your beloved King James had far more blood on his hands. Not least that of an innocent young mother burned as a witch."

That was not one of his most triumphant moments Lindsay had to admit, and regretted not being present to persuade the king to show mercy to Jinty.

"And Marion is prepared to pay in gold if necessary. That's how much she loved *her* Davie," Elisabeth had reproached him. "Though there were times when I would have gladly throttled Beaton myself, I realised it was his deep desire to save our Church from heresy that drove him, but what about you, Davie? Tell me truthfully, did you have a hand in Beaton's murder?"

Lindsay shrugged. "The Bloody Cardinal signed his own death warrant. Every time he signed his name to an execution order."

"That is the answer of a courtier and diplomat. And makar. You may not have struck the deathblow but you've aye been a skilled master of revels, planning and directing the actions of others. I only ask because of something Lady Marion mentioned. That all the clerics seemed to have spirited themselves away that fatal day except for one Franciscan friar. Perhaps Friar Lazarus had resurrected himself?"

Lindsay gave a wry laugh. "All I will say is that thon friar was as much a monk as Beaton was a cardinal."

As he attempted to chew through the beef or horse or whatever flesh that was served at supper that evening, the image of Beaton's unburied body, pickled in salt and piled over with dung, came unbidden to Lindsay. Heavy doses of salt and vinegar failed to disguise either the rank smell or the brackish, bitter taste. He picked at his meat, praying that it hadn't been tainted with miasma from the dungeons or from the plague.

"How long do you intend the corpse of the corrupt cardinal to rot in the cellar?" he asked his dining companions.

"Until the day of doom," John Leslie asserted.

"Until hell freezes over," William Kirkcaldy maintained.

"Ah!" Lindsay muttered, "Then you are braver men than me. For while the cardinal's body lies unburied, you'll never be at peace. His restless spirit will haunt you for ever more."

As he lowered his head to attack his meat, he was pleased to note that the superstitious rebels were blanching and flinching at his words.

"Aye, you may be right," John Rough, the Ayrshire preacher, readily agreed. "For I believe that the foul fiend of hell, Auld Nick himself, may have us in his evil clutches."

Since the siege had begun, more than one hundred and fifty people had entered the castle. Some were dedicated to their cause, but many were hangers-on: beggars, vagrants and the like who had heard that the English were supporting the rebels with money and supplies.

"They have come, not for the glory of God but for gold," he complained. And when Lindsay remarked on the drunken bodies littering the streets, Rough exclaimed, "Drinking is the least of it. It's the debauchery and whoring that is weeding us out. This disease that has befallen us is not the plague, but the venereal pox. Something has to be done," he bellowed, thumping the table with his fist. "If word gets out that St. Andrews has become the Sodom and Gomorrah of our age, our cause will be lost."

His eyes misted over as he appealed to Lindsay. "Our ship is rudderless. Without guidance, this ship of fools will lose its way and sink fast. Sir David, you are the very man to lead us. Join us now and steer them in the right path. You have condemned the corruption of the Roman Catholic Church in your *Satire*. Denounce the depravity here too. They will listen to you."

Lindsay pointed to his hoary head, "I'm gey old for grand gestures. I'm not the one to lead you forward but, if you'll trust my judgment, I ken the very man who can."

IX

A Dolent Death

> And see ye not that bonnie road,
> That winds about the fernie brae?
> That is the road to fair Elfland,
> Where thou and I this night maun gae.
> *The Ballad of Thomas the Rhymer,* Traditional

St. Mary's Abbey, 21 March 1547

The flickering candles at the base of the icon cast an eerie light on the Black Madonna with the infant that had been wrenched from her arms now clumsily bound against her chest with a hempen rope. Elisabeth had drawn up a stool, more comfortable than kneeling at the *prie-dieu*, to pour her heart out to the Virgin. She had never disciplined herself to learn prayers by heart for, if truth be told, she had little faith in their magical power. She had seen little evidence of heaven ever paying heed to their endless chants in Latin.

At times she envied the certainty with which the pious Sister Agnes practised her faith, but then the religious life had not been of her choosing. Besides, if the all-knowing, all-seeing God had already determined everything that would ever happen, where was the use in praying? All her struggles to impose her will, to change the course of her life, had been thwarted; whereas Betsy's simple belief in destiny was proving to be true. What will be will be. What's for you will no go by you.

And Betsy wouldn't thank her for her prayers. She knew her time was up and was resigned to pass over into the twilight world of the spirit. She'd left instructions as detailed as the Roman Catholic last rites for dealing with her death. No priest, no prayers and no pity. Her last wish was to bid farewell to her loved ones but would he come in time?

If she couldn't pray for Betsy, then she would try to pray for John. Implore the Mother of Christ to lead him back to the fold. Divert him from the road to perdition. But the ballad of True Thomas kept trespassing into her *Pater Nosters*.

> And see ye not that braid braid road,
> That lies across that lily leven?
> That is the path of wickedness
> Though some call it the road to heaven.

Pressing her eyelids against her eyeballs, Elisabeth concentrated all her thoughts on John. For a few moments there was nothing but darkness, endless black. Then, as the gloom slowly cleared, a tiny white figure appeared, floating away from her along a tunnel, receding into a distant radiance. As the weird feeling engulfed her, she knew that once he reached that eerie luminescence, he'd be lost forever, never to return.

With all her strength, she urged him to turn round and come back to her, but another, stronger power was drawing him towards the light. In this struggle of wills she felt as if her head would burst, but she couldn't let go: Come back! Come back to me, John! Don't go! A flash of light seemed to explode in her head. Colours flashed in front of her eyes. Suddenly there was no opposition, no resistance. She had lost sight of him. He was gone. All went black.

"Lisbeth! I'm here! Can you hear me? Wake up!"

Dazed and breathing heavily, she struggled to raise her eyelids. As the mist slowly cleared from her eyes, she realised she'd toppled from the stool and was lying on the cold stone floor. Lindsay was kneeling over her, splashing her face with fusty smelling water from the font. His worried face was sepulchral grey as he hugged her close. Drained and wabbit, she leant in gratefully towards him and closed her eyes. Whatever will be, will be, she muttered to herself. The holy water might have revived her but she crinkled her nose when he tried to make her drink some. How many filthy fingers had been dunked in it?

"Have you brought him?"

"Aye, he's here."

"Thank you for that, Davie."

In the corner of the outer chamber, Betsy lay cocooned in her cot. Over the last year or so she'd shrunk to the size of a wizened waif with weakened legs and a humpit back. Her auld bones were crumbling away was her self-diagnosis and she had no cure for that. Dust to dust she'd said, a wry smile flitting over her desiccated lips. Her wrinkled hands were parchment thin and spotted like the paper of ancient books. Since she was no longer able to swallow, Agnes dipped a cloth in a beaker of diluted *aquavitae* to moisten her lips. Incense burned in holders to keep away the smell of death.

"She'll have no priest," Sister Agnes face's was contorted with concern. "Nor the last rites." Wringing her hands, she bowed her head to whisper a guilty confession. Worried that, if Betsy were to depart this world unshriven, in a state of original sin, she had taken the liberty of baptising her with holy water. "But, John, perhaps you could ... Even a short prayer?"

Knox gave a wan smile. No longer believing either in the existence of purgatory, where sinners languished till Judgement Day unless released by prayer and indulgences, or limbo, for unbaptised bairns and heathens, the fate of Betsy's soul also troubled him. If anyone deserved God's grace, it was Betsy who should be destined for eternal salvation, no matter what – baptised or unbaptised.

"I'll stay with her now. You have some rest."

But Agnes still hung about, agitated. "Have you any word from Sister Katherine?" she asked timidly. "I ... we ... we've heard nothing."

Neither had he. And it shamed him that she, a woman, had shown far more courage then he had. She'd stayed with Wishart until grim death whereas he had slunk away like a wounded, fear-stricken bear, spending the long, lonely dark winter hiding in safe houses all over the Lothians. His time in the wilderness was not a worthy episode.

"Is it true?" Sister Agnes's throat tightened as she dared to ask. "Is it true that she has fled for safety to Ayrshire ..." she paused before adding, "with Widow Ker?" A painful notion, judging by the frown on her flushed face and the tears welling in her eyes. "Tell me, John, please. Will she ever come back?"

Knox couldn't console her. He didn't know. Sister Agnes crossed herself and left.

As he bent towards the cot, Betsy's eyelids flickered.

"Is that you Meg?" she muttered.

He followed her gaze towards the Orkney chair by the fireside. Meg's chair, that Betsy had brought from Hailes, was empty but were those eyes, clouded to the present world, already seeing beyond to the next?

"No, it's me. John."

With no belief in the Romish last rites, what succour could he offer his beloved Betsy in her final hours? But kindly, warm and comforting Betsy, who had loved him with a mother's unconditional love, now sought to soothe him. He could only think to stroke her forehead.

"Johnnie," she murmured. "My wee laddie."

Her clawlike hand grabbed his finger and held on to it. Her puckered lips twitched restlessly as if recounting a long tale.

"I'm here, Betsy." His voice was husky as he choked back tears.

"Don't greet any tears for me, son. It's my time."

Betsy Learmont, whose stories of the past were so scrambled with ballads, tales and superstitions that the truth was obscured, was facing the final reality. Did she hold the secret? Could she see beyond the veil?

"Betsy," he whispered, anxious for some guidance, "what am I to do? What is my fate to be?"

Knox feared the future. Wishart had bade him lay down his two-handed sword and take up the torch, for there must be one who would continue the flame of enlightenment and reform. If you come with me it shall be extinguished, he'd said, but what should he do? Stay in Scotland and risk being burnt at the stake? Flee to Germany where sympathisers would shelter him until it was safe to return? Would that be seen as the coward's way out?

"Words no swords." Betsy squeezed his finger tightly and began to mutter the words of the Fairy Queen:

"O see ye not yon narrow road,

So thick beset with thorns and briars?

That is the path of righteousness,

Though after it but few enquires."

Betsy broke off and then said, "Tell it to me, Johnnie. True Thomas, tell it to me, laddie."

Hesitantly at first, Knox began whispering the lines of the legend, with Betsy filling in when he stumbled or forgot.

"My tongue is mine ain," true Thomas said:

"A goodly gift ye would gie to me!"

In the chapel, Lindsay helped Elisabeth to her feet.

"It's a blessing that Wishart is dead, for now we can pick up where we left off." She gave her head a good shake, adjusted her wimple and pushed back the strands of hair that had escaped.

"A blessing?" Lindsay blurted. "How many people did Wishart burn at the stake?" He then tried to calm his voice. "Surely it's an even greater blessing that Beaton is dead."

She gave Lindsay a long, hard look. "Did he have a dolent death?" she taunted, her words carefully chosen to let him know that she'd read his poem. *The Tragedy of the Cardinal* expressed no sympathy for Beaton's assassination and, not only did it absolve the murderers, but judged them to be divinely inspired.

Recognising words he'd written, a shadow of a smile passed over Lindsay's face, lined with worry and age. "And now that his reign of terror is over, it is crucial for us to carry on making reforms within the Church."

"For you, perhaps, but not John." Elisabeth pursed her lips. "I forbid you to take him back with you. You're to blame for his abandoning the priesthood. Ever since yon *Satire* of yours, he's fancied himself as Divine Correction, doughty Diligence or some such other daft conceit. Well, it's high time he dropped the play-acting." Now that the colour had flooded back into her cheeks and her eyes shone, she was ready to wrestle for Knox's immortal soul if necessary. "He needs time to clear his dirling head of these dangerous ideas. Heresy is hearsay! He's become so fey, as if he's been blasted by a fairy wind. He can stay here until all this ... mayhem blows over."

Lindsay snorted. "Play-acting! Mayhem! Is that how you see the most important reformation taking place in the Church in all its centuries of history! You want to pull John back towards the dying Church and I'm pushing him towards ideas which will breathe new life into its sluggish soul."

"Is that how *you* see it?" Elisabeth sneered. "Well, I won't let you do it, Davie," she declared, for only she could save Knox from this pernicious path that would lead to burning at the stake or the gallows. "John shall go to France. To Cardinal de Guise. Under his guidance, John will be made to see sense. He shall become a bishop and then – who kens? – even a cardinal one day, and then John will have *real* power to make those changes you're so keen on." She turned to go but he grabbed her arm.

"Listen to me Lisbeth. John is a man of what, thirty years? Old enough and clever enough to make up his own mind, and here we are squabbling over him as if he were a three-year-old bairn."

His words stopped her dead. Still feeling giddy from her recent dwam, she began to sway. As Lindsay caught hold of her, she gazed at him, desperation in her eyes.

"But, Davie you don't understand. To me that's what he is. My bairn. John is not just my godson." Her voice became ragged as she forced out the words. "He's … my … son."

The light of life was fading fast from Betsy's befuddled eyes but, seeing her lips move, he leant in closer to hear her.

"Lungs fit for a preacher," she muttered mysteriously.

Uncertain how to reply, Knox tried to remember more lines from the ballad:

> "Betide me weal, betide me woe,
> That weird shall never daunton me."

His stammering recitation seemed to please her, for a faint smile flitted over her lips before Betsy closed her eyelids for the last time. With tears clouding his eyes, Knox kissed her gently on her cooling forehead. He watched her chest rise and fall, lower and lower each time, as her breathing become more and more shallow. Whenever there was a long pause, he considered calling for Agnes, but Betsy clung on with surprising strength to his finger. The candle spluttered and guttered. Sitting in the gloaming, he could hear voices coming from the prioress's chamber.

Elisabeth and Lindsay had left the chapel by the secret passageway to her chamber. As she leant against the stone mullion to cool her flushed cheek, he poured her a good measure of cognac.

"So," Lindsay began, "Sister Maryoth's story was true? That you were with child?"

"Aye, I had a bairn, Davie," she began warily, her shoulders curved, her arms tightly crossed over her chest as she strove to keep the polished nut of grief intact in its neatly sewn pocket. "A wee laddie. A son." Unspoken for all this time, these words, soaked in tears came spilling out, burning her cheeks. Lindsay hesitated, yearning but not daring to place his hands on her shoulders. "But I thought you said you'd lost him."

St.Mary's Abbey, 1528

Betsy kept her head bowed as she sat twiddling her thumbs nervously in the lap of her apron. There was aye a shoogly stone at everybody's door and this one might stop Elisabeth in her tracks.

"What I'm about to tell you might change your mind or it might no."

She took a deep breath which whistled in her throat.

"I've borne this secret like a skelf in my side for many a year, thinking whether I should tell you, or take it with me to the grave."

But now if Lisbeth was leaving and she might never see her again, it was time to tell her the truth. Elisabeth's memory of the birth was hazy: she'd made sure of that. As soon as her waters had broken, Betsy had given her a potion that dulled the pain and made her drowsy. Not even the ferocious yell her laddie gave as he tumbled into the world roused her from her drugged doze.

"Lungs fit for a preacher," Betsy had mumbled cheerlessly. She had been sorely aggrieved at being made to promise Prior Hepburn that she would deal with the bairn as soon as it was born. Splash it with caller water to baptise it, he'd said and then do the needful. The easiest and quickest way to do away with an unwanted or sickly wean was to press on the bone at the back of its neck and pull the head back swiftly. But she had no heart to throttle this braw wee fighter and send him prematurely to kingdom come. God's heavenly choir would have to wait for its trumpeter.

"So I gave him to Maggie Knox to suckle. The widow was rich in milk but poor in silver and so was glad enough to take in him."

"How can you be sure John isn't her own bairn?"

"Oh, I'm sure. The poor wee mite you breathed life into was a changeling. I should have snapped its head off there and then or just let him die for want of breath but for your pleading and the promise you made to his mother. Pity that thon scarth had ever seen the light of day."

"Scarth?" Elisabeth queried.

"That's what we cry those creatures that are neither one thing nor the other, neither lad nor lass. Shrivelled by the fairy blast, afore he even took his first breath so your blast of air couldn't save him. He failed to thrive and so it was a mercy when he slipped away at last."

All the while Elisabeth could hardly believe what Betsy was saying: it sounded as fanciful as one of her tales. Wheezing with the effort of the telling, Betsy wiped her brow and took another breath. "Aye, she kept your son and brought him up as her own until she passed away, poor lass. She never got o'er her man's death."

Elisabeth leapt to her feet, too quickly, for the sudden rush of blood to her head made her feel giddy. Tapsalteerie! Whigmaleerie!

"Betsy! What are you saying?"

"What do you think? John is your own son. With his mother's thrawn head and his father's glib tongue. Aye, and Hepburn lungs," she said nodding her head. "Fit for a preacher."

While confessing all this, Elisabeth had stood with her back to Lindsay, sipping her brandy.

"So, then, it was true that Harry Cockburn," he broke off, "that he ravished you?"

She drained the goblet of cognac before answering.

"That's what I let them think at the time, naïve creature that I was," she began, a glimmer of a sarcastic smile on her lips, "in order to save *your* skin that my uncle, all riled up, was ready to flay. And to wipe that smug smirk off Maryoth's scheming face. Nay, you may cast me as being as wanton or as sensual as one of your dames, but I'm sorry to disappoint you. The only man I've ever lain with, the only man I've ever had carnal dalliance with, is you, Davie Lindsay."

"What?" he pressed his fingers against his temples to ease the crushing thought. "So what are you telling me…?"

"That John is my son." Her voice began to waver. "Your son. Our son."

"And you never told me, Lisbeth? Why?"

She sucked in her breath.

"I was going to tell you. After I learnt about it from Betsy, when we were planning to elope. Again. At the time I thought we'd take John with us so that we three would be together. Our wee family. An indivisible trinity," she scoffed. "That was before I learnt about Jessie and before I realised that you'd already made your choice. Since King James would always have first claim on you, I made *my* choice and kept John for myself."

Lindsay nodded. Her accusation was justified.

"And have you told him?"

"Nay, and now I'm thinking that perhaps I should have. But the time never seemed right. After you left, he became so thrawn and bull-horned in his contempt that I feared he might hate me, blame me, if I told him. I didn't want to lose his respect, his love." She gave a little laugh. "I was his Madonna but he didn't know he was my child! And I made him solemnly swear that he wouldn't follow the path of heresy. The one you, his own father, are determined to lead him down. If he's taken from me …" she tailed off, unable to bring herself to admit that her life, her future would have no meaning. "Mind the grief that engulfed you when you lost your beloved monarchs? That's how I feel now. Bereft."

"Lisbeth, I'm sorry," was all he could manage to say. Lost for words, the silver-tongued poet kept shaking his head and apologising. "So sorry. If only I'd known. If only you'd told me. No wonder you can never forgive me."

He moved towards her and, as their eyes locked, he caught a fleeting glimpse of her pent-up pain, a fleck of grief in her ferny green eyes. For a split second it seemed possible that, by holding her close, he could breach her defence wall and share her sorrow. Perhaps even begin again where they always seemed to be leaving off. Now that he was free, of both king and wife, they could spend their remaining years together, with John, their son – their future.

Just as he was about to say all this, Elisabeth blinked and looked away. Throwing back her shoulders and straightening up she confronted him: once more the efficient, capable prioress.

"Well, what's done is done, Davie Lindsay. No use picking over old scabs, as Betsy would say." Feigning a cheery smile, she licked the salt tears collecting at the corners of her mouth and drained the cognac.

"But what is to be done, Lisbeth?" Lindsay was running his fingers through his hair, still struggling to come to terms with this startling revelation.

"All I ask, Davie, is that you don't take John away from me."

She stood facing him, arms crossed, waiting for him to give his consent. The tense pall of silence was becoming unbearable until the heavy curtain between the two chambers was drawn back. Knox seemed hardly aware of their presence as he moved between them like a wraith towards the window.

"Betsy asked me to open all the doors and windows," he said bleakly, tears staining his cheeks. "To let her spirit gang free."

X

Gethsemane

O my Father, if it be possible,
let this cup pass from me.
Matthew XXVI:39

St. Andrews Parish Church, Ascension Sunday 1547

Shameless snores reverberated throughout the nave from those in the congregation who had nodded off. Knox didn't blame them. He, too, was finding it difficult to stay awake as the preacher rambled on, dropping his listeners off along the way. At his side, his three lads yawned and fidgeted on their stools, unable to follow John Rough's lengthy, convoluted argument. Rough by name and rough by learning as he'd be the first to admit, the Ayrshire preacher was a man of the heart not of the head. He knew only too well that his unpolished sermons failed to command the crowd's attention and had pleaded with Knox to preach, but he had always refused. Besides, his principal concern was the education of his pupils, the only reason he'd agreed to come to the besieged castle of St. Andrews.

Now as his attention wandered away from the sermon, he wondered if it had been the right thing to do. Warned after Beaton's murder that the new Archbishop Hamilton was planning to arrest him, Knox had considered fleeing to Germany, but Hugh Douglas and John Cockburn were loath to lose their sons" tutor.

"Why not join the Castilians in St. Andrews? And take your lads with you?" Lindsay had suggested. "Not only will you be safer there, but your presence will help to quell the anarchy that is threatening to overwhelm their cause until the English army – expected any day – arrives. That way you can continue to teach your bairns."

Late on Maundy Thursday evening, they had huddled in a cove near Aberlady, waiting for the boat that was to ferry them across to Fife under cover of darkness. When a rough fishing coble emerged from the mist, they took off their shoes and waded through the shallows towards it.

"Welcome aboard, Johnnie." The burly skipper slapped him on the back and shook his arm firmly.

Knox hadn't seen his brother for many years and it took him a few seconds to recognise the full-bearded, weather-beaten sailor.

"And do you mind this braw laddie?" He hauled over the waif Knox had rescued with his sister, Isabelle. "Jamie's got a sturdy pair of sea shanks," he said, smacking him on the back of the legs before sending him off.

"I'm only a humble fisherman, Johnnie, but I hear you're to become a fisher of

313

men," William went on. "So never fear. Now you're one of our select band, we'll aye be behind you."

Towards midnight William lowered the sail. "It's bad luck to sail on Good Friday," he told him, "but seeing we've sworn to get you there somehow… "

As he and his bosun took to the oars, he signalled for Knox and his lads to take up the spare ones. "The more the merrier and the swifter the sooner," he grinned.

Early on Good Friday morning, they landed near Earlsferry where a cart was waiting to transport them overland. Holding out a blistered hand to his brother, Knox said, "I pray I never have to pull an oar again. May God be with you, brother."

William gave a deep, throaty laugh and, hugging Knox in a manly embrace, bade him God speed.

Very early on Easter Sunday morning, the builder's cart that carried Knox and his bairns into the castle was then used to smuggle out the salt-sodden corpse of Beaton. A fitting end for the proud Romish potentate, steeped in the puddle of papistry, Knox had sneered.

But now he was beginning to regret having brought his lads to this city of sin where sloth, drunkenness and fornication were rife. This Sodom and Gomorrah was no place for young men. To keep his lads away from temptations of the flesh, he'd established a rigorous regime in the parish church that served as his schoolhouse and had invited anyone wishing to learn to come along to his lessons.

"You are clearly called by God." Henry Balnaves was impressed, not only by Knox's expositions of the Scripture and Calvin's Catechism, but his teaching of Latin and Greek authors. This experienced civil servant, a procurator in the consistorial courts, had plans to establish a religious settlement of the type being set up in England. Knox would be a valuable recruit.

Well aware of his inadequacies, John Rough tried to persuade Knox to take to the pulpit. "You have a voice for preaching, not me," he said, "and a gift for putting in plain words the message of the Gospels."

Knox could not agree. It was one thing to teach Lutheran doctrines to the few, but another to take on the more responsible rôle of preacher to the many. It would lead, at the very least, to persecution and exile and, at worst, to an agonising death like Wishart's. Nor did he wish to appear presumptuous. But then, he fretted, was he being deliberately deaf to his call? And how would God communicate his will? With a hallowed whisper in his lug?

The sudden change of pitch in Rough's tone from a dull drone to a thunderous bellow startled Knox and all those around him. Nodding heads shook themselves awake and looked up in astonishment at Rough who seemed to be raising a lather about the power of the congregation to elect ministers of the church.

"Brother, be not offended!" he bawled. "In the name of God, and of his Son, Jesus Christ, and in the name of these present, I charge you not to refuse this holy vocation."

His lads were squirming on their stools, stifling sniggers as Knox turned to see where the pointing finger led.

"Hearken to the very last words of the Blessed Christ on his Ascension: Go out into the world and preach the gospel to the whole of creation: he who believes and is baptised will be saved; he who refuses belief will be condemned ..."

Aware that these words were being directed at him, a spine-chilling wave of fear flooded through him. Cold sweat soused his forehead, his palms became clammy and the blood roared in his ears. He blinked away unwelcome tears, dangerously welling in his eyes and, opening his mouth to answer, found he could not speak. Despite swallowing hard and moistening his lips, his voice sounded strangely muffled as he addressed the congregation.

"Truly, is this your charge to me? And do you approve this vocation?"

"Aye, and we approve it," they answered with one voice.

His eyes darkened as the pillars of the nave closed in on him. Rough's gruff voice echoed from a deep chasm. He could feel fiery flames lapping his ankles and licking his legs. Rising to his feet, he struggled to steady himself and then, lest his shaking legs crumple beneath him, he hurtled down the aisle, past David Lindsay and Henry Balnaves, their mouths agape.

For several days he endured his personal agony locked in his room but, as he did with Christ in the Garden of Gethsemane, God remained silent. Knox heard no reassuring call, no response to his prayers. Answer came there none. Only the voice of his own conscience tormented him, taunting him for being a coward, a feardie-gowk. He, who had been so proud to bear the two-handed sword, threatening to smite anyone who dared to harm his master, had then dropped it at the first sign of trouble. In the footsteps of the apostle Peter, after his brave show of cutting off the soldier's ear, he'd also gone on to deny his Lord thrice.

Petrified by a deep sense of foreboding – or was it cowardice? – he had watched the swirling January fog swallow up the tall, stooping figure of his master. The spot on his cheek where Wishart had kissed him farewell, burned with shame, an eternal stigma that would never wash away. Then he'd abandoned him at his trial and crucifixion.

And now the third and final betrayal: refusing to take up the torch for his master. In this he was even more blameworthy than Bothwell, labelled Judas Iscariot by many for delivering up Wishart to Beaton. But, like Judas, weak-willed Bothwell could be forgiven for he had only done what he had to do, whereas Knox had been weighed in the balance and found wanting. He wasn't brave enough to die for his faith: *Timor mortis conturbat me.*

Outside his door, David Lindsay had set up camp to wait.

"John," he called through the keyhole. "Do you mind when we first met? The long hours we spent discussing how to reform the Church? You said that preaching was vital to inform the lay-folk. For few can read but all might hear, isn't that what you said?" When there was no reply he went on. "I jalouse you're praying for guidance, for a sign. But think on this. Does God not make use of unlikely messengers?"

Knox listened in silence, willing him to go away. *Lord I am not worthy. O Father, take this chalice from me.*

"The time has come, John. The folk are waiting. Your life's journey has led you to the steps of the pulpit. You cannot flee your fate."

Ascension Sunday, the time for death and mourning was making way for the season of resurrection, rebirth and renewal of the spirit. What were Betsy's last words? *Lungs fit for a preacher.* Well, then, Father, not *my* will, but thine be done. He unsnecked the door and let Lindsay in.

XI

Nunraw

Choose thy counsel of the most sapient,
Without regard to blood, riches or rent.
The Testament of the Papingo
Sir David Lindsay, 16th Century

St.Mary's Abbey, May 1547

"The English are coming! The English are coming!"

Jean Hamilton's high-pitched shrieks as she ran about the courtyard threatened to spread panic and mayhem. "We will be murdered! Raped! Roughly wooed!" she bawled.

On her next turn of the courtyard, she ran full pelt into Elisabeth who grabbed her firmly by the shoulders. Glaikit Jeanie had inherited the Hamilton slack jaw and thick drooling lips which could make her look fey or daft or sleekit or all three: living proof that years of interbreeding produced unhealthy offspring.

"Now, now Jeanie, no need for false alarms."

"But it thays tho here!" she lisped, waving a pamphlet above her head.

A claim the prioress found hard to believe for, whatever cant the pamphlet was promoting, unlearned and unteachable Jeanie wouldn't be able to read it.

"But we will be! The English are pagan heathens! They want to grab the queen. And she's promised to my brother."

"Mind, your father is in command of the soldiers, Jeanie. He will see that no harm comes to us."

Jeanie thought for a moment her thick lips slowly broadened into a self-important smile.

"Aye, and he will thave uth from the English for the Lord ith on our thide."

"If that is true, Jeanie, then all the more reason to stay calm. Be brave and your father will be proud of you." How she would love to slap her silly face, but she dare not incur Arran's wrath. Instead, she prised the pamphlet from the girl's sweaty grasp, tucked it into her sleeve and went to meet her guest.

The Lord Governor of Scotland was enjoying their hospitality, munching on dainties and slurping one of Sister Agnes's famous liqueurs. He twirled the empty goblet in his fingers, squinting his eyes to examine it.

"My Jeanie is used to eating with the best cutlery from the finest crockery. She has complained that you won't let her use the gilt knives and silver forks I sent her," the Earl of Arran whinged.

"Your gifts, however generous, are much too extravagant for a fourteen-year-old.

317

May I remind you, lord governor, that this is a Cistercian nunnery in Haddington, and not the court of the de Medicis in Florence."

Though spoilt Jeanie Hamilton strutted around the cloister as if it were a Renaissance palace, drawing envious glances from the other girls at her expensive velvet cloak trimmed with gold thread that trailed behind her sweeping the cobbles. Chattering like a nest of fledglings they huddled together and clyped about her kists full of costly clothes and jewellery and other expensive gifts from her indulgent father.

"Nothing is too good for my bonnie Jeanie," Arran replied, his eyes dewy with adoration. "Whatever her heart desires she shall have."

But not out of his own pocket, Elisabeth was tempted to add, for it rankled that he blatantly funded his generous gifts to his bonnie wee Jeanie from the Scots" public purse and English gold.

For twa-fangelt Arran had changed sides more often than his clothes and Queen Marie no longer trusted him. He was to blame, in her view, for not stopping Hertford's troops as they laid waste and set fire to all towns and villages along the coast on their way to Edinburgh. Not satisfied with looting, pillaging and raping the capital, they then destroyed the Abbey of Holyrood and desecrated the tomb of her husband, James V, and her sons. To the shock of the unshockable "cock of the north", the Earl of Huntly, who didn't so much dislike the match with Edward of England as the rough manner of the wooing which had intensified after the death of Henry VIII.

And now, in exchange for money and advancement, Arran was conspiring with Somerset to snatch the young Queen Mary and send her to England to be married to the boy King Edward. If that fell through, he proposed to betroth her to his own son.

"But now down to business. It has come to my attention that, er … as Prioress of St. Mary's Abbey, you are under an ancient engagement either to keep the fortlet of Nunraw from their auld enemies of England and er … all others … er… " Arran peered through shortsighted eyes as he ran a sticky finger down the tattered parchment. "And that you shall not deliver er … said place to any manner of persons than me as lord governor, or cause it to be razed to the ground, so that no habitationer may benefit from er … that time forth er … " he stuttered with a tongue too big for his mouth.

Elisabeth raised her eyes to heaven. And I am to take orders from this flichty birkie of dubious birth, she thought resentfully. A weak, silly man who hid his stupidity under the mangled language of officiousness but who, nevertheless, could be dangerous.

"Pray tell me, my lord governor," she opened her arms in a gesture of supplication, "how would you advise us, weak, defenceless sisters of religion to defend this important fortalice and then – God forbid that the English attack us – to destroy it? That is, of course, if they do not rape and murder us first."

Arran's brow furrowed as he struggled with her question. "You must remove yourselves to Nunraw, Dame Prioress. Forthwith. It is an ancient ruling."

If he was planning to requisition the abbey for his troops, she'd rather he spat it out, for then she could negotiate conditions.

"And, furthermore, I need to ensure the safety of my daughter. I have no wish for another of my bairns to be seized."

She bristled. So that was it. The selfish hypocrite was prepared to gamble with the queen's life but would move heaven and earth – or the nunnery at least – to safeguard that of his spoilt darling. She pressed her hands together, seemingly in a gesture of prayer but in an effort to curb her anger.

"I understand your concern, but surely Jeanie will be safer here, at St.Mary's, where you and the brave Scots army can defend us." She feigned an innocent smile. "Forbye, the fortlet of Nunraw is nothing more than a primitive keep. We will not only be isolated there but without supplies, without water, without defence."

Arran frowned as he considered this. His bonnie Jeanie would not fare well without her comforts. Sensing his uncertainty, Elisabeth's voice brimmed with helpless pleading.

"And will you, as our governor and chief lord, help us, weak sisters in Christ, to arrange our flitting?"

He nodded hesitantly, wary of what he might be agreeing to.

"Let me see, how many horses and carts will we need? The bedridden and the lame will have to be moved and, of course, our sisters, and then all maids and serving lasses and scullions." Elisabeth began counting on her fingers. "And our young maidens with all their baggage. We cannot expect genteel daughters of the gentry, such as Lady Jean, to leave behind their belongings," she added with a sideways glance, "and of course an armed guard to escort us."

As the list grew, Arran's slack jaw sagged even more and his shortsighted eyes boggled. "At such a perilous time, when danger threatens the whole nation, it is most generous of you to spare soldiers and transport. However, the greater sacrifice lies in your willingness to place the safety of our little community above the well-being of your troops."

A baffled frown creased his brow as he struggled to follow her reasoning.

"For, if we are to be moved to Nunraw, our sisters will not be on hand to nurse and tend your wounded soldiers."

XII

The Paraclete

And they were all filled with the Holy Ghost
and began to speak with other tongues.

The Acts II:4

Pentecost Sunday, 1547

Knox hovered at the door of the vestry and fumbled in the pocket of his gown for the phial. Lindsay's gift – the power of speechmaking – could only be activated he believed, by these precious drops.

"As soon as you open your mouth you will know whether or no God has chosen you," Lindsay had declared, "and to fan the flames of divine inspiration, sip this to loosen your tongue."

Appreciating that anxiety rather than fear was crippling Knox, Lindsay had been prescribing laudanum. A few miniscule drops at a time were enough to stave off an attack of the cringes and allay his gnawing doubt that Satan was puffing him up with self-pride. Lindsay had come across this remedy at one of the European courts and prescribed it not only to twitchy players who needed calming down before confronting an audience but to himself. Knox clearly suffered from the same frailty. He was his father's son, after all.

Over the past week, the makar of plays had been helping Knox to write and rehearse his sermon.

"Think on how I taught you to act as Divine Correction in my *Satire*. Now you are no longer John Knox the Catholic priest, but John Knox, preacher and reformer. This is the part you must play from now on. Forget your past."

At Lindsay's cue, Knox took a deep breath and mounted the steps to the pulpit. Wasting no time, he began raging against the false teachings of the Romish Church, denouncing the pope as the Anti-Christ and Whore of Babylon and roundly condemning the doctrines of clerical celibacy, fasting, purgatory and the Mass. His powerful sermon, packed full of imagery from the Book of Daniel and the Epistles of St.Paul, pleased many of the congregation.

"Master George Wishart spoke never so plainly, and yet he was burnt. Even so will this one be," John Leslie feared.

"This is even more successful than we'd hoped, Henry Balnaves remarked. "Your knack as a playwright has paid off, Sir David."

"Aye, well …" While they were both thrilled at his performance, Lindsay was less so. In spite of Elisabeth's wishes he had gone ahead and lured Knox to the pulpit.

On his advice, Knox had taken the Book of Daniel as his inspiration, condemning pilgrimages, pardons and priests as being wicked and unnecessary trappings, but then he'd gone on to argue that good deeds did not guarantee eternal salvation: that Christ's blood purged all our sins and that man was justified by faith alone.

This was going too far. Lindsay had assumed that he could direct Knox's thinking and divert his radical ideas into reforming the Roman Catholic Church but Knox had seriously deviated from the script. It was clear to Lindsay that, while he was still clinging desperately to the branches of the withered fig tree, Knox was hacking at the roots. He had a mind of his own. Like someone else he knew. Lindsay was crushed.

Taking the congregation's positive reaction as the sign he was looking for, there was no stopping Knox. He had found his voice: and not only lungs fit for a preacher but those of a thundering prophet of the Old Testament. From then on, Knox preached a sermon every Sunday, filling the kirk not only with those cooped up in the castle, but with folk from the city and university of St. Andrews and beyond. But it could not continue.

Early one Sunday morning, while walking up the aisle of the parish kirk, Lindsay noticed that, although Passiontide and Holy Week were long past, all the saints" statues were covered in the purple cloaks that signified mourning for the crucified Christ. In the middle of the nave, Knox was spreading a white cloth over a trestle table.

"What are you doing?"

"This," Knox explained, laying out goblets and plates, "is the Holy Table of the Lord. Where priest and layman, noble and commoner, stout citizen and broken man will break bread together and pass the common cup from hand to hand. Unlike the papish church, we evangelicals shall treat John the Commonweal as an equal at the table of the Lord."

Lindsay nodded slowly. He could hardly disagree with his own words.

"They mean to silence you, John."

"How so? Condemn and burn me? Like they did to Master Wishart?"

"Nay," Lindsay replied, "not so drastic. To make sure you have no opportunity of disseminating heresy beyond the castle walls, they are going to prevent you from preaching on Sundays. Dean Annan is making arrangements for preachers from the abbey and the university to occupy the pulpit every Sunday from now on."

Knox guffawed. "Well, I won't let them gag the true word of God. Sunday may be dedicated to the Lord but every day is the Lord's Day. I will preach on every other day of the week."

Lindsay shook his head. "You won't be allowed to, John. To expose the heresy of your propositions, you are to be challenged to a religious duel."

Knox snorted. "A duel! Against whom? Dean Annan?"

"Nay, he dares not joust with you. He is sending in his champion, that doughty debater, sub-prior Winram."

"Then I shall win," Knox replied confidently, his dark blue eyes gleaming. Not only because his training as a notary had equipped him to argue and dispute every point of an argument but because as, one of God's elect, he had unshakeable faith in his convictions. Not so, he suspected with Winram who, ever since meeting Wishart, had been wavering in his beliefs. The truth for the friar, once so crystal clear was murky.

Thus, when called before the convention of Dominican and Franciscans in the yard of St. Leonard's College, Knox refused to defend himself against the "grey friars and black fiends'. Instead, playing devil's advocate he asked, "Can any person here prove that any one of the nine articles was inconsistent with the truth of God?"

Annan hissed at Winram, "Go on! Trounce the heretic."

With great reluctance the sub-prior stuttered and stammered his points, becoming more and more dispirited as Knox outwitted him every time. Aware that he was beaten, Winram called on one of the other Franciscans to carry on the dispute. Friar Arbuckle, too, was soon outsmarted, being driven – to the dismay of his fellows – to the astounding statement as heretical as any of Knox's own, that the apostles had not received the Holy Ghost until after they had written their epistles.

"I fear Friar Arbuckle is so wandered in the mist of his own arguments that he has fallen in a foul mire," Knox scoffed. "The Abbot of Unreason in the season of misrule has more coherent arguments than these so-called learned minds of the Church."

XIII

Black Saturday

> Though love be hot, yet in ane man of age
> It kindles nocht so soon as in youtheid.
> *The Treatise of the Twa Marrit Women and the Widow*
> William Dunbar, 15th–16th Century

St.Mary's Abbey, 8 September 1547

Wheesht! Wheesht! Haud yer wheesht! Elisabeth silently pleaded as the peal of bells from St.Mary's Kirk jangled in her skull. She sank her head into the soft pillow, pulling it round her ears to muffle the scunnersome sound. But the carillon persisted, not only in honour of St.Mary, but as a call to arms for the townsfolk, warning them that the English forces were on their way. There would be no procession for the Miracle of the Flood today. Instead the Black Madonna had been taken for safekeeping to St.Mary's Kirk where a Mass imploring Our Lady's intercession in the coming conflict would be celebrated.

Elisabeth would not be joining them. Vivid nightmares had brought on a pounding migraine. At the mirk hour of the morning, the macabre procession of hamstrung corpses jigging their dance of death had tormented her rest, with the leering skull at its head jeering. *"At Pinkie Cleuch there shall be spilt, much gentle blood that day. Let the quick of the earth live in hope but they will die in despair."*

She must have cried out for Sister Agnes came running. After changing Elisabeth's sweat sodden nightdress, she'd prepared a tisane of feverfew to soothe her thudding head. Fluttering anxiously like an agitated mort-heid moth at a taper, she'd been loath to leave her, but Elisabeth was glad to be left alone.

"You go and sing your praises to the Madonna. Pray for victory over the heathen English."

"And for our young queen to be delivered safely to France," Agnes added.

Whether through prayer or witchcraft, Catherine de Medici had, after ten fruitless years of consulting doctors, astrologers and even sorcerers, at last given birth to her first son in January 1544. Though delicate and undersized – a result of the gruesome potions the Italian witch had taken or the pox – the puny prince had managed to survive to the age of four, and it was this precious prize, the dauphin, that the French King Henri was gallantly offering to the Queen of Scots.

Not without a fight from his rival, the nine-year-old King Edward, under the protection of the Duke of Somerset. Even more determined to enforce the Treaty of Greenwich, his manner of wooing was proving more sophisticated than that of the

323

recently departed Henry VIII. Not content with attacking on several fronts, Protector Somerset was waging a war of words in a series of epistles and proclamations. Almighty God had come down firmly on the English side, so claimed the pamphlet that Elisabeth had confiscated from Jean Hamilton.

Had he not manifest his will in the deaths of King James and his two sons, leaving a girl queen so perfect a match for England's boy king? And such a union would not only divert the Scots from following a false religion but would free them from false friends, their so-called ancient allies, the villainous French. Elisabeth's first instinct had been to consign the polemical pamphlet to the flames but she had kept it – just in case.

After pulling the bed curtains together to shield the light slicing through the prioress's eyelids, Agnes had left for Mass. Elisabeth slipped off her muslin cap and massaged the deep crease in her forehead left by the starched linen wimple. Brushing her hair, she noticed that not only was it losing its lustre – no wonder, being forever crushed beneath the tight-fitting cap – but that it was now spun through with silver. No point in denying or regretting it – she was growing old. Now that the tight band crushing her scalp had eased, she hoped to doze off.

A soft click alerted her. The panel of the secret entrance in the garderobe was being opened and a slight draught stirred the bed-curtains. She lay quietly, holding her breath. All the sisters had gone to Mass and the scullery maids would be gossiping idly in the kitchen. She was alone. The English wouldn't have appeared so silently. They would have rampaged their way through the abbey running amok, breaking down doors, looting and pillaging. Thieves, then, assuming the abbey to be deserted, but how could they have found the secret passage? She had nothing to defend herself with: not even her wooden crucifix. Better to lie still and feign sleep. With luck they might not notice her. She clasped her hands together on top of the coverlet and let her breath slip softly through parted lips.

A chair shoogled and then the bed-curtains twitched, letting in a chink of light. She took a deep breath. It might be her last. Sensing someone standing over her, she fought the desire to open her eyes but, raising her eyelids ever so slightly, she could peek through from underneath her eyelashes. Holding her breath, she lay as rigid as a corpse.

But when the shadowy figure leant over, first stroking her hair and then brushing her forehead with his lips, she gave an astonished squeal. As the grey friar sprang backwards, his cowl slipped down.

"Davie Lindsay, you ghoul! You scared me half to death!"

"Lisbeth! It's you! And you're alive!"

"No thanks to you. This trick of yours is becoming a habit. Twice in a lifetime is two times too often."

"And you affrighted me. Lying there as still and pale as a corpse with your hair spread out on the pillow like that, I thought you were dead."

In his friar's guise, Lindsay had sneaked in unseen along the secret passage from the chapel for he needed to speak with her. The shock of seeing her like this, however, was making him tremble and he gripped the bedpost to steady his shaking hands. Seeing his face as grey as his monk's habit, she patted the bed beside her, inviting him to join her. They lay quietly for a while, like two figures carved on a marble sarcophagus, only the rise and fall of their chests revealing signs of life.

"Here we are, lying together like a lang-marrit couple," she sniffed. "Me an ancient crone and you an auld birkie."

"Or even a larbar. And I'll not take offence if you tell me so now," he sighed. "After all this time – how long has it been?"

She began counting up. "Why, this will be thirty-four years almost to the day of our handfasting! The year of Flodden! When we plighted our troth and promised to keep trust. Do you mind Davie?"

He minded only too well. Raising the spectre of Flodden brought back painful memories of that tragic time and now, with the English army at their gate, the country was under threat once again.

"And I fear that once again we will be crushed," he said morosely.

Elisabeth could not disagree for, newly woken from her nightmare, she, too, felt a deep sense of foreboding. She repeated the lines that had come to her in her dream about blood being spilt at Pinkie Cleuch.

"One of True Thomas's prophecies I seem to mind Betsy saying."

Lindsay shook his head. There would aye be portents and omens. Recently he'd heard one that was said to foretell a victory at Gladsmuir but since he wasn't convinced, he wouldn't raise Lisbeth's hopes by telling her.

> Here shall be gladismore that shall glad us all
> It shall be gladyng of our glee
> It shalbe gladmore wherever it fall
> But not gladmore by the sea.

"Folk are aye fabricating facts to back up their tale," he moaned. "Let's be done with omens for I have some news." He raised himself up onto his elbow to gaze down on her.

"Good news, I hope," she said but his furrowed brow told her otherwise.

"From St. Andrews."

When his hand sought hers, she didn't pull away but held onto it tightly, bracing herself to hear the worst.

"John has been taken captive."

"Oh!" She let out a little sigh of relief. So he was still alive.

Worn down after long months of plague, hunger and constant bombardment the besieged Castilians had surrendered to the French under the command of Admiral Leo Strozzi, Prior of Capua. After agreeing to their conditions, this cousin of Catherine de Medici immediately broke his pledge. Nothing Lindsay could say, not even appealing to his sense of honour, could change the admiral's mind: in fact, his pleas had been met with scornful guffaws. "We do not barter with godless heathens," he'd replied sternly before throwing back his head and laughing. "If this new religion makes men so naïve and soft-headed, then I doubt we will have much to fear from them."

It wasn't only the Castilians who had been duped. Furious for being a fool to trust the perfidious French, Lindsay was ashamed to tell Elisabeth that, on his advice, the rebels had given themselves up. So far Strozzi had spared their lives but could they now trust him to honour his promise to show mercy?

"When I last saw him, John was being bundled off to the galleys with the other Castilians."

She'd been lying still, but then her eyes flew open and she slapped a hand to her splitting head. "The gallows? What? To hang him?"

"Nay. The galleys. We must be thankful for small mercies," Lindsay said, as much to reassure her as himself. "At least Strozzi hasn't handed them over to the Scots to be burned at the stake. Instead, they will be shipped off to prison in France and remain in captivity while we negotiate to exchange hostages." Seeing her face light up at this, he shook his head. "But there may be scant hope for John. Being a priest and scholar and not of noble birth, then …"

"Then we must acknowledge him as such!" Elisabeth struggled to sit up. "We must tell them who he is. That *we* are his parents. John is as noble as any of the Stewart bastards or the spawn of spineless Arran. I'm not afeart. Are you? I shall confess everything to Queen Marie. She'll understand. She knows well enough what it is like to lose a son."

She fixed a look of such intense determination on him that he wavered. A pang of regret at having to add to his bonnie thistledown's grief gripped his heart and sweat dampened his brow. He lowered his eyelids, unable to meet her eyes shining with hope.

"But not, alas, one who is a known heretic and traitor. The queen mother is unlikely to show him mercy."

"If John is in France then I will go to him. Nay, we will both go. You have his ear, Davie. He will listen to you. Talk him out of this reformist nonsense. He may be more willing to hearken to us after a spell in prison has tempered his zeal." Though the thought of his confinement in the kind of dank, dark dungeon where Jinty and Bothwell had been shackled chilled her.

Her false hope made Lindsay feel the worst possible hunker-slider. Being a heretic and a hostage of little worth, Knox's punishment would be to toil at the oars as a galley slave. Struggling to regulate his hirpling heartbeat he pulled her in closer. His lips gently brushed her hair as he whispered into her ear. "There's nothing we can do, Lisbeth, except watch and wait."

"Nay, nay! We cannot let him fall foul of such a fate! You must do something! You're to blame for all this!" Just how much of a rôle had Lindsay as *eminence grise* played in all the plots and intrigues over the years, she would like to know.

He held her firmly while she shook her head back and forth. When she had worn herself out he released his grip and fumbled in his pouch. "Lisbeth, will you take this?"

She flinched as he held out his pinkie.

"Not for yourself, for I know fine you'll refuse it, but to keep safe for John until he comes back."

The engraved skull on the gold ring glinted in a beam of sunshine as it birled round the tip of his finger. The king's ring that had circled so many hapless fingers had proved to be no lucky talisman. She shook her head. "Misfortune has befallen all who've worn it, Davie."

"That's if you believe in auld wives" tales, Lisbeth. Our fate isn't shaped by baubles and bangles."

"Then give it to him yourself. You're his father."

"If God spares me, I will, but I'm no longer young and God alone knows how long I have left." From his pallid countenance she couldn't tell whether he was being sincere or playing for sympathy. Davie Lindsay had aye been a skilful performer.

"Enough of the doom-laden blethers, you auld larbar. I'll keep it safe till the day we can both give it to him. And tell him the truth. Together."

XIV

The Galley Slave

Priesties content you noo, noo,
Priesties content ye noo.
Norman and his company
Have filled the galleys fu'.
Song, 16th Century

A French Galley, Autumn 1547

Would he never escape the clutches of St.Mary? Knox frowned. Fate was playing a malicious trick on him, imprisoning him in a vessel named *Nôtre Dame*. On board the two-masted French galley 180 slaves or *forsairs* took it in turns to toil relentlessly at the oars since their sails were of no use in the lashing seas of the Bay of Biscay. Because of the equinoctial gales that threatened to drive them inshore, the awnings that screened the galley slaves were also furled, exposing them to merciless hammering by the Atlantic waves. Nor did the uniform, a sleeveless brown jerkin, give much protection against the elements or the knout. Sodden with sweat and sea-water, the coarse canvas cloth clung pitilessly to their cracked peeling skin, rubbing salt into the running sores and weeping weals that never healed.

When first put to the oar Knox, the smallest and weakest, had toiled to keep time with the other four *forsairs* chained by the leg to their bench. Because of his small stature he was placed at the outboard end of the oar and so he didn't have to heave himself up on tiptoe to take his stroke like those at the inboard end. At least he was further away from the dreaded *comite*. The overseer strode up and down the central *coursier* that ran from stem to stern of the ship wielding a whip ready to use on laggards for a steady rhythm of rowing had to be maintained at all times.

After months at the oars, the muscles in the dominie's arms had strengthened but thick calluses covered his scholar's hands and Knox worried whether he'd ever be able to pick up a quill again. That was the kind of thought he had to drive out: he had to remain resolute, not only for himself but also for his fellow Castilians. Fearing that losing track of time would mean losing his mind he started keeping a rudimentary diary, scratching a notch each day on his oar.

Crack! The force of the blow propelled him forward and he struck his forehead against his oar. He nearly blacked out but the tip of the knout whipping sharply across his back and his bare arms roused him.

"My God, my God, why dost thou forsake me?"

Wearily Knox lifted his head. James Balfour, a fellow Castilian was bent over his oar, his spine racked by sobs. His bench-mates were cussing and swearing at him for lagging at the oar, because they too, and anyone else who got in the way of the whip, were being flayed unsparingly by the overseer. Knox put out a hand and patted his shoulder.

"Never abandon hope, Balfour," he urged, his voice thick from the lash.

"Even Christ on the cross lost hope," Jamie sobbed.

Their overseer, a muscular Moor, leant over and grabbed Balfour by his matted, straggly hair and pulled his head back. Stinging tears flowed down the runnels of the cracked skin of his shrunken face.

"Which would you sooner have? Your unwashed corpse thrown overboard or fed to the rats down below?" the overseer threatened, letting go of his head to thud against his oar.

Down below, the bowels of the ship housed the hospital, ostensibly for the recovery of those stricken with disease or weakness but in fact a filthy hole where the afflicted were thrown, often never to come out again. Since the slaves were either criminals or heretics, their lives were expendable. When galley fever was rife, many victims preferred to die toiling at the oar than be hurled into the charnel house where the ship's rats scampered over the bodies sniffing out weakness. Then they would begin gnawing at the eyes, it was said.

"Jamie, keep in mind Christ's suffering and passion on his *Via Sacra*," Knox wheezed. "Consider this as your *via dolorosa*. The oar is your cross and with each pull of the oar ... another step on the long road to ..."

"Golgotha and death!" Balfour wailed in despair.

"Nay," Knox panted with the effort of speaking and rowing, "to resurrection ... of the spirit. Never forget Wishart and Patrick Hamilton," Knox urged him. "Our suffering is as nought compared to the final agonies of those martyrs for the faith."

After another lash of the knout, Balfour heaved himself up and pulled down on the oar. Once they were swept into the rhythm of rowing, Knox chanted psalms to keep their spirits up. The mindless repetition of the rosary or endless litanies might have brought comfort, but no such popish profanities would ever pass his lips again.

By the end of September they had reached Nantes at the mouth of the River Loire where they were to moor for the winter: the shallow freeboard of the galleys rendered them unsuitable for voyages in high, wintry seas. Until their winter quarters on shore were ready, the slaves were kept on board, chained to the oar, their only shelter against the chilly night air being underneath the awnings used to protect them against the harsh summer sun. Though most of their time was spent mending ropes and sails and carrying out essential repairs, Knox was surprised when the Scots were allowed pens and paper. Some concession must have been reached. Fortunately, his hands were not so wasted that he could not correspond with Henry Balnaves, confined in comparative comfort in the Castle of Rouen, and those Castilians incarcerted on Mont Saint-Michel. The knowledge that he was not a lone voice crying in the wilderness inspired Knox and spurred him on to hone his thoughts and compose religious tracts and letters.

Though the Castilians had survived their baptism of fire that did not prevent the French crew from trying to convert the heretics back to the Roman faith. On Saturdays, they lined up the Castilians with the other Christian galley slaves, to sing the *Salve Regina* in front of *Nôtre Dame,* an image of Our Lady crudely painted on a rough board and nailed to the mast. The Scots, however, steadfastly resisted her charms and turned their backs on the idol, drawing their hoods over their heads and covering their ears. On Sundays, they refused to attend Mass, and on Mondays they were flogged.

"Do you not worship the prophet Christ?" the Moor asked, mystified as to why the Scots were being ostracised. Being told that, indeed, they were followers of the true teachings of Jesus Christ, he was still confused. Surely there could be no questioning the word of the prophet?

"His Word has been corrupted," Knox explained, "and in our struggle to find the way back to the true path we are being tested. God is pushing us to the limit of our physical endurance so that, once delivered from this bondage, we shall be invigorated with renewed will and strength to carry out his purpose. Of that I have no doubt, for it has been ordained. And God's will *shall* prevail," Knox assured him.

This the Moor did understand. To him, all Christians were infidels, yet in Knox's fatalism and capacity for suffering, he recognised qualities that he'd believed peculiar to his own, Islamic faith. Everything is ordained. Everything is as it should be. By the will of Allah.

8 December 1547

"Kiss her, *hérétique*," the lieutenant bellowed. "Save your damned soul, you son of Satan and kiss. For this is Our Lady's Feast Day."

The French sailors had burst into the Castilians" *bagne,* a crudely built barrack on the riverbank where the forsairs were quartered for the winter. After an all-night drinking spree the *argousin* and his crew were seeking more fun. In the early dawn mist, they forced the Scots *hérétiques* onto the foredeck to pay their respects to the image of *Nôtre Dame.* The lieutenant took particular delight in tormenting Knox who, as a fluent French speaker – thanks to Sister Agnes's tuition –could always be relied upon to answer back. He removed the painted icon from the nail and thrust it into the heretic's face.

"Trouble me not," Knox said, shrinking away from the sailor's brandy breath. "For I will not worship a graven image."

"You shall pay due honour to Christ's Blessed Mother," the *argousin* insisted and forced the icon between the heretic's manacled hands. A triumphant cheer rose from the rest of the crew. "Now kiss her, you spawn of the devil."

For a moment it looked as if the heretic were praying to the idol between his hands. As the crew fell silent waiting for him to obey, Knox suddenly swerved sideways and pitched the icon overboard into the Loire as if it were a burning skivet. Then he turned to address his companions in Scots.

"Let Our Lady now save herself," he jeered. "Being so holy she should sink, but since she's light enough, she'll swim."

The Scots tried to hide their sniggers for, if the French understood that a "light" woman meant one of easy virtue, a slattern, Knox would be severely punished for his blasphemy. From then on, however, the *argousin* and his crew left the irredeemable Scots heretics to their own damnation.

XV

The Treaty of Haddington

What is fortune, wha drives the dett so fast?
We wat there is baith well and wicked chance.
Fickle Fortune
Henry the Minstrel, 15th Century

St. Mary's Abbey, 4 July 1548

The two girls had to stand on tiptoe to peer over the parapet of the abbey bell-tower. All around and as far as they could see the countryside was ravaged: black gaps in woods slashed for timber gawped like an auld crone's toothless mouth; deep trenches gashed long, vicious scars in fields and meadows while fortifications and ditches steadily encircled the town like a noose. The English were digging themselves in well and truly. From the lofty bastion of the garrison's headquarters being built nearby, a soldier waved to them.

"Douk down!" Isabelle shouted. "For if thon English devil sees us, he'll cast his evil spell o'er us and turn us to whinstane."

Jeanie hunkered down and stuck her thumb in her mouth, her shortsighted eyes widening in terror in her doughy face. Whatever Isabelle said must be true for she knew everything. Brought to the abbey by Knox, the penniless orphan lass had been named and claimed by Sister Agnes who had taught her all about plants and herbs and healing and let her help out in the infirmary. Isabelle could not only concoct poisons that could kill folk, she could also cure them with magic potions. And she could speak French and even understand Latin, languages which were just gibble-gabble to Jean. Isabelle was wise beyond her years.

"The English are heathen devils," she continued to torment her, "with horns and tails and cloven hooves!" From the corner of her eye she could see Jeanie's bottom lip trembling and, though Sister Agnes had taught her a chant to ward off evil spirits – something like *abominomalo diabolo* – she wasn't going to use it to console the earl's vauntie daughter.

"Hearken!" she shrieked as Jean clapped her hands over her ears and jolted at a thunderous explosion from the English cannon. "That's their fiendish mouths spouting fire and brimstone. But you're surely not afeart, Jeanie Juniper? You're the brave governor's daughter."

"And he will thave us," Jean lisped, whey-faced and quaking. "He'll be here thoon. He gave his word." With that she scrambled to her feet and twirled off down the turnpike stair.

"If Errant Arran had stood firm on the field of Pinkie Cleuch, all this could have been avoided," Elisabeth blurted, unable to conceal her bitterness

So much for the confident governor, gloriously arrayed in gleaming new armour, who had ridden out to lead one of the largest hosts in Scottish history: so much for his well-prepared trenchworks and well-oiled field artillery train: so much for the priests and monks, geared up and armed for battle, who strode among the ten thousand men mustered along the banks of the River Esk, spurring them on to fight the devil's own: for the legions of hell, their number swollen with experienced mercenaries and highly trained cavalry, had might on their side.

If the constant gunfire from the English fleet in the Firth of Forth could split ears in Haddington, then it swiftly shattered the brains and the resolve of the Scottish host. When the foot soldiers, fleeing a shock charge by heavy horse, had dashed for the safety of the marsh or of Arthur's Seat only to be ridden down and slaughtered, Arran had panicked and fled the field. On Black Saturday, while the Esk ran red with the gore of ten thousand Scots, the streets of Edinburgh flowed with the seventy tuns of beer Somerset had ordered for the victorious English troops. Thomas the Rhymer's prophecy had come true.

"And then our bold lord governor was forced to flee again – from the wrath of Edinburgh wives who vowed to stone him to death," Elisabeth sneered. "How I wish I'd been there to cast the first stone."

"Only those who are without sin may do so," Queen Marie said quietly.

"Oh, for the pleasure of pelting errant Arran's hide, I would gladly believe myself to be unsullied."

"I fear your heart is desperately wicked, *ma chère amie*," the queen laughed. "Or at least *très méchant*."

"Or, as the Scots would say, Your Grace: as mischant as Auld Mischanter."

The queen giggled and then heaved a sigh.

"I should be grateful that Governor Arran has persuaded the stubborn Scots lairds to sign our Treaty," she said, her voice tinged with regret, for it meant that she would soon have to bid farewell to her beloved daughter. While the Scots had at last agreed to Mary's betrothal to the dauphin, she was to be kept safe in France until her marriage, far away from the thieving English heathens.

"Only because of the rewards your King Henri has offered our brave governor; the promise of a wealthy French bride for his son, Lord James, and, more importantly, the Duchy of Châtelherault and a generous pension for himself," Elisabeth reminded her.

Before they changed their minds, parliament had been summoned to the abbey at Haddington to ratify the Franco-Scottish Treaty. The soldiers setting up camp on the banks of the Tyne were being hampered by the wranglesome three estates squabbling over who should be assigned the largest, most lavishly equipped tent – until a diminutive French nun began haranguing them. Lay aside their pride and vanity she remonstrated, for the biggest tents would be needed for a makeshift infirmary to tend the wounded from the inevitable conflict.

Thon master of diplomacy, David Lindsay, should be here to placate them, Elisabeth thought, but his valuable skills were being put to use in Denmark where, as a member of the Scottish embassy, he was ostensibly negotiating a trade treaty but in reality requesting assistance against attack from the English.

Seeing the fluttering flags and pennants of the gaily-coloured tents and pavilions – used in times of peace for spectacles and pageants – brought memories of the Tournament of the Wild Knight flooding back. Closing her eyes, Elisabeth savoured that moment when Lindsay had whirled her high in the air. Never again would she experience such giddy excitement. No more wheeling and whooping. No more birling.

Perhaps it would have been safer to retreat to Nunraw, she thought, giving herself a shake, but the English had seized all the strongholds in the area including Yester, Hailes and Nunraw. Queen Marie was also concerned. Although French troops had landed at Leith in over a hundred vessels and were on their way to Haddington, she feared that there would be too few men and not enough provisions. The siege would be a long one.

"But that should not affect Her Grace, Elisabeth pointed out. As soon as she had signed the Treaty, Queen Marie would set out for Dumbarton Castle where her daughter was waiting. Having dropped off the French troops at Leith, the galleys were sailing round the north coast of Scotland to the Clyde estuary to pick up the young Queen of Scots and take her to France.

"How furious Protector Somerset will be when he finds out that his precious prize has been snatched from under his nose." Queen Marie gave a quiet chuckle.

"And we shall miss you too when you leave, Your Grace," Elisabeth said sadly.

Marie de Guise furrowed her high, noble brow. "I'm not leaving," she declared. However strongly her De Guise relatives had urged her to abandon the wild Scots to their own devices, however much she pined to return to her motherland and however many torments lay ahead, she would be staying in Scotland. "I must safeguard my daughter's inheritance at all costs. If I leave, the Scottish lords will be easily won over to the Protestant cause. Not for any religious conviction, but for English gold," she added ruefully.

Stumbling over the uneven ground, Sister Agnes came scuttling over to them. Clinging onto her skirts, red-faced Isabelle seemed about to burst into tears.

"Jeanie has disappeared!" Agnes gasped.

Isabelle bowed her head as she explained how she'd scoured the abbey for Jeanie. Too ashamed to admit that it might be her fault for filling her simple soul with dread, she sobbed out her fears that the feckless lass might have fallen down a well or into the river.

"We shall have to call out the guard," Agnes said, gathering the weeping orphan lass in her arms.

"Not yet," Elisabeth replied. The fewer who knew about it the better – so as not to alert the English who might scoop her up and hold her for ransom – and certainly not her father who'd never cease casting it up to them.

Crowds were streaming through the streets of Haddington where a barricade had been put up round the market square. There was almost a carnival atmosphere as musicians, tumblers and assorted street entertainers, taking advantage of the impromptu audience, began to perform under the cautious eye of English soldiers on patrol.

Jeanie had come to a standstill. She balanced on one leg, sucking her thumb and twirling a lock of hair into a ringlet, for she had lost one of her slippers and her pretty lace-trimmed bonnet. Barefoot urchins in filthy rags were pointing at her and daring each other to run up and tug at her satin skirt with their clarty hands. She glanced around, terrified in case one of the horned English devils leapt out at her. Tears welled in her eyes. Where was her father?

Across the street an important looking man in a smart uniform sat astride a snorting stallion. She began to limp towards him when a stout woman caught hold of her arm. The sharp, acidic smell from her clothes stung Jeanie's nostrils but the woman had a kindly smile and sparkling eyes.

"Come away here, my bonnie lassie. Have you lost your mother?" she whispered in her ear. Her sour breath stank of ale. Jeanie wrinkled her nose.

"I'm looking for my father. He's the governor."

"Is he, indeed, my bonnie bird? Well, thon's the English governor up there. You don't want to get trampled under his hooves." Jeanie shuddered, not daring to look and see if they were cloven or if fire and brimstone were spewing from his great gob.

"Don't fash, lassie. Bessie here will take care of you," she wheedled, rubbing the satin of her gown between her forefinger and thumb while casting a calculating eye over her expensive calf slipper.

"And I've lost my shoe," Jeanie whined.

"And I wager it cost a pretty penny. I should ken, for I'm a tanner's wife. Come, my lass, I'll help you look for it. And to sweeten our search, I'll buy us a dainty or two."

As she tried to lure her away, the crowd suddenly surged forward and pushed them up against the barricade. In the makeshift ring, two soldiers brandishing swords and bucklers were circling each other. As the first clang of sword clashing on sword rang out, the tanner's wife asked, "What's going on?"

"Two of our lads stationed at Yester," a spectator replied. "Grey could have had them both hanged and that would have been the end of it, instead he's putting on a show for us. To make us think the English believe in fair play." He hawked up a gob of spittle that narrowly missed Jeanie's one remaining slipper. "Thon foul-tongued Newton was caught cussing the King of England's blessed name but, instead of crawing about it, the cowardly poltroon's putting the blame onto Hamilton."

Jean's ears pricked up. Hamilton? Did that mean her father was here? She clung onto the barricade, resisting the woman's attempts to prise her knuckles away.

Unable to push their way through, Elisabeth and Agnes were circling the densely packed mob, hoping to catch a glimpse of Jeanie's stylish lace-trimmed bonnet. A sudden hush fell over the raucous rabble as the falsely accused Hamilton finally forced the false-tongued Newton against the flimsy barricade. The crowd held their breath, not daring to distract their champion as he drew his sword back ready to slay the sleekit slanderer.

"Thlay him, brave Hamilton! Thlay him!" a shrill, girlish voice piped up from behind the barricade.

For a split second Hamilton hesitated and, turning his head slightly in the direction of the cry, presented his exposed thrapple to his opponent. In a trice, Newton plunged his sword into Hamilton's windpipe, piercing right through to the back of his neck, and then wrenched it out to sink it deep into the stricken man's chest.

Jeanie Hamilton's wide eyes gawped as the blood spurted like a fountain, spattering her satin gown and splashing her calf leather slipper and white stockings. She stood petrified, spittle drooling from the corners of her mouth as she sucked on her thumb. Sensing that the furious mob might turn on them, the tanner's wife slunk off through the crowd, muttering that the sappie-heided lass was fey.

But the rabble were baying for the blood of the sliddery Newton, who was cowering on his knees before the English Governor Grey, claiming the right of the law of arms to be set free. A barricade of English soldiers, arms linked, held back the outraged mob to let Newton mount his horse and ride off. Only when Grey gave an imperceptible nod to three mounted knights who set off after him did the crowd calm down. Justice would be served after all.

Elisabeth pushed her way through the mob to drag Jeanie away. Blissfully unaware of causing a man's death, she was intent on rubbing at the bloodstains on her pretty gown. How Elisabeth longed to shake the gormless lass until her bones rattled and her teeth clattered, but what would that serve? That a man's life could depend on the whim of a capricious wee lass leading everyone a merry dance, only confirmed the fickleness of fate.

XVI

In the End is my Beginning

> Farewell, ye lemand lamps of lustiness
> Of fair Scotland, adieu my ladies all.
> *The Testament of Squire Meldrum*
> Sir David Lindsay, 16th Century

A French Galley, July 1548

Sweating and straining at the oars, the rowers listened, ears on the prick, for the crack of the whip that signalled the end of their shift. Then they flopped across their oars, too exhausted to be irritated by the flapping wings of gulls diving into the slops and splattering them with guano. Before he could rest, Knox used his ragged thumbnail to scratch out a mark on his oar. Another notch, another day over. In late spring the galleys had been fitted out, French soldiers had trooped on board and they had set sail once again into the turbulent Bay of Biscay. To where, they were not told.

He slumped over his oar, wrinkling his nose at the foul stench from the sludge sloshing about under his feet, and shut his eyes to blot out the sight of it at least. When he'd enquired where he might relieve himself, the Moor had laughed gustily as if he'd never heard anything so funny in all his life.

"Unless you've brought your own chamber pot, you'll piss and shit where you sit."

Young lads scuttled like cockroaches under their benches to sluice away this bree of urine, faeces and vomit. Today the stench curdled his stomach and he wanted to retch. The thought of food made him feel sick but he took his scran bowl when it was passed along: he wasn't ready to donate his rations to his starving mates yet.

Thankfully today's offering wasn't gruel, a greasy sludge of oil and beans that stuck in his craw and which even the sour, brackish water couldn't sluice down. It was a thin watery skiddle boiled up from scrapings and peelings, which, if nothing else, would slake his drouth. He nibbled round the dry, fusty biscuit, spitting out weevils that had wormed their way into it. To force the crumbs down his gullet, he had to keep gulping and when the ladle was passed round, he slurped at the musty rainwater until it slittered down his chin. He had to eat and drink otherwise he risked being flung into the hospital. He would not die in harness.

The next morning he could hardly raise his hand, never mind lift his arms to row. The smell of vomit clogged his nose and his face was swathed in sweat. All night a constant flux – spewing up green bile at one end and dribbling a skittery mess from the other – had sapped his strength and left him steeping in his own stinking midden. When he tried to stand up, he blacked out, falling forward and hitting his head on the oar.

The Moor overseer unchained him, eased him onto the gangway and slapped his face a few times to revive him. He summoned the French surgeon who, on seeing who it was, just shook his head and left. The Scotch *hérétique* was already dead in his eyes and deserved no treatment. He was lowered down into the dreaded hospital from where no-one came out alive. Around him in the cramped space emaciated bodies writhed in their death throes, calling out to their various gods for mercy: Allah. Jehovah. Almighty God.

The galley glided silently along, enshrouded in a thick, impenetrable mist that muffled the sound of the creaking vessel. He was utterly alone in the eerie silence. The sea and the sky had blended into a mirky greyness but then, as the hazy outline of the Craig of Bass loomed out of the haar, his spirits lifted. North Berwick must be nearby, and soon they would be within reach of Aberlady.

Unseen in the mist, he slipped his scrawny leg through the leg-iron and slithered quietly into the icy waters of the Forth. The coldness knocked the breath out of him. He plunged deeper and deeper beneath the waves, spinning and spiralling downwards towards the darkness. Desperate for air he flailed out with his arms and legs upwards before his lungs burst. As he opened his mouth he retched out briny seawater and bilious green gaw. He grabbed hold of a piece of flotsam floating past and gratefully wrapped himself around it.

How long he dozed bobbing on the waves, he couldn't tell, but when he came to, he was no longer clutching a plain board but the statue of the Black Madonna. Ferny fronds of maiden's hair caressed her simpering lips and slimy bladderwrack coiled around her crudely painted face. The hard wood slowly yielded becoming as soft as womanly flesh under his fingers. The Madonna was changing into a mermaid before his eyes, with a long, lewd figure and fish tail. With a shudder of disgust he thrust away the profane icon and then kicked and splashed his way towards the wide bay of Aberlady. As he waded through the shallows to the shore, he could see the familiar outline of the Garleton hills in the background: a light breeze carried the sounds of a welcoming peal from St.Mary's Abbey. A short walk home and freedom.

The rays of the morning sun burned through the haar and lit up a figure coming down the brae towards him, arms beckoning. But when he tried to move, it was as if lead weights were dragging his legs down. His breath came in short bursts and he could hear the blood booming in his ears. He couldn't lift his feet out of the quicksand that was swaddling his feet. He threw up his arms in a vain attempt to slow the swamp that was swiftly sucking him down. Then he saw her face.

The Queen of Heaven, radiant and divine, her face shining with her beatific smile, her arms outstretched in a gesture of compassion. Gratefully he reached out, but as he clasped her blessed hand, the slender fingers blackened into writhing tentacles. Her compassionate smile twisted and warped into the lecherous leer of the gypsy girl and then the gruesome grimace of the Black Madonna.

As if bitten by the serpent, he dropped her hand and opened his mouth to scream, but thick evil-smelling slime slid down his throat and squeezed against his eyelids. With a slurp he slipped into the smothering darkness. A wave of cold seawater suddenly splashed across his face.

"Master Knox!" Master Knox! Wake up! You must wake up!"

With great effort he opened heavy-lidded eyes and blinked a few times. James Balfour was kneeling over him, wiping his face with a cloth.

"Forgive me, but you were so feverish, the Moor told me to douse you with water." Appalled at the surgeon's lack of compassion, the Moorish overseer had released Balfour from his chains to tend to his compatriot in his last hours.

So he was still here. Lying on a bare board in the stinking hold of the galley with only a threadbare blanket to cover his nakedness: Jonah in the belly of the whale.

"We've passed North Berwick and we'll be within sight of St.Andrews ere long," Balfour said, trying to sound optimistic.

"Aye," Knox mumbled. "I can hear the bells."

"Bells? You must still be dreaming."

"Aye, well, whatever dream I was having, it is now over," Knox replied. "Thanks be to God." Raising himself up onto his elbows he tried to get to his feet. Every bone ached and his head dirled but he was desperate for at least a glimpse of St.Andrews, perhaps his last. Balfour asked the Moor if he could take Knox up on deck. St.Andrews was a holy city, he explained.

"As Mecca is for us. *Allah Akbar.*"

With Balfour pushing his legs and the Moor pulling his arms, Knox struggled up the rope ladder. Never a large man, he seemed to have shrunk. Scranky-shankit and bow-backit – could this gaunt, shrivelled old body be his? Streaks of grey in his straggly hair and unkempt beard daubed him as brockit as a badger. The sun and wind had etched deep lines on his face and hunger had scooped hollows in his cheeks. He had descended into the hellhole as one man and come out another.

The first blast of the bitter east wind nearly blew the frail Knox over and the salt spray stung his eyes. Craning his scrawny neck, he could just about make out the spires of St.Andrews rising out of the Scottish mist, and yonder the steeple of the church where God had first opened his mouth in public.

"And you shall do so again," Balfour declared.

His eyes watering from the salt spray, Knox bowed his head. Aye, he would that. Now that he was one of God's elect, he wouldn't depart this life until he had preached there again.

Since Knox was not deemed fit enough to take up his oar he was given respite. Although the hospital was hardly the most suitable place to convalesce, he was allowed out on deck during the day. After sailing round the north coast of Scotland, the galley would be setting anchor soon and he'd be able to gather his strength, the Moor assured him.

"We're taking on a most precious cargo. Of utmost secrecy. Your Scottish gold, perhaps, or your crown jewels."

Coaxing daft Jeanie Hamilton onto the gangplank was no easy task as she wriggled in Elisabeth's hand like a squirming tiddler. If children from noble families were to accompany the young queen, then the Earl of Arran insisted that his son and daughter be among them. But the fushionless lad was too unwell to travel, while the spoilt lass was digging her heels in at the end of the pier, snivelling that monstrous sea creatures dwelling in the deep would drag her down.

"Come on." Lady Fleming took Jeanie firmly by the hand and hauled her up onto the deck. "No more girning. You're not a bairn. See how Her Grace, the queen, so bravely trotted up the gangplank and she's only five. Set an example to the younger lassies."

She led her over to a group of younger girls, in matching costumes and bonnets, chattering excitedly. Left a widow after Lord Fleming was killed at Pinkie, Jenny Stewart, with her mother's flaming hair and her father's fiery temper, was to act as chaperone to Queen Mary. She left Jeanie with the four Maries, one of whom being her own daughter, and then turned her charm on the French skipper. Since the winds were against them and it might be days before they set sail, she begged leave to go back ashore. But the skipper was unyielding: all passengers had to stay on board.

"He's a true sailor, thon tarry breeks," she grumbled to Elisabeth. "No doubt the auld sea dog favours heaving his mast with his bosun's mate," she sneered and flounced off to supervise her charges. The five-year-old Queen of Scots and her new playmates were chasing each other in a game of tig round the narrow gangways that ran round both sides of the ship, connecting prow to stern.

Elisabeth made her way to forecastle at the prow of the ship where sailors were loading supplies into the cabins underneath. On the foredeck, Margaret Erskine, another Pinkie widow, was bidding farewell to her seventeen-year-old son being sent to study at the Sorbonne in Paris. The morose-looking James Stewart stood stiffly, glancing shiftily sideways, as his mother harangued him in a quiet but firm voice. Never forget whose son he was, never forget that he was the queen's elder brother and never let himself be pushed aside by the bullying French. And be prepared for the day when Her Grace – his sister, mind – had need of him, for she would, of that Margaret Erskine was certain. Then, pinning his arms to his side, she pressed him roughly against that oft-admired bosom.

A sudden pang of envy struck Elisabeth as she witnessed this brusque hug between mother and son. Squalls of wind intensified the pitch and yaw of the boat making her feel queasy: the murky water lapping the sides of the shallow boat seemed to be welling up. She grasped hold of the rail and focussed her eyes on the landmark of Dumbarton Rock to steady her reeling head. From the castle, unable to bear protracted farewells from her daughter, Marie de Guise would be watching and waiting.

"*Vous êtes malade, Abbesse?*" The skipper was gazing at her with concern. Elisabeth shook her head. She only wanted to look round the galley. "To make sure your royal passenger travels in comfort?" he said. "Never fear, Abbess. Your precious child queen, our dauphin's betrothed, will be well sheltered from any storms." He pointed to the stern of the ship where sailors were erecting a tent on the captain's deck. The other passengers, he explained, would berth under awnings on the gangways during the voyage.

What about the sailors? There didn't seem enough space for the jostling crew.

"There are cabins – but not enough for all the mariners – but since they work in shifts they can share a berth or bed down wherever they can. The slaves have to sleep at the oar. That's all those murderers and heretics deserve so don't waste any prayers on their damned souls, Sister," he said by way of farewell.

Elisabeth thanked him and then began to grope her way along the rail. The sour stench rising from the lower deck stung her nostrils: she wished she had a nosegay or a muslin cloth to cover her nose but she forced herself to look down. She scanned the scraggy, gaunt bodies of galley slaves slumped over their oars or sprawled across their benches. Was this the miserable existence Knox had to endure? she was thinking, when a sudden, sharp noise made her jump. A strong-armed Moor had cracked a whip to rouse the dozing *forsairs*. She flinched. A barefooted lad, wearing only a pair of tattered breeks and a red cap came out of a cabin underneath the foredeck, struggling to carry a pail. He thumped it down and began ladling slops into wooden bowls, passing them among the slaves who slurped greedily at the pigswill.

The Moor laid down his whip and, balancing like a tightrope walker, edged his way along the *corsair* between the benches. With both hands he heaved at an iron ring and yanked open a hatch in the deck. Then he knelt down and positioned his strong arms underneath the oxters of the captive to pull him out of the lower depths. Blinded by sunlight, the slave staggered for a moment before the Moor led him, stumbling over his shackles, along the gangway. Then he propped him up against a coil of ropes in front of the cabin. With a weary nod of thanks, the captive stretched out his legs, raised his face to the sun and gulped down lungfuls of fresh air.

Elisabeth's heart squeezed in pain: she felt a sickening lurch in the pit of her stomach. The weird feeling of foreboding that had haunted her all her life now threatened to overwhelm her. She clenched her fingers round the rail to keep herself from fainting. Now was not the time to fall into a swoon for, despite the scraggy beard and the matted hair, she recognised him. Sunk deep into their sockets Knox's unmistakeable blue eyes shone out more intensely against his weather-beaten skin.

A sharp stab of pity for the torture he must be suffering pierced her heart, but that would all end soon. She would go immediately to Queen Marie and petition for his release. Then she would take John home and nurse him back to health – salve his wounds and heal his scars – but most of all she would give him the love she'd kept back all these years. A mother's love. Witnessing Margaret Erksine with her son had taught her that. Whatever her faults, the royal mistress had never deprived *her* son of his birthright.

John Knox had a right to know who his parents were: however upsetting it might be. She wouldn't wait – like her father had – until *her* deathbed to tell him the truth. And he should be given the chance to decide his own future. With no wish to be a prioress, had she not railed against her fate? She, of all people, should have realised all this. Who was she to accuse Lindsay of sending Knox down the path of perdition, when she was no less guilty in her determination to manipulate his destiny? Knox may have been coerced, rather than forced, into Holy Orders but he'd been given few other options: bishop or cardinal were hardly choices.

Well, that would all change now. Let him leave the Church if he wished – she would seek a papal dispensation for him – but not to follow a false path. He should start a new life: marry a loving wife who would bear him children; live the life she'd been denied. Placing her hand on her chest, she could feel, underneath her sark, the lovers" knot with the king's ring pressing against her heart.

"John!" she called out.

Knox blinked a few times and then looked up to see a dark figure silhouetted against the sky. The woman clothed with the sun. The Queen of Heaven, her face forever imprinted on his memory, but now in his dreamlike state he was seeing her as she was the first time he set eyes on her, with the multi-hued Paraclete on her arm. Once again he experienced an intense desire to touch her soft hands, smell her lavender oil and sense her warm, sweet breath as she placed a soft kiss on his cheek. As great weariness overwhelmed him, he felt his spirit weaken and his resolve begin to melt away.

"John!" she called out more urgently. "John! Recant now and you can go free!"

He stiffened at her words. This woman clothed in the sun was not a vision, but a delusion. Not the Queen of Heaven but the Queen of Elfland, tempting him away from the right path:

> For that is the path of wickedness,
> Though some call it the road to heaven.

The Whore of Babylon in the guise of the prioress was trying to seduce him with her feminine wiles and he had almost succumbed. For, Almighty God, in his infinite wisdom, knew full well the love that Knox still harboured for his godmother and had set him one last test. Knox knew that he must forever harden his heart against such temptation. Never again would he drop his guard. He would never recant, he would: *Keep Tryst*.

Elisabeth had begun to clamber down a ladder leading down to the lower deck but as soon as she reached the bottom rung she was overpowered by muscular arms the colour of burnt chestnut. Waggling her head from side to side, straining to see over his shoulder, she grappled with the Moor in a macabre dance.

Knox's eyes narrowed to needle points of piercing blue. He raised his shackled hand not in blessing but in warning. He pursed his lips and mouthed the words: Go. In the name of God, go. And then he pressed his eyelids tight shut.

As her legs buckled beneath her, the Moor threw her over his shoulder and carried her up the ladder. Then, when she tried to go back, he picked her up again and swung her round. For an instant she was the thirteen-year-old Lisbeth again, being whirled round by Lindsay, the world and her future whirling in front of her eyes. Tapsalteerie. Whigmaleerie.

As the Moor urged her towards the gangplank, she kept looking back and calling out plaintively, "My son! That's my son!" But her words were borne away by the breeze.

7 August 1548

With favourable winds at last, the fleet of galleys lifted anchor and prepared to leave the Firth of Clyde. Three mothers stood on Dumbarton pier, gazing out to sea and clinging on for a last glimpse of the galleys: *Stabat Mater dolorosa*. At Elisabeth's side and resolutely apart from Margaret Erskine, Marie de Guise stood firm, steadfastly refusing to show tears in front of her auld enemy. Only when they left the pier did she share her grief with the prioress.

"Shall I ever see my beloved daughter again?" she said softly. "If only…"

"There's no sense in wishing that life could be otherwise, Your Grace. What will be, will be," Elisabeth replied in an effort to comfort the desolate queen mother, but that was not what she believed. Although Knox may have dismissed her this time, she had not given up hope. For the day would come when he would turn to her again and she would regain his trust. But until then she must: *Endure Fort*.

The queen mother was nodding, "Wise words, *ma chère soeur*. And what is that saying the Scots are so fond of? About submitting to fate?" She pondered for a moment before moistening her lips to pronounce in her best Scots tongue, "You maun dree your weird."

Author's Note

Nearly all of the principal characters in this novel existed in real life, apart from a few who are fictional: Betsy Learmont, Kate Hepburn, and Sister Agnes. The events are mostly based on historical fact with a liberal use of artistic licence in their interpretation.

The main liberty is taken with the central relationship of John Knox, Elisabeth Hepburn and Sir David Lindsay, which, although a matter of conjecture, is not beyond the bounds of possibility.

Knox was notoriously reticent about his early life and he first appears in the written records as a Notary Apostolic on 13 December 1540. While some of his biographical details have been disputed, it is now accepted that he was born in Giffordgate by Haddington in 1513 or 1514, but his parentage remains obscure. He and his brother William were orphaned at an early age and, while Knox described himself as "a man of base estate and condition", some biographers consider that his family must have had reasonable financial resources to send him to St. Andrews University. Knox also mentions strong kinship with the Earls of Bothwell – the Hepburns of Hailes Castle – but, as far as he was concerned, he was born again when the Reformist preacher, George Wishart, pulled him from the "puddle of papistry'.

Elisabeth Hepburn appears in the records as Prioress of St. Mary's Abbey from around 1520 till 1563. Described in one document as the daughter of an Augustinian canon and in another as the kinswoman of John Hepburn, Prior of St. Andrews, she is assumed to be the prior's natural daughter. Hepburn requested from Archbishop Forman her appointment as prioress – at the very young age of twenty-three – overruling the election by the nuns of their own nominee, M. H., presumed to be Mariota, or Maryoth, Hay. In an entry in the Haddington Protocol Books of June 1541, Elisabeth is accused of "carnal dalliance" with one Harry Cockburn. She is also recorded in the Accounts of the Lord High Treasurer of Scotland as riding to the hunt with the court of James V.

The young king's tutor, Sir David Lindsay of the Mount and Garleton, who later served at court as herald and diplomat, was a renowned poet and playwright. His famous work, *Ane Satire of the Three Estates,* is a scathing attack on the corrupt practices of the Roman Catholic Church and one of the clergy he ridicules for scandalous behaviour is the Prioress. She then defends herself by cursing those friends who compelled her to be a nun and "would not let her marry". Did he base his character on the free spirited, real-life prioress, Elisabeth Hepburn? And could Knox have inspired – or even played the part of – Divine Correction, God's avenging angel, sent to instigate reform, and John the Commonweal, who takes up the cause of the Poor Man?

Lindsay certainly encountered Knox in St.Andrews Castle in 1547 when he encouraged him to preach against the antichrist of Rome, and the parallels between the imagery of this sermon and Lindsay's poem, *The Monarch,* are too striking to be simply coincidental. While it has been acknowledged that Knox appears to have exerted a decisive influence on Lindsay's reformist ideas, it is also likely that theirs was a close, mutual relationship that began much earlier, with the older poet inspiring the younger cleric.

All three could have met around 1527 when Lindsay was exiled to his property at Garleton near Haddington where Knox was a pupil at the grammar school and Elisabeth was prioress at St.Mary's Abbey. These coincidences form the springboard for a plot that interweaves documented fact with inspired guesswork. This novel is an attempt to shed light on the early, formative years of one of the most influential figures in Scottish history, John Knox.

Acknowledgments

I would like to thank all those friends, family and colleagues whose help, comments and moral and practical support have contributed to the production of this book.

Among the many reference sources I consulted, I am indebted to the following whose thorough research has proved invaluable – but I accept full responsibility for my interpretation of their facts.

Transactions of the East Lothian and Field Naturalists" Society; Ishbel C. M. Barnes, *Janet Kennedy, Royal Mistress;* Jamie Cameron, *James V;* Carol Edington, *Court and Culture in Renaissance Scotland;* Roderick Graham, *John Knox – Democrat;* Stewart Lamont, *The Swordbearer;* Rosalind K. Marshall, *Mary of Guise; John Knox;* Marcus Merriman, *The Rough Wooings;* Pamela E. Ritchie, *Mary of Guise in Scotland;* Gerald Urwin, *Feat of Arms: The Siege of Haddington.*

For practical help, thanks are due to Eric Glendinning of Haddington's History Society, the staff at Haddington Library and the John Gray Centre, Tyne & Esk Writers, Betsy Dyer, Gerald and Margaret Urwin, and my fellow writers at our Saturday meetings.

For their moral support over the years, I owe a special debt of thanks to Altyn Bazarova, Mary Buckley, Alison Girdwood, Peter Keating, Valerie Shaw, Ruth and Chris Thornton, the Carlung book group and last, but not least, the Gilroy family.

Grateful thanks also to Dana Celeste Robinson and the team at Knox Robinson Publishing for guiding me along the path to publication.

Finally, words are not enough to express my thanks to Matt Macpherson for his unfailing support and patience.

THE

WELLS

The Hope Trilogy
Book One

Patrick Gooch

KNOX ROBINSON
PUBLISHING
London • New York

The Kent Countryside, 1736

The horses were changed at a coaching inn in Chelsfield, a hamlet situated on the rolling ridges of the North Downs. Thereafter, good time was made over the next leg to the Grange Inn at Riverhead. In a shady courtyard, the favoured passengers were offered beef, ale, port wine, and cheese from a laden table. Not having eaten since breakfast, Marius devoured a full platter with relish. The horses were replaced, and they boarded to continue their journey. However, no more than minutes passed before the coach came to a rocking halt below the town of Sevenoakes.

"It's too much fer the 'orses," the coachman called. "Yer'll 'ave to take yer baggage, and walk to the top o" the "ill."

Not a welcome command. Walking off a heavy meal by carrying baggage uphill on a warm summer's day was not what the passengers had envisaged. With ill grace, the coach seats slowly emptied, baggage was retrieved, and in ones and twos, they wearily commenced their upward journey. Marius found himself handed down both his own and Mrs Johnson's voluminous carpet bag.

"How far is it to the top, driver?" asked Brown, adjusting his frock coat and squaring his hat and wig over a reddening face.

"No more 'an three-quarters o" a mile, sir. Yer'll find us by the 'orse trough and pump in the middle o" the town."

With a click of the tongue, a flick of the reins, the coachman encouraged the team forward, and the now unburdened coach climbed slowly from view.

The pace varied. The column of walkers lengthened as it wound its way up the hillside. Carrying Mrs Johnson's bag, Marius was obliged to walk beside her. Not given to exercise, the gentlewoman's progress was slow and they were soon bringing up the rear, stopping frequently on the incline.

"I wish I could pretend I was taken by the view," Mrs Johnson said breathlessly. "But I'm afraid, sir, the heat is conspiring against me."

On one occasion Mrs Johnson rested on a convenient milestone. "I am not sure what I would have done if I had needed to carry my bag as well," she said in a relieved tone.

"Dr Hope, if I may be so bold," she said, leaning forward and touching his arm with her fan. "I have the strongest impression all is not well. Is something disturbing you?"

Marius smiled ruefully. He would have preferred to keep his private concerns from fellow-passengers.

"If I appear preoccupied, madam, it has nothing to do with present company. More a reflection of my work. In fact, the reason I am making this journey is to distance myself from it. Mr Jordan was right, I am a physician, but not a contented one."

Mrs Johnson was silent for several minutes. Marius thought the conversation was done. Then she enquired. "What does your family advise?"

"I have never seen fit to raise such matters with them, madam," he replied stiffly.

They continued their upward journey. Marius knew he had responded harshly. Yet Mrs Johnson had not been overly inquisitive. When in company, was it not natural to converse in such a manner? Need he have been so cutting in his reply?

As he trudged beside the gentlewoman, Marius realised that this was how he had always reacted. He thought back to earlier times with the family. Whilst the others would discuss their troubles openly, invariably he would leave the room if conversations took a serious turn. He had always revelled in his brothers' and sisters' triumphs, given sympathy when setbacks arose. More than any member of the family, Marius had been anxious to retain the idyll of home life. If there were moments causing upset, so they were hidden away, repressed, until the threat went away.

In childhood, they were rarely of lasting concern. Gradually, it became his way of dealing with personal agonies. Put them out of mind. Allowing them to intrude was to acknowledge their existence.

However, Marius was slowly coming to accept that as one became older, so it became difficult to isolate yourself from the world. Problems dismissed do not melt away. On the contrary, they grow in magnitude. The situation now facing him at the hospital was one such example. Was this visit to The Wells another occasion when he was fleeing from an issue?

As the roadway levelled out on the approaches to the town, Mrs Johnson was able to catch her breath.

"I'm sorry if you thought I was prying into your affairs, " she murmured.

Marius immediately regretted his sharpness of tone.

"Madam, please accept my apologies. Making that untimely remark was more a condemnation of myself."

Hesitating for a moment, he then said something foreign to his nature.

"May I confide something to you, Mrs Johnson?"

"I may appear a chatty soul, Dr Hope," she replied with a faint smile. "However, it is not in my nature to reveal a confidence."

Thus it was, as they walked towards the pump in Sevenoakes, Marius found himself recounting the setbacks facing him at the hospital.

"I am a physician in charge of one of the wards at St.Bartholomew's Hospital," he said reflectively. "I treat ailments such as smallpox, typhoid fever, and even periodic outbreaks of bubonic plague."

He hesitated, a flicker of irony crossed his face. "I take satisfaction from my work. But more and more, I am of the opinion that whilst some branches of medicine are progressing in leaps and bounds, many of the treatments we employ are still largely guesswork."

For a moment he wondered if he should unburden himself upon the woman.

"Carry on, Dr Hope."

"Increasingly, I have felt I was treating the symptoms not the causes. Whenever, I have broached the subject with the chief physician, he has declared I was not employed as a medical evangelist. I was there to alleviate pain and suffering, to cure the patients in my charge . . . and I was not doing a particularly good job."

He stopped to change round the baggage he was carrying.

"We practise blood letting of course, use cold compresses and vapour burners. I try to keep patients with the same disease apart from others. But I am convinced there is more we could be doing.

"Even as a student, when assessing contagions I was convinced crowded, unsanitary conditions encouraged the spread of disease. At first, I thought my tutors considered the idea misdirected. I realise now though they might accept the premise, to them it was inconsequential. The majority of patients receiving attention at St. Bartholomew's do not come from deprived backgrounds."

They stopped once more some way short of the coach. There was little need to hurry, the coachmen were reloading the baggage, the passengers slaking their thirsts at the pump.

"In many respects, the chief physician was right," Marius observed. "I was not curing many people. I tried numerous remedies of my own devising, but to no great avail. We do little, other than make patients comfortable, and hope their maladies subside."

Marius glanced at his companion. "Forgive me, Mrs Johnson, may I provide you with some water?"

Mrs Johnson smiled her acceptance, and he walked over to the fountain and returned with a metal cup.

"I came to realise," he continued, "that I was not only casting doubt on the chief physician's judgement, but also his attitude to the prevention of disease. Perhaps, the last was a more sensitive issue," reflected Marius. "For the past year I know I have been an irritation in my repeated requests for change. I wanted the hospital authorities to search for ways to eradicate a number of diseases rather than provide ineffectual treatments.

"Matters came to a head ten days ago, during St. Bartholomew's Fair. This is held just outside the hospital gates, and attracts a wondrous array of stalls and visitors. There are fortune-tellers, sideshows, strolling musicians, shies, trinket sellers, dancers. The whole square is decorated with coloured garlands."

He stopped for a moment, vividly recalling the welcome diversion from the demands of the hospital. But as the glimmer of past thoughts died, his mouth took on a firmer set.

"After the fair, a gentleman was admitted to my ward suffering a high fever. His companions, who brought him to the hospital, were unable to give an explanation of his condition."

Marius made to pick up their bags, stooping to take hold of the handles.

"On examination, I noticed a small area of broken skin on his left side. Looking at his chemise and waistcoat, there were matching marks on both garments. I spoke with his friends asking if he had been near an animal. Immediately several of them muttered, "St.Bartholomew's Fair"."

They neared the coach, which was making ready to continue its journey.

"Strolling around the fair, they had happened upon a musician with a performing monkey. They had teased the animal, much to the annoyance of the owner. It would appear he had snatched up his instrument, and at the first notes, the monkey had leapt at the victim. His name was Doughty, Francis Doughty. The animal had clung briefly to his chest before returning to its perch. At the time, no one realised it had bitten him."

Marius remembered clearly the day Francis Doughty had been placed in one of the beds.

"I was at a loss to recommend the appropriate treatment. His pulse rate and temperature soared. His skin turned yellow, and open sores appeared all over his body. I applied our usual regimens. Alas, after three days of agony, Mr Doughty died," he mumbled, lost in his thoughts.

"Perhaps it was for the best. I have never seen a disease of such virulence."

Their footsteps slowed. Marius was absorbed in his recollections.

"This may sound gruesome, Mrs Johnson, but in severe causes of death, I often remove and dispose of those organs which are diseased. Mr Doughty was so consumed with an attack of unknown origin, frankly, I thought it best to be rid of the whole body," Marius said in a troubled voice.

"In my concern, perhaps I was less than considerate in my handling of the incident. When his family came to the hospital, I put my recommendation to them. They were appalled, and adamant in their refusal. What is more, despite my protestations, the hospital authorities sided with their decision."

As the memories returned, a pained expression crossed his face.

"They even wanted a night-time funeral. I know it's fashionable these days. Many believe it adds to the occasion, with blazing torches, candles, prayers and hymns offered up in the half-light. Burial arrangers say it allows for mourners more easily to express their grief."

Marius recalled he had washed his hands of the whole affair. At least, so he had thought.

"Two days later I happened to be passing the students' quarters, and paid a visit to the anatomy room. To my horror, there was Mr Doughty stretched out on the dissection table, with the anatomist, Dr Curtis, in full flow."

He glanced anxiously at Mrs Johnson. Common sights to him could be upsetting to others. " Forgive me, I often forget how macabre it must sound."

"Go on, Dr Hope," Mrs Johnson said in a quiet voice.

He looked at her uncertainly.

"Well, I accept that Curtis might not have known the provenance of the body. Cadavers usually acquired by hospitals are those of criminals. However, there are times when they are procured from other sources. I am well aware that bodies snatched from graveyards often reappear in mortuaries. It's an abominable practice, hospital authorities should be more diligent."

He stopped for a moment, again glancing sideways to see if he had disturbed her.

"What happened, Dr Hope?" she prompted.

The memory came flooding back.

Marius had stood in the doorway. Unseen, as Curtis, in that keening whine of a voice, had lectured. "This cadaver appears to have suffered from an unknown malady, so we must take precautions."

In outrage, Marius had called out. "Pray, what precautions do you recommend, Dr Curtis?"

"Ah, Dr Hope, welcome to the room from which you so often excused yourself in the past," Curtis had answered bitingly. "I cannot be expected to know all the facts of this body's ailments. But, we shall employ vapour burners and the students in the front row will wear cloths dampened with vinegar over their mouths."

"I tell you now that is not sufficient!" Marius had shouted. "Less than two days ago, this man died in terrible agony from an unknown cause. His body should not even have been interred, it should have been incinerated. You are jeopardising everyone in the whole building by your flagrant disregard!"

"I did not suffer your irrational ideas as a student, and I certainly do not intend to take notice of them now. Leave immediately!" Curtis had cried, beside himself in anger.

After that, events had moved swiftly. The hospital governors had interviewed Marius the next day. For his part, he had despaired of ever making them see the obvious. He was advised to adjust to the methods set for the good of the hospital or seek employment elsewhere. The chief physician had insisted he come to his senses.

He recounted this to the woman who had stopped and was now looking up into his face. The last words had been said in such a dispirited voice, that Mrs Johnson reached out to touch his arm. They stood together for several minutes, each silent with their thoughts.

Then Mrs Johnson remarked, "We must give the matter serious consideration, Doctor. I can appreciate the attitude of the hospital, not that I agree with it mind.

What you have done is confuse them. You have asked them to choose between the observance of good medicine and their more practical interests."

She smiled. "I believe you did the right thing in leaving. It will allow for a fresh view of the situation. If you would permit, I would welcome discussing the matter further."

With that she plucked her carpet bag from his hand.

"Come, sir," she declared. "Now we must repair with the others to The Wells."